Cthulhu Fhcon

Jennifer Brozek • Kat Richardson • M.J. Stoumbos
David Boop • M. Todd Gallowglas • Frances Pauli
Frank Martin • Jason R. Frei • John Lance
Hank Schwaeble • Irene Radford • Russell Nohelty •
G.R. Theron • Olivia Baxter Hudson • Rhiannon Louve
Elizabeth Guizzetti • Paul DeStefano • A.R.R. Ash
Peter J. Wacks

Edited by Frog Jones

Impulsive
Walrus

CARTOON PRINTED WITH PERMISSION FROM S. S. JULIAN

Aaron Waltmann • Abby Braunsdorf • Adam Goldstein • Amanda Esch • Cheeser • Christian Dannie Storgaard • Clayton W. Mann • Cliff Winnig • Colleen Feeney • Curtis Frye • Dan V. • Dead Fishie • Edward M. Kovel • Elizabeth Guizzetti • Ella Ananeva • Eric 'Hedgehog' Coles • Eric Priehs • Frontman • Genevieve Slunka • Glenn Slate and cows • Guy Edwards • Ilene Tsuruoka • Janka Hobbs • Jeff Lewis • Jennifer Flora Black • Jess Leigh Unrein • Joe Gillis • Joel Gilbert • Krysi • Linden Vimislik • Mike Jack Stoumbos • MissJerseyBlue • Mr. Kitty • Niels Starfari • Noeli Gifford • Paul Anguiano • Paul Popernack • Radars Game Room • Rebecca Cook • Rhiannon "Gibbitt" Rhys-Jones • Rosamaria Cirelli • Ruth Ann Orlansky • Sanan Kolva • Shawn • Sheri Budrow • Sonse Cahuni • Stephanie Breiding • Susan Wilson • Tim Lonegan • Vulpine • Walter Weiss •

ONE OF THE MANY singular things about H. P. Lovecraft (1890–1937) is the extent to which his work has inspired other writers to elaborate upon his conceptions. This phenomenon began even in Lovecraft's own day, with such of his colleagues as Frank Belknap Long, Clark Ashton Smith, Donald Wandrei, Robert E. Howard, Robert Bloch, Fritz Leiber, and especially August Derleth writing tales that riffed on key aspects of Lovecraft's evolving mythos. After Lovecraft's death, Derleth became both Lovecraft's publisher and his most devoted partisan; but, sadly, he failed to understand the true essence of his friend's creation. Lovecraft's work is fueled by several key motifs that he worked and reworked in tale after tale: cosmicism, or the suggestion of the vast gulfs of space and time and the resulting inconsequence of humanity within those realms; hereditary degeneration, or the possibility of human beings reversing the course of evolution and lapsing into a state of primitive savagery; the horrors emerging out of history and landscape; and the uniquely existential horror of psychic transference or replacement.

Over the last several decades, writers ranging from Ramsey Campbell to Caitlín R. Kiernan have grasped the true essence of Lovecraft's work and have produced novels and tales that pay due homage to the dreamer from Providence, R.I., while at the same time expressing their own originality. Much the same can be said of the stories in this volume, by a diverse cadre of contemporary writers.

Some of these writers play on certain sub-themes in Lovecraft's work, such as the idea of extraterrestrial language. This concept is embodied in the name of his most celebrated creation, Cthulhu. It is in "The Call of Cthulhu" that Lovecraft both introduces that baleful entity from outer space (now trapped in his stone city of R'lyeh under the waters of the Pacific Ocean) and devises such phrases from the R'lyehian language as *"Ph'nglui mglw'nafh Cthulhu R'lyeh wgah'nagl fhtagn"* ("In his house at R'lyeh dead Cthulhu waits dreaming"). In a letter Lovecraft makes the key point that the very name Cthulhu "is supposed to represent a fumbling human attempt to catch the phonetics of an *absolutely non-human* word. The name of the hellish entity was invented by beings whose vocal organs were not like man's, hence it has no relation to the human speech equipment. The syllables were determined by a physiological equipment wholly unlike ours, *hence could never be uttered perfectly by human throats.*"

It will be observed that many authors in this volume take a less than reverential view toward Lovecraft and his creations. Indeed, the element of humor can be said to predominate in this book. Even this can be seen as a covert tribute to Lovecraft; for it is a great mistake to think that he was a dour, humorless New Englander who never cracked a smile. His tales are full of puns, in-jokes (such as a reference to Clark Ashton Smith as "Atlantean high-priest Klarkash-Ton"), and so on. "Herbert West—Reanimator," "The Hound," and several others are both horror tales and parodies of the horror tale. Some of his lesser tales are even more overtly comical, such as the hilarious "Sweet Ermengarde," a send-up of the sentimental romances prevalent in his day.

And if the science fiction convention—another element in this volume—is something that postdated Lovecraft's lifetime, it should be noted that he was an enthusiast of similar gatherings, especially among the members of the amateur journalism movement, which he had joined in 1914 and to which he remained devoted for the rest of his life. It was at such a convention in 1921 that he met his future wife, Sonia H. Greene. During his years in New York (1924–26), Lovecraft happily hosted meetings of the Kalem Club—a group of friends whose last names all began with K, L, or M. He was scrupulous in securing toothsome sweets for his friends, along with coffee (which he secured by taking an aluminum pail to a nearby deli and having it filled with the hot beverage), served on his best china. To be sure, Lovecraft could be the life of the party when he chose.

It is refreshing to see contemporary authors look at Lovecraft's work as both the terrifying cosmic horror that it is but also as the source of a lot of fun. Perhaps that is the best way his work can remain alive in the twenty-first century.

—S. T. JOSHI

CONTENTS

INTRODUCTION
Frog Jones

There is nothing in the world quite like a science fiction convention.

I'm not talking about big, commercialized comic cons. Those are fun in their own way. I'm talking about the smaller conventions. The ones put on by hard-working, and largely unheralded, fans who do it for no reason other than they love science fiction, they love fantasy, and they want to celebrate that with other people.

I've been to countless of them, and every time I go I feel like I'm coming home again. It's a community. And simply being in that place, at that time, means you have so much in common with everyone else there. The things that the outer world might judge one for—the things that we keep in tight when we go about our day jobs and live our lives—it can all come flying out at the con. Our friends, our family—it's all there.

Each one of them stands out in my mind as having its own personality. I'm not going to name them, here, but there's a con we go to where the rule is that everything will get weird, and the trick is to roll with it. There's a con we go to that's a little more highbrow than it should be, and there's the con we called home that's now passed into history after COVID. (I'll name that one; goodbye, Spocon).

And there's the one that's cursed.

This convention happens in a hotel that is, in fact, next to a body of water. And the hotel is truly designed to be a thing of madness. It's as though the architect wanted to make it as difficult as possible to navigate the twists and turns of the hallways. I'm not actually sure why this was desirable, but it's a good quarter-mile walk from the front desk to the elevator.

The first time we attended this hotel, the dealer's room was positioned in the basement. And on day two of the convention, the grey water pipes from the hotel kitchen broke, causing an unexpected water feature on the carpet directly in front of the dealer room.

One that smelled exactly how you'd expect the grey water pipes to smell.

Needless to say, the scent of old grease, rotten food, and just a hint of human waste created a wall in front of the dealer's room that only the most dedicated of nerds were willing to pass through. It had something of a negative impact on sales.

This is, to date, possibly the worst experience I've had at a convention. Sitting in a room devoid of customers before a table full of books that I'm not going to be able to sell to anyone. And yet...and yet, we had fun with it. We authors began speaking with each other. And we'd look out on the back deck (yes, this hotel basement has a back deck. Thing of madness, remember?) at the dark, swirling waters before us.

And really, we came to what I still believe is the only reasonable conclusion.

The hotel in which we were staying had been designed and constructed not by some architect in the early 70's who'd been dropping acid at the time (this theory being the prevalent one prior to our sewage-coated insight). No, the hotel had been built with intent. The madness of its design had been calculated.

And something lurked in the waters before us.

This, by the way, is what happens when you stick a bunch of speculative fiction authors in an enclosed room, fill that room with the foulest scent imaginable, and then remove all chance of them selling anything to anyone. They start telling stories about the situation to one another. In the end, we all agreed that the hotel definitely served as an altar to a Lovecraftian beast slumbering in the waters beyond.

A couple of factions emerged around whether the purpose of said altar was to summon or confine said beast—we had to agree to disagree there. But whatever the reason, we knew, down to our bones, that our series of misfortunes had nothing to do with random chance. No, we were merely pawns in a single move of a cosmic game of horror and insanity.

It says something of us that we consider this scenario preferable to simply getting the raw end of the stick and having a bad sales day. I choose not to linger overmuch on this point, though, as self-reflection has never been a pleasant experience for me.

Nevertheless, I have said it before and I will say it again; one must be careful when speaking to authors. I've said it; I apparently have yet to learn my lesson. Because invariably, someone will take this sort of storytelling and speak the words that should strike true horror into the heart of any who listen.

"This would make an amazing anthology."

And so, for the third time, I have set my quill as an author aside for the greater good. When the spirit of creativity strikes authors, one can but attempt to harness it and guide it into a single volume.

What all of us have in common is our love for the small literary convention. The fans – you, reader, are included in this—who appreciate what we do. The ability to interact with you and to present ourselves to you is an honor each and every time we do it. The thankless, grueling work put on by the various concoms to bring us all together for this weekend of magic and wonder.

This volume serves to honor all of that in the way we can do best. By unleashing an Old God on a literary convention and letting things take their natural course. What course that is has been determined by the author. Some of it is comic, some horrific, and much of it both.

n

But as the madness of a science fiction convention runs straight into the madness of the Old Ones, it's hard to stay sane.

So embrace the madness. Put that con badge around your neck, take out your program, and get ready to be an unabashed nerd. Because you're about to attend Cthulhu FhCon.

Observations of a LARP in Three Acts

Jennifer Brozek

About the Author: JENNIFER BROZEK is a wordslinger and optimist, an author, media tie-in writer, an editor, and a collector of antique occult literature. She believes the best thing about being a full-time freelance publishing industry professional, is the fact that she gets to choose which 60 hours of the week she works. In-between cuddling her cats, writing, and editing, Jennifer is an active member of SFWA, HWA, and IAMTW. She keeps a tight writing and editing schedule and credits her husband with being the best sounding board ever. Visit Jennifer's worlds at jenniferbrozek.com or on Twitter: @JenniferBrozek.

Observations of a LARP in Three Acts
Jennifer Brozek

One: The Beginning of the End

Lori pointed to her phone at the convention programming schedule. "Look at that: a LARP I can play in instead of running. It's been forever." They stood in the lobby of a new-to-them hotel on the middle of an island in the middle of a coastal city. The entire building screamed 1980s with its incomprehensible corridors, "discreet" signage, and outrageously patterned carpet that made one dizzy if you stared at it for too long. None of that dulled the excitement of a new convention experience.

Bill looked over her shoulder and read aloud.

"'*Things of the Water: a modern day Mythos LARP designed to transport you to another world. Full immersion. Locked room mystery. 25 slots.*' It starts soon. First come, first serve, no doubt."

"Things of the Water, eh?" Rob mused. "Maybe we could play together instead of being pitted against each other by a cruel and uncaring LARP master."

Lori smiled. "I resemble that remark. So, you wanna play?"

"Absolutely." Rob grinned. "Let's do it."

Thirty minutes later, they stood in a large ballroom.

1

Lori took it all in; it seemed decked out like a cross between a cave and a masonic temple with all sorts of props and set dressing. "I approve. This shows that the LARP coordinator has put some serious work into the story. Who is this guy again?"

Rob shrugged. "His name is Devon Shire. Never heard of him before this con. Maybe he's new to the area."

The LARP coordinator rang a bell to get everyone's attention. As the deep bong of the heavy brass bell faded, Devon raised his hands. "Welcome to *Things of the Water*. This is a full immersion LARP and a literal locked room mystery. Once we begin, you cannot leave and return. The doors will be locked. If you leave, you are out of the LARP for the rest of the evening. We have 25 slots and 30 sign-ups. If you cannot guarantee that you'll be here for the full five hours, I'd prefer you not to stay. Be kind to your fellow LARPers."

He pointed to the left. "And before anyone asks... bathrooms are over there. Now, if you cannot stay for the entire evening, please step aside. The rest of you please lineup here."

As the crowd muttered and moved, Bill leaned down to Lori. "Tough GM. But not a bad idea for a locked room mystery."

Lori nodded. "But not kind to the smokers in the group."

"They can deal. Go have a quick one then tough it out for the evening."

The three of them made it to the middle of the line. Lori watched Devon work. Professional interest, of course. Something to bring back to her wife and fellow LARP coordinator. It looked like he was doing the standard "what do you want to play" set of questions. However, as they almost reached the head of the line, she realized he was doing something a little more interesting.

Devon held a clipboard and a pen. "Name?"

"Dan VanVoorhis."

"Birthday month?"

Dan paused before answering. "February."

Devon looked up with interest. "Another February birthday. Good. I'll have to figure out which one of you is younger."

"Why?"

Devon wrote something down. "Part of the randomization scheme. What kind of character do you like to play?"

Dan shrugged. "I'm easy, just not cheap. Whatever. Or a chaos factor."

"Alright. Do me a favor, stand over there by that lovely lady with the long dark hair. Her name is Frontman Gil. I'll have to talk to both of you about something *interesting*."

Lori, Bill, and Rob looked at each other. They all glanced at Dan and then back at each other again, smiling. The same thought ran through their minds: keep an eye on Dan VanVoorhis and Frontman Gil. See what is so "interesting" about them.

"Who's next?" Devon asked.

Bill stepped up. "We are." He gestured to himself then Rob and Lori. "We'd all like to play something together."

"Oh?"

"We never get to. A certain GM," he pointed at Lori, "never lets us team up."

Devon cocked his head to one side. "Why not?"

Lori scoffed. "I know better." Then she sighed. "They're good. We all are."

Rob eyed her with a look that clearly asked, *Why did you tell him that?*

"I see. Thank you for your candor. What are your birthday months?"

Bill answered for all of them. "December."

"All of you? That's handy." He tapped the clipboard with his pen. "Tell me, would you rather play True

Believers or those trying to stop them?"

Bill glanced at Rob and Lori.

Lori answered, "If you're asking if we want to play the good guys or the bad guys, give us the cultists any day of the week. We'll get it done."

Devon smirked. "Well then, True Believers it is."

Two: A Fateful Interruption

@@@

Lori sidled up to Rob. "Did you get it?"

He nodded and showed her a small frog statue. The frog was made of a blue stone, probably sodalite, and sat on an obsidian base. The whole thing was about an inch around and three inches high. "You get yours?"

"Of course." She didn't bother to show him her statue. It was similar to his, though her frog was made from a green stone—adventurine, she thought—on a black base. Scanning the ballroom made cave-like with dim lights and muted decorations, she looked for Bill.

There was a lot going on. As far as she could tell, there were at least four main plotlines: a forbidden romance, a stolen artifact, an assassin who had killed multiple characters with authorities looking for the culprit—she thought Deirdre was playing the assassin—and a cultist ritual that she and her friends needed to gather items for.

Right now, she didn't see anyone who was trying to stop the cultist ritual. It was almost too easy. That was one of the problems with LARPs. Sometimes a person you depended on to do the right thing just didn't live up to expectations. It sucked when it happened in one of her LARPs. Then again, failure was always an option and she always prepared for it. She just hoped that Devon had also prepared for it.

There.

Bill extricated himself from a knot of people and made

his way to them. He took a circuitous route, passing by the LARP coordinator and giving him a significant look. Devon acknowledged him with a nod and continued on with whatever he was doing with Frontman Gil and Dan VanVoorhis.

"Got it," he breathed when he arrived. He pulled his frog statue out of his pocket and showed them. It looked like the rest except for the fact that his frog appeared to be obsidian like its base. "Now what?"

Looking at her character sheet, Lori said, "Now we do the ritual. Then the True Believers win. Or at least, we succeed at our part."

Rob glanced around. "If we get interrupted, we have to start over. Let's do this quick."

They chose their ritual location and sat down, then placed the statues together. The three frog statues sat together with their backs to each other, facing the three players who sat around them. One by one, they spoke the ritual words written on their cards. First Rob, then Lori, then Bill. There would be three sets of three, each led by a different person.

"Culn r'luh sgn'wahl."
"Culn r'luh sgn'wahl."
"Culn r'luh sgn'wahl."

Lori turned over her card as Rob began the next set of ritual phrases.

"Goka cgo ch'ftaghu."

She opened her mouth to speak but before she could utter a word, a dark shape loomed over them and a hand reached down and knocked over the frog statues. A large static charge from the black frog statue caused the stranger to jerk back from them.

"Hey!" Rob's voice was sharp but low toned, designed to both be menacing and unobtrusive. It was a skill he'd honed over many years of LARPing where secrecy was the name of the game. "What's your deal?"

"You can't complete the ritual. It'll open a portal to R'lyeh. An actual portal with monsters and horrors beyond imagining. You'll all die." The speaker was a tall woman dressed in an odd motley of clothing: a graphic t-shirt over what looked like buckskin pants and motorcycle boots. Her blonde hair was bound in a long braid fastened with rawhide and plastic barrettes.

At this point, Bill grabbed all of the frog statues and cupped them in a protective grip as the three of them stood up and faced the stranger. Bill stepped back, letting Rob and Lori speak for him. Lori was familiar with this game. She would be good cop and Rob would be, well, Rob.

"I'm not sure what you're talking about...," she read the woman's nametag, "Hinter."

"This isn't a game," Hinter snarled, keeping her voice as low as Rob did, matching his menacing tone. "This is a setup. You're being duped into opening a portal. Someone here will die tonight, maybe a lot of you, and it will be your fault."

The woman sounded so convinced that Lori glanced at Rob and Bill, wordlessly asking if they were in danger from her. Bill shifted back, indicating yes while Rob took a step forward, also indicating yes.

"This isn't funny," he said.

"It's not meant to be funny. You do this ritual, someone dies."

Lori raised her hand in an "out of character" sign before asking, "Uh, are you for real? Because, honestly your acting's off the charts if not. Kudos for that."

Hinter scowled at her. "I am 'for real' trying to save your life and the lives of everyone else in here. Don't you get it? You w—" She broke off as she glanced over Lori's shoulder.

Lori looked back and saw Devon talking to another player, moving towards them.

"Don't complete the ritual," Hinter hissed, her eyes on Devon. "For all our sakes. I have enough to worry about as is." She whirled away and moved into the next knot of players.

Bill shook his head. "Hell of an NPC. Scared the crap out of me."

Rob watched her move through the room, breaking up the small groups of people, interrupting anything they were doing. "Yeah. Or crazier than a shithouse rat."

Lori decided it wasn't her LARP thus not her monkey, not her circus. Looking at her cards, she asked, "Where's the little pyramid? It's part of the ritual. It's supposed to go in the center of the frogs."

Rob smacked a hand to his forehead. "I've got it. I'm sorry. I forgot it in my pocket."

Lori glanced to where she saw Hinter last. She caught the woman disappearing into the bathroom with Devon on her heels. "Well, we need it. Good thing Hinter showed up, or we would've done the ritual wrong. I guess she's an NPC after all. Hint...Hinter."

Bill pointed to a corner. "Let's set up over there. No more interruptions. I want to win."

Three: An End is Also a Beginning

"Chrii ilyaa n'ghft n'gha uaaah..." Lori, Rob, and Bill finished in unison and grinned at each other.

The atmosphere of the room changed. Immediately, the dim lights began to flicker, as a small bright light about a handsbreadth wide appeared on the singular cleared wall in the ballroom. The temperature in the large room dropped into something moist and chill.

As the small orb of light grew, it dimmed into a glowing circle less blinding and more alien. The circle stopped growing when it reached the height of a tall man. Within it, shadows danced on cavern walls lit with glowing lichen. Shadows of inhuman, bipedal creatures. The edges of the circle continued to strobe, making it hard to see what the creatures actually looked like.

Bill and Rob stepped in front of Lori as she gave a soft squeak of surprise and fear. The rest of the LARPers drew back from the wall with the same murmurs of shock and fear, leaving Devon standing in the middle of the room. In front of him were Dan and Frontman. He leaned forward and whispered to them. Both players nodded and the three of them walked towards the wall.

As they got close, both Dan and Frontman faltered. Devon put his hands on the backs of their necks and guided them forward. Even from where she was, Lori could see that neither of the players wanted to approach the glowing circle or the alien creatures within.

"No...no...no..." Lori whispered as she realized something was very, very wrong. She swore she could smell them—the alien creatures—wet, musty, moldy, rotten. Every bad smell conjured up from a clogged sink once it was unplugged wafted through the room.

With a sudden push, Devon sent Dan and Frontman tumbling forward into and *through* the wall. Both of them screamed high shrieks of fear as those alien creatures— black, chitinous, bulbous—moved faster than the eye could see and grabbed the hapless players and pulled them *somewhere else.*

Devon stepped forward, muttering an incomprehensible language in a low tone. Before he reached the circle, the bathroom door slammed open. Half the LARPers in the ballroom yelped or screamed with surprise and scrambled away from that side of the room. In the doorway, Hinter stood, bruised and bleeding. "STOP!" she shouted and strode forward.

"You're too late, woman." Devon made a rapid series of signs towards her. "It's done. Tsathoggua will be fed! He will be fed well tonight on all of them."

Hinter fended off the signs with hand signals of her own. Her stomping steps became a run as Devon crossed the circle from the ballroom into the cave, running now. Without hesitation, she followed him into that other world, but stopped on the other side. "That abomination will starve," she shouted as she raised a hand.

Devon paused, small in the distance. He saw something none of the others could see and shouted, "No!"

"Yes!" Hinter turned and threw something at the watching crowd.

It never reached them. Instead, whatever it was—small and round—struck the center of the hole in the wall and stopped. It hung there for a moment, glinting in the strobing light of the opening's edge, then the circle stuttered and disappeared along with Devon, Hinter, and those alien creatures. The ballroom fell into darkness.

For several long moments, no one moved or spoke. Lori found herself clutching Rob and Bill's arms. "Holy crap," she whispered.

With that soft acknowledgment that they were all still alive and still here, the room broke out in excited whispers and movement. They milled about, waiting for the LARP coordinator to reappear and make some sort of announcement about the end of the game.

Bill looked around. "Where is he?"

Lori shook her head, letting go of her friends. "I don't know." She didn't want to say what she was thinking—that Devon wasn't here anymore and neither were the two sacrifices or Hinter who had tried to stop it. "Rob, get the lights."

Rob nodded and threaded his way through the room to the wall. There was a collective gasp and wince at the suddenly bright room after hours of dim light. Everyone looked around, looking for the LARP coordinator.

A voice from the right asked, "Is that it? Is the game

over?"

The room rumbled with the same question. No one was willing to leave without hearing the end credits where the LARP coordinator usually told the room the end result of all of the stories that had happened. But as Devon wasn't here, no one knew what to do.

Lori saw that the entire playership avoided the wall where the circle, *the portal*, had appeared. Her stomach roiled at the thought that it had been an actual, real portal, that those alien creatures existed, and that the two players—Frontman Gil and Dan VanVoorhis—were gone, sacrificed to something unpronounceable.

Bill shook his head. "How the hell did he do it?"

Rob, who had returned to their side, shrugged. "Video. Obviously. That's why they kept that one wall clear and the lights dim. It was really effective."

"No kidding. I about wet myself."

Lori knew it wasn't a video projected on the wall. There were no shadows interrupting the scene. She'd tried that trick a couple of times and it hadn't worked well enough. She didn't say anything. Her attention was caught on something small and round on the floor next to the wall where the...circle...had been.

She walked over to it, Rob and Bill trailing behind her as they talked about the game. Picking it up, Lori saw that it looked like a bronze coin, roughhewn and worn with age. One side had writing on it rubbed into something unreadable. The other had a stick with five branches; three on one side, two on the other. The coin felt smooth and precious in a way she couldn't explain. She put it in her pocket.

Rob tilted his head. "What's that?"

Lori turned to the wall. There was a faint circle of dirt on it as tall as Bill. "I guess that's where the portal was."

Bill shook his head. "Someone's gonna get fined. Let's get out of here."

Rob touched the edge of the circle then looked at his fingertips. They came away dirty. He shuddered and rubbed his hand on his jeans. "Yeah. Let's go. It was a good game. Terrible ending."

Bill beckoned. "I've got just the thing. A "Hail the Deep" room party. I picked up a flyer earlier. I hear Sarah and Josh run the wildest room parties around here."

Lori followed them out of the room, her hands in her pockets, not certain what to think or how to feel. The only thing she knew was that the *Things of the Water* LARP had not actually been a game, and she'd had a part in what had happened. She didn't know what to do now, but as she squeezed the coin in her pocket, she knew she had a clue of where to look.

END

Temp-to-Perm

Kat Richardson

About the Author: KAT RICHARDSON is currently wandering loose through the mountains of Western Washington in a trailer with two dogs and a husband. It's even her own husband. Along the way she has been a journalist, actor, singer, costumer, writing instructor, seller of beanie babies, and a freelance editor and writing coach. She is the author of nine bestselling novels in the Greywalker series, one award-winning SF novel, a load of short stories, and a few unspeakable things that live in an electronic trunk. Trust me, it's better that way....

Temp-to-Perm

Kat Richardson

The Royal Western Hotel lounged on the riverbank two miles above the salt marsh like a colossal, headless reptile, curving as the water curved, all concrete bones with steel stripes on green glass skin. From the water side, the serpent appeared to be melting into the cement walls that imprisoned the river for the length of its passage through town. Opinions varied whether the building was a triumph of 1970s brutalism or just a monstrosity.

But even more than that, the Royal Western had a *Reputation*: strange events seemed to cluster to it, odd happenings, visits by people destined to become notorious, suicides, and disappearances.... The longer it crouched on the river bank, the more opinion swayed toward the unpleasant, but never enough to risk setting the river free by tearing the building and its walls down. Who knew what lurked in the hotel's water-bound gut—aside from the mundane machinery and processes that kept it running? Could be anything. But that day, it happened to be a hiring interview—its own special horror.

"And why do you want to work here?" Mrs. Aiken, the Head of Housekeeping and Janitorial, asked.

The girl—who was called Evelyn—replied, "My family used to travel a lot and we stayed here a couple times when I was a kid. I just kinda love the place."

15

"You understand this is a temp-to-perm position?"

Evelyn nodded. She was short and stocky, wore her hair in a complex braided style that made her head look large and round, and had lightly freckled skin of a shade that could be called olive only if you had never seen one. She knew she wasn't pretty, but no one really cared what the cleaning staff looked like, did they? She also knew that temp-to-perm meant the hotel could fire her anytime it wanted. "Yes, and I'm fine with that," she said.

Mrs. Aiken nodded in a perfunctory manner as she straightened up her paperwork. "Good, good. I'm glad you're able to start right away. RiverCon begins this weekend—our first big event of the Spring season. It's a Sci-Fi convention and they can be a little... weird, so I want to get you up to speed before the early attendees start arriving on Wednesday." She sent a tight smile in Evelyn's direction without meeting her eyes.

Evelyn noticed the Head of Housekeeping never looked too long at her, shifting her focus back to her paperwork, or her supply cupboards, or... pretty much anything. She didn't hold that against the woman; she was used to it. Though Mrs. Aiken had no cause to look down her nose at Evelyn, being a pale, stringy-limbed hag with a face only a mother barracuda could love.

"I'm really grateful for the chance," Evelyn said.

Mrs. Aiken inclined her head once again. Evelyn thought she looked like one of the bobble-head dolls the gift shop sold, stiff and dumbly nodding without meaning. "Well, if it works out, we'll make you permanent here. So." The Head of Housekeeping snapped the paperwork into a clipboard with a pen dangling from it on a curly plastic cord, rose to her stork-like height, and started across the room, talking over her shoulder. "Let's get your uniform and gear, and you can get going. You'll be working with Oscar and Tulia for the first day or two until you get your bearings—the hotel has a convoluted layout and it takes a while to get used to. It is easier to understand if you start down here in the mechanical areas."

Housekeeping was on the first subfloor at the back of the Royal Western. It had a row of glass brick at the top of the wall through which murky sunlight filtered past a film of algae and the occasional splash of brown river water. The glass was part of a diamond-scale pattern on the side of the hotel that faced the river, letting in moving, watery light, and lending a weird ambience to Mrs. Aiken's kingdom of cleaning supplies and dustless efficiency.

The Head of Housekeeping walked quickly, assigning Evelyn uniforms and equipment, naming and pointing out all the supply cupboards, and leading her to the cart corral. "You'll have cart six. It's the big one on the left," Mrs. Aiken said, and pointed at a utility cart with a collection of mops, brooms, and other janitorial pole arms in a rack on one end, and gray fabric attached to the frame with hooks to hide buckets and less-attractive gear stored on the bottom of two shelves. "It's a heavier duty unit than the regular housekeeping carts for guest rooms, since you're on clean-up and janitorial crew. Keeping it stocked and tidy is part of your duty. Now, we'll head to the dressing room. I'll assign you a locker, and then you can change and go meet your 'training buddies'." Mrs. Aiken clearly didn't care for the term—Evelyn imagined HR had invented it in a fit of "employee-friendliness."

The staff dressing room was stuffy and smelled of bleach struggling to overcome the odor of constant wetness and poor ventilation. The Head of Housekeeping stared at Evelyn for a moment as they stood in front of her newly-assigned locker, then held out her clipboard. "Sign the form on the top—it acknowledges that you've got all the equipment I assigned you."

Evelyn did as she was told and returned the clipboard to Mrs. Aiken, who signed something herself, pulled the page off the clip, and handed it back. "I hope you'll be with us for a long time, Evelyn," she said, then turned sharply and marched out. Back to her den, Evelyn thought.

She dressed in one of her two dark green uniforms and went to find Oscar and Tulia. Was it weird that she was excited? Maybe. But she really, really needed this job.

Thursday was Evelyn's first time on dawn duty—which started with the pool area. The concrete around the pool and down to the fence at the edge of the river walk was pink in the sunrise light, and it even looked kind of pretty that way. So far, Evelyn found all the tasks simple. Physical labor had never bothered her.

She watched Tulia and Oscar as they stood in the doorway of Cabana 1's shower room. Tulia's dozens of black-and-white extension braids looked blood-streaked in the dawn light, and her brown skin ruddy, while big, bald Oscar stood to her left like a sandstone monument. They were a good couple—they claimed they weren't, but when they stood like that, some part of one always touched the other and they seemed to melt together at the intersection, as if they were one person in a two-part body. It gave Evelyn joy.

Tulia had her hands on her hips, one elbow pressing to Oscar's beefy bicep. "Terrific," Tulia muttered. "Neon hair dye in the baths. Why can't the SFF fans do their hair Vampire Red at home?"

"Or least not here," Oscar added, glancing over his shoulder at Evelyn, " 'cause red stains by the pool freak the guests like none of your business. You're gonna need the Heavy Bucket, Li'l Evie."

He'd given her the nickname on first meeting and, like so many things, Evelyn didn't mind. She *did* mind the bucket, though; it wasn't actually heavy, but rather filled with bottles of heavy-duty cleaning chemicals that would run into the river or leach into ground water and poison everything. She despised that.

"Gross," she muttered under her breath as she dragged the bucket of horror toward the shower.

"Hey," Oscar said, "don't let no management hear you complaining. They don't care how it get done, so long's it *get done*. Hm?" Tulia gave her a narrow look at the same time, as if to drive an extra nail into the message.

"Yes, Oscar," Evelyn said, passing between them.

He offered one of his crooked smiles. "I know you get it. Don't forget gloves and mask. That stuff *nasty*!"

Evelyn snickered and stopped at the edge of the stained white tile. She sniffed and bent down to get a better look at the dark red mess. It was hard to smell it over the scent of morning river fog curling up from the water and creeping across the concrete. She pursed her lips and frowned as she sniffed again, then glanced over her shoulder. "That's not hair dye."

Tulia cocked her head and raised her eyebrow. "Then what is it?"

Evelyn shrugged. "Blood. C'mon, you knew that."

"Well," said Tulia, turning her gaze on Oscar, "what do you think?"

Oscar grinned, showing a lot of nicotine-yellowed teeth. "Smart cookie. Now what you gonna do, Evie?"

"Clean up. Duh. But I'm wondering where the guy is, 'cause that's a lot of red."

Oscar shrugged. "Well, he ain't here, so don't worry about it."

Evelyn shrugged. "Fine. Why don't you guys do the restocking—y'know: the easy stuff—while I scrub-a-dub-dub?"

Oscar laughed while Tulia smiled. "A'right," he said. "You scrub." And they started for the cabinets.

Evelyn knelt down between the Heavy Bucket and the stain and, once her buddies had turned their backs, she put her hands flat down in the blood. "Did you meet my father?" she whispered.

The blood stirred and flowed toward her, crawling under her fingernails and up her arms, beneath her uniform until there was only a thin, wet slick of pinkish goo on the floor. Evelyn took a damp rag from the bucket and mopped up the last of the stain with a frown. She didn't notice Tulia watching from the corners of her eyes.

The next bloody mess—in the Grand Ballroom— caused quite a stir and forced RiverCon's opening night party to relocate to the River View Ballroom on the second floor. Most of the people who saw the stain were incapable of recognizing it for what it was, and the rest conspired to say nothing. The convention-goers complained loudly about having to go up the stairs and elevators after they'd already come down, and many got lost in the upper hallways, which were incapable of running straight for any great distance lengthwise. A few of them eventually found a conveniently unlocked small meeting room and had a party of their own, which resulted in hastily-scribbled paper badge ribbons that read "LostCon ConCom."

Evelyn had volunteered to clean up in the ballroom while Oscar and Tulia helped the catering and AV staff move everything, and set it up elsewhere.

She brought the Heavy Bucket, but, again, only set it down and knelt beside the stain while everyone else was busy with their own tasks. "Did you know my mother?" she asked the blood as she took it into herself. If it replied, no one but Evelyn heard.

There was another stain by the pool early Friday morning, but this one was out in the open by the river walk gate.

Evelyn, Oscar, and Tulia stood by the gate while the river churned and rippled on the other side, and stared at the stain for a minute in the mauve-streaked, green-grey dawn. "Where do they go?" asked Evelyn.

Tulia replied, "Who go?"

"The lost, the missing. These blood donors."

"Ain't nobody gone missing," Oscar said.

"I'd bet someone has. Not one of us. One of the SFF fans, maybe."

Tulia shook her head. "Nobody's gonna tell us that. Besides, it's none of our business. We just clean up. Which you better get to, missy."

"I don't want to wash all these chemicals into the water," Evelyn said. "Couldn't we just rinse it away if we have a strong enough hose?"

Tulia and Oscar stood side-by-side between her and the nearest standpipe. They also blocked the view of anyone looking toward them from the hotel, and there was no one yet jogging along the walk who might see. "Why?" Tulia asked. "You can clean it up without that. I saw you do it yesterday."

Oscar nodded, and Evelyn cringed away. "I didn't do anything..."

Tulia shook her head, her braids swishing like water weeds in a deep current. "Don't even, girl."

Evelyn let her shoulders slump. "All right, but I don't want you to watch."

"Why not?" Oscar asked.

"It's private!"

He chuckled and turned his back, linking his arm with Tulia's when she did the same. "I still know you here, Li'l Evie."

"I know..."

She glared at their backs for a moment before she knelt down to talk to the blood. "Were you my sister?" she whispered to it, and it began to flow...

When Oscar and Tulia turned around, the stain was gone, and Evelyn stood glaring at them with her arms crossed over her chest.

"I told you I visited here when I was a kid."

"You sure about that?" Oscar asked.

"Don't be a jerk, Oscar. I came with my folks."

"And then...?" Tulia asked.

"I disappeared for three days. I don't remember it. I don't think anyone does. But that's why I'm here, and that's all I want to say about it!"

Oscar said, "But that ain't all there is to say."

Evelyn knew her mouth looked like a long, hard scar in her face—she knew the feeling of that stubborn, angry expression she'd worn so often. "You're not real friends," she said, picking up the Heavy Bucket and carrying it to the utility cart. " 'You're just my 'training buddies,' and I'm not telling you any more. Let's get back to work."

Tulia and Oscar exchanged frowns, but didn't ask for more. They wound their arms together and followed her.

Evelyn found the next mess Saturday morning on her way to check in for her shift. The blood was spread and oozing around the maintenance entrance from the parking garage. She dropped down next to it with a hard sigh. She rubbed her hands over her head—her hair felt as heavy as waterlogged coils of rope and her eyes were hot and gritty. With slumping shoulders, she put her palms down into the stain and stared at it, murmuring, "Would you be my brother?"

This time the blood shivered, but didn't move to join her.

From a shadow Tulia said, "Someone's missing."

Evelyn raised her head slowly. "Is it Oscar?"

"No. But you got to go see Mrs. Aiken. Right now."

Evelyn got to her feet. "What? Does she think this is my fault? Because—"

"I'm coming with you."

"Of course you are," Evelyn said with an annoyed sigh. She marched toward the doorway, knowing she looked angry from the stiffness of her face and the way her teeth hurt from grinding together.

The bloody mess squirmed, unseen, and oozed after them.

It was not the way she'd gone before, and yet it was. Past the first door, the air was damp and the lighting was lower than normal, but Evelyn could see another door; it lead to the stairs. She hurried toward it and started a descent into long narrow rooms of pumps and pipes that kept the river water from rising through the building to slowly drown it.

She went on.

The pump room gave way to smaller corridors that lay deep in the retaining walls, twisting as the building above turned to follow the river. And the light grew steadily dimmer as the floor grew wetter, but Evelyn kept going. She could hear Tulia making small splashing sounds behind her as they went, but she didn't turn back to see her. She had to see Mrs. Aiken. Had to.

Her hair was saturated with dripping water, and so heavy that she reached up to loosen it, letting long loops fall around her shoulders and down her back. She felt bigger, as if she were expanding into the wet and the dark. The cold was strangely welcome, and welcoming.

She started running, Tulia splashing behind.

The next door covered a curtain of river weeds that swayed and swirled through a sheen of uncanny water. Evelyn burst through and into a cavern clawed from the riverbank. Water pushed against the walls, but neither flowed nor was absorbed. Great stones had tumbled into the space long ago and now rested on the cavern floor as algae-covered pews, an altar, and a font that bubbled deep indigo fluid over its lip to ooze slowly to the ground.

Mrs. Aiken stood in between the altar and the pews. She looked more like a barracuda now, her eyes bulbous above a pointed maw full of sharp teeth. Her limbs were ribbed and segmented like horsetail, surging up through her form and bursting out in hundreds of thin, green fronds in place of hair. Beyond the altar, the Great Mystery awaited: a dark current of water in which a bleak, many-armed form fluttered and writhed.

Her voice came as a wet gargling noise. "What a surprise to see you again at last—you took your time, Evelyn. Didn't you think I would remember you?"

Hands clenched into fists by her side, Evelyn replied in the same, if less-sure, manner, "Why would I think that? I remembered you every time I closed my eyes. Why did you take Oscar?"

Mrs. Aiken made a terrible face. "I would never touch him!"

"But you took my family. And I came to get them back."

"The Great One took them. I am only Its Handmaid."

"Well, you suck at it. You can't even run this hotel without people knowing weird shit happens here. Half the con kids are spooked and ready to leave early. I'd say that's pretty lousy management."

"You're challenging me?" Mrs. Aiken was agog, which would have been more impressive if someone with a fish face ever *didn't* look agog. "One tiny dry-lander?"

"Me and my family," Evelyn replied. She opened her fists and the blood she had collected flowed out of her hands and mingled with the strange slow mess that had followed them from the parking garage. Where the running gore hit the rising water on the floor of the cavern, four eldritch creatures of mud and blood, reed and bone, and magic older than Mankind rose: knots of tentacles, beaks, and unholy eyes, over and around which the river flowed in loving strokes.

Evelyn's monstrosities raised a mighty wave within the cavern and rushed toward Mrs. Aiken as one great and awesome swell bent on destruction.

"Stop." A huge voice like the sea's own boom on lonely shores, in vile harmony with another—alien and wild—froze the wave in place.

Poised at the moment before it breaks, the wave hung over Mrs. Aiken, who huddled into an abject ball at its base, while Evelyn spun, staring around the room to find the source of the voice. She looked toward the Great Mystery, where the river curtain had split open and something that was not quite Oscar slipped out to glide across the water on a dozen boneless, spatulate arms.

And Tulia, seeping and flowing through the water with her braids streaming behind as waving strands of blood-streaked sawgrass, joined him in front of the altar. They wove half-and-half into each other.

A mad bubbling that was knowledge more than sound bled into Evelyn's mind. *"Correction Is Our Purview, Little Evie And We Are Very Disappointed. Your Performance Has Been Unsatisfactory For Some Time, Mrs. Aiken, But Baiting Our Newest Member Of Staff Is Inexcusable."*

"I only tried to bring her into the fold, Great One," Mrs. Aiken whimpered from the floor, head still bowed.

"We Prefer To Be Called Management. As You Know."

"Yes, Management. I'm sorry."

"Is That An Apology?"

"Of course, Management."

"To Evie."

"For what?" Mrs. Aiken shrieked, jerking her head up and staring at the awful thing that was Management.

"For killing my family! For tormenting me!" Evelyn cried out. "And you're a lousy Housekeeper, and a worse boss!"

"I am the Handmaid!" Mrs. Aiken spluttered. "It was done for you, Great— uh... Management."

The water in the cavern heaved in a massive sigh. "*Pitiful,*" Management bubbled. "*We Do Not Accept Unwilling Sacrifice, Nor Do We Require Unpaid Overtime. Termination Is Our Only Option.*"

The interwoven beings that were Management turned to Evelyn. "*Do You Require Retribution, Little Evie?*"

Evelyn's braids had begun to writhe and coil themselves back onto her head, her mouth had become wider—almost splitting the lower part of her face from the rest, and she looked at Management with huge yellow eyes that glowed in the strange darkness. "Well, duh. That's what I came for."

Her wave of blood and fury fell upon Mrs. Aiken and swept the other woman away into the Great Mystery.

"*Much Better,*" said Management. "*Don't You Agree?*"

"Umm... Sort of. But have you seen the state of this place?"

"*How Would You Feel About A Promotion?*"

Evelyn thought about it and shrugged. "Well, I *did* come to clean house..."

END

RetCon

M. J. Stoumbos

About the Author: M. J. STOUMBOS is a 1st-place winner of the Writers of the Future contest and the author of the space opera series THIS FINE CREW. His work has appeared in a number of anthologies and collections, including *Street Magic*, *Galactic Stew*, and *Dragon Writers* alongside Brandon Sanderson. Mike Jack teaches high school composition and fiction writing, as well as goal-setting workshops for adults. He also writes articles and essays for TheBookBreak.com and other groups. You can find him at MikeJackStoumbos.com or @MJStoumbos on Twitter.

RetCon

M. J. Stoumbos

Screams of terror and anguish erupted from every corridor of the cursed castle, as I ran for my life along the garish red carpet. Newly stained clusters of deep scarlet created variations in the design—as did the bodies.

The only sound that overtook the caterwauls of human lungs was the stretching and shredding of the building's foundations, more like angered groans than rumbles, tilting the floor underfoot, ripping away sections behind me.

I banked at the corner, then skidded to a hasty halt, seeing a gap of at least twenty feet which had collapsed into rubble.

Frantically spinning, searching for options, I spotted one window—it bowed for a half-second, then buckled under strain. Tiny shards of glass darted toward me, and I barely managed to shield my face.

Then, before I could pick a direction, the floor ratcheted down, so suddenly I dropped to one knee, slicing through slacks and into skin.

When I raised my eyes from my bloodied leg, I saw something almost majestic through the broken window: a pristine mountain, the centerpiece of the distant horizon, framed by a lush forest of blue-green fir trees, and separated from me by a river.

—then the floor collapsed entirely, ushering me swiftly down into crushing darkness, faster than even gravity should be allowed to carry me.

I woke to a jarring sensation when the car rocked on uneven beams of the old but sturdy bridge. Not that I needed the extra encouragement into consciousness, but striking my forehead against the window did the trick. "Jesus!"

"Blasphemy," muttered the other gent in the back seat of the luxury sedan—which ought to have been a much smoother ride. Not that he was particularly religious, or even Christian, but my manager, CJ Patel, had this thing about the power of words. He gave the slightest shake of his head, but did not otherwise look up from his tablet. It displayed one of those organizer apps, that tracks the far-too-many tasks and potential events we would hit this weekend. "Did you have a good nap?"

"Um...." My throat felt raw, like I'd been sleeping for months and not minutes. "Had the craziest dream. Are we close?"

From the front seat, our uber driver piped back, "We've crossed onto the island, so just a few minutes more to the hotel and *Slash on the Rocks*." She sounded inconveniently chipper for such an early hour, but I had to get used to that. Soon, I'd be neck-deep in a sea of twisted, macabre superfans.

I looked out the car window and, for a weird second, was grateful to see it intact. Letting the dream's visceral terror ebb away, I instead focused on the well-groomed and isolated island. The bridge wasn't too far behind us, but I could still see where the land sloped into ravine. Even in the morning twilight, the spruces lining the opposite shore appeared majestic. I could imagine how their aesthetic might appeal if they dripped with blood.

"Des," said CJ, pulling my attention, "I've worked out your schedule for the convention." His accent drew on both his Indian heritage and finishing school flair, resulting in an iconic mix of intriguingly exotic Fortune-500—a remark which CJ called "accurate, but a tad racist." He kept me in check that way. He pointed a slender index finger at the various tabs and organizers on his screen. "Panels, autographs, merch-rep, VIP luncheon, and downtime. And of course, opening address today."

I noticed the driver's eyes in the rearview, a look of recognition, not yet voiced.

"Any chance of another nap before all of that?" I asked, but CJ just handed me a thermos.

"Coffee, black." CJ Patel was many wonderful things, but few would describe his manner as compassionate. I rounded up to *direct* and *efficient*, rather than *cold*.

"Do you mind if I drink coffee back here?" I asked the driver.

"Go ahead!" she blurted, her excited eyes locked on mine in the mirror. Good thing we were going so slowly up the switchbacks or she might have taken us over the edge.

Of course, when our destination came into view, all three heads turned forward and stared.

The hotel itself was more like a castle, and could have inspired any horror writer worth his salt. At first glance, it had a fancy, looming quality, with far too many floors and extra rooms, and a twisted split-level look when you tried to line up windows from one wing to another. Though only viewing from one side, I made out four distinct turrets around the corners, surrounding a grand-lodge centerpiece with an old-fashion gothic mansion roof threatening the sky above.

Even in the brightening morning, I half-expected a cheesy bolt of lightning to shriek across the blue canvas sky to set the scene.

"This is kickass," I observed.

"Agreed," said CJ. "They weren't kidding when they said they'd managed a better venue than last year."

He sounded so impressed, I had to wonder if he were being smug. After all, it was a legitimate gothic mansion on a rocky island accessible by only one bridge. In other words, perfect. "Did you book this place?"

He laughed. "I am afraid I cannot take the credit. But I did manage to get you the best room in the house."

"Uh-huh." I knew the drill: the headliner was promised the "grandest suite," but hotels often told several people they were getting the best room, assuming we'd never bother to compare them. In theory, if any fans did get lucky enough to score a suite invite, they probably wouldn't waste time comparing square footage.

"Where do you want me to park?" she asked.

"Anywhere," I replied, but CJ took the metaphorical wheel.

"Follow the arrows, where it says *Guests*."

Though *guest* would usually mean anyone at a hotel, this weekend, it meant people like me: pros who made special, advertised appearances at conventions. The banner over the general entrance had this garish, silver-age comic-book lettering with cartoon blood splattered across the words "Welcome to Slash on the Rocks."

We pulled into the parking lot closest to the "Featured Guests" side entrance, where more cars were unloading merch. My publisher had already shipped boxes of the books to the site, so I just had to drag my sleepy self out and up the ramp.

As we disembarked—CJ taking his personal suitcase, and me wielding a less ornate duffle—the driver worked up enough courage to ask, "Hey, are you Desmond Macaulay?"

"Guilty," I replied, my expression too charming to be subtle, even under dark glasses and hood.

"Oh my god, can you—" She rummaged in her glovebox. "Can you sign something for me?"

CJ tried to intercept with, "Actually—"

But I said, "Sure."

"I don't have a copy, but..." She produced and handed me a small, lavender notepad, bordered with stick-figure butterflies.

I held back a laugh at the juxtaposition. Not everyday you get the autograph of a horror author and illustration on the kind of stationery your grandmother keeps by the landline.

CJ supported his suitcase with one hand and planted the other firmly on his hip, while he waited impatiently for me to sign. "You know, we're charging for those inside." I couldn't tell if the remark was to me or her.

But I'd already autographed, free of charge.

"Thank you so much!" said our driver, and almost ended the exchange on a very positive note, until, "One more thing. I just need to know—for the new season, you're going to bring back Jennifer, aren't you?"

Any chance of humor sloughed off my face. The pressuring gut punch of every online forum throughout the summer, petitions to rewrite the rules of the series in order to revive the character who'd died. I felt like I'd had this conversation a hundred times already, and the mention provided nausea, foreboding, or just plain annoyance.

This time CJ intervened, grabbing me by the elbow to pull me along. "We're needed inside." He gave a curt nod to the driver. "Thank you!"

"Okay, bye! Have a good convention!" she called after.

As soon as the uber had started away, CJ said, "You should've charged her."

"Oh, come on, it's a little signature."

"It's not free anymore. Not at events like this."

I breathed in through my nose and then huffed out

through my mouth, knowing he was right. It was one of those *be-careful-what-you-wish-for* things. No one could have predicted how much my paranormal mystery series would take off, and that conventions would keep upping the price point to get signed pictures with me. It made me feel a little silly, but it also got me guest-of-honor status at castles on islands.

Before we went in, I allowed myself one last satisfying scan of the grounds, taking in the slope toward the river and the tree-line on the far bank. Maybe it was the last remnant of my nap speaking, but I had the briefest impression of a pair of eyes—like a coyote's—looking back at me. Of course, I blinked and they'd gone, but the little hint of ominousness was the final touch to help me feel right at home.

The lobby was just as impressive as the exterior, and somehow just cozy enough to feel familiar—perhaps more due to convention trimmings than architecture. The twin stairways, curved around the center of the room, giving the whole space a grand circular illusion, which was augmented by carpet's design and a crystal chandelier above. Otherwise, most fixtures had been updated or covered for the occasion. The ornate, historical trappings were adorned with posters and cutouts of the greatest (and localest) in horror fiction. Many blown-up paintings and book covers, the odd musician or minor TV star standee, and of course my series: *Vladimir Holmes*. The cover of my first issue, with the greatest vampire detective the worlds had ever known, took up a massive display, and by it stood my own cardboard likeness, labeled, *Desmond Macaulay—Guest of Honor*.

CJ had the tact not to accuse me of this, but I often frequented small venues to feel like a big fish. The poster version of me wore hair a little longer than my current cut, as well as a dark-blue suit. A precisely trimmed, jet-black goatee framed the confident face, staring back at the less-polished me.

My hooded sweatshirt, dark sunglasses, and two-days' stubble didn't mar me beyond recognition. The concierge spotted us and scurried over with words of welcome, then quickly summoned the young man who'd be my handler— the convention minion assigned to the talent.

This kid, as bright-eyed and bushy-tailed as they come, had round, freckled cheeks just begging to be illustrated. He exuded the impression that he'd not only requested to work with me but had cashed in every favor to do so.

Unfortunately, it didn't take two minutes for him to eagerly ask, "How are you going to bring back Jennifer? All my friends and I are talking about it. Our favorite theory—"

I groaned loudly enough to stop him mid-sentence. Sometimes I maintained poise and patience for this kind of thing, but for some reason, I was feeling particularly drained today, and just couldn't entertain the conversation for what felt like the thousandth time. "She's not coming back."

The fanboy's face fell, as surely as if I'd run a dagger through his favorite anime plushie.

CJ, who'd been speaking to the concierge, paused to stare at me. The look was chilling, *damning* even, for I'd just alienated a reader.

"Look," I said, a little more evenly and maturely, "sometimes, even in supernatural series, characters can die and not come back to life." Even this seemed to miss, coming off more patronizing and sarcastic, despite intended sincerity. I noticed more spectators, at this point all volunteers or other pros, watching the conversation. I felt as if I were giving my keynote early, a preview of things to come. Some were already whispering—even the pros— and I'd seen far too many people say it to not recognize the name *Jennifer* on someone's lips.

The freckled fanboy sputtered a faltering, "But..."

I stepped back, farther into the center of the lobby. Standing between curved stairways on the carpet's centerpiece sigil, I told him—and anyone in earshot. "In last season's final issue, Jennifer died—not just died, but exploded into banefire, incinerating her soul. It's just not possible for anyone to—"

A crunching noise cut me off, drawing my attention to a sudden crack in the wall. Several people gasped and dropped or huddled for fear of an earthquake, but the floor did not noticeably rattle. One dark little door under the spidering crack had twisted in its frame, and off popped its little gold-painted "Maintenance" label, in a manner almost comical.

The concierge asked, "Is everyone okay?" and, amid *yes*es, several chuckled in relief.

Nursing an eerie suspicion, I stared at the crack above the door, until someone yelled, "Look out!"

I managed to raise my gaze just in time to see another circle—now less ornate, but somehow more organic as it fell, splaying the dangling bobbles in random directions, like the patterns of a human iris in extreme close up.

My perspective afforded me that brief, beautiful view, until the chandelier crushed me.

@@@

I woke to a jarring sensation when the car rocked, so much I banged my forehead against the window. "Jesus!"

"Blasphemy," muttered CJ.

Before he could ask if I'd had a good nap, I surged forward, catching my collarbone in the seatbelt and clutching my chest with one hand. Had I been entirely awake, I might have come up with something more eloquent than, "Chandelier!"

Of course, there was no chandelier in sight, and the view from the sedan up the hill was serene in the thinning fog, which faded faster than the dream. It took CJ the rest of the drive up the way to reassure me that I was fully awake and not impaled. Our driver was too weirded out to ask me anything as we exited the uber.

"It was too freaky," I told CJ in the gravel parking lot, whispering so the other unloading pros wouldn't assume I was a complete nut. "Like actually being killed at *Slash on the Rocks.*"

"More traumatic or inspirational?" asked CJ, clearly hoping I'd pick the latter.

Either way, with each step and each semi-sarcastic remark from my manager, I felt like I was putting distance between myself and the dream. That is until I went inside.

I had toured many mansions and castles—honest tax-deductible research for a vampire detective series—and they certainly did not *all blend together.* They were distinct in size, shape, color, feel.

But this castle—whose name I didn't even know, on some island in a river—was far too familiar. This went beyond deja vu; I'd have called the castle a dead ringer, and I'm the kind of nerd who knows where that term comes from. Worst of all, when I looked up, I saw the massive chandelier, suspended above a circular pattern in the carpet like some kind of religious seal.

I must have stood with my mouth open for too long, because CJ intervened. "Des, I think we should just get you to the show floor and set up."

I nodded, keeping one eye on the chandelier as I shuffled my steps away from its circle of light.

"Let me introduce you to your assistant," said CJ, indicating the convention minion who would be my handler, a young man with a huge smile and freckled cheeks—who, just then, was the most terrifying image I'd ever witnessed.

"Oh, no!" burst from my throat like projectile vomit. I tried to rein in. "No, no, no—Thank you—No."

With no follow-up comment, I marched away from the

lobby.

@@@

Fortunately, the rest of the castle didn't remind me as immediately of dreamt-up death. While I couldn't totally shake the familiarity, I settled down enough to get to work. Headliner or not (windfall success or not) I was still going to be professional; professionals give speeches and sell books.

CJ remained eerily quiet and calm while we draped black blankets over cheap folding tables and set up the issues of the comics in neat, eye-catching stacks. The production value had increased over the years, leading up to the most recent—my best sold, and best rated issue, even with the character death that so many people wanted me to undo.

And when we unrolled the banner, a six-foot graphic of the main characters, the now-dead Jennifer glared back at me, her green eyes narrowed and determined. Of course, I'd drawn her that way, just like I'd drawn the hero beside her, Vladimir Holmes, who wore the same beard but was taller, darker, and much more attractive than me, by design. Reminders that the series was, after all, a work of fiction.

"You might consider what your fans want," said CJ. "Give them some candy instead of spinach."

"I'm not in the business of candy," I said. "And they'll get over it. It's not like the series started with Jennifer, and it's done great since issue one."

CJ nodded, and abandoned the brief attempt to convince me. He knew as well as I that my graphic novels were still continuing to top the sales rankings. He may have questioned whether I made a literal deal with the devil to make this happen, but CJ always left the content of the series in my capable hands.

He didn't even look over the opening speech—simply

wished me luck and sent me up to the podium.

The castle's auditorium had that lovely ancient theatre feel and smell. The lights were bright enough to prevent me from seeing the audience in detail. Like the lobby, though, keynote addresses seemed dreadfully similar and often boring.

I delivered this one swiftly, keeping it short to not get in the way of the real programming. Everything was going fine, but my eyes kept adjusting, until I could see those of the audience, and then the familiarity grew stronger, overwhelmingly so.

I'd finished and was about to hand off the microphone to the host, when someone called. "Hey! How're you gonna bring back Jennifer?"

Renditions began playing through my mind, times when I had said, *That can wait til the panel* or *Come find me on the show floor.* In this reality, I froze.

But doing nothing fixed nothing. The adience member then shouted, "Bring back Jennifer!" And on repeat, gathered more, until the crowd, in one voice, were chanting, "Bring back Jennifer! Bring back Jennifer!"

Armed with only a microphone and the slipping confidence that I was the author in control of the series, I snapped. *"She's just a character!"*

There was a collective gasp, from everyone in the room, as if under a spell, recoiling backwards from this terrible report simultaneously. It was eerie how much they could get swept up in inane pop culture—and that's coming from the author.

"Jennifer is a two-dimensional creation from my mind, and she's gone, dead, and there's nothing in her universe that can bring her back!" I panted, seethed, practically frothed at the mouth, and I heard myself saying slight variations on the same theme in a thousand renditions of my keynote address. It always preceded destruction.

This time, one of those bright stagelights flared, as

the old oils and dusts overheated enough to ignite. The fire jetted and spread, cascading along the ceiling and dripping chunks down to the floor. Each seat and handrail seemed impossibly flammable, overwhelming the people nearby, who—dashed from the spell—tried to run but with nowhere safe to go, not on this island.

I *knew* in that moment, I'd seen this auditorium fill with fire, water, wind. I'd seen the upper floors, the stairways, every turret destroyed. I'd heard that roar from underground.

It was the purest cacophony of chaos I had ever known; I only hoped to remember it next time.

"I'm serious!" I told CJ, as our car once again approached the haunted mansion. "I'm in a literal time-loop where everyone is being killed."

The driver seemed to be scanning for hidden cameras, in case of a public prank.

"Des, *Slasher on the Rocks* is too immature a pun, even for you."

"This isn't a joke, CJ, and it's not a slasher either. I'm talking earthquakes, the ground swallowing us, bolts of lightning, floods!" Even I had to admit that the list ended anti-climatically, and what I could remember of the flood deaths were more boring than cool.

"Okay, I think you've let your imagination run rampant," said CJ, as we pulled into the parking lot, the tires crunching through loose gravel. "Now, let's go inside before we're in butterfly net territory."

I was developing other retorts as we exited the vehicle, but all felt too silly to be believed. If I were CJ, I wouldn't buy them either.

Then the driver leaned over and asked, "Hey, Mister Macaulay, are you going to bring back Jennifer?"

"No!" I hollered, balling my hands into fists. "No, she's

dead and she's not coming back. Find someone else to ship!"

Just then, a chorus of snarls interrupted from over the ridge. CJ and the driver both cried out in alarm when they saw a swarm of coyotes charging up the hill toward the parking lot.

I might have run or fought on other renditions. This time rolled my eyes and sat crosslegged on the ground, while anyone in earshot raced futilely for safety.

Funny thing, when I placed my bare palms on the actual rocks, I felt something strange: a kind of tremor and a faint, deep groan. But this wasn't an earthquake; this cataclysm would be carried out by coyotes, one of whom was already dragging CJ by the ankle.

Looking down, I noticed a distinct orange glow, slivering up through the pieces of gravel. Then, my vision was interrupted by a coyote's jaw.

It hardly mattered whether I'd done this ten times or a thousand. The lobby was both new and familiar, as I looked down from the lofted second floor and made the declaration. The words rolled off my tongue, another crushing rejection of all my fans' (and Jennifer's) hope.

This time, when rumbling began, I was ready. Though my physical body had never experienced this, my mind understood it.

I ran, not to the emergency exit, but the stairs *down.* Down was closer to the source. Going up wouldn't work, going out wouldn't work, but down would.

Even then, I couldn't explain exactly how I knew, but the terrain was familiar to me. I knew to jump to the left in order to avoid crashing into somebody and getting us both too tangled to escape. I knew to skid to a halt before a chandelier shattered to the lobby floor in front of me.

I needed to know. Something underground had been

controlling everything. And it would be through that dark little maintenance door and the stairs behind it.

Water already trickled down, courtesy of a rising river outside, but I moved faster than they would flood.

The dark stairway's walls were a mix of mottled cement and exposed rebar. Rickety hanging lightbulbs slashed dim beams onto wooden steps that probably hadn't seen service in generations.

I wondered if this path was new, if I'd ever made it this far before. Then, a gut urge told me to stagger my step, to switch left and right feet. I'd chosen correctly: a large nail stuck out of one of the boards, precisely where I would have stepped—and had undoubtedly trod before.

So I'd pierced my foot on this stair at least once, maybe many times more. But I didn't stop; maybe this time, I'd win.

A few inches of water had filled the bottom, but the smell was more putrid than what could be managed by fresh river water. The aroma of ancient tombs, a leviathan's belly, or a living volcano.

And, yes, there stood another door. Barely holding back the water on my side and allowing a sliver of light from the other.

I tried the handle, but it was locked. Still, like everything this far below, the wood was ancient. So, with a roar of exertion, I shoved my shoulder through, feeling aged wood crunch and split, and eventually give way to an otherworldly orange glow.

My feet half-stumbled forward, in confusion and maybe awe. For, beyond the door, was nothing constructed by man. A precipice, a rocky cliff, charcoal black, and pointing its sharpened shard to the source. And there floated... a wonder that could scarcely be described and never accurately drawn in a single still frame.

It was, among other things, a grand eye, floating in an abyss, some unknowable distance from the precipice.

The glow within the pupil backlit gross tendrils, which from a greater distance could appear like the patterns of a human iris. No arms or articulating tentacles spread from the eye, but some changing number of hooks pressed out through the meat around that iris, reaching forward and pulling on... something, beyond my ken.

The hooks manipulated ribbons of impossibly colored smoke, threads stretching up into darkness, toward the surface of the *real* world. This giant, floating eye pulled the puppet strings of the island from below.

I felt like I was observing the strands of fate, but it scarcely mattered if I was right—about anything, the being's construction or its powers. I just needed to end the loop.

"Yoooouuu disturb me..." drawled a voice, from nowhere—and everywhere, and made me want to drop to my knees, weeping in supplication, or to vomit in my mouth. As a horror writer, I resisted both.

"I disturbed you?" I asked. Maybe I should have started with something more polite and reverent, but my manners must have faded several deaths ago. "*I* distrubed *you*? You've been killing me." I paused to check myself. "It was you, wasn't it?"

I'd never seen a floating orange eye reluctantly nod, but the gesture was too big to miss.

"Okay. Well, before you get all high-and-mighty about me waking you up, maybe you should have assumed this would be a consequence of putting a *horror writer*—" I stressed, pointing both forefingers at myself. "—through a hell loop. I was bound to figure it out."

"No," grumbled the being, in a tone I could tell was more annoyed than wrathful or awe-inspiring. "You did not wake me. I would not sleep through any of this. Not when you have come to my convention. Why would I slumber through my own conjured entertainment?"

Some bizarre internal logic followed: if this ancient

monster had summoned everyone here for its own amusement, it probably wouldn't nod off.

"I mean, *your choices disturb me, AUTHOR!*" This sounded like an accusation, as if calling me 'author' would force me to apologize.

Instead, I laughed.

"What is so funny?" it demanded, causing me to laugh harder.

"*My* choices? What about your choices? You're killing everyone here and resetting time. Over what?"

"This—is—important! You have a responsibility to your characters and your world—as do *we* to *yours*."

This was a new concept, that a god might consider me another deity, but of the world I wrote. "This is about my series? No, wait, specifically what I'm planning next season. Well—Geez, if you wanted me to change the plan, why not a memo? Why not send CJ a tip?"

"It doesn't work that way! I maneuver the strands and threads of people's fate."

"Okay," I said, interrupting before it could go into a long diatribe about being older than time or something, "but this has got to be the most elaborate way to tell me you want something without ever actually telling me what you want."

"Isn't it obvious?" it asked, and, in a way, it was.

I had been trying to deny it for... well, for as many times as I'd died. But I'd only been delaying the inevitable conclusion.

"You must bring back *JENNIFER!*" It's voice warbled in such tragic passion. "I cannot rest since Jennifer has exploded. My eye does not shut. My gaze does not falter for many mortal months, and many hundreds of iterations beyond that!"

"You too?" I blinked. "I mean, she was a good character. A total hottie, badass shapeshifter, who rejected the throes of any thrall. But she's a character. She died. And the story continues."

"But not without Jennifer!" it bellowed, in a manner somewhere between Godzilla and a Dalek, and put enough pressure on my ears to trigger sudden popping. Immense but fleeting pain gave way to a trickle of blood down the lobe and my neck.

But I'd been through too much to give in so easily. "Excuse me?" I countered. "You're demanding I change my series for you?"

"You little worm," sneered the eye. "You ungrateful cur! *Your* series?!? *I* made it possible. If not for me, your pathetic rag never would have seen more than two issues. I made you. I created your success; I twisted the limelight to shine on you, and led millions to your story who would have never known your name. I pushed the waves into motion for you to become phenomenal, and in turn you serve me by drawing."

The last piece fell into place. I had indeed sold my soul. In as close to a literal sense as I'd ever imagined. While this explained a lot, it was, unfortunately, a little insulting, and encouraged—shall we say—resistance. "And what if I don't make the change? Will you just keep killing everyone? If you do, you'll never get to see next season anyway, and isn't a season without Jennifer better than no season at all?" I knew I was tempting whatever the hell version of fate is called, but I figured I had little to lose. If I died here, who's to say I wouldn't just come back and resume the conversation?

The eye did not leap out and strangle me with hooks or tendrils, not yet at least, so I had its attention.

"Look," I went on, "I wrote and illustrated the end of a season, in which a favorite character died, and people were still clamouring for more. Because there will be more! Something else will happen, another character will happen. Besides that, my series doesn't actually change you at all. You're infinite, immortal—probably. I mean, you can control whether this island collapses in on itself and kills everybody. So why do you care about a graphic novel?"

The eye shifted, and moaned, like a toddler starting to pout even though there was no logic to the umbrage it was feeling.

"Seriously," I pressed, "why do you need me to change it? Why can't you just create what you want?"

The eye turned away from me, and scrunched as close to closed as it could manage without lids, then let out an anguished cry of, "I can't draw!" In an instant, the giant eye went from terrifying primal god to distraught muppet.

"I have tried," it went on, "but I do not have the appendages. And when I try to force minions by seizing their minds, they do not have the motor control, they do not take my creative suggestions, they do not produce the images I need! To live forever..." it sighed, "and to fall short of mortal talent. It shames me."

My eyebrows could have lifted my feet from the charred rock. This god needed me to write and illustrate the series. This god also had hooks into my soul, which I'd traded away through endless prayers for success as an author-illustrator.

I was a god-damned Faustian author, but I also held a bargaining chip, a get-out-of-soul-jail card if I played it right... "Seems to me we're at an impasse."

"An impasse?"

"Yeah. You won't let time resume until I bring back Jennifer, but I can't change the laws of my universe without damaging its integrity. I mean you, of all fans, know that Jennifer was blasted into oblivion, and was completely destroyed beyond any hope of return."

"True..."

"So, if you want me to pull a massive ret-con, you have to do something for me," I said, hoping the eye couldn't hear how fast my heart was thudding. "Release me, let me go from whatever ownership you have on my soul, and I swear to you, on pain of whatever you'd do to me, that I will bring back Jennifer and keep her alive and in the story for another five seasons at least."

"Ten!" it countered.

"Deal!" I said, amazed that it hadn't said a hundred and not trying to offend it again. "If I'm alive and working for the next ten years, Jennifer will be too."

It hummed, mused to itself, in a cacophony that sounded like a million angry bees. Then, "Deal."

I felt relief—but only for an instant, when I realized there was still one chore left to do in this lifetime. "You have to reset the island again, don't you?"

I'd never before seen a giant eye shrug. "Last time," it promised.

The eye flared open, tendrils waggling. Several articulating hooks shot toward me. My very last hope was that I wouldn't remember the sensations of being eaten by that eye.

@@@

I woke to a jarring sensation of a rocking car and a forehead against the window. "Owww..." I groaned.

"You look like hell," remarked CJ.

"Been there," I said. The driver's eyes flicked toward me, then back to the road. I scooted forward and asked her, "Hey, do you read *Vladimir Holmes*?"

"Ohmygod, yes! Are you Desmond Macaulay?"

"Yeah." I bit my lip and swallowed a particularly stubborn pill, without making eye contact with CJ. "What would you think of us bringing back Jennifer next season?"

Though I'm loath to use the term, she squeed. "I knew it! I knew she couldn't be gone. How are you going to do it?"

I expected CJ to chide me for giving away secrets to

non-paying customers, but he too shifted in his seat, facing me with sudden interest. "Yes, how? You'd said it was impossible."

"It was... or so everyone thought. But she's coming back. And as for how," I cleared my throat, "*that* will remain a mystery."

When I stepped out of the car into the morning light, I have to admit that everything seemed brighter this time around, less likely to become enveloped in sudden evil fog.

As soon as our driver had started away, CJ took the opportunity to check in. "So you're finally giving your readers some candy to counter all the spinach."

"Seems like."

"Mm-hmm. Smart. But you don't really know how you're going to bring her back, do you?"

I grinned and shook my head. "Not yet. Maybe I'll have an alternate universe, or we'll find out that the version who got killed was a duplicate golem. Or maybe a time loop to reset what went wrong."

CJ actually sneered at that idea. "That's overplayed. Besides, you already ruled out the other two possibilities, so if you do revive the character, you might have to change the rules of your universe."

I shrugged, musing about exactly how I work this announcement into my speech, but finally grateful for the opportunity to move forward. "Sometimes it's what you have to do to appease your fans."

"Glad to hear it," said CJ, "if you tick them off, they'll eat you alive."

END

David Boop

About the Author: DAVID BOOP is an author, editor, screenwriter and award-winning essayist. His debut novel was the sci-fi/noir, *She Murdered Me with Science*. His follow-up, *The Soul Changers*, is a Victorian Horror based on the Savage Worlds RPG, *Rippers Resurrected*. Wolfpack Publishing released his weird western mosaic novel, *The Drowned Horse Chronicle – Volume One* in 2022.

David edited the bestselling weird western anthology series starting with *Straight Outta Tombstone*, and recently released his first space western anthology, *Gunfight on Europa Station*. He's worked with characters such as Predator, The Green Hornet, Kolchak, the Black Bat, and Veronica Mars.

Find out more at Davidboop.com, Facebook.com/dboop. updates,Twitter @david_boop, or www.longshot-productions. net.

I See Stars of Green...
David Boop

Buster Hideo couldn't believe his good luck. Of all the volunteer staff for Helluvacon©, he was chosen, if by destiny, to be the guest liaison. He hadn't particularly known what the job had entailed when he raised his hand during position volunteering. Quite the opposite, really. He hoped someone would explain what a guest liaison did. The con chair, however, had listed off his duties vaguely. She must've guessed he was familiar with them, seeing as he'd raised his hand and all.

The only reason Buster wanted the position was that it gave him exclusive access to his favorite author of all-time, Stefen Proust. Proust's novels were the stuff that dreams (and nightmares) were made of. Buster ate every word the flamboyant author wrote thanks to his fannish father, who first read Proust's books to him as a child, but then later encouraged Buster to read on his own as he grew up.

Epic fantasy.

Comedic Science fiction.

Even touching into the macabre with his most recent works.

Helluvacon® would be the first time Buster got to meet his writer idol. As he navigated the always-under-construction highway to the airport, he grew nervous.

What if they didn't connect? What if Proust was in one of his legendary bad moods? What if Buster had a booger hanging from his nose?

After Buster parked and checked himself in the side-view mirror for the third time, confirming no hangers, he walked briskly into the main terminal. He unfolded the sign he'd made last night which had Proust's name printed on it, along with the con's logo: a she-devil in a *Sailor Moon* cosplay. He pushed his way forward through the crowd of people waiting for their loved ones to ascend from the arriving trams.

Buster spotted the Cavalier's hat coming up the escalator first. You couldn't miss it if you tried. It was like a black hole that inevitably drew your eyes to it with intense gravitational forces. Ebon as midnight, the brim extended out from Proust's head easily in a twelve-inch radius on one side, while the other side was pinned up against the crown. A feather—that could have only come from a Great Eagle of Tolkien lore—arced out from the trim like a bright, white fountain.

Adding to the jaunty pirate appearance, Proust carried the look from the hat down, with long, wavy, gray hair and a bushy mustache extending past a soul patch on his chin.

Proust wore a white tunic under a brown leather coat of the type custom-made at a Renaissance faire. Matching pants and boots, completed the look. As Proust stepped from the escalator, he carried with him his musical instrument case.

Buster grinned. Inside the case would rest "Yseld," Proust's lute who created the second half of his legend as a genius filker. The singer-songwriter had as many musical Guest of Honor credits as Author GOHs. Proust wrote fantasy ballads based on his books, other people's books, movies, history, and some just born of his imagination. Buster owned his one and only album and played it on repeat in the background as he studied for his college classes. Each song was like a whole novel unto itself. Proust's concert would be Saturday night of Helluvacon™.

Prost scanned the expectant crowd, found Buster, strode toward him with purpose and asked in his raspy voice, "Where can a guy go to smoke a cigarette in this place?"

@@@

"Mind if I smoke in your car? I'll crack a window."

That would be the third cigarette Proust smoked since he arrived. One while waiting for his luggage. One outside the car as Buster loaded that luggage into the trunk. And now, another.

"Sure." Buster didn't smoke, but he already smelled like a pack-a-day user. "So, Mr. Proust, excited for the convention?" He immediately regretted the question.

Proust answered magnanimously. "Of course. I mean, one con is not really different than the other, but I think this one will be special."

Feeling encouraged, Buster continued, "What's different about Helluvacon¿" He caught the author grinning out of the corner of his eye.

"Ah, yes. Well, I've been to this hotel before, many years ago. I attended the first con there."

Helluvacon✳ had been held at the Columba Riverbeach Hotel for thirty-three years. The property's private owners had resisted recessions, attempted buy-outs, weather damage, and the like. Even the city tried to seize it, claiming "eminent domain," but the owners successfully sued to greatly increase the asking price and the city gave up.

"That's fascinating," Buster exclaimed, again, mentally slamming his head against the wall. *Chill out, dude!* He thought.

"Indeed," Proust replied. "I loved this hotel back in the day. Never found another hotel like it."

Buster knew exactly what the GOH meant. The Riverbeach's design was atypical and sort of counter-intuitive. Most hotels started at the front lobby and spread out equally to the sides, that way no one ever had to walk far to their room. Not the Riverbeach, though. The hallways branched off in several different directions, and then connected up in the conference center in the back, looking over the St. Columkille River. Often, con attendees became lost trying to find a panel room or the con suite.

"Buster, huh? Parents didn't like you?"

The young man chuckled. "It's not my real name. My dad was really into mech anime when I was little. He'd put it on in the background when he watched me in the evenings. I guess I got fascinated with the *Buster Gundam* and ran around blasting imaginary things yelling, 'I'm a 'Buster!' 'I'm a Buster!'"

"Cute story." Proust returned his attention to his cig and looking out the window.

They continued with the small talk such as Buster asking questions about Proust's work-in-progress, his latest tour, and the like. All too soon, they pulled up to the hotel. Buster gathered up the author's gear and let Proust lead the way to the front desk.

Nostalgia widened Proust's eyes as he spun slowly around scanning the lobby. Woodcarvings circled the trim around the top of the walls near the ceiling. They depicted an ancient sea battle between sailors and giant leviathans. The monsters, Buster always thought, looked very Kaiju to him and less mythological.

"Ah," Proust said with a sigh. "The Great St. Columkille Battle. Seventy-four men died protecting the village of Columba from demons that'd risen up from the river bottom to feed."

Buster cocked his head. "What? That's not the ocean? I've never heard that story before."

Proust got into line for the front desk. "Yeah, there's a lot about history they don't teach anymore. Science, too." Proust loved astronomy, according to his biography.

The author left the statement there, as if that said it all. Buster wondered if he was messing with him, ultimately deciding he was. Proust was a master storyteller and, despite feeling picked on, a warm feeling enveloped him. His favorite author had chosen to fuck with him, and that made Buster happy.

Until...

"Hi, Stefen Proust checking in. I'm warning you, I'm going to smoke in my room, so just go ahead and apply the fine now, so I can pay it now. That way the con isn't billed for my filthy habit."

Oh, man. Con Com really didn't prepare me for this.

After that kerfuffle, the rest of the first day went fine. The Con Chair came down and settled accounts for Proust, then Buster took his luggage to his room and allowed the grand master to settle in, rest, and grab another smoke before opening ceremonies.

At the first event, Proust was his usual mix of charming, flirtatious, and most of all, entertaining. He performed a quick number for the audience in which he thanked everyone for honoring him with being a GOH. There were, of course, three other GOHs, including a science GOH, art GOH, and fan GOH, but Proust stole the show.

Buster was responsible for all of the GOHs in some way, but the expectation was to focus on Proust, unless something else came up.

Right before the ceremony ended, Buster stepped on stage and handed each a gift bag he'd been required to arrange. Again, with very little prep beforehand, he had messaged each guest and asked them a series of questions. Inside the bag, they found their favorite snacks and a beautiful faux-jade figure of their spirit animal.

Proust, digging into his bag, raised an eyebrow at Buster, who smirked.

"I might wait until I get back to my room to dig through this. I have panels to get to," he apologized, but the audience urged him on. Never wanting to disappoint a crowd, Proust pulled out his "treat": a pint bottle of *Writer's Tears.*

The Con Chair glared at Buster from her seat. Her guest liaison shrugged and mouthed, *That's what he said was his favorite snack.* She continued to shoot Buster daggers, but became distracted when Proust inhaled sharply.

He held in his hand an intricately carved miniature *Manta*, a water Kaiju that Buster had slipped in there from his private collection. He wasn't going to give his idol some *tchotchke*. No, Buster wanted him to have something personal as a thanks for all the hours he'd spent living in the man's imagination.

For his part, Proust seemed really surprised and grateful. He thanked everyone and winked at Buster.

After that, Proust had two panels on writing. Buster planned to help him navigate the labyrinthine hallways, but the GOH showed he knew his way through them even better than his liaison. Panels successfully finished, Proust returned to his room.

Before stepping through the door, he motioned Buster to join him. "Come in," he offered as he opened the sliding glass door to his balcony.

Buster entered as Proust lit up what would be the first of many cigarettes. "Why don't you grab that bottle and pour us a shot of the Irish whiskey you were so kind to present to me?" Then, he paused. "You're old enough to drink, right?"

Buster countered, "I bought it, didn't I?"

Proust laughed. "Age never stopped me when I was young. I figured you were the resourceful type."

The young, but completely legal, man poured them each a healthy dose of the booze. When he stepped out onto the balcony, he found Proust admiring the wooden figure.

"You didn't buy this at some comic book store, did you?"

Handing the author his drink, Buster explained. "No, sir. For my senior trip, my parents and I went to Japan. As it so happened, we showed up on the first day of the Shibuya Renaissance festival." He blushed a bit. "Something about that figure spoke to me. I'm not *just* into giant mechs. I also *love* Kaiju."

Proust nodded. "We didn't have fancy names like that when *Godzilla* first came out, but I really connected with the message: respect nature...or be destroyed by it." He tipped his hat at Buster. "Thank you."

Buster blushed more.

Through the night, friends and peers visited Proust's room, which induced more drinking, more singing, and a lot more smoking. At times, the author would get a distant look in his eyes, as if the night brought back memories of that first HelluvaconX he attended. Some staff and attendees were still around from then, though none in the same form. They talked of aging, friends long gone. There was hugging, some kissing, but by 2 A.M., Proust shuffled them all out so he could have one last smoke and go to bed.

When Buster, the last, made to leave, Proust called to him from the balcony, where he leaned out looking at the night sky. "Did you know that our sun is actually green?"

Buster stopped and returned to stand beside the author.

"Green? I thought it looked yellow?"

"It actually looks white, if you could see it with the naked eye, because it burns so hot. The gases in our atmosphere scatter the wavelengths so we perceive yellow sun, blue sky." Proust pointed at a random star. "No, when I say green, I'm talking temperatures. Stars like our sun put out heat that's based on an RGB color index: blue hotter, red cooler, green–just right."

Buster, now engaged, asked, "Like RGB for TV monitors?"

"Yup, just like that. Our Sol is emitting heat that could best be described as 'green' on the index. Fascinating, huh?"

"Yessir, it is."

Proust frowned. "Stop with the 'yessir' bullshit. It's Stefen, okay?"

Buster agreed he would try. He excused himself, knowing Saturday would be a long day. He left Proust there, on the balcony, cigarette in hand, gazing at the stars, lost in his musings.

Proust sat on two panels leading up to his concert that evening. Buster watched on as the GOH showed up an entitled self-published author who claimed to know how the publishing industry worked. He used surgical precision as he disected their points. His fans in the audience cheered him on with laughter or the passé "Burn!" Fans of the author he eviscerated typed scathing reviews via their cells to the social media platform *du jour*. Buster doubted Proust even cared. He spent very little time online, letting his poly-partners handle most of his posts and email. The author currently had three, all dedicated to allowing him to focus on his latest work.

During his GOH talk, Proust revealed that the novel he'd just turned in was his darkest to date: a post-apocalyptic tale of mankind run amuck. He titled it, *A*

Wise Man's Hell.

"I call it a survival guide to the world we're heading for," he said with sly grin. "It's clear we've doomed our reality. So, how do we navigate the next? What are the rules?"

Someone raised a hand. "Isn't that what McCarthy did in his book?"

Proust leaned forward, a twinkle in his eye. "Sure, but he didn't go far enough. In mine, I'll take you places that the monsters in your nightmares see in *their* nightmares."

That made Buster uncomfortable. Sure, he wasn't opposed to dark fantasy, but the way his idol talked, it sounded full-on horror. Horror had never been a genre Buster dove into heavily. He preferred stories where the hero defeated evil, not just survived it.

Talk over, Proust handed Buster his room keycard.

"Can you go get Yseld for me? I'm going outside for a smoke. I'll tune her in main events before tonight, then I need to meet some fans for dinner."

Buster accepted his charge with enthusiasm.

Stepping into the hotel room, Buster scanned for Yseld's case, finding it on the desk. Buster gazed down at the fine ironwood case that'd been custom built with Yseld. Giving into impulse, Buster flipped the two locks to take a look inside the case, reasoning that he had to make sure she was in there. Replicated ancient Mesopotamia designs that Proust had discovered while researching his earlier books, she was as much art as instrument.

Yseld stunned. Shaped like an almond, and as deep a brown as one, eleven strings—nine in the center and two on either side—begged to be plucked.

Buster looked around the room, then to the door. Feeling safe, and knowing that Proust would be tuning her soon anyway, Buster picked Yseld up and held her lovingly. She felt warm to his touch, like a girlfriend sliding in under his arm. Positioning the lute as he'd seen

Proust do in videos, Buster laid a hand across her strings and strummed, just once.

The images searing his mind and replacing all thoughts with visions of blinding horror. Demons, large as skyscrapers, devastated cities. People died instantly from their touch, or were scooped up and devoured by the handful. The demons chewed their soft flesh, then spit their bones like sunflower seed shells. The Kaiju's destruction in movies paled in comparison to evil emanating from theses creatures' every pore. Some, not consumed, driven mad, tore their flesh from their bodies, or gouged their eyes out. Many…so very many…killed themselves in waves much as lemmings. Survivors became slaves to the demon masters.

All save for one.

A cloaked figure stood atop a mountain. He held Yseld in his hands and, as he played, the old ones danced joyfully over the world. He didn't so much control them, no mere mortal could completely, but amused the Old Ones enough to let him live.

No, not just live, Buster felt, but live forever.

Free of pain.

Free of age and disease.

Women, men, worshiped at his feet to gain his favor, and he let them. This was the future he wanted. To be the source of all joy in the world, to free it from human control, and return it to the reality that once had been.

And above, in the sky: a green sun.

When Buster dropped Yseld, she landed on Proust's bed, but he fell hard to the floor. He curled into a ball, trying to block the images from his mind, but they played over and over like a video meme you couldn't get to stop. He'd witnessed his family, his friends die in agonizing ways. No one was safe. No politician. No priest. No millionaire. All were fodder before the ancient ones.

Some semblance of sanity returned to Buster when his cell, which lay on the floor next to him, buzzed. The text was Proust asking if he'd had any trouble getting Yseld. Climbing unsteadily to his feet, Buster typed a quick "had to use restroom," then returned Yseld to her case. He noticed a folded piece of paper. Drawing it out, he found a handwritten sheet of music. The lyrics were of no language Buster had ever seen, but intermixed with the regular notes were strange symbols. Greek. Latin. Aramaic. And some undecipherable.

The final song Proust planned to play that night. The final song of Helluvacon☉; the final song for all of humanity.

☉☉☉

After Buster threw up in Proust's bathroom, and cleaned up any evidence of it, he felt stable. Sealing Yseld back in her case, he checked himself in the mirror, putting on his best fake smile.

He brought the case to Proust and then excused himself quickly, claiming other GOHs were upset he was spending so much time with the filker.

Motherfilker is more like it.

Proust understood but, with concern, asked, "You'll be at the concert tonight, I hope?"

Buster nodded. That would start in three hours, giving people time to dine and con services time to clear out chairs from main events and open the large blinds that looked out over the river.

Proust would sit on a low riser while attendees laid about on pillows or cushions surrounding him. The filk circle was a time-honored tradition, but the way the main hall was positioned, it would give whatever Proust planned to summon an easily accessible buffet.

Sitting on the bed in his room, Buster pulled his knees to his chest and rocked. No one would believe him. He barely even believed him. If he hadn't seen it in his own mind...

Why did I see it? Why did Yseld show me that? Doesn't the lute belong to him?

Buster thought how easy it was to personify an inanimate object. Yseld wasn't a living thing, right?

Right?

He pulled open his laptop and searched for the name Yseld.

Yseld — faerie. One of the gandharva, semi-immortal musicians believed to sing songs that could tame gods. Men sought her power by trapping her in musical instruments, forcing her to do their bidding. [translated from ancient Sanskrit. See references below.]

Then Yseld the lute wasn't just a lute, was she? The bastard Proust had actually trapped a fae inside of it. That's how he planned to control whatever beast lay at the bottom of the St. Columkille River.

But the wiki said control, not bring forth. So how did he plan to awaken the creature?

Buster remembered the symbols on the sheet music. He searched for a few and discovered they corresponded to hieroglyphic numbers throughout history. When he googled them, Buster realized those glyphs correlated to weather conditions. They could create or remove gasses in the air. Certain symbols removed oxygen, others hydrogen. Proust could customize the atmosphere! His mind, still overwhelmed from Yseld's warning, swam with all the data. It was too much. Demons. Stars. Music.

Stars. Green stars.

What had Proust told him? Our sun was a green star. Something about those symbols would trigger a change in our air, which would then release the krakens, per se.

Helluvacon♉ was ground zero for the apocalypse!

Looking at his watch, Buster knew he didn't have much time left. His googlefu had taken up the dinner hour. Attendees would be trickling their way back and soon the dealer's room would be closing for the night.

The dealer's room!

The Huckster's Room at Helluvacon✷ had one of the best selections of unusual items outside a comic-con. If any item could stop the destruction of humanity, it would be there.

Most of the attendees, guests, and staff of Helluvacon♋ sat on cushions (or ADA chairs where requested) in the main events hall. The opened blinds revealed the slow-rolling St. Columkille River behind Proust. A full moon hung at the top of the large glass windows, just above the city of Columba. Nearly three-quarters of a million people went about their lives, blissfully unaware. Their deaths would be the dinner bell for the Old Ones when Proust pulled his celestial stunt.

Buster couldn't make a move until Proust actually started his song. He knew that Yseld's message to him was a warning. She was the key.

The liaison had ignored all the texts from the Con Chair and the rest of the staff, demanding he report in. Buster hadn't had much time to arm himself before the dealer's room closed, it had to be enough.

Proust finished a number and bowed with the applause. "Thank you. That was *The Stream of Consciousness Brew*, a favorite at many of the taverns I've played in." He took in the crowd with a gaze Buster thought contained a strange mix of sorrow and compassion. "We've come to my final number." Disappointment exuded from the crowd. "Well, the final song for human ears, none-the-less." Proust sat and started a story, as he did before each song. "You see, I was diagnosed with inoperable and terminal pancreatic cancer about six months ago, ironically, just before I got your invite to be Helluvacon♎'s Guest of Honor."

Waves of shock and disbelief swept through the crowd. Some of Proust's friends began to cry. Buster watched as the Con Chair issued hushed orders to the staff, preparing for what she suspected would happen next.

Buster chuckled. *You've got no idea what's going to happen next.*

Proust held up a hand to silence the crowd. "Wait," he begged. "It's not all bad news. At least not for me. You see, I attended the first Helluvacon☾ here some thirty years ago, and when I did, I found the myth of The Great St. Columkille Battle fascinating. I decided that it'd make a fine subject for a novel, so I researched it and discovered it wasn't a myth. It actually happened!" Proust stood and paced around the riser. He explained to the confused audience, "Men had fought a giant river god named Dagon. They not-so-much 'beat him' as 'cast a spell that changed the atmosphere so the sun no longer appeared green.' That's what put the Old Ones to sleep."

He paused, looked out over the stunned faces, and backtracked. "That's right. I hadn't told you. You see the sun's actually gre—" He waved the thought away. "You know what? Never mind. I'm running out of time. Let me cut to the chase. Dagon is powerful and has the power to heal or destroy. I'm going to wake him up, you see, and get him to heal me."

A majority of the crowd breathed audible sighs of relief. Others laughed, finally "getting the joke." This was just another Proust tale leading into his next song. A few even cheered.

Proust cocked his head. "What? Oh, you think I'm... No, I'm not..." He hung his head resignedly. "Doesn't really matter, does it? You came to hear me perform, and I never leave an audience unsatisfied." He returned to his seat, positioned Yseld, and said, "For my final number, a new composition I call, *Green Skies Tonight.*"

Proust played beautifully, magically even, leading into the first stanza. The haunting melody ionized the air with notes of sadness, of tragedy. Before he sung a word, his audience found despair welling inside them. They grew agitated, wanting to leave, Buster could see that, but were compelled to stay. When he hit the first stanza, Proust sung words that no ear there had ever heard, but somehow understood.

The tale recalled a time before recorded history when the first gods walked the earth. They created mankind to be their slaves, their food, and their amusement. Lesser beings, feeling pity on the poor humans, taught the humans to fight back, to steal the power away from the Old Ones, and take the world for themselves.

But the gods left warnings of their return, hidden within all the races of mankind, and in those warnings were symbols, keys to return the world to the way it was.

Proust played strange notes on Yseld and glowing icons appeared hovering above his head.

☽ ♎ ♋ ♉ ✗ 👁 Ⱶ ∧ ¿ ℧

A green film slowly slid across the moon's surface like an eclipse. The reflection of a sun no longer yellow, no longer white, but green as the Old Ones intended. The river boiled. Plumes of steam geysered upwards like Old Faithful.

A form rose from the St. Columkille, silhouetted in emerald shadows. It stood like a human, but that was the only similarity. Enormous lidless orange eyes, oval-shaped and with black pupils, stared into the hall. Gills sucked in air, and Dagon's veins pulsed neon-blue under mottled-green skin. It towered over the hotel and leaned in close to the windows, its fish-like face filling the entire view.

The attendees finally screamed and raced for the exits, only to find the doors had been barred by the hotel staff while they'd focused on Proust's concert.

Buster expected that. No matter. He'd hidden before the concert started and, as his former idol finished his swan song, he knew it was his time to act.

Buster stepped out from behind the racks of chairs

that'd been stacked to the side for the concert. He clanked more than he'd liked, but he hadn't had much of a choice in the dealer's room.

The people trying to knock down doors hadn't noticed him yet, but Proust did.

"Buster?" Proust blinked. "You're still here?"

Buster nodded.

"You touched Yseld, didn't you? And you still stayed?" Proust shook his head disapprovingly. "You could've run. Could've lived, at least for awhile."

Countering, Buster said, "I couldn't do that. Boy, when they say, 'Never meet your idols,' they weren't kidding."

That made Proust laugh. "You came to stop me, huh? Delusions of being a hero?" The filker stood, Yseld firmly clutched in his hand. "In *that* gear, of all things?"

Buster looked down at himself. While he'd had plenty of choice of weapons, protection had been limited. The only thing in his size was a suit of hand-forged samurai armor. The smith had only applied a primer to it, so far, with plans to finish painting it on Sunday as a demonstration. The helmet, also not finished, contained a half-face shield, which only covered Buster's mouth, but not his eyes.

The young man stood in the middle of the main events hall in what would be recognized by many fans as Gundam-chic.

Buster pointed a gauntleted finger at Proust. "You taught me what it means to be a hero. In your books. In your songs. I'm sorry you're dying, but that doesn't give you the right to destroy everything."

Proust scowled. "The right? What right does humanity have to do that? I'm not destroying the world. I'm freeing her." He hooked a thumb back at Dagon, who hadn't moved yet, possibly enthralled by Yseld "He'll create sluggoths to clean the oceans. Others of his kind will repair the skies...level the cities. This world will return to the paradise it once was."

"At the cost of humanity," Buster challenged. "At the cost of *your* humanity."

Shrugging, Proust prepared to play. "Better than dying, kid. But you'll find that out soon."

Buster raced forward, but the armor wasn't built for speed.

Proust strummed Yseld.

Dagon yelled.

The windows shattered.

The force of Dagon's voice blew the audience to the back of main events. People careened into one another. Wails of the damaged and dying filled the hall, becoming accompaniment to Yseld's music.

Buster stood. The weight of his suit held him fast against the wind. When Dagon's howl subsided, Buster ran at Proust. Reaching the dais, Buster jumped and came down on the wide-eyed author. He knocked Yseld from his hands, sending the lute spinning across the floor.

Proust fell backwards, scrambling crablike away from Buster.

"You don't understand," he said. "You don't know what I've seen through Yseld." Tears flowed down his cheeks. "I want to live to see a healed world. I want..." The words caught in his throat. "I want to live!"

"And I," Buster said, "want my Manta figure back." He could see the bulge in Proust's vest, so he pulled the wooden figure out. "You don't deserve this."

At that moment, Dagon's hand reached into the hall and two massive fingers pinched Proust at the waist. The GOH howled in agony as Dagon dragged him backwards. Outside, the Old One lifted Buster's former idol up and stared directly at him. Words sounded in everyone's mind though Dagon's lips never moved.

"Control us, would you?" The deep, soul-rending

voice made many people in the main events vomit. "You insignificant being?"

Sensing what was about to happen, Proust pulled out a flask from his vest, uncapped it, and chugged the whiskey. When it was empty, he looked Dagon in the eye and said, "Eat me."

So, Dagon did.

Buster, gut torn to pieces, watched as a Cavalier's hat drifted down onto the floor in front of him. His hero had fallen, but he hadn't. Not yet. Buster picked up Yseld and walked to stand in front of the glassless windows. He set the lute down as Dagon addressed him.

"And you? Are you someone who believes he can kill a god?"

"Me?" The young man answered. "No, I'm no god-killer."

Reaching behind him, he drew the double-bladed axe he'd acquired from the dealer's room. He held it in both hands above the lute, and prayed that once he freed Yseld, she would stop Dagon and any other Old Ones before they woke up.

With a lopsided grin, he yelled, "I'm a god-*Buster*!"

END

WHEN CONVENTION AND ELDRITCH TIMES CONVERGE

M. TODD GALLOWGLAS

About the Author: A man known by his friends to be a bit too clever for his own good, M. Todd Gallowglas is a hybrid-author (with mainstream and alternative publications), storyteller, and educator from Northern California. He has written over 20 books including novels, short story collections, poetry collections, and non-fiction books. He holds a Bachelor of Arts in Creative Writing from San Francisco State University, a Master of Fine Arts in Fiction from Sierra Nevada College, and a Master in Fine Arts in Poetry from the University of Nevada Reno, Tahoe. His traditional storytelling show at Renaissance Faires, Celtic Festivals, and geeky conventions has mesmerized audiences for over thirty years. When not writing, Gallowglas is an avid gamer, enjoys ballroom dancing (swing, blues, and tango are his favorites), and adores coffee. Lots and lots of coffee.

When Convention and Eldritch Times Converge
M. Todd Gallowglas

The convention starts in the usual, banal way, as
most of this kind do. Attendees greet old friends,
merciful in their ignorance, unaware of the dreadful
thing slumbering beneath their feet. Edward M. Kovel stands
in line for registration, his mind keeps considering
the manuscript back in his hotel room. Edward's
world moves forward one step at a time, until, *May
I see your I.D., sir?* He doesn't know what to
think when he discovers his wallet
is in the wrong pocket—his left pocket.
The fact of this behavioral oddity and Edward's
inability to remember this anomalous shift
of behavior continues to plague him when he walks
the convention halls. Each time another
human catches Edward's attention, his
mind snaps momentarily and temporarily back
to this present but soon regressed to earlier moments to
correlate exactly when and why he'd shifted pockets.
All attendees suffer similar distracts from the hotel shifting
its halls and rooms, subtly and minutely,
contents of its architecture changing out of context.

Between two rivers, the haunted hotel looms,
its corridors twist in a sinister dance,
echoes of terror in labyrinthine rooms.

M. TODD GALLOWGLAS

In the hotel's halls, past and present play,
echoes and whispers with eldritch spite.
A convention trapped in a strange dismay,
Lost in corridors that twist out of sight.

I—what   strange concept of   human psyche—
am—only considered in past tense once time has
forced an individual
into   future, which now becomes   present.
Speech fails   convention attendees
because language cannot articulate what
men fail to notice. Machinations
of beings who exist in realms beyond
science and reason always
have more patience and perspective   Machiavelli
refused
to contemplate. Whispers resonate: *Cast off your shells,*
follow   hopes and dreams
my follow nerds, whose imaginings cry louder than any
advice offered by amateur armchair academics
without any empirical evidence to support
knowing what's best for you.
Why do you even try to remember lives outside these halls?

Echoes and whispers with eldritch spite,
Minds entangled in mad whisper's embrace,
Lost in corridors turn and twist out of sight,
Seeking exits that don't exist in this maze.

Strange echoes haunt each corridor and booth,
and fannish minds in wonderment derail,
where between two rivers, the hotel stands aloof.

Bear with it. Bear with it, Edward M. Koval repeats
in his

mind. He thinks   feeling of walls leaning
closely together is due to   social anxiety
That plagues most of this community from time to time.
I got this, Edward tells himself, I got this. I
did this last year and the year before.
Not   Edward   any of   attendees will let themselves
see, truly notice,   happenings in
any given moment only   few paces away. Reality,
actual reality, beyond what any congoers might want, beyond
visual tap dances their psyches make   avoid noticing
horror,   reality of walls leaning
at them,   corners shifting directions,   sending
the attendees to wander, only arriving at rooms when panels
end,   restaurant when it closes,   to the bar after last call.

Minds entangled in mad whisper's embrace,
when reality blurs with fiction's lore,

in the hotel walls, where ancient terrors move,
bringing sidewise realms, where realities frail,
in between these walls, air grows tense, uncouth.

Fans seek exits from intra-dimensional maze,
Yet remain trapped without any hotel doors.

May comes round again   again.
The months cycle.   con extends beyond every
merciful temporal confines benevolent
gods placed upon humans   give them
if/then, cause   effect rationality.
Indeed, Edward M. Kovel wanders here,
there,   everywhere. Never questioning where else he might
be. Not working   his manuscript.   hotel   con   each become
such   integral part   his psyche, his
guard let down, so far down,   manuscript might   not exist.
Those fans he sees, engage   small talk   hours,
hours,   hours about   pop culture they love,

when is   next book, movie, show, game coming.
No care   concern   worry   how some
power might   might not affect   outcome
of where attendees wind up, regardless where
the hotel map decides   point out, you are here.
Willpower is   strange phenomenon. Some claim you   it
or you don't. It   depends   what situations reality
drug   person through. Edward's will is such
that when he is engaged   writing
the universe   fling slings   arrows,   Edward's
cunning could dance   dodge away   nudge each
of   distractions deftly aside. However, put
man   nearly any other situation when   universe
devises   torment him,   he
can not
keep his attention   anything other   distraction, thinking, *Save
me   plague of woes.* except now, moving
from one place   another, his mind slips past
the need   willpower   escape because this is con.   great
chasm grows   grows between what is expected
of him outside these walls rather   within. Even
sleep evades him   he never notices returning   his room.

When reality blurs with fiction's lore,
attendees gather, with their dreams aloof,
and remain trapped without any hotel doors
in the never-aging halls, the fans play.
In the forever convention, souls never stray
from this architecture beyond rational detail,
deep under the hotel's shadowy roof.

Let me think, Edward M. Koval thinks. *Let*
me think. He recalls times when he   think   pray.   *I*
pray?   whom do I pray?
That is a question
if answered might solve this vast riddle.
I want to pray, Edward thinks. *Let me think,   whom*

do I pray   ? I do
not remember how   think   pray. How did I
survive   thinking praying? How did I find myself
this wandering, wandering, wandering . . ? He recalls
manuscript hard drive, waiting to be finished. He thinks,
My situation... my manuscript... waiting   my computer...
waiting
executors   my imagination.
May comes   again...   again... Edward
put his mind, what little will power, throws
caution   ag'oth   find his way back   his room
before it will be   late
audacity   aosmina'emh   his manuscript
and imagination might
see   end   nag eadhyrr wandering. Is
that   rub,   way out?
It seemed preposterous.   halls, Edward
meets attendees trying   engage   small talk.
No! Edward snaps. He has the oekiar, has
other,   important business   nerdy small talk. His
eye spies his prize   end   hallway, only   few   steps

in the hotel's ancient halls, shadows play,
echoes of cosmic whispers in the night,
in a Purgatory, wandering from hall to hall,
eldritch whispers of fhtagn wail,
the air grows tense, within these walls,
boundaries blurs, reality becomes a spoof,
the convention twists, sanities turn pale,
in shadows deep, the hotel stands aloof,
within these walls, the air grows uncouth.
a convention trapped in a strange dismay,
lost in corridors that twist out of sight.

Edward's M. Koval's world moves
forward one step at a time, until,
May I flae'hgan your I.D., sir?

He doesn't know what to think
when he discovers his wallet
is in the wrong pocket—his left pocket.

And that takes his mind away from his manuscript

again
again
again

May I flae'hgan your I.D., sir?

    END.

THE RATS OF UNDERSTORY B

FRANCES PAULI

About the Author: FRANCES PAULI writes books about animals, hybrids, aliens, shifters, and occasionally ordinary humans. She enjoys a good convention as much as the next author, though thankfully, any dark gods she's encountered in the hallways have been easily banished without the need for transformation. She knows better than to read from books that whisper to you, in particular when left unattended. You can find her works at: francespauli.com and most of the usual places one finds books. Almost all of them are safe to read from.

THE RATS OF UNDERSTORY B
FRANCES PAULI

HARRISON FELTON WAS a published author. The large
rolling suitcase he dragged behind him was full of proof—
twenty-five shiny, newly printed copies of his first novel,
A Temple To My Indecision. His publisher had only
charged him $19.95 per copy, and they'd assured him the
misspelling of his name would be handled long before he
had to order another dozen. It bothered him if he thought
too long about it, so he brushed the slight aside and
focused his energy on the trek he was making.

Garish gold and purple carpeting lined the hallways
of the hotel. It was stained in places, worn down the
middle, and displayed a pattern that seemed to shift a
little each time he passed a branching corridor. Harrison
was beginning to believe he'd taken a wrong turn, in fact,
but the paper fliers taped to the hotel walls insisted the
author readings were on this level.

The bottom level. Two elevator buttons below the one
labeled: Parking Garage.

The convention program had agreed with the room
assignment, though the name seemed odd. The conference
rooms upstairs had names like Rowan and Hazel, but
the author readings were in Understory. Harris snorted.
This was his first convention as a published author, and
he hadn't wanted to complain. Still, as he navigated the

labyrinthine corridors, scanning ahead for the next sign, and noting that he took more and more steps between spotting them, Harris began to wonder how any of his readers were supposed to find him down here.

He checked his watch. In his eagerness, he'd begun his trek with a full twenty minutes to spare. Now, he had five before his reading was supposed to begin. He twisted to face the long, empty hallway behind him. Not a soul wandered into view. No cosplayer. No eager fan. Not even another author with a suitcase full of newly printed books.

Harris turned back and frowned. The carpet had shifted again, but he hadn't been moving this time. He hadn't turned or changed hallways, nor could he see any sign of a seam. Yet only moments ago the pattern had clearly been formed of large, off kilter polka dots. Now it boasted a series of skinny stars. He squinted at his feet, scanning for the place where the rug had changed.

Soft voices dragged his gaze upward again. From somewhere ahead, he caught the muffled sounds of conversation. Perhaps, his readers had beat him to the panel room. Harrison stood tall and marched forward, certain his audience already waited for him in Understory A.

He hurried his feet over the stars, and he scrunched his nose as the hallway began to smell of dusky mold. Not surprising, considering the hotel sat in the middle of a river. The lights flickered as he followed the next sign to the right, and the stars shrank into pinpricks. Harrison dragged his novels eagerly toward the sound of voices. He stopped in front of two closed doors, and the conversation ceased as if it sensed his arrival.

A final flier sagged on the wall between the rooms. One corner had come free of its tape, so that the words "Author Readings" leaned at a slant to the left. Plastic plates set into the wall read "Understory A" and "Understory B", and to Harrison's dismay, the voices had come from the wrong one.

Another author must be reading in room B, but the fact that an audience had, in fact, shown up bolstered him. Perhaps they would move rooms once the first reading ended. He checked his watch and panicked. Only one minute to go.

Harrison opened the door to Understory A. The lights were out, and for a second, he thought the carpet was glowing. Hundreds of tiny lights twinkled around the room's floor, blinking at him as if he gazed up at the night sky. When he stepped into the room, however, they winked out. Harrison groped for a light switch, and when he flicked it upwards, the room was illuminated.

He frowned at the carpet. Large circles again, not stars. Four rows of chairs had been arranged with an aisle down their center. At the front of the room, a long table waited. Harrison dragged his case forward, unzipped it, and began unpacking *A Temple To My Indecision* in a series of stacks and towers designed to show off the cover he'd paid two-hundred and fifty dollars for.

He pulled one chair out from behind the table and sat just to the side of his books to wait. The voices next door filtered through the adjoining wall, but they sounded hushed, almost rhythmic now. The reading should be done, he figured. The audience would be asking their final questions, chatting, and making their departure.

He should prop open his door. He should stand in the hall maybe, invite the crowd from next door to stick around for his panel. As he waffled, the voices fell silent. Not in the way a conversation dies, slowly and naturally one note at a time. No. The sound simply stopped, snuffed out as suddenly as a candle between damp fingertips.

Harrison frowned. He glared at the door. It had been stupid to let it swing shut behind him, but it hadn't fully closed. He could see a strip of hallway through the crack, and the flutter of lights as bodies passed in front of them.

Quickly, he sprang from the chair and trotted back down the aisle. He hadn't spent five years of his life writing a novel to give up here, at the threshold of his success. Harrison hustled for the door, and just as he cleared the last row of chairs, he tripped, sprawling forward with his arms windmilling.

He hit the carpet and lay there, dazed for a moment, his breath hitching and his foot caught on the metal leg of a chair. How had he managed that? He frowned at the overturned seat. It hadn't leaped out and snagged him, yet he could have sworn the aisle was clear a moment earlier. With a groan, he pushed himself to his feet and shook off the impact.

Then, Harrison scurried into the hallway.

It was empty. The voices had long since gone, and though the corridor stretched a good twenty feet in both directions, not a single soul could be seen marching away. Silence lay over the hotel, thick as the musty smell coming through the walls.

Harrison pushed open the door to Understory B, half expecting to find a crowd. It was as empty as its twin. The only sign the room had been inhabited was a book left lying on the table up front. A single book, left behind no doubt, as a freebie.

He'd thought of a similar tactic himself, but what good would a sample do if there was no one around to claim it?

He wandered to the table and examined his competitor's product. The cover was ghastly, a solid black field with only the faintest hint of a face on it. It looked like horror, but without any contrast to the image, it was hard to tell. He'd have asked the artist to make it more visible, and he'd definitely have rejected that font.

Still, there was something compelling about a hardback book. The guy had spent some dough on that, and the book was thick, a good two hundred pages longer than Harrison's. Maybe that was the secret to drawing an audience? Maybe *A Temple To My Indecision* was too short.

Harrison picked up the book and sat in one of the vacant chairs. He flipped open the cover, admiring the internal art. Not cheap. It gave the book a historic feel, a weight to it that felt good on the eyes. Riffling the pages, Harrison admired the thick paper, the tight binding, and the perfect, uniform margins. He stopped on a random page, squinting at the text.

Something about this book had drawn a crowd, and fancy packaging aside, he believed it had to do with the story. Everything came down to story in the end. If there was something magical about this one which drew fans, Harrison wanted to possess it.

He began to read, struggling over some of the names and made-up words. There were a lot of those. After a few paragraphs he stopped trying to suss out the pronunciation and just let his mouth approximate the syllables. The story itself seemed thin, much thinner than *Temple's*. In fact, it read like a laundry list of random esoteric promises.

"Under the darkness, I lie," Harrison read. "Beneath the fathoms, and only the hand of *asphomemital* may raise me. The gate of stars is open, and I am the heart's sun. Gross." He skimmed forward a few pages, searching for anything more coherent. "This is terrible."

On page 369, he found a poem. It was italicized, or he'd have missed it, and it had been printed opposite a picture that seemed to be made of nothing but squiggly lines. Harrison squinted at it for a moment, but the image made his head hurt.

He read the poem instead.

"For all the power at your command, I shall defend and honor. To release the shadow. To know all things. Change me, oh...." He tried the name three different ways, unsure if any were correct. "Change me and I will serve thee. I choose my form, my truth, in the embodiment of..."

Something skittered in Harrison's peripheral vision. He turned his head, scanned the floor between the chairs. The room seemed darker, somehow, and he could smell something else besides mold, something foul, like food on the very edge of going rancid.

Harrison closed the book. He stood and set it back down on the table. Part of him wanted to take it, but truly, he was not a fan of horror. He turned away just as a low, furry body darted across the aisle.

"Rat!" Harrison shouted. He shuffled back, slamming into the table, and knocking the book off. It tumbled, end over end, falling but never quite hitting the floor. Harrison watched it until his head spun. Wind rushed in his ears, the darkness swelled and swept over him, and he was falling too.

The rat scampered across a field of stars. It was frightened, but it couldn't quite remember what chased it. Its long bald tail tingled with danger, however, and it could feel the need to run in every whisker. Something hissed far over its head, and the sound rose and fell like a song.

Working its paws faster, the rat ran for the nearest wall and turned, streaking against the line where the starry rug met textured beige. Its body zinged with a primal terror, and its beady eyes caught another movement just ahead. Another rat ran from the hissing, and when it reached the wall, it vanished.

Escape. The rat aimed its low head at the spot where its kin had gone and threw itself forward. The wall sped past. The hissing grew into a howl. A crack appeared in the baseboard, and the rat flung itself against the gap. It was a tight fit. He breathed out and flattened his long body, wiggling frantically until he popped free on the far side.

There, when comforting darkness surrounded him, he stopped, sat up on his haunches and sniffed the air. The space behind the wall was narrow enough for his whiskers to touch both sides, and it smelled of fungus and other rats. Though the sounds still rose and fell in the room outside, his sense of danger had ebbed instantly. Now, only curiosity replaced it.

He'd seen another rat come this way, and a short series of sniffs told him in which direction a rat had most recently passed. He smelled no food, nor did he remember which way he'd been going before the singing began. He had nothing to do but follow, so he scampered after the other rat, running between the walls, and only stopping when he lost the scent to sit and sniff it out again.

The trail led him into branching spaces, up over fat wires and down through cracks into lower areas. He ducked nails and squeezed between boards, climbing through a narrow trench, at last, into a wide space filled with other rodents.

Their squeaks echoed in the darkness, and his sharp eyes made out the shifting of bodies, the pinprick glow of a hundred eyes. Many scents mixed into a bouquet of musk and fur, a comforting aroma that suggested safety even though he had no idea if he'd come here before.

It felt right, and when he sulked into their midst, the other rats made room for him. A few touched their noses to his, and their squeaky voices welcomed him to the group. "Greetings." Nose touch, "Greetings, greetings friend."

The rat squeaked back. Their eager reception warmed him. Their furry bodies brushed against his, and everyone's tail threaded over and under everyone else's. He moved through the mob, saying his hellos and tapping his nose to any offered muzzle, and he began to feel that this was, in fact, exactly where he'd been going. He belonged here.

As he went, a familiar scent tickled his whiskers. He moved toward it, murmuring his, "greetings, greetings, friend," as he went until the smell was too strong and his tongue too heavy with hunger. He chased the aroma to a cleared area beneath a squat pipe. There, a fat black rat hunkered over a long, sleek tube of meat.

"Mine," the black rat hissed.

"Hot dog," he said back.

"What's that?" The massive owner of the hot dog sprang forward. "I'm Azmodel," he said. "This food is mine."

"It's a hot dog, Azmodel" the rat said.

"What's a hot dog?"

"I'm not sure." He squinted at the food, certain that it was, in fact, a hot dog, and even more oddly, that he preferred his with mustard. "Food, I think."

"Yeah, it is," Azmodel said. "And it's mine. You're new, so I won't bite you today."

"Thank you," the rat said.

"What's your name?" Azmodel asked.

"I'm not sure," the rat said, thinking that perhaps "Mustard" was not a *something*, but a *someone* he liked to have hotdogs with.

"You haven't been to the gate?" Azmodel sat taller, tucking his paws beneath his chin, and aiming his round ears up and forward. "You haven't been named yet?"

"I'm new." The rat lowered his head in shame. He had no name, and no idea where this gate was.

Azmodel looked longingly at his hot dog, then shrugged and turned away from the food. "I'll take you," he said. "The gate is the only thing that matters."

The rat followed Azmodel, surprised that the bigger rat would abandon his meal to help. If it was more important than food, he figured, the gate must be worth seeing. They skirted the edge of the open area, hugging dark walls where thick black mold grew beneath dripping pipes. Azmodel led him through another chink in the wall, but this one led to a long tunnel, down a ramp that turned one way and then the other, and eventually, out onto a hard, stone staircase.

Something in the rat's brain suggested "subbasement", but the word sounded far too ridiculous to utter aloud. Additionally, the stairs they bounded down seemed to be vibrating. The air reeked of something other than mold, something that carried the pungent sweetness of death. A soft hissing echoed in his ears, growing louder as they descended, and it felt wholly off topic to point out that he knew where they were.

Azmodel continued into the subbasement, bouncing in the open without any sign of fear. He led the way between much larger pipes, past a sign that read: Boiler Room, and into a long hallway with no lights. Here the hissing twisted into a voice, a chant with words that did not register in any language.

"The gate is ahead," Azmodel said. "You'll love it."

The rat was beginning to doubt that, but his new friend's enthusiasm bled over into his furry body. He bounded in Azmodel's wake, down a final short series of steps, and into a room entirely made of stone. Moss clung to its high ceiling. Roots broke through the concrete near its foundation, and the smell of death swirled in a palpable fog through the air.

The gate stood in the center of the room. It faced an enormous metal grid set into the wall, beyond which the dark river swirled past. The water hissed and burbled, sounding like many, distant voices all speaking at once.

"Glorious," Azmodel said.

Come closer, a voice like claws on glass ordered.

The rat moved without meaning to, scampering up to the crumbling archway. It was made of jet-black stones, supported by a pair of twisting beams and crowned with an arch that came to a sharp point. Or rather, it should have.

Something had shattered portions of the structure, and the arch crumbled on one side. The right pillar, too, had whole chunks missing from it, though from the look of it, someone had been slowly, painstakingly rebuilding that section.

Closer.

Azmodel gave him a friendly nudge with one shoulder. *Come, new one.*

The rat took a step closer to the gate.

"He needs a name," Azmodel announced.

In the rat's brain a word fluttered past, something he felt he should have reached for, kept close and for himself. It was too quick however, and he lost it even before he could shape it in his mind.

You will be Zephilum, the voice hissed. *Builder of the gate.*

Those words clung to him, settling like a heavy blanket across his furry back. He *was* Zephilum, and he would build the gate. The gate was glorious. The gate was the only thing that mattered.

Zephilum scampered toward a pile of tiny, shattered bits of jet, eager to begin. Azmodel appeared in his way, shaking his head, and working his paws beneath his chin.

"Not now," he said. "It's time to eat and sleep."

"But the gate?" Zephilum took a short step to the side.

"Tonight," Azmodel said.

Zephilum followed him reluctantly back to the steps, his belly empty, and his eyes heavy. He still stopped at the top and gazed back with longing. He would eat and sleep, but only so that he could build. Only so that he'd have the strength to lift those black stones into place, fit each fragment carefully into its rightful spot, and see the arch perfect and whole again.

@@@

Zephilum worked beside Azmodel and their friend Brathwin. It was slow work, building. Each fragment had to be sorted from the pile and fit back into exactly the place it had come from. The black gate was a puzzle, and some nights they were lucky to put half a dozen bits back together before it was time to stop and rest.

The gate was patient.

On a good day, he could see the stone rising, mark where the pillar had ended and where it was now. The progress satisfied and frustrated him. Always, he felt the urgency pushing behind his thoughts, the need to be finished and fully repaired.

That purpose drove him for many days. It slept beside him in the nesting area, where all the furry bodies packed around him could not match the warmth of his desire to build. It whispered in his ears while he nibbled the food they found in the hotel hallways. Crumbs and crusts, chips, and cast-off remnants of the feasts above. The building possessed him, as it did the rest, and Zephilum worked with the frenzy of ten rats. They all did.

Slowly, the gate grew, and the rats bonded over its progress. They became of one mind, one family of furry siblings desperate to see the job finished. It was all they thought of, and it was all Zephilum cared about.

Until the day he saw the book again.

He was returning to the nesting area with Brathwin, the slender gray female who worked and slept between he and Azmodel. The black rat had remained in the eating area longer than usual, And Zephilum was enjoying the company of the female alone as they retreated to sleep. They'd been discussing the day's work, and the largest hunk of stone they'd managed to fit into place since Zephilum's arrival.

As they entered the nesting area, they passed a trio of pale females dragging a fat, familiar novel.

"Mine," Zephilum squeaked, and without thinking,

leaped onto the book and hissed defensively. "My book."

"It's prime nesting material," one of the females argued. "Stupid male. Get off of it."

"This is my novel." Zephilum hunkered lower atop *A Temple To My Indecision.* He read the title, admiring the bold font, the smooth gold gradient, and the way his cover artist had made it look embossed even on a glossy finish. He read the author's name below, and he remembered.

"I am Harrison Felton," he said. He was not a rat; he was an author. He was the author of this book, of *A Temple To My Indecision*, and he was not about to let rats gnaw its pages for their sleeping. "I wrote this."

More rats gathered around them, sniffing the air, and flicking their ears forward to catch the drama. Brathwin stood on the tips of her rear paws, and her whiskers twitched as she measured the seriousness of the situation.

"Rats don't write," she said. "They build."

"I'm not supposed to be a rat," Harrison said. In the back of his mind, the voice from the gate hissed, but he shoved it aside easily now, with his novel to bolster him. "And this is not nesting material, it's a story."

"Prove it," one of the other females squeaked. "Show us this story."

"I will," Harrison said. He jumped down from his book and scurried to the right side. Using his paws and his muzzle too, he lifted the front cover, the title page, and the dedication. Then he pushed them aside, crawling up and under the front matter as if it were a tent.

Harrison used his rat body to open his novel, and when Chapter One spread open before him, he perched in the center of page 1 and began to read.

"It was a dark and stormy night," he said. "Isn't that a great beginning?"

The rats scooted closer to the book. Brathwin's beady eyes gleamed up at him. Many disc ears swiveled in his direction, an attentive, if tiny audience. Harrison groomed his whiskers with both paws and sat proudly atop his book. It was better than *no* audience, he decided, and settled in to tell his tale.

His audience grew as rumors of the book spread. Each time he opened *A Temple To My Indecision*, Harrison found a larger crowd packed in around the book. Their eyes twinkled like stars, focused and attentive, fixed on him.

By night, the rats built the gate, and Harrison worked alongside them, caught in the grip of the building spell. By day, he read from his book, one chapter at a time. All the rats gathered to listen. They followed the story well enough, and by the time he'd gotten to chapter six, they were hooked.

Soon, they were approaching him with questions during building hours. Harrison would be forced to stop his work to answer, to explain a human term, or to deal with the usual questions about where his motivation came from or whether one of the characters was based on any of them.

He took his fame in stride, only puffing up slightly when he heard them debate who the villain was or argue about which male the female character should choose to mate with. It all boiled down to finding your audience, he reasoned, and now that *Temple* had a solid fanbase, the last thing he wanted was to get a swelled head.

Despite knowing he was not supposed to be a rat, the combination of the gate's spell and his sudden celebrity kept thoughts of humanity at bay. Then, Harrison got to Chapter Ten.

"You can trust me," Harrison read in the voice he'd adopted for his dashing hero. "I won't let you down... this time."

The rat crowd broke into murmurs at this. Half their

number was rooting for the hero, and the other half the plucky-but-less-attractive best friend. Harrison grinned at the ruckus and continued in his heroine's voice, which he believed had only gotten better for all the practice.

"You know I want to," Harrison purred. "One look in your eyes and all I want is to forgive you, but..."

He reached the bottom of the page and frowned.

"But what?" Several voices in the crowd squeaked together.

"There's a page missing," Harrison said.

The rats squealed in horror.

"I can sum up," he added quickly. "You see, he convinces her to go with him and then—"

"Wait!"

One squeak rose above the others. Harrison stood as tall as he could, leveraging his tail for balance and staring out over the gathered crowd. Someone shoved their way forward, pushing the others aside as they went. The rats parted, and Brathwin stood alone beside Harrison's book.

"I know where the missing page is," she said.

Harrison jumped down from his novel, and the gray female led him across the nesting area, through a gap in the baseboards, and down a space between walls where he'd never traveled before. Brathwin slowed, twisting her ears forward and tilting her head to one side. A soft scuffling sound filtered through the wall ahead. Together, they crept up to a rat-sized hole. Brathwin poked her head through, then popped back out and nodded.

"He's in there."

"Who?" Harrison asked.

"Azmodel," she said. "He's trying to learn to read."

Harrison sat up and twisted his paws beneath his chin. His whiskers tightened. He sensed trouble was afoot, but now that he knew he was *not* a rat, all he could think was, "preposterous."

He followed Brathwin through the hole, and they

emerged into a small chamber, a pocket of space between the walls, twice as large as the usual tunnels. There, Azmodel sat atop a large black book. He'd propped a page from *A Temple To My Indecision* against one wall, and was squinting at it until his beady eyes watered.

Brathwin scampered over to the studious rat. Azmodel sat up and glared at Harrison. Harrison gaped at the big black book.

"What's he doing here?" Azmodel's squeak sounded far less friendly than usual.

"He needs that page," Brathwin said. "So we know what happens next."

"Actually," Harrison said. "I need that big black book."

"No." Azmodel bounded forward, his huge furry body rising to its hind paws between Harrison and the tome. "That book is mine," he said.

"You don't want it." Harrison backpedaled, disturbed by how small and squeaky his voice sounded. "Trust me."

"Give him the page from his book," Brathwin said sensibly. "And you can keep the black one."

"No." Harrison and Azmodel spoke at once.

"Boys," Brathwin sighed.

"I need the black book," Harrison said.

"Teach me to read." Azmodel lowered and twitched his long nose. "And I'll give it to you."

"Why do you want to read?" Harrison was pretty sure that a rat brain could not learn to read English. He was almost certain that the only reason he'd been able to was because he was not, really, a rat. He was also convinced Azmodel would rather chew the thing to shreds than let him have it.

"You read," Azmodel snarled. "And they love you."

His beady eyes drifted ever so quickly toward Brathwin.

"I can't teach you to read," Harrison said, flinching when the bigger rat hunkered forward. "B-but I think I can offer you something even better."

"No tricks." Azmodel's eyes turned flinty, two daggers in the darkness.

"No," Harrison said, wishing there was more room to step backwards. His tail already kinked against the wall behind him. "No tricks, but if you let me have that book, you can be rid of me completely."

Brathwin sniffed loudly.

Azmodel rubbed his paws together and let his ears fall far forward. "I'm listening," he said.

"Not here." Harrison remembered that a human man did not fit in the space between walls. "Help me drag it to the room where you found it."

For a moment, he thought the rat would argue. Azmodel had clearly had enough of him, however, and the temptation to evict Harrison was too strong. Brathwin refused to help, fleeing back into the hole in the wall, but between them, Azmodel and Harrison lifted the book which had turned him into a rat. They dragged it under the pipes and over the wires, stood it up and pushed it through the narrow spaces, and eventually, hauled it into a corridor with a carpet that looked like stars.

"This is far enough," Harrison said. The convention had ended days ago, and the hallway was plenty big. "We need to find the page with the squiggly lines."

"There are lots of them," Azmodel said. "They make my head hurt."

"I'll do it." Harrison set the book down and skittered to the right side. He hesitated before crawling into *these* pages. He could hear the whispers already, the sound like far-off voices. With a deep breath for a rat, he poked his nose beneath the cover, and crawled up into the paper.

Azmodel watched from a distance at first, but as Harrison struggled to turn each page, the other rat grew bolder, eventually climbing up beside him. Like small, furry acrobats, they flipped through the black book, and every time an illustration appeared, Harrison stopped to examine the pages.

It took far longer than he expected, for the book was vast, and the writing on the paper seemed to shuffle around when he looked at it. He felt the power in the tome pulling at him, drawing the rat to the surface, and pushing the man lower. He might stay, it whispered to him, curl up in a warm nest with Brathwin and forget this nonsense.

"There's one," Azmodel said, laying his body across the pages and forcing the book all the way open.

Harrison looked at the squiggling illustration, and the book hissed. He looked at the poem opposite, and his mind cleared. "Of course," he said. "You see, I stopped there and then, I said 'rat'. It makes perfect sense."

"If you say so," Azmodel said.

"Just watch, and everything will be clear." Harrison gathered his courage. "You might want to step a little away."

Azmodel dived off the book and scampered to a nearby wall to watch. Harrison sat on his haunches, aimed his beady eyes at the page, and read the poem aloud. He said each word carefully, pronounced the name just as the hissing in his brain suggested. And because he knew how tricky words could be, he was very careful to end with, "the embodiment of *my original human self.*"

Harrison Felton stood in the subbasement. He faced the black gate and examined the progress his rats had made over the last year. After returning to his human shape, he'd torn down a good fourth of the right pillar. Now it stood nearly complete again. They'd been working hard, building, as only those possessed by evil could.

He'd have to do more this year.

No.

Harrison cranked the volume on his earbuds to drown

out the voice and the river. Quickly, he removed the fragmented stone, placing it handful by handful back into the rats' pile of rubble. While he worked, he listened to the new audio version of *Temple*. When he finished there was even less of the gate intact than last time.

Which should keep them busy for another year.

It was bad enough they possessed the grimoire. Harrison was certain letting the rats finish would be a very bad idea. Wiping his palms on his trousers, he stood, examined the black stone, then turned his back on it. A suitcase full of his books waited at the top of the steps, re-edited and recovered when he got his rights back and went indie. He left the subbasement dragging them behind him.

To his surprise, there were three people waiting for him in Understory B. Harrison greeted them and sat down, pulling out a few copies of *Temple* and laying them haphazardly on the front table. He opened his personal copy and eyed the audience.

"Welcome," he said.

The carpet twisted and turned to stars. Something low and quick moved in his peripheral vision.

"Today I'll be reading from my first novel," Harrison smiled at the girl dressed like an anime sailor. "But many of you will be happy to hear the second book is coming out soon."

The cosplayer looked at her companion, then at the only other person in the room, an older gentleman wearing fuzzy cat's ears.

"We'll begin with chapter ten," Harrison said. "If someone could please get the lights."

The sailor girl stood, then paused and looked a question at him.

"I always read in the dark," Harrison said. "Author eccentricities, you know."

She shrugged and scooted to the doorway, flicking

the lights off and casting the Understory into darkness. Harrison tapped his LED clip, and a faint glow illuminated *A Temple To My Indifference*. Around the room, pinprick lights blinked near the baseboards. A sea of stars washed from the spaces between the walls, drawn from their nests and their dreams of building, to hear the rest of his story.

His audience had arrived. His true fans gathered in the darkness, and Harrison opened his book to Chapter Ten and began to read.

END

ARTIST ALLEY AWAKENING

FRANK MARTIN

About the Author: FRANK MARTIN is a comic writer & author who is not as crazy as his work makes him out to be. Since his writing career began he's had multiple short stories published in horror anthologies by numerous indie publications. Frank has also had comic shorts appear in the "fluff noir" anthology series *Torsobear* & the all-ages horror anthology *Cthulhu is Hard to Spell*. Frank also wrote & produced the comic anthology series *Modern Testament*, which featured a wide ensemble of artists throughout its four volumes. Frank's novels include the YA sci-fi thriller *Predestiny* published by Crossroads Press, the lake monster tale *Oscawana* published by Severed Press, among others. Frank currently lives in New York with his wife and three kids.

ARTIST ALLEY AWAKENING
FRANK MARTIN

For as long as I can remember I've feared sharing my art with the world. I drew as a little girl, studied my craft in college, and even attempted to make a career out of it. But one problem remained: I was too shy to put myself out there. I didn't have a website or references. Not even a business card. I needed to do something, anything, to kickstart my job prospects.

Then I heard of Island Con.

Of course, I'd never tabled at a convention before. How could I sit there with all those people walking by, glancing over my work, contemplating, critiquing, judging? Just the thought filled me with trembling anxiety.

The online horror community buzzed with excitement about this show. Apparently it took place at an abandoned river hotel, and tickets were selling for a ridiculous amount of money. Tables in their sprawling artist alley, however, were free. I couldn't believe it. I just had to fill out an application and submit my portfolio. Apparently, a committee selected artists based on their work. Not their clout or standing in the community. Just skill and skill alone.

So you could imagine my surprise when I got in.

I felt ecstatic. This could become the big break I pined for. So with a little encouragement from my parents and friends, I packed a bag for the one-day event and hit the road.

The river was in the middle of nowhere, but anyone headed to the convention stood out like a sore thumb. We travelled together like a herd in a giant migration, all of us packed into the sole steamboat that ferried people to and from the island. I waited three trips before I finally had a chance to board. I'd never heard of a con being so hard to get to, but it paid off once the hotel came into view.

It looked as if the island formed just for this large three-story building. There was barely any room for the dock. I'd read that the hotel arrived decades ago as a destination spot but couldn't book a single guest. You couldn't tell that by looking at it, though. The structure glossed in pristine white, but its patchwork design reminded me of something Dr. Frankenstein might build. Thick columns stood positioned on either side of the entrance like a plantation, yet odd looking gargoyles perched along the roof resembled a gothic cathedral. Every other window shined with stained glass, and the others were clear and rounded like an art deco funhouse.

I could've stood on the dock for an hour just admiring the hotel's architecture, but the flowing crowd pushed me forward into the building. I thought I would've stood in line forever before getting my table, but it moved quicker than I thought. Before I knew it, I met a masked man in a dark, purple robe.

"Welcome to Island Con," he greeted in a deep, raspy voice.

The mask was a dull white with a strange green line weaving through it at random. If I didn't know any better, I could've sworn I stared a tentacle.

"Hi," I said with an awkward wave. "I'm Tabitha Roberts. I have a table in artist alley."

He nodded slowly. "Yes, Ms. Roberts. You'll set up at table 4H."

"You know my table number off the top of your head?"

"Of course. Island Con takes great pride in its artists."

This guy could've impressed me, if he didn't creep me out so much. "Thank...you."

I strolled past him, bag still slung around my shoulder, and entered the convention floor. It instantly took my breath away. I entered a big wide open space with balconies connecting all the rooms above. The ground floor hosted the main convention area. Surprisingly, the artist alley looked more like an artist avenue. Tables of illustrators wrapped around the entire room. If I didn't know any better, I would've sworn it took up eighty percent of the space. Maybe more.

Vendors started setting up in the middle, but they seemed pretty hard to get to, almost as if the layout were designed for the artists and artists alone. I've never visited a convention before, but I'd never heard of anything quite like this.

I found my table, set up my stuff, and waited. A short time later, attendees for the day's event began pouring in.

The place quickly became cosplayers galore. The show was horror themed, so movie monsters roamed everywhere I could see. A couple comic super heroes, but mostly just a lot of blood and gore. I loved it.

The strangest of the bunch being a group of people in robes. They reminded me of the masked man that gave me my table number, but their robes looked different. Darker and grungier. Authentic, I would say, as if they tossed around in a dryer a few hundred times with rocks.

The robed group wandered around almost aimlessly, but I didn't get a good look at them until one stopped at my table.

"Salutations," a voice said from deep inside the robe. It sounded grainy and distant, like it spoke through a voice modulator.

I smiled, though my nervous jitters probably made it

look more like a cringe. "Umm. Hi."

I stared into the darkness inside the hood, but I couldn't see a face. Coupled with the distorted voice, I had no idea if they were a man or woman. Whoever they were, these cosplayers knew their stuff.

"Your work is…"

The hood looked up and over my head, examining the charcoal portraits I had displayed behind me. "Exxxxquisite.

"Thanks. Do you work here?"

"I would like to commission you for a piece," they said, ignoring my question.

"Sure. My rates are—"

"Whatever the cost," they interrupted, "I'll double it."

Wow. I'd heard stories about conventions where artist alley was pushed into a corner, barely an afterthought and completely ignored by guests. I considered myself lucky that my first show prioritized artists so much.

"That's very generous of you. What do you need?"

The robed figure's chest rose and fell, not exactly breathing, but filling itself with pride. "A god."

Dramatic much? I really wanted the work, but grimaced and shook my head. "Sorry. I don't do religious pieces."

"Good. Because this god isn't bound by dogma."

I opened my mouth to reply, but they spoke up before I had a chance. "He's everywhere and nowhere. A force of nature that answers only to the universe herself. He's timeless. Eternal. An Old God in every sense of the word."

Curiosity got the better of me. Although odd, my mysterious patron certainly seemed intriguing. I just had to know more. "What does he look like?"

"You already know. All you have to do is close your eyes and believe."

I waited for them to go on, but they didn't. The robed figure just stood perfectly still and stared at me through the void in the hood. They wouldn't move so much as a muscle, so I obliged. What was the worst that could happen?

I closed my eyes and thought of this weird god even though I had no idea what it looked like. Then something strange happened. The blackness in the back of my eyelids started to move. It whirled and swirled until a mass began to take shape.

A long, slithering tentacle stretched towards me. Then another. And another. A head popped up from the darkness. It looked large and bulbous, covered in eyes and a singular mouth. Inside sat a circular set of jagged teeth, and the entire creature rose up from the depths of my imagination, unleashing a near deafening roar that silenced the convention's constant commotion.

"Hey," I said as my eyes shot open. "How did you..."

But the robed figured was gone, replaced by several crisp hundred dollar bills on the table. Too late to back out now. My mysterious patron paid in full. Now I had no choice but to deliver. I took out my stuff and got to work.

I struggled at first. The image of this "god" was fleeting. Usually I could see a drawing in my mind's eye with ease, but this figure would only wash over me in glimpses. It reminded me of an object buried ashore that become more and more revealed as the tide came in to drag away the mud.

Soon charcoal had drenched the page, and I found the god had revealed himself to me in full. My pencil danced wildly across the page, possessed with inspiration. The entire convention drifted to the background. There was no chatter. No guests wandering in front of my table. Just me, my art, and the god that linked us.

I finished much quicker than I thought; so fast I practically felt out of breath. I placed the commission on the table and stood to admire it. It was beautiful in the most terrifying way possible. I almost couldn't believe I could create such an amalgamation of horror and wonder. I would've thought it unimaginable if I hadn't created it myself. I hated appraising my own work, but I dared to wonder if some might call it a masterpiece.

Once I sat back down I realized just how much the drawing took out of me. My legs shook, and the beginnings of a headache pounded in my forehead. I needed a walk to reset myself, so I put the commission away, grabbed a snack, and headed out to explore the rest of the convention.

It seemed crazy to watch so many artists at their tables, working diligently on their commissions. I had never seen so many illustrators in one place, not even at college, and to get into this show they all must've worked insanely hard.

I moved closer to get a better look at what they worked on, and I almost choked at what I saw. They were drawing my commission. Every last one of them. Not my commission, specifically. Each artist gave the drawings their own style and flare. But it was definitely the same creature, the god my robed patron demanded of me.

I couldn't believe it. Had those cosplayers went around asking everyone to draw the same thing? I needed to know and approached an overweight bearded artist to find out.

"Hi." I said as friendly as possible.

He kept his eyes down, never bothering to look up from the commission he hadn't finished. "Go away. I'm busy."

"Yeah," I sighed. "I can see that."

After a moment, the artist finally gazed up with annoyed, leering eyes. "So then why are you still standing here?"

"I was wondering..." My finger drifted up to point at his work. "Who commissioned you to draw that?"

"Some weirdo in a robe," he replied. "Just dropped a butt load of cash on the table and—"

I heard all I needed to and walked off before he had chance to finish.

Something strange seemed to be going on. There was always the chance that an eclectic art aficionado would spend an absurd amount of money to have every artist draw the same picture...but I doubted it. What other explanation could it be, though?

Then, as if I had an answer arrived on cue, the entire hotel began to shake. Everyone stopped in their tracks, firmly planting their feet on the carpeted floor, myself included. Though I couldn't imagine why. The ground beneath us trembled. Was it an earthquake? On an island? In the middle of a river? I had no idea.

I looked around for any of those robed figures but they were gone. None were in sight. Then a voice spoke from above.

"Can you feel him?" it shouted "His presence in the air?"

We all looked up and found the masked man standing on a table. It just now occurred to me that he resembled the person that commissioned the drawing, but only slightly. He seemed more grounded and real, not just some ephemeral figure that might vanish without a trace.

"He's growing stronger and will soon grace us with his presence," he preached to the guests.

Everyone stood kind of spellbound by the strange turn of events. The entire room continued to quake, but someone needed to step up. I guess that someone had to be me.

"What's happening?" I asked. "What did you do?"

He looked down at me and I saw two very human eyes within the mask. "I built this place to worship him, so that he may one day rise from his slumber. He just needed followers."

He then turned his attention back to the crowd as a whole. "No one came, though. A god can't exist without worship. So other plans had to be made."

"You held this event to make us worship your god?"

I couldn't see his face, but I imagined an arrogant smirk behind it. "I did no such thing. He arranged it all."

"He brought you here," the masked man continued, "organized this entire charade from the depths below us. He knew he couldn't make you pray to him. You had to worship willingly. But through your art, however…"

He then raised his arms and looked to the ceiling, testifying for all to hear. "You gave him all the love he desired."

The rumbling wouldn't let up, and screams reverberated around the convention floor. The masked man stood like a statue, and several cosplayers, all dressed ironically as super heroes, climbed up on the table to tackle him to the floor.

The man's mask fell off in the struggle, revealing an old, weathered face etched with wrinkles. He looked elderly, practically near death, but he didn't resist as several of the heroes pinned him down.

"You can attack me all you want," he shouted, "but it won't matter. He lives. He lives!"

The man's voice carried across the room, followed by a loud, demonic shriek outside the hotel's walls. The windows suddenly shattered, and a swarm of gigantic tentacles invaded the convention floor. Large, slimy limbs raged wildly out control. The scared screams in the room turned to panicked shrieks of terror as the tentacles waved at random. Some struck people, sending them flying into the walls. Others slammed the floor, cracking it in half.

Sheer pandemonium took over.

"What do we do?!" someone shouted beside me. I looked over to find the artist I had questioned earlier. "What do we do?!"

I thought for a moment, trying to remember the masked man's words. Then it all became clear.

"The art," I told him. We have to destroy it."

The man swallowed, clearly distraught by my suggestion. "But...it's my best work."

"What's more important?" I scoffed. "One piece of art or being responsible for summoning a giant river god monster?"

He swallowed again, this time followed by a rapid nod.

"Spread the word," I ordered and sent him on his way.

I watched as the artist rushed to his table, grabbed the commission he'd been working on, and ripped it in half. He then went to the table next door and told that artist to do the same.

One by one, each artist in attendance grabbed their drawing and destroyed it. And also one by one, the tentacles began to retreat. The monster outside roared again, but this time it sounded different. Not so much a triumphant howl but a cry of pain. The plan worked. The god grew weaker.

The artists continued to destroy their work, ripping tons of paper to shreds. By the time the final tentacle pulled away, a healthy serving of torn paper covered the floor. The terrified screams all turned to sighs of relief, and, oddly enough, hugs of gratitude.

It felt strange joining the celebration. Not because I was shy. I'd gotten over that the moment the building started to shake. No, I felt strange because out of everyone, my drawing still sat safely tucked away at my table. I just couldn't bring myself to destroy it. How could I? It was a masterpiece, after all.

END

Under Sanctuary's Watchful Gaze

Jason R. Frei

About the Author: JASON R. FREI lives in Eastern Pennsylvania where he works as a therapist with children and adolescents. He writes speculative fiction culled from the experiences of his life and those he works with. He blends science fiction, fantasy and horror into new creations. Visit him online: https://facebook.com/odinstones.

UNDER SANCTUARY'S WATCHFUL GAZE
JASON R. FREI

"I cast fireball." Roary sat back with his arms crossed and a smug look on his face. Orange Cheetos dust powdered the front of his black star-speckled robe.

"Hold up." Mitchell whined in a nasally voice. "Can't you delay until after my turn? The fireball will hit me along with the mummies."

Roary smirked. "Not my problem. You ran in there without consulting any of us."

"That's my job, dumbass—"

Roary slammed his fists down on the table. "It's *Dumas*, you oaf!"

Priscilla giggled and shifted in her chair to keep the tail of her large, unflattering fox fursuit from bunching. "What's the skill check for fireball, Sir Dumas?"

Roary glared at her for a moment and then smiled. The girl was talking to him and he didn't want to ruin any chance he had with her.

He tipped his head in a mock bow. "The check is dexterity, my fair Oriana."

She curtsied in her chair. "Since I delayed my turn, I'll take it now and cast Cat's Grace on the mighty Dalnyr. Maybe he can make the save with a bit more dex."

Mitchell brightened up. "Thank you kindly, my lady."

Kenny laughed. "For once, I'm glad I didn't rush in."

Mitchell grimaced at him. "Rogues don't rush in. They just kind of skulk around the shadows and wait until someone's back is turned."

Kenny's face turned red as the others laughed.

"I'll have a heal or rez ready if it's needed," said Aaron Waltmann. He spun his twenty-sided dice on one of its corners.

Randy wiped his glasses on the front of his shirt and sighed. When he first heard of the Dungeon Master gig at TableTopCon, he jumped at the chance. His regular Saturday night group bored him. They wanted pre-made campaigns and took way too long to make a single move. TTC offered him the chance to try out his own fantasy world with a new group eager for adventure. Randy was one of five offered the position.

Unlike most cons, his stay at the legendary Hotel Sanctuary was included, along with comped meals and a contracted salary. He would have done it just for the chance to stay at the hotel.

Sanctuary, as it was called, was built in the early 1980's on Petty Island, in the middle of the Delaware River between Philadelphia, Pennsylvania and Camden, New Jersey. Designed and built by Kristof Varner, a purported contemporary of Aleister Crowley, it was rumored that he and four friends disappeared the night of the hotel's opening and were never heard from again.

The hotel was renowned for its architecture. Grotesque and lewd gargoyles engaged in vulgar and indecent acts lined the roof of the thirteen story gothic style building. By some odd property in the stonework, rain that dripped down its edifice turned the color of blood until it reached the ground. Demons, succubi and creatures of eld peeked out from the masonry and appeared to dance and cavort through the night. Large panes of stained glass surrounded the upper levels, depicting grisly scenes of murder, sacrifice and supplication to unknown gods.

The interior of the hotel spread out in such disarray as to cause madness. Jet-black marble staircases sometimes led directly into walls with no openings. Blood-red lacquered doors opened onto solid expanses of black and gold facades. Footsteps clicked and echoed weirdly off of polished granite floors giving the impression of ghostly treadings across halls and on different floors from where they came. Some of the guest rooms were oddly shaped of five or more walls while other rooms appeared to contain unusual angles that hid great areas of unattainable space.

"Well?" asked Priscilla, pulling Randy from his musings.

"Sorry, travelers," said Randy is his best Olde English voice. "I must have nodded off whilst you were bickering amongst yourselves." He flashed a winsome smile and both Priscilla and Aaron blushed.

Roary glowered at the DM. "Are you gonna roll to save or daydream the rest of the night?"

"You are quite correct, Sir Dumas." Randy tipped his head toward Roary.

Dice clattered across the table as Randy rolled for the two mummies. One of the die spun on a point as it landed on a one and Roary fist pumped into the air. The other die was a low roll and the rest of the group cheered.

A third die, dark blue with white swirls, bounced around a leather mat as Mitchell rolled for his save—and it came up a twelve. "Let's see," said Mitchell. "Normally, my Dexterity bonus is plus two, but with that Cat's Grace spell on that's another two...so sixteen." He looked up at Randy expectantly.

"The DC on the nose," said Randy. The gang whooped again.

Randy cleared his throat. "Sir Dumas chants softly as his hands begin to glow. With a shout and a point, a bright streak flies from his fingertips and lands directly in between the two mummies. The mummy to the right

110

of Dalnyr the Great incinerates instantly and falls into a pile of ash. The mummy in front of him shrieks as he is engulfed in flames. As the mummy begins to crumble, Dalnyr spies a leather-bound book nestled inside its chest. The barbarian dodges deftly to the right, pulling the book directly from the heart of flame before the mummy disintegrates."

The band of heroes cheered and a small gathering of convention goers whistled and clapped for them. Randy was well known as one of the most skilled of storytellers and always drew a group, whether it was of players or just sightseers interested in a good tale.

Randy produced a book from a bag at his feet and passed it over to Mitchell. Puckered black leather stretched around a slim book. Its yellowed pages were thick and blank.

"It's empty," said Mitchell, flipping through the pages.

"Can I see?" asked Roary. His eyes gleamed with envy. Mitchell passed the book over.

Roary turned the pages slowly, one at a time. "I cast detect magic," he said.

Randy nodded his head. "What languages do you know?"

Roary picked up his character sheet and looked it over. "Uh...Common, Elvish, Abyssal and Deep Speech."

Randy's eyebrows arched. He gestured for the book and Roary gave it over. Randy pulled a Zippo from his pocket, flicked the striker and waved the flame back and forth under one of the pages. Randy gave the book back.

"You notice a stanza of words in R'lyehian, a subset of Deep Speech, on one of the pages."

The players gathered around the book, as did the crowd of observers. Rust red words in a thin, spiky handwriting now appeared on the page.

nafl'fhtagn ehye ot ot fhtagn mgepog
ng mggoka thy agl llll shuggothh

> *syha'h l' darken shuggog*
> *llll gn'th'bthnk ng n'ghanglui*
> *mg ahog fhtagn ahor nog*
> *uh'eor n'gha ng mgehye*

Roary looked up at Randy questioningly.

The DM smiled. "It says 'Rise, oh Sleeper of the Deep, and take thy place among men, forever to darken the world with blood and disease. No more sleep shall come, only death and destruction.' "

A piercing squeal sounded in the gaming hall, causing everyone around the table to jump.

"Sorry, folks," came a voice over the loudspeaker. "It is ten minutes to midnight and we will be closing the hall until tomorrow morning. The pub will be open until two and you are free to roam the many twists and turns of the hotel for as long as you like."

The crowd grumbled and the adventurers packed up their belongings for the night.

Randy dropped his Olde English dialect and switched back to his Southern one. "Since y'all are spending the next few days with me, how about we get a few beers and check out the hotel?"

Aaron lowered his head and twisted his hands together. "Can...can I come too?"

Randy instantly liked Aaron. He remembered being so nervous at his first con. He put his hand on Aaron's shoulder and squeezed. "You're an important part of the troop Terinval, so of course."

Aaron smiled and his eyes grew big. "Your accents are great, by the way."

After the group gathered their backpacks, they got drinks from the bar and wandered through the first floor of the Sanctuary. Randy gave a thrilling back story to the hotel and outlined some of the more infamous events to

112

have happened.

Roary pulled a long drag from his beer and almost choked on it. When he recovered, he asked "Was the builder really a magician, like a freemason?"

Randy chuckled. "Freemasons were a secret fraternity, but they weren't magicians. Varner was a member of the Ordo Templi Orientis. The OTO was an occult group that researched magic and practiced rituals based on sex in order to gain power. Rumors have persisted that the order performed these powerful rituals to summon creatures from other dimensions."

"That sounds like a load of crap," said Mitchell. He visibly swayed from the half-pint of beer he'd drunk.

Priscilla huffed. "It's the basis of the entire game we're playing."

"Yeah," said Mitchell, "but it's just a game. There's nothing real about it."

A small cough came from the back of the group and everyone turned. Aaron half-raised his hand in the air. Randy nodded at him.

"Rumor has it that Varner and his associates went into the basement on opening night to perform some ritual. Some of the guests described a lot of weird noises throughout the evening, and just after midnight, the entire hotel shook like it was in an earthquake."

Kenny giggled. "Sounds like some real good sex magic."

This caused the entire group to break out into laughter. Roary turned to the wall and pretended to hump it. Priscilla, laughing, pushed Roary against the wall to help him along. The robed wizard lost his balance and grabbed onto a wall sconce. The sconce twisted in his grip and an audible crunch echoed in the corridor. A moment later, part of the wall slid inward revealing a set of carved stone stairs leading down into the dark.

Randy gasped and then a smile split his face from ear to ear.

"Y'all found one of the secret passages!"

Mitchell high-fived Aaron and Kenny. Roary and Priscilla hugged and then pulled apart quickly. Both of their faces were scarlet.

"Let's check it out," said Kenny, and stepped into the entryway.

Aaron balked. "Shouldn't we tell the front desk or something?"

"It's pitch black in there too," said Priscilla.

Randy took a moment to ponder. His face lit up and he hurriedly rummaged through his backpack. He pulled out a large, thick candle in a smoky gray jar. With a flick of his wrist, he lit the candle with his Zippo.

"Better?" he asked Priscilla.

She gave a small curtsy. "You first, fearless leader."

Randy looked over at Aaron and raised his eyebrows. Aaron nodded. The six adventurers made their way down the stairs.

֍֍֍

The candle's flame intensified in the darkness and lit the way down the stairs. Shadows jumped across the smooth, barren walls creating the illusion of lurkers at the threshold of human existence. The air grew cold and moisture slicked the surface of the walls and steps as they descended.

The stairwell seemed to spiral in on itself as it plunged downward. At times, the companions found themselves walking single-file, and other times they walked in a single line, shoulder-to-shoulder. When they finally made it to the bottom, cold sweat ran in runnels down their faces and backs.

At the bottom of the stairs, they entered into a cavernous room. A three-foot high urn of polished black metal sat inside the entranceway. The acrid smell of oil emanated from it. Randy tipped his candle into the urn.

Flames spread around the room in a shallow channel from the base of the urn, lighting up the cavern.

The room itself was not large, but a trick of the light and sound within gave it the impression of being cosmically massive. The black walls sloped upward, producing a domed ceiling dotted with small white pinpricks, creating the appearance of a night sky. A burbling sound, like swift water, filled the chamber.

In the center of the room stood a capped well slightly taller than the now-lit urn. It was covered in moss and slime, giving it a sickly, greenish color. The sound of the water seemed to originate from within it.

Around the perimeter of the well stood five bizarre statues. They were vulturine in appearance. Half-spread wings stood out from each bird-like creature. Serpentine necks twined out from between the wings and horrid demon-like heads sprouted from them. The statues were of an odd metallic-like rock, each being a different color—green, white, orange, red and black. At the base of each beast laid a dusty robe.

"My God!" said Randy. He turned to the group. "Do you know what this is?"

"It's creepy, is what it is," said Mitchell. He stared at the eyes of one of the vulturine statues.

"What is this place?" asked Priscilla.

Randy's mouth hung open as he took it all in and then said, "I studied philosophy in college. My specialty was occult religions. That's where I learned about Sanctuary. For my thesis, I researched different esoteric practices and focused specifically on cults of the Great Old Ones found in forbidden books, like the _Necronomicon,_ the _Unaussprechlichen Kulten_, and the _Cthäat Aquadingen_."

"What are you talking about?" asked Roary.

"They are... grimoires of a sort, spell books, used to summon god-like creatures from another dimension, like the OTO tried. I recognize these statues from some of those books. They are the Vaeyen. They are guardians who keep the Great Old One Cyäegha bound in his own universe so he can't get to ours."

Kenny picked up one of the robes. "Why would these statues need clothes?"

Aaron smacked his forehead. The sound of it echoed through the chamber. "Of course. Varner and his friends must have been a part of some cult who wanted to summon this being."

"No, no, no" said Randy. "I think they did the opposite and kept it from coming through."

"So, you're saying that these statues are actually Varner and his buddies?" Mitchell poked at one of the demon heads.

Randy thrust his hand out at Mitchell. "Don't touch them!"

The head of the green vulture statue crumbled at Mitchell's touch. This caused a chain reaction in all of the statues, causing them to instantly decay into dust.

Mitchell looked at the others. "Oops."

The lid on the well thumped as if something beat on it from beneath. The flames around the room flared brightly and then dropped down to a soft glow. The lid thumped again even harder and then flew straight up into the air like a cork from a wine bottle.

The sound of water grew in its intensity and suddenly burbled up and overran the top of the well. Where it hit the flame, it hissed and turned to steam. A cloud of fog developed around the well, obscuring it from view.

"We should get out of here," said Randy.

The group turned to run, but the opening to the stairs was nowhere to be found. A squelching, sloshing sound susurrated from the center of the heavy mist. Dark shapes played behind the gloom. A stench of raw sewage and decay pervaded the room. Kenny gagged.

The fires brightened again, chasing away the cloud.

116

No more water spilled from the well, but a nebulous shape began to ooze its way out. The sloshing sound grew louder as the shape gathered its form.

A throng of thick, black worm-like appendages rose from the pit in the center of the room. In the center of the mass rested a massive eye. The green double iris glinted with madness and rage.

The adventurers ran in all directions, searching frantically for a way out of the room. The beast roared and its extremities whipped out. A tentacle of the massive creature whipped out and slammed into Roary's, sending his body flailing through the air like a plastic bag on a windy day. His body hit the wall with such force that the stone underneath cracked. His limp body slid to the floor, leaving a red streak in its wake.

Priscilla screamed as a tentacle wrapped around her ankle. Mitchell fished a pocketknife out of his backpack and slashed at the limb. Viscous green fluid spurted from the wound and it released Priscilla. Kenny zig-zagged around the room, dodging tentacles that slapped and swung at his moving body. He felt like the rogue Terinval in one of their campaigns. He watched as a great limb swung toward him. He ducked at exactly the right moment only to collide headfirst into Randy who was running the opposite direction.

Randy grabbed Kenny and picked him up from the floor.

"Have you seen my backpack?" asked Randy.

"Forget your backpack, man. We need to get out of here."

"No!" Randy shook Kenny. "That creature, Cyäegha, has opened a portal to another realm. If we don't get him back in, more will come."

"What are we supposed to do against something like that?" Kenny was close to tears.

"We need to recite the Vach-Viraj incantation. I have

a copy of it in my backpack. The stanza from the book in the campaign was written in R'lyehian. I have several incantations from the forbidden books written in that book."

"Fine. What's your backpack look like?"

"It's dark green with D&D buttons all over the front of it. Find the others and get my bag. I'll try to keep Cyäegha's attention."

Kenny sped off to find the others. Randy picked up one of the discarded robes and plunged a corner of it in the flames. The robe caught fire and Randy waved it around.

"Hey!" he shouted at the creature. "Over here, ugly!"

Cyäegha turned its eye toward Randy and twisted its deformed body toward him. It regarded him with a bestial intelligence.

Aaron ran up to Randy, the missing backpack in his grip. Randy nodded his head.

"I need you to get the leather book from the campaign earlier tonight."

Aaron emptied the bag on the ground and grabbed the book.

"Turn to the last page and pass it carefully over the flames. You'll see writing appear."

Aaron did as he was told, almost burning the book in his haste. The spiky red writing developed after a few passes. Mitchell, Priscilla and Kenny joined them.

"What's next?" asked Aaron.

Cyäegha watched the small group warily. Randy kept the flaming part of the robe high and carefully tore strips from the unburned fabric. He explained the plan as he did this.

"That new stanza is the Vach-Viraj, an incantation that the cultists used to both supplicate Cyäegha and keep him bound in his own plane. Ordinarily, we would need a Tikkoun Elixir, something similar to holy water, but I believe Varner and his associates performed their ritual here because the Delaware River is consecrated. I won't go into the story now, but just believe me.

"I want each of you to take a strip of cloth and set it ablaze. Spread out around the foul beast and keep it busy by waving the fire in the air. I will read the incantation and that should send it back down the well. We'll have to figure out a way to close it, but we'll get to that later."

The four adventurers took their strips of cloth and set them on fire. They then spread out around the well. Cyäegha spun quickly around from member to member, watching them with his great horrible eye.

Randy looked down at the book, wet his lips and began to read.

"Ya na kadishtu nilgh'ri stell'bsna Nyogtha, K'yarnak phlegethor l'ebumna syha'h n'ghft, Ya hai kadishtu ep r'luh-eeh Nyogtha eeh, S'uhn-ngh athg li'hee orr'e syha'h."

The words came out thick and strange, not readily made for human lips. Fortunately, as a GM who put care into his craft, Randy had practiced them before a mirror many times over.

Their sound bounded off the walls and reverberated throughout the cavern. Cyäegha was silent through the reading, but an agitation spread through the Great Old God's body. The tentacles writhed and twisted. Gaps appeared between them and the vast expanse of that other space intruded on this world.

When the last echo died away, each member began to glow a different color—green for Priscilla, white for Aaron, orange for Randy, red for Mitchell and black for Kenny. The glows intensified, enveloping their bodies and obscuring their features.

A high-pitched hum sounded around the chamber. It rose in crescendo and beams of light radiated from the companions, bursting out and striking the turbulent body of Cyäegha. With a great sucking sound, the body of the Great Old One shattered. Its worm-like appendages dropped into the well and the colossal green eye burst in a slimy explosion. Immense gouts of water thrust out from the well, filling the cavern.

As violently as the water poured forth, it receded back into the well just as quickly. It pulled Roary's body down the well along with it. Chunks of rock shed themselves from the wall and rushed along with the water, fusing together to cover the top of the well.

The fires burned out from the deluge and left the room in an eerie silence. The only clues left in the chamber to suggest that anyone had been there were five glistening vulturine statues, softly glowing in muted hues.

A scream split the night on the shore of Petty Island. A couple on a romantic stroll were startled as a bedraggled form crawled out of the river and collapsed. Police soon arrived and found Roary on the precipice of death. Gripped in his hands was the puckered black leather-bound journal. Upon inspection, the journal's pages were blank.

Roary never fully recovered. He rarely spoke and when he did, it was gibberish to those around him, sounding foreign and ill-fitting. The black journal stayed tucked under his arm at all times. He avoided waterways, except for once a year, when he checked into the Hotel Sanctuary. He always stayed for three days, but none of the hotel staff ever saw him leave his room.

END

Awaken! Arise!
T-shirts For Fifty-Five!

John Lance

About the Author: JOHN LANCE lives in New England with his lovely wife and daughters. He enjoys spending time with his family, reading, writing, and working in his garden. His stories have appeared in *Crunchy with Ketchup*, *Wight Christmas*, and *Raygun Retro*. His website is: http://www.johnmlance.com/

Awaken! Arise! T-shirts For Fifty-Five!
John Lance

We awake!
The ice is gone. Retreated? Did the star expand?
Impossible to say. Impossible to know.
Yet.
Hunger! Ravenous! It has been so long. We must hunt!
Scout first.
Hunt!
Reconnaissance. Investigate. Understand.
Then hunt?
Then hunt.
The river is low but the cave still shelters us.
There is something else. Above. Not there when we fell
asleep.
A structure. Primitive. Confining. Restrictive.
Like something a child would build.
It only uses three dimensions.
A stupid child.
There are no others nearby. Only us. We are alone.
Out of time.
Out of place.
Better to have remained asleep.
Why did we awake?
We don't care. We are alone. Alone in the dark.
We woke because we heard something.

Our name.
There it is again.
"Nagowraith."
Above us. Inside the structure. And there are other noises. Grunting. Babbling. Chaotic cacophony.
No, not chaos. There is rhythm. Cadence. There is...
Meaning?
How strange. Unexpected. Curious.
How simple.
Communication via sound waves within a limited spectrum. Easy to interpret. Easy to comprehend.
"Awaken Nagowraith. Awaken and arise!"
Many voices. Chanting. They are many, but not like we are many. They are singles.
How foolish. How silly. How droll.
"Thank you for joining me in our morning ritual. A reminder, the breakfast service is from 8 to 9. Souvenir t-shirts are available for fifty-five dollars at the main booth, get them while the getting is good. And our first panel starts at 9:30 sharp, so be there on time or be fed to Cthulu."
The Destroyer?! Here?!
Back to the dark. Hide. Be safe.
But we will starve. We are ravenous. We must feed.
Wait! Something is coming.

"Did you see this one?" Jillian asked, holding out her phone.

"Of course, I saw it. I took it. I took all the pictures," Ben replied without bothering to look at the screen. Being Jillian's Instagram documentarian could get a little wearing.

"You didn't take this one," Jillian replied, her cherry lips pursed in her patented pout.

Ben sighed. "'Sorry, let me see."

It was a selfie of Jillian and some sort of squid-bat thing. The angle of the photo perfectly flattered Jillian's blond hair, wide green eyes, and bright smile. The monster was almost an afterthought.

"It took Joe three months to build the mask," Jillian said.

"And Joe is?"

"The guy in the costume, duh," Jillian rolled her eyes.

"Right. Sorry. Should have had a cup of coffee. Which I would have had if we had gone to breakfast after the opening ceremony rather than sneak down here to the basement. What do you think Toby, can we go eat and then come back and finish, um, whatever it is we're doing?"

"For the hundredth time, refer to me as *Professor Rice*. And we're looking for the secret entrance to the lost Chamber of the Nagowraith," Toby replied. He was wearing a top hat, cape, and monocle, like some English gentleman from the late 1800s. Only the flashlight he held was out of place.

Ben, who was dressed in jeans and a sweatshirt, looked blankly at Toby.

Toby rolled his eyes and glanced at Jillian for sympathy. Jillian was too busy scrolling on her phone to notice.

With a sigh, Toby said, "Just look for something bearing the mark of Cthulu."

Ben nodded. "Sure, and a Cthulu is…"

"The octopus! The octopus monster! It's like you never even heard of the Elder Things or read any of the stories before! Why did you even bother coming to this convention to begin with?"

It was a question Ben had asked himself multiple times since checking into the old hotel last night. Maine in the middle of March was even colder than he had anticipated. Like most normal college seniors, Ben planned to spend Spring Break in Fort Lauderdale, or Cancun, or any other warm place with beaches. But Toby wanted to attend this weird convention, and where Toby went his twin, Jillian followed. And where Jillian went...

Jillian touched Ben's arm and he felt a familiar shiver up his spine.

"Don't take it personally, Benny. Toby..."

"Professor Rice," Toby interjected.

"Fine, the obscure-character-known-as-Professor Rice."

"Thank you."

"...has been spending too much time on the message boards, particularly the one claiming the Elder Things are real and all the stories and movies are coded messages between cult members. Then he read the post about the Chamber of the Nagowraith being here at the Con and he's been chomping at the bit to be the first one to find it ever since. It's a whole new Old One. Plus, it'll make for a great set of Instagram posts."

Ben—who hated being called Benny—sighed. "I'll go look behind the furnace."

The basement's weak track lighting cast everything in sinister shadow. Patio furniture tucked in among the water pipes morphed into grasping claws. Pool noodles scattered among boxes of holiday decorations became tentacle towers. And the patter of small mouse paws echoed around the cluttered space like slapping talons.

"Found it!" Toby called, pointing at a small, aqua-green squid head with disturbingly human eyes painted on a cement brick.

"Cool," Jillian exclaimed and snapped a picture.

"Don't you post that," Toby said.

"But..."

"Do you want everyone else coming down here and wrecking it?"

Jillian sniffed.

Toby rolled his eyes. "Just wait until we see what's

down there. Then you can do a whole montage."

"Fine."

"The paint looks fresh," Ben observed.

"I'm sure they added it for the Con," Jillian said.

"Guys, you're wrecking the whole immersion of the experience," Toby protested.

"Right, sorry," Ben said. "So how do we get to the chamber, Professor? Press the brick and the secret door opens?"

"Maybe if we were in a Scooby Doo cartoon," Toby snorted as he placed his hand lightly against the block, which sank into the wall. They heard a click and a portion of the wall swung open.

Toby cleared his throat. "I thought we would need to solve a puzzle or something."

"Maybe next time don't be so quick to dis Scooby Doo, eh?" Ben replied. Peeking through the dark doorway, he said, "We'll need our flashlights after all."

"Oooo, this is so exciting. Here, take this," Jillian handed Ben her phone, although he hardly recognized it with the LED and shotgun microphone attached to the top. "Hold it in landscape mode and follow me and Toby."

Ben was about to protest, but then realized the LED light was brighter than his flashlight.

Toby started down the stairs and Jillian and Ben hurried to catch up. The stairway corkscrewed down, making it difficult for Ben to keep both Toby and Jillian in the camera frame. Ben erred on keeping the focus on Jillian. The door closed behind them.

"It's kind of spooky. And it's getting warmer, which is weird. What do you think we'll find at the bottom? A mysterious temple? A forbidden altar?" Jillian threw a steady stream of chatter over her shoulder, though Ben knew it was for the camera's benefit, not his.

"Doesn't really seem like the sort of stairway that ends in mystery," Ben replied, running his hand along the smooth concrete walls and noting the clean, gray steps. "Probably takes us to the laundry."

Toby pulled up short. "Do you hear that?"

"Hear what?" Jillian asked.

"Shhh!" Toby frowned.

Ben strained his ears. Eventually he heard the noise as well. Wet, labored breathing and loud, stomping steps.

"What is that?" Jillian asked with alarm.

The steps stopped. "Hello?" a weak voice echoed up the stairway.

After a moment's hesitation, Toby replied, "Hello?"

The stomping began again, and a heavy set, red faced young man stumbled into view. "Oh, thank goodness! Both my flashlight and my phone died. What are the odds, right?" He waved his plastic flashlight to emphasize his point.

The man was dressed like a European explorer, complete with pith helmet, khaki shorts, and a handlebar mustache.

Noticing Toby's top hat and cape, the man said, "Professor Rice, I presume."

Toby gave a polite chuckle. "I like your Professor Atwood. Few people get the mustache right."

"Thank you. My real-life name is Kenny, by the way."

Toby performed introductions, then nonchalantly asked, "So, Kenny, did you reach the bottom?"

Kenny grinned. "You mean, was I the first person to crack the seal on the Chamber of the Nagowraith and learn its terrible secrets? Sadly, no, though I think I was close. The cement steps change to stone stairs a little further on. Be careful, by the way, those are slippery." He pointed at a bruise on his knee.

"Do you want to join us?" Ben asked, because it was the polite thing to do, but also to see the disapproving look on Toby's face.

The man smiled and dabbed some sweat from his chin.

"Thanks, but I've had enough early morning adventuring. I'm going to hit the breakfast bar and try again later, after I get a lot of spare batteries."

"Take my flashlight. I'm good with the camera light," Ben handed Kenny the flashlight from his pocket.

"Thank you. Maybe I'll see you later at one of the panels."

They watched as Kenny disappeared up the staircase.

"Come on, Kenny looked like a talker. Who knows how much longer we'll have this to ourselves," Toby said.

Though Ben would never admit it to Toby or Jillian, he was feeling curious, excited even, to discover what awaited. It didn't take long for the cement stairs to give way to slate. Soon after they reached a door with a tentacled face painted on it.

"I hope there's another way up," Ben muttered, rubbing his sore thighs.

"Ready? Here we go," Toby pushed the door open and they stepped into an immense cavern.

"Huh, I was kind of expecting more," Ben said, tracking the camera around the landscape. Admittedly, Ben's experience with caves was limited. But other than some big stalactites and tall stalagmites, there wasn't really anything notable except a shallow stream.

"Kind of anti-climactic," Jillian said.

"What's that?" Toby pointed at a cloud of lights rising from the stream.

"It looks like the night sky," Jillian said.

Wisps of silver connecting the lights made Ben think of a cobweb covered in dew. "Okay, I take it back, that is cool," he said.

"I was expecting more tentacles," Toby said, disappointed.

So hungry.

"What did you say?" Ben asked.

"That wasn't me," Toby replied. "Jillian?"

Jillian pointed. "I think it was the, umm, lights."

Must feed! Must devour!

"Um, Toby, is the Nagowraith a, ummm, good guy?" Ben asked.

Toby rolled his eyes, "I told you, the Nagowraith is a whole new Elder Thing. No one knows anything about it."

"Fine! Are Elder Things nice?"

"No."

"This may have been a bad idea," Jillian whispered, backing away from the lights. Her flashlight began to flicker, then went dark. Toby's quickly followed.

Hungry!

The LED on the camera dimmed as the cloud of lights brightened. They expanded, changing colors as they grew. Red, blue, green, and yellow danced in the dark.

Jillian screamed.

Torches along the walls suddenly sprang to life and revealed an ornate altar. A man holding a dagger overhead and wearing blood-red robes decorated with black glyphs stood behind it.

"Great Nagowraith, it is I that have awoken you! Devour these sacrifices! Restore your strength! And share with me your dark knowledge of eternal life!"

"Isn't that the master of ceremonies from this morning?" Ben asked.

"Wow, they had me going there," Jillian smiled in relief.

Devour? Consume? What?

"Them! Rend the meat from their bones! Tear their flesh and be reborn!" the priest pointed at Ben and his friends.

"Seems a bit drastic don't you think?" joked Ben.

"Shhhh, you're wrecking it," Toby replied.

"Sorry, my bad," Ben gave the priest a thumbs up. "You're doing great."

"Oh, I get it, it's a riddle. We have to figure out what

the Nagowraith eats," Jillian said.

Toby snapped his fingers. "Right. They did something similar at TerrorCon two years ago. There was a whole mystery part. Let's see, when the Nagowraith appeared the flashlights and LED stopped working. It must eat light."

"Then why are the torches still lit?" Ben asked.

"You can use fluorescent or incandescent lights to grow plants but you can't use firelight. Maybe the Nagowraith is similar," Jillian said. Seeing the looks on Ben and Toby's faces she added, "And you guys said a minor in horticulture was a waste of time."

"Fair enough," Toby said.

"The Nagowraith is a plant?" Ben said.

Jillian shrugged, "Or plant-like. If it's hungry, we should just take it outside and expose it to sunlight."

Ben groaned. "I can't climb all those stairs again. Hey you, cult guy!"

"Ben what are you doing? You're going to get us banned from the Con."

"If that's the master of ceremony, and he beat us down here, there must be a faster, easier, way up."

"They hate breaking character!" Toby said in a harsh stage whisper.

"Look, the Nagowraith is starving. Hell, it's even shrinking. Which is a nice effect by the way. If we're going to, you know, save it," Ben used air quotes, "then we got to move fast."

"He's got a point," Jillian said.

"Fine. But we can at least do it correctly," Toby replied. Slipping into a terrible English accent, Toby addressed the cult priest. "I say, pardon me old chap, but could you kindly direct us to a lift that would take us to the surface? We wish to restore this poor emaciated Nagowraith to its full glory by exposing it to sunlight."

The cowled figure pushed back his hood to reveal

a baby-faced man with receding black hair and thick glasses. "Do you really think that will work?"

"Umm, indubitably, or my name isn't Professor Rice," Toby said,

"Nice touch," Ben whispered.

"The service elevator goes to the roof. We could use that."

Hungry.

"I know, I know," Jillian tried unsuccessfully to pet the lights. "Just follow us and we'll get you something to eat."

They followed the priest to the elevator. When the doors opened, the elevator's overhead lights began to dim.

"Wait, don't eat the light," Jillian said.

Why!?!?!

"I can't ride in the elevator in the dark. It would be too freaky. If you just wait a little longer, you'll be able to eat until your, um, heart's content. If you have a heart."

For a moment, the lights of the Nagowraith blinked and shifted colors like a spastic rainbow before returning to more muted hues.

We will wait. We have been very patient. But we are starving.

"I know, I promise, it will be worth it," Jillian said.

The group piled into the elevator and the priest pressed the button for the roof. They found themselves standing inside the Nagowraith. The skein of lights drifted around them like a nebula and there was the oppressive scent of wintergreen.

"It's like a Christmas tree threw up in here," Ben said.

"Don't be rude," Jillian hushed him.

They watched the floors go past. Jillian fiddled with her hair, checking for split ends. Toby adjusted his monocle. The priest stared straight ahead, refusing to acknowledge the others.

"Sooo, been living under the hotel long?" Ben asked

one of the lights.

Eons. Millennium. Before the dawn of your species.

"That's a long time."

Yes. A long time. In the dark. Asleep. Waiting. Hungry in the dark.

The overhead light flickered.

"Now, now just a few minutes more," Jilliian said. To Ben she whispered, "Get the camera ready." Then she casually slipped to the front of the car so she could be the first one out.

The doors opened and the bright morning light streamed in.

So fresh! So delicious!

The Nagowraith swarmed onto the roof top. It swirled and sparkled.

Jillian rushed out to stand inside the cloud of lights, her arms held out wide as she spun slowly in a circle. Her eyes were closed and her head tilted slightly so that the sun landed fully on her face while the Nagowraith twinkled around her.

"She does know how to set a scene," Ben admitted as he zoomed the camera in on her.

"Uh huh," Toby said, not even glancing at his sister. "That is one happy Nagowraith."

"Now who's breaking character," Ben said.

Toby gave a half smile, then grunted as the priest shoved past him.

"Now that you've feasted, share your knowledge with me! Tell me the key to eternal life!" The priest cried.

"Got to give him props for sticking with the bit," Ben said.

Soooooooo good! More! More! We must feed!

"Is it me or are the lights getting even bigger?" Toby asked.

"It looks like I'm in a bubble bath!" Jillian said, holding out her hand, trying to entice one of the colored orbs to alight on her finger.

Suddenly one of the lights popped, spattering the group with a yellow, snotty liquid that smelled like microwaved fish.

"Ew! Ectoplasm!" Toby said.

MOOOOOORRRRREEE!!

Another light popped.

"My hair!" Jillian cried.

"Agh! Some got in my mouth!" Ben gagged, then threw up all over Toby.

"Stop! Stop! You have to stop gorging yourself!" The priest shouted.

YUMMMY!

The remaining globes exploded in a torrent of mucus.

"Agh! This was a new outfit!" Jillian sobbed as she dashed past Ben to the shelter of the elevator.

The priest, his robes soaked, his glasses covered in slime, sank to his knees.

"I don't suppose there's another Nagowraith?" Ben asked as he wiped the camera phone with the one dry part of his sweatshirt.

The priest shook his head.

"Ah well, a really great show. I am going to need to hop in the shower though," he walked back to the elevator.

"That was awesome. I've never seen anything like it. I'm definitely coming back next year. See you around the booths," Toby clapped the priest on the shoulder before following Ben and his sister.

A single, blinking light drifted past.

Soooo full!

Landing on the roof, it popped.

END

Quite The Following

Hank Schwaeble

About the Author: HANK SCHWAEBLE is a horror, thriller and suspense writer whose credits include Damnable (Berkley/Jove), which won the Bram Stoker Award for Best First Novel, and Diabolical (Berkley/Jove), as well as The Angel of the Abyss and the horror-noir collection American Nocturne, both re-released in 2021. His latest collection, Moonless Nocturne, was slated for publication in 2022 from Esker & Riddle.

A graduate of the University of Florida and Vanderbilt Law School, Hank is a practicing attorney and former Air Force officer and special agent for the Air Force Office of Special Investigations. He was a distinguished graduate from the Air Force Special Investigations Academy, graduated first in his class from the Defense Language

Institute's Japanese Language Course, and was an editor of the law review at Vanderbilt where he won four American Jurisprudence Awards.

In addition to reading and writing, Hank enjoys keeping in shape and playing guitar. Hank and his wife, fellow writer Rhodi Hawk, make their home near Houston, Texas. He is currently working on his next novel.

QUITE THE FOLLOWING

HANK SCHWAEBLE

Kemper Baldwin studied the scene with the jaded eye of a weary deserter, staring at the man with the long hair on the angled rock, at the black duster flowing in the alien wind, at the rocket-shaped gun above the man's head and the scantily clad women with distressed expressions strewn in various states of repose near his feet. Behind them, to the right, he spied a regal woman wearing a windswept crown of fierce golden horns atop an immense, tusked beast poised to descend upon the lot. He ran his eyes one final time over the giant orb in the sky silhouetting them all, and thought, *there's gotta be a special place in hell for whoever signed me up for this.*

He watched the sharpie in his hand write the name of that responsible party he had in mind with an extravagant flourish across the worn cover before finishing with his trademark stab-and-slash, a move that delighted fans who failed to see it for the gesture of thinly veiled spite that it was.

"Thanks!" said the young man in the puffy shirt. He had a bright sash tied around his waist and a metal eyepiece enhancement extending from a headband covering one eye, a nod to some sort of space pirate character Kemper recognized as vaguely familiar but which didn't interest him enough to place. "Picked this up for a steal! *The*

137

Queen Out Of Time. Your first cover! This means so much to me!"

"I'm sure it does," Kemper said. The broad smile plastered on his face did not reach his eyes. "Treasure it for all time."

"You're my second favorite artist," Space Pirate said. "Right behind..."

Don't say it, Kemper thought. *Don't you fucking say it. If I hear that name one more time—*

"... Philip Franzer."

Kemper maintained eye contact without saying a word. *Franzer.* Why did they always drop that name? It made no sense. Their styles were nothing alike. Franzer used thinned out oils and scuffed brushing, bursts of color and diffused details. Nothing like the sketched authenticity Kemper employed, the use of shade and earth tones, the sense of life detailed in each face. He felt his nostrils flare, then he dropped his eyes to his watch to make it clear the interaction was over.

The second hand trudged forward one agonizing tick at a time, refusing to speed up no matter how hard he willed it to. Fourteen more minutes, then he'd be able to feign a tight schedule, stand, and pantomime his apologies, and presumably be rescued by his handler.

He sensed the presence of the next person in line and raised his head with a sigh, started to force his mouth into a rictus grin, and then caught the scent of perfume, a musky, sweet fragrance, jasmine pedals on a cupcake.

"I'm so very glad to finally meet you," she said.

The woman standing across from him was not what he expected. She was tall and shaped like a bikini model, with an outfit—if you could call it one—that covered about as many square inches, little more than a few chains accented by strategic lappets of silk.

"The pleasure's all mine," he said, his smile this time relatively understated, but genuine.

She placed a three-by-five glossy card on the table in front of him. "I wouldn't be so sure about that."

Her hair cascaded in dark red curls and waves that flowed over a silver and gold tiara-type of headdress. She held his gaze with hazel-green eyes and stretched her mouth into a beaming curve that accentuated prominent cheeks and a jaw that formed a tight triangle.

"I'm Deandra," she said. "I'm a big fan of your work."

Well, damn. He wanted to make a witty comment, something suggestive, flirtatious, but he held back. He'd caught heat for that kind of thing in the past and the truth was he needed these kinds of gigs. Advancements in desktop graphic design had brutalized the market. Or, more precisely, his share of it. He pulled the cap off his sharpie and lowered his eyes to the print, then stopped.

"Where did you find this?"

The woman's expression turned enigmatic and she raised an eyebrow skyward. "Like I said, I'm a big fan. I think you're this generation's..."

He clenched his jaw, felt his molars grind together.

"Edward Hopper," she said.

The words stopped him cold. It had been years—decades, more likely—since he'd heard himself described that way. A yawning gap due to some misguided editor's attempt to give him credit he didn't want. Credit and, of course, that damn award.

"Your play with light, the use of shadow and cityscapes to call attention to the contradiction of people as social and isolated at the same time. It's just brilliant."

He looked at the print again, a promotional card from an exhibition in Soho. He searched his recollection—had to be over thirty years ago. '*Escapes.*' One of his early works, an urban alley at night cloaked in darkness except for a dim triangle of illumination from a streetlamp, an open apartment window to the right framing a woman at a table, drink in one hand, forehead resting in the palm of her other, cigarette wedged between two fingers. The legs of a man visible in the background, protruding off a bed or couch, either passed out or quite possibly dead.

On the other side of the alley, across the chasm of darkness, a figure sits on a fire escape, shrouded in shadow, all but hidden from view, visible upon close inspection. But just barely. To most observers who study it he seems young, intense, patient. He's watching the woman through the open window, his intentions and mood completely indecipherable. Whether he was a witness to a crime, a would-be perpetrator, or simply a voyeur, no one could be sure.

A critic once hailed it as "a modern masterpiece of urban mood and mystery, a reminder of the complexity of the human experience that, like life, raises more questions than it answers."

"Thank you," he said, his voice faintly cracking as he signed the print with uncharacteristic care along the white bottom border. "That's very kind of you to say."

"No," she said. "It's not." With a subtle flash of her eyes and teeth, she turned and walked away, the small, sheer silk curtain veiling her buttocks fluttering with each step.

Eleven-thirty arrived, better late than never. Yasmine showed up with it as if she'd timed her steps to his Rolex.

"Sorry, folks," she said, addressing the couple dozen or so people still in line. "We have to clear the space. But Mr. Baldwin is scheduled to be available for another signing tomorrow, as well as later this afternoon at a private event, for those of you invited."

Kemper stood and stretched. He knew he should feel bad for the people who'd waited but were now being turned away. He also knew with even more certainty that he wasn't being paid enough to do more than the minimum. If they wanted his autograph so badly, they could buy one of his prints and see him in a few hours, or whatever it was they needed to do to get an invitation.

At Yasmine's request, he followed her to the hallway, where she made a notation on her clipboard. She adjusted her glasses and looked up, courteous and professional, all business.

"I trust you haven't had any problems?"

"No, everything's been... fine."

She nodded, glancing down at her papers. She was a good deal shorter than him, slightly on the plump side, with dark, smooth skin and caramel eyes and a bit of a dowdy look to her clothes. At first blush, her hair stood out, short, bronze and probably, in his estimation— looking down on it from that close—a wig, as it seemed to cover her head like a sculpted helmet.

"Your next event is at two p.m. in the Zemblanity Room."

He panned the area, throngs of people passing by, arterial flow moving in spurts, Jedis and Stormtroopers, aliens and cartoon characters, galactic warriors and Starfleet officers.

"The what room?"

"*Zemblanity.* It refers to... discoveries that are made by design. The room is a new addition."

"If you say so. Where is it?"

"We'll find you when the time comes. Can I get you anything?"

He gave the question some thought, mostly about how to phrase the subject he'd been wanting to broach. "I seem to be missing some of my drink tokens."

She maintained the same countenance through her blinks, obviously not believing a word of that assertion, but discrete enough not to let it show. The way he saw it, he wasn't exactly lying. He was indeed missing three of the four he'd been given, as they were last seen in the possession of the bartender in the main lounge.

"I will try to get you some more this afternoon, after the event. If you remind me."

Not what he'd hoped to hear, but he supposed he could hold out till then.

"You have just under two hours until the reception, so please feel free to enjoy lunch in the River Cafe or the Blue Oyster, if you'd prefer finer dining. Be sure to charge the meal to your room."

Except for the drinks, he reminded himself. They didn't allow those to be charged. Not since a Guest of Honor ran up a nine-hundred-dollar tab one year to go with the steak he'd barely touched. Or so the story went.

"I'll be fine."

"I wish I could say feel free to take in some of the sights and explore the city, but we request our invited guests not leave the island while events are still pending, as ferry access can be tricky. Though the schedule says they run hourly, that's not reliable. I know it doesn't look far, and I suppose some think they could throw a rock and hit the shoreline, but there's only one boat making the run and we would hate to have you miss your signature event."

Not as much as I would, he thought. Selling prints was the only chance he had to make extra cash above the couple grand he got for showing up.

"I understand," he said.

"Well, if there's nothing else, I trust you can find your way back to the lobby, and from there to your room. If you do decide to wander, there's a diagram on the back of the convention brochure. Just don't leave the building."

"Speaking of that, what's the story with the layout here? Seems like it was built for King Midas."

She smiled. "The architect—the whole design team, really—was tasked with creating plans for a hotel that would bring a dream of the original owner to life. He was very specific."

"His dream was to own a hotel with weird angles and

sudden corners and corridors that branch off to nowhere?"

"Not that kind of dream. A literal one. Morris Livingston always claimed he had a dream where he was in hotel that was destined to be the single most important structure in human history. That he explored every detail of it for what seemed like hours and hours, and that when he woke he knew he had to build it. He sold everything he had, borrowed every penny he could, and bought this tiny river island. He mortgaged himself to his eyeballs to build this place specifically to match the one in his dream, right down to the most minute detail. He disappeared in 1988, shortly after it was completed."

"I supposed we're left to infer the stress of it caused him drop out of sight, spend the rest of his days on the streets or in some remote cabin somewhere."

"According to some, yes. But others believe the day before it opened, he ventured to the top floor, an open area apparently intended for special events and galas, stripped himself naked, then put his mouth over the barrel of a shotgun and pressed the trigger with his toe. His lenders and investors pressured and bribed officials to cover it up, fearing they'd be stuck with a worthless piece of land if the public knew the truth. Or so some claim."

"Lovely. Must be fun explaining that to wedding parties."

"Oh, that's not a problem. Except for the occasional private event, it's strictly off limits."

"I'll make a note of it. Avoid the Penthouse-slash-Killing Floor."

She let out a wry chuckle. "Only those who are supposed to can find it. There's no way to enter through open stairs or guest elevators. It's limited to private staff access and authorized guests. But feel free to investigate and explore. We pride ourselves on the uniqueness of the hotel's layout and the numerous points of architectural interest."

Well, he thought, *I guess that means I won't be offered a tour.* Not that he minded, as he had no particular interest in one. He had no particular interest in anything, except perhaps finding a drink.

Yasmine departed after another reminder not to leave the hotel, making more notations on her clipboard as she trundled away. He was looking around, trying to decide where to go, which consisted mostly of deciding where he might use his remaining drink tokens, when he caught sight of the redhead through a few layers of convention goers. She was crossing the hall, entering one of the rooms.

He took in a breath. Maybe there was one other thing that interested him.

He headed in that direction, hoping that whatever was going on in there included a bar.

He pushed on one of the double doors and found himself in the gaming room.

The size and activity caused him to stop and take stock. A gamy smell invaded his nostrils, the funk of bodies and breaths and an assortment of perfumed fragrances intended to cover them up. He looked around to see row upon row of tables filled the middle of the rectangular space, a few feet separating each, people seated around almost all of them, spectators milling about, looking over shoulders. Along the far wall, the head, neck and front legs of a dragon protruded from an elaborate depiction of the rest of it, complete with a background graphic of rugged terrain and a castle high on a hill, the feature set up for people to take selfies, and several were doing just that, some brandishing swords, others feigning terror. He panned his eyes from one side of the room to the other, his gaze sweeping over the bearded men behind decorated screens and bespectacled women rolling dice and thin people and fat people and all types in between engrossed in similar actions. A woman in a cloak waved a wand over a table while a short, portly man in a leather helmet pointed to a rule book. There were people dressed as superheroes moving pieces around boards and people in khakis and numerous others in t-shirts and jeans positioned at video game consoles clustered along the walls. Convention regulars and obvious newcomers and enthusiasts of all shapes and sizes and various skin tones. Most, especially the men, seemed to be in poor shape and had bad complexions, the prevailing mien of them sloppy and unkempt. Had they ever heard of a gym? Or a salad?

His own thoughts gave him pause, and he wondered why his reaction was so harsh. Had he always held such contempt for these people? This fandom? And why did he have any at all? He hadn't exactly been the high school quarterback himself—was a quiet, somewhat broody teen, bookish and resentfully dismissive of anyone who seemed to be more popular than he was, which was just about everyone. And in those younger days he was far closer in his tastes, appearance and temperament to the typical person in this crowd, so why did he harbor these feelings toward them? An unsettling conclusion came to him. It was because they *did* remind him of himself, of who he was—with one gargantuan difference. By and large, these people seemed happy.

It felt like a gut punch, admitting that. But looking at them, it was inescapable. They were smiling, clapping, laughing. Sharing comments, excitedly reacting to meaningless things like dice rolls and imaginary battle outcomes. These were people enjoying games, enjoying friends. Enjoying life. These were the people who enjoyed things like his artwork.

And he hated them for it.

He shook himself back to the moment, unsure how long he'd been standing there. Glancing about, he caught sight of the redhead in the skimpy costume not too far away. Deandra, he reminded himself. She was standing to his left several yards off, engaged in friendly conversation with a small group, not looking his way or giving any indication she'd seen him.

With a casual turn he moved to his right, putting some more distance between them, hoping to find a way to occupy himself that would allow her to notice him.

"Care to try your luck, Sir? Test your powers of prognostication?"

Kemper looked over to see a man standing behind a curved table taking up a corner space of the room, set off somewhat from the other activities. He was tall, somewhat stooped, with a long neck and a prominent Adam's apple. His short black hair was combed flat with a sharp part and its edges formed a triangle at the peak of his forehead. There was a beak-like curve to his pronounced nose, made all the more conspicuous due to his weak chin, and the pockmarks on his cheeks were like the shallow craters of an alien moon.

"Excuse me?" Kemper said.

"A simple game, sir. No money involved. Just a test, to see how in tune you are with the forces that power our vast and mysterious cosmos through which we all must travel as we pass our time on this plane." The man stared at Kemper with small, intense eyes and there was a hint of a smirk to the thin line formed by his lips.

"I don't have much time," Kemper said, glancing back over his shoulder. The young woman was still part of the group conversation, standing just to the opposite side of the doors, looking as comfortable as earlier in her skin, which was exposed in all but a few places. "I only came in to look around."

He retrieved a laminated card attached to a lanyard from his pocket, showing it for no particular reason other than the vague sense that identifying himself as a Guest of Honor might somehow offer an explanation.

"Ah, yes," the man said, his gaze not quite dropping to look. "But I think you'll find you're particularly suited to this challenge. We are all mere vessels, channeling the energies of time and space that surround us. Our talents and the products of it are a manifestation of the particular connection we have to the endless and the infinite. But do not worry, this will only take a few seconds."

Kemper tossed another glance over his shoulder, saw her still there, still engaged. He let out a breath. "Okay, what do I do?"

The man raised a deck of cards, oversized, maybe four inches by seven. "Please request a number of cards to be dealt, not less than two, nor more than twenty."

"Six," he said, seizing the first number that came to mind.

The man dealt six of the cards onto the table in front of Kemper in a line, face down, each sitting a couple of inches from the one next to it. The back of each card bore a strange symbol, redolent of a pictogram. It seemed both weirdly familiar and completely foreign to him, like a simple stick with angled branches.

"Surely, you are familiar with the works of the master, H.P. Lovecraft?"

An odd question, Kemper thought, and one that caused him to hesitate. "Yes, of course," he said.

One of the works he was best known for—if not *the* work he was best known for—was the cover of an anniversary edition of *The Encyclopedia of H.P. Lovecraft, Complete and Unabridged.* His design featured an enormous creature emerging from a misty, shadowy fog, its presence unmistakable but its precise aspect and contours inscrutable. The suggestion of a limb here, a claw there, appendages intertwined with wisps of vapor in unexpected places, coupled with what was perhaps a star or the moon but what could be an alert and searching eye peeking through the ether. Enthusiasts raved over the way it supposedly captured the true essence of the author's vision, how it reflected the cold and indifferent terror of his cosmic mythology.

Kemper had always been amused by the praise—when he wasn't annoyed by it—considering he hadn't so much as read the introduction. He'd merely glanced at the table of contents and let his imagination take care of the rest.

Of course, that happened to be the work that led the do-gooder editor, so impressed by the piece Kemper provided, to disregard his request for anonymity. That condition had governed all his prior work, but that editor gave him full credit by name *and* actively lobbyed organizations that gave out awards.

And, of course, Kemper won.

His name was immediately linked to numerous other covers that started receiving renewed interest and fan attention. This put his art in high demand for conventions, magazines and graphic novels, loved by seemingly every corner of the art-consuming world.

Except, of course, for the one he'd been working toward his entire life.

His scheduled kick-off exhibition of his "Alley Ways" collection at a prestigious San Francisco gallery suddenly ran into a scheduling conflict, and the few that agreed to host him after that drew little interest from the market. He had been initially packaged and sold as a fresh talent, a newly-discovered and brilliant virtuoso of contemporary realism. As it turned out, the snobby denizens of the world of fine art weren't interested in paying top dollar for the paintings of a pulp artist who had for years paid the rent by drawing spaceships and ray guns and alien beasts. Apparently, they wanted their starving artists to actually *starve.*

"Each card in front of you contains a symbol, a representation identified in the works of Mr. Lovecraft.

Each is different. I will show you cards one at a time from the remaining deck and you point to the card in front of you that you believe matches it."

"A magic trick?"

"Not a trick. A challenge. A test to see how many you can correctly predict."

Kemper shrugged. He chanced another glance over his shoulder, saw Deandra still talking with the small group, another person approaching and being greeted with smiles and hugs.

"Why not?" he said.

The man raised a card, showing its face to Kemper. It depicted a simple, stylistic design, a circle with a black center, like a bullseye, and eight legs extending out in various lengths, curling into gentle hooks.

This is stupid, he thought, quickly losing what little interest he'd started with. He dropped a finger onto the farthest card to his right and gave it a tap. The man placed the card face up on top of it, then drew another.

The next card had a circle with what looked to Kemper like a snake jumping out of water, curled in a crescent shape, but with its body split so that another line mirrored its shape and folded back onto itself. He gave his head a shake and chuckled, then randomly tapped the card farthest to his left.

Before the man showed the next card, Kemper said, "Just so you know, I'm not feeling anything. No visions, no sensing. Tell you what, to speed this along, just deal the cards here, here, here and here."

The man looked at him as if taking his measure and held his gaze, then he tilted his head and dealt them in the order demonstrated.

Kemper sucked in an impatient breath and let it out. "Now what?"

"Now, we show your results." The man reached toward the cards farthest to Kemper's left, but Kemper grabbed his wrist before he could touch them.

"Allow me," Kemper said, sensing the trick coming.

The man shrugged and dipped his head before pulling his hand back. Kemper glanced over his shoulder to see Deandra begin to pull away from the gathering, extending an arm and appearing to say her good-byes. She looked in his direction as she started for the doors and he quickly turned away.

"The cards, sir."

"Uh, right." He flipped over the first and second pairs, then stopped, spreading each apart to get a clear look at the faces. Then he flipped over the remaining four sets in quick succession and did the same.

"You switched them while I wasn't paying attention," Kemper said, looking up.

"No, Sir. It is not my place to deceive in such a manner, and I would not resort to such a crude sleight if it were. Besides, you do not really believe what you say."

"There's no way... it's not possible."

"In the infinite expanses of our universe, all things are possible. It is simply a question of where and when."

Kemper looked down at the cards again and blinked. Not only did each of the paired cards contain the same symbol, the cards that had been set out face down also contained a name and description of what the figure represented. One letter on each card was capitalized and in bold, regardless of where it appeared in the word or name. The first one on the left contained the name *Bo**K**rug,* described as "The Slayer of Sarnath." The K was larger than the other letters and set in boldface type. The next card contained the name *Ran-T**E**goth,* "The First to Wake," with the E conspicuously more pronounced. Each pair contained a matching symbol, each bottom card a single oversized letter in bold print in the name or text.

In the order they appeared in front of him, those letters spelled *KEMPER.*

"Okay, I'm stumped. You're good."

"I am merely the dealer. It is you who has the attention of the Old Ones."

"Uh, okay." Kemper shook his head, then chanced another glance over his shoulder. Deandra was no longer in sight.

He stepped back from the table and scanned the room, sweeping his gaze over the tables, the video consoles, the huge dragon partly protruding from the mural on the back wall. With her revealing costume and distinctive red hair, she'd be impossible to miss.

"I've got to run," he said, tossing the words as he stepped quickly toward the doors.

"Of course," the man said. As Kemper hurried away, he thought he'd heard him add, *"See you soon."*

Kemper pushed through a door and spilled out into the hallway. There were people talking and loitering in pairs and trios and walking in various directions. Among the many in faded t-shirts and torn jeans moved costumed explorers and would-be aliens and one Lost In Space robot. He looked to his left and his right, registering faces, searching for red-hair or lots of skin. Nothing.

His head snapped back to his right. A hint of a bare leg, a flutter of diaphanous silk, both disappearing behind the corner. He headed that way, forcing himself not to break into a sprint.

Why? he asked himself. Why was he chasing this woman? Because she was beautiful? Sexy? Her provocative costume? There were plenty of other women—and a number of men—dressed in similarly revealing costumes. Besides that, she was probably half his age, possibly younger. Did he really think she was interested in some convention hook-up with a guy likely older than her father?

No, he knew that wasn't it. It was because of what she'd said to him, because of the artwork card she'd brought.

Because she thought of him as—*knew* him as—a genuine artist. It had been many, many years since anyone had mentioned his early works, his serious paintings. He wanted to talk to her, hear how his art affected her, what drew her to it. He wanted to find that feeling again, that sense of deep meaning and connection through his art.

The fact she was attractive, well, he had to admit that didn't hurt, either.

He pivoted around the corner and looked down a long, empty hall. He broke into a jog and stopped midstride as he came even with an alcove with furniture where two men and a woman were seated, chatting. They each turned their heads, all quizzical smiles and curious expressions. Before he could ask if they'd seen a woman pass by, he heard a noise from further down the hall, the clank and thunk of a door closing. He nodded politely and hurried on until he reached the end where the hall cornered into a short doorway recess with a large wooden door. Above the door, a debossed sign read *Zemblanity Room* in thick bronze lettering.

So I'm a little early, he thought, figuring Yasmine should have told him to avoid the room if showing up ahead of schedule was a problem.

The door had a round brass knob the size of a baseball. It opened slightly inward when he gave the knob a light twist. Beyond the door, nothing was visible, only tar-black shadow. He pressed the wood and peeked around as it crept open. He got the sense of an enormous space beyond, a feeling of cavernousness, but there was no way to tell because the room was shrouded in an inky pitch of complete darkness, all of it, except for one small area directly ahead, illuminated in a cone of white light.

In the center of the circle, stood the dealer from the gaming room, standing at an almost identical table. Or perhaps the same one.

"Ah, Mr. Baldwin," he said, gesturing. "I've been

waiting."

"I was... I thought I saw someone come in here."

"Please, join me. We did not have a chance to finish."

Kemper looked to each side, his gaze stymied by the impenetrable lightlessness. "How did you get back here so quickly?"

"Time moves in different ways for each of us. Please, step forward, so we may continue."

"That's okay," Kemper said. He backpedaled and started to pull on the door. "I was just looking for someone."

"You'll have a chance to see her again, if you will simply complete the challenge. I promise."

Kemper stopped. He stared at the man glowing in the spotlight. *This is another magic trick*, he thought, quieting the voice urging him to turn around, to leave. *Maybe she's part of it. Maybe she's watching from the shadows.*

There was only one way to find out.

He pushed the door as far open as it would go, holding it there and checking to make sure it didn't start to swing shut once he let go. Satisfied, he moved forward and stood in front of the table.

"Do you do this for all Guests of Honor, or just me?"

The man smiled but said nothing. He held out a deck of cards similar to the ones he'd used in the gaming room and fanned them out face-down on the table.

"Choose," he said.

"You're asking me to pick a card?"

"This is your true test," the man said. "To see if you are worthy."

He didn't like the sound of that, but also didn't like the idea that his worth was in question. A test of worthiness? Worthy of what? He decided the question was beneath him, and that the best way to demonstrate how meaningless he considered the whole thing was by playing along like he didn't care. He raised a finger and plunged it down without giving it any thought, only to stop before it landed. Kemper remembered reading about magic tricks as a kid, about how magicians are able to will someone to pick a particular card using quirks of psychology. Good ones could make it seem totally natural, use average tendencies, steer people with things as innocent as word choice.

No, he thought. You're overthinking it. And what did it matter? Just get it over with.

He poked his finger on the card next to the one he'd originally targeted.

The man slid the cards away from either side of it into separate stacks, Kemper's finger still pressing down on his selection. Then the man picked up the two stacks and joined them together. He turned the deck over and fanned it out on the table for Kemper to see.

The faces were white. All of them. Completely blank.

Kemper looked down at the card beneath his finger and flipped it over. It was not blank.

"You, Sir," the man said, smiling broadly. "Are truly special. Everything we hoped for. All hail Azathoth!"

Before Kemper could respond, he felt the floor shift beneath him, buckling his legs. He was moving; the whole room, he realized, was moving, ascending, an elevator sensation, only faster. Then just as abruptly, it stopped.

He regained his balance and glanced about to find he was now near the edge of what looked like a vast, round area, a dark auditorium of sorts, rimmed by one continuous series of heavily tinted glass windows set a bit higher than could be seen out of and circling the entirety of the space. The air was cool and thick with a dank, earthy miasma, a mix of mold, must and fish. Before he could speak, torches sparked one by one, curving along the room's perimeter, their tops erupting into flame. The torches were set in holders protruding from narrow sections of wall between the tall windows that stretched up to a domed ceiling with a circular skylight at its center, a dark gray sky visible beyond it.

The sight of people gave him a jolt. Dozens of them, all garbed in ankle-length tunics the color of pale sand and gathered round the center of the room. The ones nearest him parted, outermost to inner, forming a wide swath leading to a round opening in the floor, perhaps eight feet in diameter, rimmed with a low masonry parapet the height of a single brick.

Above the hole, Deandra, still wearing her skimpy costume, hung from leather straps looped around each wrist, suspended from a crude wood sawhorse-type frame over the hole, a pair of six-foot tall legs on each side with a single spit spanned between them, her feet lower than the floor around her. The straps holding her were each wrapped once around the spit in opposite directions, held in place by a pair of tunic-clad men, one on each side.

Deandra made eye contact with him, her face lighting up, lips parting and mouth stretching wide.

"I knew you would come!" she said. "I knew you were the one!"

Rubbing his eyes and blinking, he was unable to make sense of what he was witnessing. Whatever this was, whatever kind of elaborate prank or extreme cosplay event he'd been thrust into, the nature of it eluded him.

He tried to conjure something clever to say, something about how funny this was, how *yes ha ha ha they sure knew how to go all-out and boy oh boy was this a good one*, but before he could think of anything, movement to his right caught his attention. He looked to see someone rising from the floor, another woman, this one dark and zaftig, a crown of sleek golden horns perched on her head. She kept rising above the floor level, higher still, as she sat atop a creature with oversized tusks that also rose into view beneath her. Startled, it took him a moment to see that the beast was not real, but a fabrication; an enormous crafted head attached to a rounded length of body on which she sat, held up by six men in tunics. The woman's arms and midriff and legs were bare, uncovered by her shimmering gold top and double-split golden skirt. Her raven hair was close-cropped tight to her scalp beneath her martial headdress. Recognition flickered briefly in his thoughts before taking hold.

"Yasmine?"

She raised a smooth leg and swiveled to a sidesaddle position as the men lowered the artificial beast, then she slid down to the ground, her golden sandals bright against the black floor. The throng of people all dropped to their knees, crouching low and bending forward. They crabbed out of her way as she moved toward Kemper.

"Was it as we hoped?" she said.

Kemper was confused until he realized she was looking at the man behind him, the dealer.

"Yes, my Queen."

Yasmine smiled. "This is a truly glorious moment," she said. She turned to face Deandra. "Are you ready, my dear? The honor awaits you."

"Yes, my Queen." Shifting her gaze to Kemper, she said. "Thank you! Now my destiny shall finally be fulfilled so that you may fulfill yours! I shall revel in the harsh embrace of the Messenger, ever grateful!"

Kemper shot glances around the room, his eyes bouncing from Deandra to Yasmine to the man behind him to Deandra again. "What the hell is going on?"

Yasmine raised her arms high. "Begin the Summoning!"

A soft hum emanated from the mass of people huddled on the floor. The hum slowly transformed into a murmur, growing louder, until it became a chant. As words started to be discernable, Yasmine began to engage in a call-and-response, hers being the only words he could understand.

"O' NYARLATHOTEP... Mighty Messenger... Hand of Azathoth... Would-be Devourer of Our World... accept this

humble Offering of your servant…"

"NYARLATHOTEP IJACEEBO!"

"We ask only that you show yourself so we may praise you and present you with this, the greatest gift of all…"

"NYARLATHOTEP TELAL ALAL… UNGOYUD MANGEIF NAGUZ!"

"We have found a Herald who shall demonstrate that the time is now, who shall present to you the true form of the god of Chaos, the Daemon Sultan, He Who Sleeps on the Black Throne…"

"IJACEEBO IJACEEBO IJACEEBO!"

"Appear, o' Ancient Pharoah of the Universe, so we may commence the Great Awakening!"

"NYARLATHOTEP EDIN NA ZU!"

The hard surface beneath Kemper began to tremble and shake. He bent his knees to keep his balance, unsure what he should do, what he could do. Scramble for an exit? Where? Run to Deandra to pull her away from the pit beneath her? Would she even let him?

The tremor stopped and for a couple of beats all was calm. Kemper straightened up, started to speak, but the words were cut off by an explosion of water from the opening. A mammoth tentacle burst upward, smashing into Deandra and destroying the wooden spit and frame suspending her. It was twice as thick as her body, with an enormous paddle on the end and hooked spikes like claws protruding from its numerous suckers. It wrapped her like a colossal anaconda, one twist enveloping her from knees to shoulders, and the paddle clamped down on her face with a wet slap. Then the entire mass of it yanked down, disappearing into the hole, Deandra and most of the broken frame and one of the men who'd been holding a strap but failed to let go whipping into the opening behind her. A faint echo throbbed briefly, then died out.

Kemper blinked, then blinked again. *"You gotta be*

shittin' me."

Yasmine raised her arms in triumph. "All hail Nyarlathotep!"

A cheer erupted from the congregation, exclamations of pure elation.

Kemper began to pan the perimeter, sweeping his gaze with an increasing sense of urgency as his pulse pounded in his temples.

"This is all possible because of you," Yasmine said, smiling wide as the celebration quieted. The group got to their feet, almost in unison, and cleared a wider path for her to approach.

"I don't understand," he said, unable to come up with anything better.

"You are the *Herald*. You are the only one who has ever captured the true essence of Azathoth, Ruler of Dreams, Unraveler of Reality."

"I... I have no idea what you're talking about."

"Your depiction, your image on the cover... we have scoured the world, looking for the One who held the key, who had the vision to see the Old Ones as they are. None could pass the tests. Then Deandra came to me, told me of her dreams. Her dreams of you. She dreamed it all, her, me, you, all of us here, like this. She showed me the product of your imagination, the glimpse you presented to the world that few understood. This gave us hope, hope that you could truly see. None has ever passed the tests. None, save you."

"Wait, are you talking about the cover for that anthology? I didn't imagine anything! I just drew something vague, something to capture the mood of the book! That's it!"

"You have been chosen. You have the Sight. Whether you realize it or not, you, and only you, can see. You can awaken *him*."

She backed away and turned, sweeping an arm in the

direction she'd come. Kemper looked beyond her, saw the creature she'd been carried in on, and for the first time it occurred to him it was the beast from *The Queen Out Of Time,* his first cover, the one he'd autographed for the person in line before Deandra. That realization was quickly trumped by another, that the outfit, the gold halter and skirt, the golden crown of horns, that was from the cover, too. But why? What did it mean? There was only one reason for it he could think of. *To honor him.*

Beyond the inanimate beast, now lying in a slouch on the floor, he saw something he hadn't noticed. He took a few steps closer to confirm what they were. An array of materials. Rows of paint tubes, an assortment of brushes, a large palette, as well as charcoal pencils and sponges and rags and spatula knives.

"All for you," Yasmine said, as if reading his thoughts.

She gestured overhead. "This shall be your canvas. This shall be where you create the greatest piece of art the world has ever known, and ever will know."

He tilted his head and stared at the ceiling, taking in the concave contours of the dome's interior, the round skylight in the center.

"Just open yourself to it. Let the waves, the signals, the forces of the Ancient Ones flow through you. Let go of all doubt. You passed the test. You are the conduit. You are the vessel. You are the *Herald.* You are the *message.*"

He told himself these people were crazy, that they stumbled across some bizarre creature and formed a demented religion, that he needed to play along until he could find a means of escape, humor them, wait for them to let down their guard. But then, gazing at the empty surface above him, for an instant, a brief glimmer of a moment, he could almost see it, could see that space filling with imagery, with swirls and shades of deep, unsettling colors. He could sense the shapes emerging, uncoiling in the depths of his mind, ready to be coaxed to the surface. That skylight no longer a mere piece of architecture, but some incomprehensible type of orifice, waiting to be birthed.

A gasp from the crowd and he turned to see an arm, slick and white, like the belly of a fish, clamp itself over the edge of the opening, followed by a leg swinging up a few feet away, Then Deandra emerged, pulling herself out and rising to her feet along the rim. Only it wasn't Deandra, even he could tell that. Her skin, which had been smooth and creamy, shimmered with a green iridescence, her hair now the blood-red of a vampire squid. But it was her eyes that were the most telling. They were swollen and black and too hollow to even look at.

The congregation dropped to the floor, bowing, and this time Yasmine joined them. Even the dealer, Kemper looked back to see, had lowered himself and averted his eyes. But not Kemper. Kemper gazed at the thing that was not Deandra for a pregnant moment, then at the assortment of paints, then looked up to the ceiling once more.

So, this, he told himself, was how it turned out. This was his calling. His destiny. As much as he wanted to turn and run, as much as he knew he should die a valiant death by fighting, by resisting, he also knew he would not. This is what would give it all meaning, this was why he'd been steered down a path he hadn't chosen, why doors had been closed and awards he didn't want bestowed.

He peered into the dead eyes of the one who was now in the form, or occupying the body, or whatever the hell it was that was not Deandra. She'd been wrong, he wanted to say to her, even though he knew she wasn't really there. He was not this or any other generation's Edward Hopper. He was something else entirely; the Michelangelo of the Apocalypse, this place his demonic Sistine Chapel.

The empty eyes stared back at him, bemused. It seemed confused as to why he was not cowering or groveling or prostrating himself like the others. It was a good question, he had to admit, but one he didn't try to answer. He shifted his gaze one more time to the arrangement of paints and brushes, then raised his eyes skyward. He knew exactly what to do.

He would start, he decided, with a shade of red.

END

STURGEON MAN AND A MERMAID

IRENE RADFORD

About the Author: IRENE RADFORD is a founding member of Book View Café. You can find a number of her books, both reprints and original titles, at the café, including the entire Pixie Chronicles Series. She has been writing stories ever since she figured out what a pencil was for. Mostly she writes fantasy and historical fantasy including the best-selling *Dragon Nimbus* Series and the masterwork *Merlin's Descendants* series. Look for her writing new historical fantasy tales as Rachel Atwood, a different take on the Robin Hood mythology in Walk the Wild with Me, from DAW Books and the sequel Outcasts of the Wildwood. In other lifetimes she writes urban fantasy as P.R. Frost or Phyllis Ames, and space opera as C.F. Bentley. Lately she ventured into Steampunk as Julia Verne St. John.

If you wish information on the latest releases from Ms Radford, under any of her pen names, you can subscribe to her newsletter: www.ireneradford.net. Or you can follow her on Facebook as Phyllis Irene Radford.

STURGEON MAN AND A MERMAID
Irene Radford

"Stupid Human!" Sturgeon Man muttered. Known as Stu among the Elder Gods, every time he spoke his own name, he couldn't help but add an almost "r" sound to the end. He was Sturgeon Man after all. Not stew like some cooked concoction humans made.

He dug deeper into the muddy riverbed as a high-powered speedboat raced above him, propellor nearly scraping the boney plates across his back. The boat missed him only because it turned a tight left turn and made a half circle to return the way it had come. He rose to the surface to see if it was safe for him to proceed. A long tail of muddy spray followed the boat and drenched people in other boats and sunbathers alike.

Stu's river was too shallow this summer for such nonsense.

Clouds and clouds of muck filled the water, devoid of small shellfish and decaying plants that might make a tasty sturgeon snack.

The time had come to return to the sea. Mating season had passed, and he'd lingered too long within the reach of human infestation. Why couldn't the invaders leave well enough alone!

He'd tolerated them when they paddled across his river, and later built small wooden bridges. The supports for the constructions attracted plants to grow around the submerged bases, and the plants attracted small fish, which in turn fed bigger fish, his natural prey.

But the new bridges had grown so huge, the supports needed to sink all the way to bedrock, destroying much of the riverbed. Now powerboats caused more damage with their whirling propellors.

Stu sported numerous scars across his boney back from battles with them. Not honorable scars earned in battle with others of his kind for mates and territory. Or lethal duels with elder gods never satisfied with their territorial limitations.

Anger propelled him upward into a full breach. He loomed over the top of the offensive boat for several seconds. The strangled look of combined wonder and fear on the faces of the boaters reminded them that he was the ancient god of this river, and all of the lesser creatures should bow down to him, truly afraid of his awesome power.

And then all three thousand pounds and thirty feet of his length began to crash back into the water, spraying the boaters with chill river water on this hot summer day.

Dozens of humans gathered on the riverbank slammed their hands together in a round of applause that soothed his anger. Not the response he expected. At least they approved of his mighty display.

Then, just as his head began to submerge again, a sparkling blue mermaid with bright pink hair sunning herself on the sand caught his attention.

She was the most beautiful thing he'd ever seen. She stirred his lust more than the swarm of female sturgeons begging him to cover their eggs with his sperm.

Mermaids didn't belong this far from the sea. Her bright colors belonged in the warm tropical oceans far to the south—much too warm for his northern thick skin and boney plates.

He must investigate.

A short time later Stu crawled out of his fish body onto the pebbly riverbank a short way upriver from where the mermaid had been absorbing sunshine. The bright sun above, unfiltered by several feet of water hurt his eyes. With a few strained thoughts he created soothing dark glasses, a bright turquoise tank top, and knee-length, floral print shorts that hung loosely from his hips. Clothing as bright and bold as his southern mermaid. Oh, and floppy sandals to protect his feet from the hot sand and blacktop above the embankment where humans walked and rode two-wheeled vehicles.

He hadn't taken his man-form in a long time, and he needed a few minutes to get used to the idea of walking. A quick look at the numerous people gathered near the mermaid reminded him that he needed to shrink the boney plates that normally protected his body into fingernails and toenails. He couldn't do much to disguise the bone spurs atop his bald pate. His chin tentacles pulled back into something resembling a sparse beard. But they remained sensitive enough to detect the electromagnetic pulse every living thing emitted. He could still sense the presence of people without seeing them.

Now to seduce the love of his life—at least until he'd mated with her. Another thing he hadn't done in a long time. Releasing his sperm to cover a lady sturgeon's eggs was a necessary biological imperative. But making love to a female of another species... that took time and patience and practice.

He looked forward to this.

But what was this? Three more mermaids had joined the first. All sparkled brightly in a rainbow of colors on their bodies and different-hued hair. Each more lovely than the last.

All of them were surrounded by a bevy of males. Mostly human-ish. Some looked as if they wore hastily put together costumes—mismatched bits of fur and leather with lots of bright and shiny metal. Not at all what he expected the current dominant species to wear.

Life, and intermingling of species would be so much easier if they all went naked.

But these humans were such puny creatures they could not rely upon real fur or scales to protect them from the elements.

At some unnoticed signal, all of the humans, ish or normal, gathered beach blankets, towels, and tote bags and ambled along a path between the artificial dunes toward a massive building with lots and lots of windows. They took his mermaid and her handmaidens away.

He had to follow.

But wait, how did the mermaid walk without shape changing so that she had legs and feet to propel her? Fish tails could not manipulate air as they did water. All of the elder gods and magical creatures had the ability to shift to their alternate form. Mermaids in particular, already half human, should be able to produce legs and feet with barely a thought. So why didn't she?

Then his mermaid and her entourage got ahead of him, not waiting for him to muddle through his twisted thoughts.

Extraneous males planted themselves between Stu and his quest.

He hung behind a group of people, mixed old and young, who strolled past the young man seated just inside the glass door that opened without a hand pushing it. But as each person passed the entry, they fumbled for a plastic envelope with a brightly colored card inserted inside. Some wore them on thongs around their neck, the women, mostly, had them attached to their totes or clipped to the waist of their clothing.

The door guard nodded at each, then returned to a hand-held device that beeped and clicked annoyingly. Stu paused until the guardian of this portal seemed absorbed in whatever the device screen showed him. But the boy was more alert than expected. He held out an arm to stop Stu. "Badge?"

"Um..." Hastily he extruded a colorful card encased in plastic—actually a film of his own waste, as plastic was beyond his powers—from the band of his shorts. "Sorry man," Stu drawled as he lifted his tank top to reveal his badge, obviously an entry pass or 'ticket', that's what humans called them. Ticket. But the boy had asked for a badge.

Now Stu was confused.

"Smart!" the boy laughed. "Any chance at all to display your abs to the babes. Hey, if I had a six-pack like yours, I'd flash it any chance I got." He pinched his flabby mid-region and jiggled it.

Too much fat to make a tasty meal.

Stu moved inward in search of his delectable mermaid.

He caught a glimpse of his mermaid's pink hair just as more doors closed trapping her in a windowless cave. He ran forward, brushing aside more costumed people in his desperate need to rescue her.

He pounded on the polished metal doors, leaving behind a dent or two. "Wait," he yelled.

"Hey, man, chill. You got an anger management problem?" queried a male voice from behind Stu. At the same time a heavy hand came down on his shoulder.

"No... no." Stu took a deep breathe, letting his lungs do their job. He hadn't realized how shallow his breaths had been, moving in the slow rhythm of gills bringing in life-giving oxygen in many places, not just his narrow mouth and nose with a limited capacity. "But... the people I need to follow got swallowed up..."

"Yeah, I know the feeling. Um... Security's on their way here now. You're gonna get us kicked out and it's only Saturday morning of the con. This shit isn't supposed to happen until after midnight tonight when everyone's drunk out of their minds. Come with me." The paunchy middle-aged man increased his pressure on Stu's shoulder and dragged him to the left, where the doors to another metal cave parted.

Before he could protest, the doors closed again, trapping Stu and his new companion inside. A panel on the right and above the doors flickered and light from behind them bounced from one to the other and back again.

The walls of the box began shaking and jerking, trying to move up and down at the same time.

"Hey, what's wrong with the elevator?" one of the other people crowding much too close to Stu, shouted. He thought it was a woman from the higher tone of her voice, but in this crowd they all seemed androgenous, like fish out of mating season when gender didn't matter and was not obvious.

Then a buzzing sound penetrated his head. His tentacles, hidden within his beard, quivered, then pulsed.

The woman who had shouted slapped her hand against the lights on the panel in front of her. The lights along the top of the door all blasted bright white, then grew dark and blank.

"Hit the emergency button and get us out of here. We'll need to take the stairs until the hotel gets this thing fixed." Stu's new friend pushed against his back, propelling him forward.

The door parted a hand width then crashed together again. They repeated this performance. Stu caught them at the apex of their opening, a hand on each side, and channeled all of his elder-god-strength into forcing them open.

Reluctantly they obeyed, like persuading a crocodilian to part with prey that would poison it. (Stupid humans were always leaving treacherous bait, like plastic rings, where

170

they shouldn't, too lazy to clean up after themselves.)

At last, the doors gave up their fight against the might of an elder god and opened, hanging a little off level.

"Hey thanks, man. I'll buy you a drink later. Meet me in the bar. I'll be there from four o'clock on." Someone slapped Stu's back and edged past him to the safety of the outside.

Stu drew in a deep breath of fresh air as if his lungs hadn't worked the entire time he'd been in this building.

Not knowing what else he should do, he followed the man who'd dragged him into that hideous cave.

"Hey, did you see the sturgeon breech in the river earlier. Man that was quite a sight, and really rare. Supposed to be a lucky omen. I'm Matt, by the way. I'm following the art show and the anime exhibits. The artist GOH is my fave in anime. She's half Japanese so she's able to blend both cultures into some of the best drawings." He thrust out his hand in a flat gesture, while flipping his badge over so that Stu could read the name at the bottom of the colorful drawing.

He had to smile at the reference to his earlier display of power. A lucky omen though? It was supposed to inspire awe in the face of impending doom.

"I'm... uh... Stu." He returned the gesture of greeting, not liking having to touch a human. Sturgeons never touched each other.

He flashed his own badge still affixed to his shorts, making sure he'd inserted his name along with copying the design.

"I cannot believe the idiocy of the staff this year," Matt said while he walked. "My roommate and I arrived separately and they put us in separate rooms and charged us the full price for both rooms. We had the same reservation number, and they couldn't see that there might be a problem. We got it all straightened out, but man, it was looking to be an excessively expensive weekend."

"I am not staying in the hotel for the entire weekend." They moved on.

"What are you looking for at the con? They've got everything this year, great writers, as well as artists, a wide variety of music, and some of the best costumes on the west coast."

Stu didn't understand half of what Matt said, but clearly the man knew what was going on in this strange collection of humans. He saw people with elaborate make-up—some robbing their faces of all color, highlighted with black mouth and eye painting—bizarre hats, extra wide skirts, and constraining torture devices around their mid-regions.

"I'm looking for a blue mermaid with pink hair."

"I think the mermaids have all come inside by now. July weekends on the Columbia River can get mighty hot."

Stu's thick skin protected him from external temperature changes, so he hadn't noticed. But summer heat might explain the presence of tropical mermaids this far north. But why so far inland? The river water was low and a bit stale-tasting but not salty. Not even brackish.

While conversing and introducing themselves, the two men climbed a flight of stairs, walked down a corridor that took three right turns and a left, then down a new flight of stairs. The tug of the river against Stu's mind grew stronger as they descended. They now walked below the level of his home waters. He breathed in the heavier air gratefully.

Then Matt led him out a heavy door to a paved courtyard containing a rectangular pool and a smaller, circular one filled with toxic chemicals. Stu gagged with every breath that burned his lungs. Matt didn't seem to notice. Ten agonizing steps later the two men entered the building, twisted through another corridor that sloped upward, then climbed a full flight of stairs, and eventually dumped them in the central hotel lobby.

Stu bent over, grasping his knees as he drew in deep breaths that almost cleansed him from poisons of the pools.

"Don't worry, you'll get used to the labyrinth after a day or two. Took me five conventions to really learn my way around. Even now I sometimes get lost."

"You must orient yourself to the river. Once the waters are in your soul you never get lost," Stu replied. He straightened and breathed normally—for a human.

"Yeah, yeah. Heard that before. But I can't swim and the only way I'll take the river into my soul is to drown."

"That can be arranged."

Matt stood tall and craned his neck, ignoring Stu's comment. "There's a woman with pink hair, but she's not a mermaid now. She's wearing ordinary cutoffs and a blue con T shirt."

Stu looked where Matt indicated, he was taller than most men in the room, reflecting his godly nature.

He found the pale woman with a sun blush on her face and upper chest that clashed with the shade of pink in her hair. Could this be his beloved mermaid shape-changed into a human? Her clothing was blue, like her fishtail, but not the same shade or sparkling.

"I don't know if that's her or not. She looks quite different now."

"Well, if she's here for costuming you can catch her at the masquerade tonight. These gals tend to pick a theme and stick close to it, even if they change clothes five times a day." Matt moved toward the side of the open area where a peculiar smell drifted toward them.

Stu wrinkled his nose in disgust.

"Hey' its past lunchtime and the sushi is half price. This place is great, the best in town, but usually more expensive than I like to pay. I may act like a teenager at a con, but that doesn't mean I have to spend like one with no thought of tomorrow. Except I hope to win my bid on a numbered print in the art show and that's going to take a hunk of my reserves. The sushi is still fresh. I'm really looking forward to this."

"You call that fresh?" Stu asked turning his back on the display of... "It's all dead. How can you call it fresh?"

"Dead, of course it's dead. Why would you want to eat live fish? Ick!" Matt shuddered all over. Then his face took on a brighter expression. "I know, you're dressing as a Klingon tonight at the masquerade and you're getting into character now. That's really cool. If you eat a live goldfish on stage, you'll gross everyone out and probably win a prize. The judges really appreciate authenticity."

Another woman wearing a grotesque headpiece that resembled a sea turtle's shell, came up beside them. She had buck teeth that made her drool a bit. Her garb looked like sturgeon skin leather and she brandished several bladed weapons that smelled of petroleum... plastic! "Personally, I'd rather drink prune juice. Now that is a warrior's drink." She stalked off, swaying her backside as if trying to entice them.

But Stu only wanted his mermaid, not this... whatever she was pretending to be.

He swung back around so he could examine the crowd more closely, seeking pink hair and sparkling blue scales. One of his tentacles escaped his scraggly beard and instinctively bristled with electricity.

A spark jumped out from his facial hair and joined with another beneath the table of dead fish. The artful display jumped and shimmied as if coming back to life. The aroma of decaying sea life filled the room like magical fog.

Dozens of people jumped up from their places, holding their noses, and moaning in disgust. "The refrigeration unit died," Matt proclaimed. "Hey, maybe now the sushi will be free!" He pushed aside people moving away from the dead fish in his eagerness to get to the delicacy.

The sound of tearing fabric, akin to a salmon trying to rid itself of a murderously baited hook, overrode the noise of the crowd exiting the space.

"Watch where you're going, turd," a broad woman wearing one of the torture devices and an excessively wide and long skirt shouted at him. She held up the ragged remnants of her dress where it had dragged the ground behind her.

"Huh?" Stu stared at the shiny textile, that now looked like a fishtail that had tangled with a motorboat.

"Good thing I've got fusible interfacing back in my room. I think I can repair it." The woman flounced off.

Stu decided this gathering was too crowded for him. He'd been out of the river long enough that his skin itched, and his throat burned. He wandered toward a less crowded area where a glass container of water and paper cups sat on a small table. Eagerly he watched a woman in T-shirt and jeans flip a lever on the glass thing to make water trickle forth into a cup. She drank it down eagerly and repeated the action. Then she moved to a nearby door with the silhouette of a human with a skirt painted on it. She leaned on the door and it slowly opened inward. She disappeared inside. That brief opening of the door allowed a whiff of strange chemicals to ooze outward.

He repeated her actions at the water carafe the moment she moved off. The chilled water crossed his parched lips and he had to spit it out again, careful to return it to his cup.

Poison!

More burning chemicals!

Without thinking he returned his full cup to the table.

"Sir! Please dump that cup in an appropriate place. No telling what kind of germs you spat into it." A woman wearing dark slacks, a white shirt, and a red vest with a plain name badge (not a colorful con identifier) frowned at him and pointed to a door with the silhouette of a male painted on it.

Not knowing what else to do, Stu carried his cup to the door and leaned on it. It obeyed his wish to open. A quick look inside revealed a line of whiter circular receptacles with metal "taps" similar to the one on the water device. Further in stood more white things along the wall. Two men relieved themselves, careful not to look at each other.

Ah. He dumped the cup of tainted water into one of the circular basins, then took the opportunity to relieve himself at the same time. One of the occupants moved to the basin and turned on a tap.

The wash of water tainted by the burning chemicals gushing forth robbed Stu of his balance and set his stomach to bouncing. This place needed to be flushed of the poisonous water. He extended his senses and found the metal pipe closest to the river. In seconds he opened valves and pulled fresh, life-giving river from its channel into the hotel. All of the hotel.

His senses righted and refreshed him. A little. He'd still been out of the water too long and needed to return to his home soon.

But he still had to find his mermaid.

And there she was, in the hallway just beyond the opening when he exited the water room. Still wearing the blue shorts and shirt, her pink hair made a significant marker that differentiated her from the two females in a tight discussion with her. "I ate too much lunch. I think I should go throw up so I can fit into this blamed costume," she said in a nasally whine. "It seemed like a good idea when I first started sewing this thing, but now I'm growing to hate it. It gets smaller every time I wear it."

There it was, the blue sparkly thing that looked like a garment with a fish tail was draped over her arm.

"You aren't a mermaid at all. Just another stupid

human out to trick me," Stu muttered to himself and marched past the females toward the stairs that would lead him to a river level exit.

Behind him, a female screamed. "EEEEeeeeewwwww! The water is polluted with river stuff. There's algae growing in it, and... and I saw a live fish swimming in it!"

"Just a little one," Stu said on a smile. "Don't you appreciate real sushi?"

"I swear this hotel is haunted by the dark Elder Gods, straight out of Lovecraft. They lurk in the river waiting to sacrifice us," the fake mermaid snarled.

Stu grinned to himself.

A few more long strides and he'd climbed the berm between his beloved river and the infestation of humans.

Seconds after diving into the water he re-emerged in a full sturgeon breech and flipped his tail in defiance of them all.

Vaguely, in the distance, he heard Matt's voice proclaim, "Another sturgeon breech! That's two in the same day. A massive lucky omen."

END

THE HORRORS OF VENDING

RUSSELL NOHELTY

About the Author: RUSSELL NOHELTY is a USA Today bestselling author, publisher, and speaker. He runs Wannabe Press (www.wannabepress.com), a small press that publishes weird books for weird people. Russell is the author of dozens of novels and graphic novels including *The Godsverse Chronicles, The Obsidian Spindle Saga*, and *Ichabod Jones: Monster Hunter*. He also edited the *Cthulhu is Hard to Spell* anthology series. To date, Russell Nohelty has raised over $325,000 on Kickstarter across over twenty projects. He has a very entertaining newsletter, which you can join at www.russellnohelty. com. He lives in Los Angeles with his wife and dogs.

THE HORRORS OF VENDING
RUSSELL NOHELTY

"You're not really doing this show are you, Shadrack?" My wife asked as I loaded the last box from the garage. She waved a green flier around in front of her. "This flier doesn't even seem like it was written by a human."

I placed the box of books in the truck and turned to her. "We talked about this, Harriet. If we want to put a down payment on our own place, then I have to do every convention that comes my way."

She looked down at the flier. "But Cthulhu Fhcon? That doesn't even make any sense. And it's on that old creepy island off the coast..."

I smiled as I walked up and grabbed her shoulders. "How bad could it be? Remember that holiday con two years go?"

She chuckled. "You mean the one where all the attendees were off playing magic all day, and there were only like ten vendors?"

I nodded. "And I still made a couple hundred bucks. Besides, if it's really that bad, I'll complain, and they'll probably give me my money back. I don't like using that trick, but I can be very intimidating."

"You do know how to beat a dead horse, my love."

I feigned offense at her. "Me?! That doesn't sound like anything I would have ever done in my whole life. How dare you."

After that, she smiled and kissed me softly on the lips. "I have a bad feeling about this."

I tapped my forehead against hers. "I have a bad feeling about every convention, but if I'm ever going to be Neil Gaiman, I need to sell a bunch of books. The only way I know how to do that is at cons."

"I know." She sighed. "Just come back in one piece, okay?"

I raised my head and kissed her on the forehead. "If that's the bar, then I think I can leap over it."

"Famous last words."

I walked to the car and closed the trunk. "I love you."

"I love you, too."

I understood Harriet's concern. I'd been running the convention circuit full time for two years. They were mostly bad these days, with some terrible sprinkled in for good measure. My first year I did a lot of business, but recently I'd been barely breaking even on table fees, let alone gas and printing costs.

That's one thing people didn't understand about conventions. Fans assumed you were a guest of the show when they came to your table, but more often than not you were stuck paying your own way. Even if they somehow comped you a table, you had to get yourself to the show, including your room and even parking.

It wasn't an easy life.

I thought that becoming a full-time author would be different. I grew up on movies where authors wore tweed coats, lived in lake houses, and only wrote one book a year. I was sold a bill of goods, and the reality was much different than that. It was a lot of supply chain management, bookkeeping, and heavy lifting. If I knew how much manual labor was involved in being an author, I would have worked out much more when I was younger.

The road to Havenhurst Hotel was cracked with

potholes, and the bridge over to the island hadn't been properly maintained in a coon's age. I'm not saying we had great roads and bridges two hours south where I lived, but these ones seemed built to keep people out. And yet...dozens of cars were on the road up to the aging hotel. My old heart smiled a bit—I hadn't just chosen a terrible convention in an awful location instead of being with my pregnant wife back at home.

That was always the worst part of conventions; the loneliness of it. My wife tried them a couple times, but she hated crowds and abhorred capitalism. Conventions were her worst nightmare. She still came every once in a while when I went out of state. But even when she was there, Harriet spent most of her time wandering around the city, seeing the sights, and having a grand old time, while I got stuck with the bill. I didn't begrudge her it since she worked hard, but my margins were abysmally thin even when she didn't come.

The songs of Jason Isbell blared from the radio as I waited to unload my car and head into the convention. They promised free parking, which was a huge help, as a weekend show could set you back $50 in parking fees alone. I recognized some of the cars and trucks in front of and behind me on the road, and we waved at each other as we waited for our chance to get into the show. It took a special type of crazy to be willing to spend all your time selling stuff to strangers, and those who ran the circuit became a sort of family in our own awkward way.

An hour after starting across the bridge, I finally pulled up to the front of the hotel. The siding looked cracked with age, paint peeling off every surface. Perhaps the ancient gothic building had been beautiful once, but those days were long gone, like a Hollywood starlet lying on her death bed.

A young man in a red blazer waved at me when I stepped out of my car. "He're for con'ven'tion, sir?"

His throat choked out each syllable like a frog trying to speak English or somebody trying to hold back vomiting with each word from their mouth. I had never heard anything like it before, but in the din of the convention, I heard several other of the staff make the same noises with their throats, so perhaps it was a dialect I wasn't familiar with.

I nodded, hesitantly. "I am. I'm a vendor. I have a trunk full of stuff to—"

He didn't let me finish before snapping his fingers to signal a bellhop in a red cap and a tarnished gold cart to rush up to me. "Sh'va'na he'lp."

"Thank you." I turned to the woman with her hair pulled up in a bun that the cap covered. "Shavana. It's nice to meet you."

"Sh'va'na," her voice croaked in the same way that the young man did.

The man in the red blazer pulled a box out of my car. "Ha've a go'od sh'ow."

He helped unload my boxes and then held out his hand for my keys. Before I could reach into my pocket to pull out a tip, he was around the car and hopping into my driver's seat. He was an odd duck, but very helpful, so I tried to stuff my feelings of confusion deep down and take the strangeness of his voice with a grain of salt.

Sh'va'na clicked her mouth several times and began shuffling inside, walking as if she had never been on dry land before. After my interaction with the young bellman, her strange mannerisms didn't seem as unique as I would have pegged them in any other situation.

"How long have you worked here?" I asked before I remembered she didn't talk much. I became content to just follow her through the lobby, where a dozen men, women, and families checked into the hotel. I hoped this meant that the weekend would be a success.

Every convention had a rhythm to it. The hardest part

184

was doing one for the first time. You never knew how much you would sell, so you had to steel yourself away for making almost nothing. My books were pretty good sellers at horror conventions, and they're all influenced by Lovecraft myths, so I had high hopes, but low expectations.

I'd been lost in thought, looking at the worn wallpaper curled at the edges for at least five minutes when I realized that we had been zigging and zagging through hallways that didn't seem to make any sense—not unless the hotel was a hundred miles long, at least. All convention centers were circuitous and hard to navigate, but I'd never seen one as confusing as this place.

Luckily, Sh'va'na seemed to know exactly where she was going, and eventually the hallway broke into a wide show floor. I worried that nobody would be able to find it, but my fears were partially alleviated when I saw my friend Tim setting up his booth a couple down from where Sh'va'na led me. He'd been the one to tell me about this convention—and he rarely did bad shows.

"Oh, thank the gods you're here, buddy," I said, shaking his hand. "I was worried you wouldn't make it."

"Are you kidding me, man?" He replied with a southern twang in his voice. "We need a new dishwasher/ I can't miss out on a way to make some money."

Tim sold old comic books and trinkets. His sales were always good, no matter where he went, as long as the people that came to the convention had a sense of nostalgia about them. And they always did.

It was easy to set up my booth. I had only published three books in my Cthulhu Howard, P.I. series, so I had only a tablecloth, some books, and a few stands to set up. To these I added a sign up for a free print for subscribing to my newsletter and bookmarks to draw people over to the table.

"You wanna go exploring?" Tim asked when I was done

setting up. "Or do you need to check in still?"

"Both, but it doesn't matter to me in what order I do them. Maybe one and then the other."

Tim thought that sounded like a good idea, so we set out back into the hotel, waving and chatting with the other vendors as we passed. I brought my own food from home, but Tim always liked having a drink at the hotel bar after set-up, so I said I would join him. I had no idea where we were as we darted left and right, but Tim seemed to be an old ham at navigating the windy corridors.

"I loved this place as a kid, man," he said when we finally reached the bar in the lobby. "My mom was a maid here before we moved down south, and I guess the directions just stayed with me, wandering these halls."

"It reminds me of the Shining," I said as a bartender brought us two beers.

"You're not wrong. Kubrick stayed here once, and it never left him."

"You're messing with me."

"Nope. I even met him once. Weird guy. I got these drinks," Tim said, pulling a twenty out and sliding it to the bartender. "Keep the change."

Tim was a generous man. He took pity on me when I started out, and showed me the ropes of conventions, helped me hone my sales pitch, and made sure I was choosing the right shows so that I didn't lose my shirt. He also knew how tough it had been for me lately.

"I just hope it's a good show, man," I said to him. "I can't have another bad one. It feels like each one is worse than the one before it."

"You'll get your mojo back," Tim said, taking a sip. "We all go through dry spells. I have a good feeling about this place. You're a great writer, and I'll bet you that your fans show up this time."

I didn't have many fans, outside of the few I met at conventions at least. I made decent sales online, but the

186

only real money was at shows for me, and that money was drying up fast.

"Yeah," I sighed, chugging my own beer. "I hope so, but I'm not as confident as you about it. Maybe I should just go back to selling shoes."

"Yuck. Don't do that. I think it'll be different this time. This is the one where you'll turn it around. I mean, it's a Cthulhu convention, and you sell a Cthulhu book. If you can't clean up here, you should get out of the selling-books business."

He said it as a joke, but it dug into my gut because that was what I feared. Tim had staked me for this show, and I owed him my table fee if I made it back. It had been a long time since I cleared three hundred dollars at a convention. I was running out of money for buying tables, and we were already barely scraping by with two, let alone a third mouth to feed in a couple of months. If things didn't turn around soon, I would have no choice but to stop chasing the dream.

After finishing our beers, I said my goodbye to Tim and went to check in for my room. The crowd had died down and I was able to walk up to a dark-skinned woman at the counter. Her hands consistently moved from place to place on her body, itching and scratching as though she had some body-wide rash.

"Hello," I said. "I'm checking in for my room. Shadrack Magilicutty. I booked—"

She held up her finger. "Sh'ad'rack."

I nodded. "Magilicutty, yes."

She looked at me for a long moment, and I swore I watched her eyes blink sideways before she looked down at her computer screen and typed very slowly onto it. "Sssss-hh-aa-ddd-raaa-ck."

"It's probably under Magilicutty," I replied, but she didn't seem to care.

"Eee'ar'ly," she groaned out to me when she finally

looked back up.

I nodded. "Yes, that's right. I know I'm early, but I was hoping to check in with my bags before the convention started and freshen up. If you have a room."

"Fi've. Th'ree. Se'e'ven," she reached down and slowly scrawled it on a piece of paper, and then turned and pulled an old, thick key off the wall. When she turned to me again she screeched into the air. "Sh'va'na."

Sh'va'na rushed forward and took the key. She pointed forward and then started to scuttle forward toward the elevator. "Sh'va'na."

The halls were nowhere less confusing upstairs, but at least the rooms were numbered. I took notes of them while we walked, and soon enough I was at my room. Sh'va'na opened the door with the key and left it in the door for me. "Sh'va'na."

I walked inside and went to hand her a tip, but by the time I turned away she was gone. Weird people worked here, but at least they were nice. I pulled the key and closed the door, before falling into the bed.

I shouldn't have even gotten a room. Two hours wasn't that far to drive every night, but Tim told me that I had to do it, and after he staked me for the table, I felt I owed it to him. Now, I regretted it.

I threw my clothes into the ancient dresser and watched the wallpaper peel as I texted with Harriet. I told her I was in the room and everything would be okay.

I wasn't sure anything would be okay.

Harriet had a decent job which paid for our mortgage, but with every weekend that passed, the baby came closer and closer. How could I let my wife care for a baby while I pursued some stupid dream?

I talked to her often about giving it up. She constantly told me that I would be miserable doing anything else, and that our child should know that her daddy loved his life...but did I love this? Did I love being gone every

188

weekend, begging people to try my books out, watching them walk around with twenty-dollar cups of root beer they would consume in ten minutes and telling me my fifteen-dollar book was too expensive? Looking through me with dead eyes like I didn't even exist? Was this really better than selling vacuums, or cell phones? At least then I didn't take it personally when people rejected me.

I must have worried myself to sleep, because the next thing I knew it was dark, and there was a banging on my door. I opened it to find Tim on the other side, smiling at me. "Come on, buddy. It's just about time."

I looked down at my watch. It was 7pm. Oh crap. I had missed a whole day at the convention. This was not good. I rushed to the door and opened it to find Tim. "Oh my god. I can't believe I missed the whole convention. Harriet is going to kill me."

"You didn't miss much," Tim said. "The real convention starts in ten minutes."

I cocked my head to one side. "I don't—the flier said it started at 11am. I was just coming to lay down for a minute and I wasted the whole day."

"Oh...yeah..." He said. "That's not the convention I wanted you to come to. Follow me. You've gotta see this."

He pulled me out of my room, confused, and bitter at myself. We zig-zagged through the halls again and made it back to the lobby. There was an eerie green glow about the whole place that was amplified by the fluorescent lights everywhere. Convention goers muddled through the halls, talking to each other, and a tightness grew in my stomach.

I had blown it.

When we got to the convention floor, I was very confused to see all the vendors still at their tables, talking to each other, chit-chatting. Usually, when the convention floor closed to attendees, the vendors rushed to the doors.

"I don't understand." The doors slammed behind me,

and it made me jump. "What's happening?"

Tim slapped me on the back. "The best convention ever is about to start. Get to your table."

I did what he said, shaking my head for a few minutes until a huge light shot down from the ceiling above us, and then turned into a calming blue. In that moment, the doors to the back of the convention floor opened and hundreds of maids and bellhops wandered inside. They all moved uncomfortably in their skin as they ambled around toward the tables, looking at the tables with a little amusement.

I watched as Sh'va'na walked through the door and ambled up to me, looking at her feet. She reached into her purse and pulled out all three volumes of my book, and a pen. "Sh'va'na."

"She wants you to sign them, mate!" Tim shouted, and I was very confused. "She's your biggest fan."

"How is that possible? She didn't say a word to me except her name! And how do you understand her?"

"We'll talk about it later." Tim waved me off. "Just sign the dang books."

I turned back to Sh'va'na and complied with her request, signing all three of her books. Then, she looked down at my table, pointed to all three of the books there, made a five with her fingers, and then nodded. "Sh'va'na."

"You want five of each?" I asked.

She nodded, and made a signing motion with her hand. "Sh'va'na."

I smiled and counted out five of each book. I signed then and she gladly paid me for them with a big smile on her face. Her teeth were sharp, like those of sharks, but her excitement was palpable. Her eyes were wide with wonder, and I swore I saw her eyes blink horizontally instead of vertically. When she had paid and scooped up her books, she turned to a group of other bellhops and showed them the books, pointing at me.

The other bellhops' eyes went wide. They rushed over to me, growling and clicking to each other. They pointed to my books, and made signing motions with their hands.

"What is happening?" I mumbled to myself.

"I told you, you just had to find your audience bud," Tim said. "You're famous in certain circles. You just had to find them."

I sold out of all my books in the first two hours, and had to dip into my excess stock from my suitcase. Once I was done with the day, I had a hundred preorders for books that I had to bring back the following morning, and had my best day at a convention ever by a wide margin.

When the bellhops were gone, and the maids had cleaned me out even more, I walked over to Tim. I handed him three hundred dollars for the table. "I think this is yours."

"Good day, then?" He asked with a wide grin.

"I have no idea what just happened."

He looked at my table. "Looks like you'll have to go home tomorrow and get more books."

"I absolutely do," I said. "Who are those people?"

"They're your fans," he replied. "And they're my people. I showed your books to my mom, and she passed them around. Everyone loves them here. You're a really talented writer."

"I swear I saw their eyes blink horizontally, man, and their teeth—I don't think they are human."

Tim pulled out a tooth from his mouth to reveal a sharp tooth underneath. Then, I watched as he blinked horizontally, and then vertically, and then horizontally again. "Is that a problem?"

"I—" I looked down at my wad of cash. "I guess not. Their money spends just like anyone else's."

"That's the right attitude. I thought you would be cool with it." He leaned forward. "You'll have to excuse Sh'va'na, and the others. They haven't been on land for very long. They'll learn how to be human more as they get to know the surface."

I placed my hands on the table. "Are they—" An idea crossed my minds too crazy to express to anyone but Tim. "—Deep Ones?"

He winced. "We don't like that term, but let us just say H.P. Lovecraft revealed many things he shouldn't have."

"Was—he a De—one of you?"

Tim placed his hand on his lips and nodded. "Luckily, people think it's just myth and legend. We have done a very good job of that."

My eyes furrowed, but I only had one question left. "Are there other cons like this?"

He chuckled. "Oh, so many."

It was a revelation. I couldn't believe that I had found a group that loved my books. I didn't even care that they were monsters. They treated my work with reverence. They rushed to me and they ran off to read the books with glee and gusto. Were they really even monsters at all, if they could make me feel like my work had value?

"How about dinner?" I asked to Tim, holding up my cash. "I'm buying."

I couldn't wait to show Harriet. She would never believe it. I barely believed it, but I wasn't going to turn up my nose at the best con day ever, or the best group of humans that I had ever met...even if they weren't human at all.

A Descent Into Depth's Bliss

G.R. Theron

About the Author: G.R. Theron is a Pacific Northwest based fantasy author, panelist, and member of the Mythopoeic Society. He is a former member of the Fairwood Writers. Educated at the University of Washington as an Ancient Historian and Classicist, his work often draws upon classical themes and mythos.

He cherishes the best writing advice he ever received from his grandfather; the truth should never get in the way of a good story.

Follow him at grtheron.com for more information.

A Descent Into Depth's Bliss
G.R. Theron

During the afternoon of a dreary spring day, the last chill of winter's breath lay in a fog that crept towards the hotel. I nursed a scotch at the hotel bar, bereft of the comfort normalcy offered and naively relieved by its absence. It was my first time at a convention, and even what I thought I knew had not prepared me for what they truly were. What truly lurked beneath in the reality that wasn't what it seemed.

I had thought conventions merely strange events where stranger people dressed up as the strangest things. Prior, when I had driven by year after year, my friends would snicker at what they saw. Who were these people so engrossed into illusionary worlds? Who were these people who dwelt in dreams? Who were they who dared to hold to wonder when others had set it aside for the material, responsible world?

To others, they were people running away from something. To me, they were running towards it.

My friends would snicker and mock and detest. As if these people's existence threatened their own. But I envied their courage, even if I had so long lacked it. The resistance to real world's redundancy held intoxicating allure.

It was a beautiful, haunting resistance that I needed to

understand. It felt like a protest to what I'd been reliably and repeatedly informed was the real world. And the real world was drab as if the world of wonder vied against that of accomplishment and status. Reliability abhorred restlessness, and in the end only fools choose a restless life over the safety of reliability. I was grimly certain that was what people meant when they said to grow up. They meant to grow small.

I hovered between the two. Those closest to me often came and, in worried whispers at private lunches, they'd voiced their unasked-for opinions. "You're wasting your time with those people."

My girlfriend's frustration was less subtle. "It's time you grew up and focused on the real world."

"How so?" I had asked, looking up from my canvas and balancing a paintbrush between two fingers. One of our friends was buying a house, which I had been informed meant starting life, and I it was not the first time nor the last that she'd broach the subject.

"Hobbies are great, but you have so much potential. Don't you want to start building an actual life?" She had laid her hand on my shoulder and brushed my hair from my eyes.

Just as predictable as their derision was my silence. Voiceless, I offered no counter. They knew my hobbies. They'd seen my art, my dragons, and my beasts. They were aware of the fanciful realms I painted and how I wouldn't pass a single book without seeing the cover.

They knew but didn't understand.

I'd grown familiar with being understood in parts, accepted in fractions. Only a fool would try to pursue a career as a cover artist. How many artists were there? Thousands upon thousands if one. There was nothing new about feigned tolerance but the comforts of being tolerated were few.

The convention's newness, however, came in many

forms. Most of all, lurking beneath, there was a vast communal exhale. As if collectively, the escapees from the mundane sighed in relief. They had come home at long last.

"You're new here," said the bartender. It wasn't a question, and he refilled my scotch without asking.

"How can you tell?" I asked.

His smile was thin, bordering on mocking without quite reaching it. "You work for the hotel?"

"No."

"Then get yourself something else to wear."

"What's wrong with this?" I asked, plucking at my sports coat and button up shirt. "I'm wearing jeans."

"Girlfriend picked it didn't she?"

I took a sip of the whiskey. "Maybe."

"She's not into...all of this...is she?" The bartender gestured to the convention with a swirl of his finger in the air.

"Um...no." I winced, imagining her here. "Not at all."

"And why are you here?"

"I want to become a cover artist," I said. "So, I read that you're supposed to go to conventions and start to network."

The bartender watched me longer than was polite and longer than was awkward until the moment passed into uncomfortable. It was then that I noticed he didn't blink. Not once. I felt small, hunted in a way that made me twitch in the barstool. It was as if he was looking through me, into me, and weighing something that I couldn't see or understand.

The lights seemed to dim then, as if a passing cloud hid the sun, or some overhead light had gone out. Dim were the sounds of the convention beyond. The ice cracked in my glass, loud in comparison. I glanced down, expecting it to be shattered, but the cubes were intact, swirling in the wake of my stilled hand.

Finally, he spoke. "No, that's not it."

"It's not?" I croaked. My throat dry, I sipped the whiskey.

"No, that's not why you're here. Not what you want."

"And what do I want?"

"You'll know by the end," said he. "Talk to me then."

Not knowing how to respond to the strange shift in conversation nor the man who, now, appeared somehow taller and larger, looming before me as if I'd been shrunk by the drink or he swelled by it, I quickly reached for my wallet. "Well, I should be going."

"It's on the house."

"Won't your manager mind? I wouldn't want you to get into trouble."

This seemed to amuse him. "No," he said. "I've been here a long time."

"At this convention?"

"All conventions."

"All?" I put my wallet away.

"Oh yes."

"When did you start?"

"That's the wrong question," he said, leaning forward. His eyes bore into mine, and again I felt the urge to run. But there was something about his gaze that pinned me to the seat and something about the deep tones of his voice that lulled my mind. Was it the drink? The strangeness of this place? His smile was almost warm. Almost. "You should ask instead at which point I end."

"Your shift?" I asked awkwardly.

"This," he said, gesturing to the convention. "When do I, when does this, when does it…end?"

"The schedule says Sunday afternoon."

"The schedule never lies but it never tells everything either," he said, leaning back. "Enjoy the convention, Seth."

"Thanks for the drink," I said.

It wasn't until I was away, among the throng of people and the din of conversation, that a question crawled into my conscious mind. How did he know my name?

The bartender's words and mannerisms haunted me. It wasn't until early in the morning, well before dawn, that my mind settled. By then the voices from the hallway beyond had quieted. The room parties seemed to operate like speakeasies; people attended simply based on knowing which rooms to go. But at that uncommon early hour, when only the wind caressing the window and the sputtering rain beyond remained, I found new understanding.

It was the job of the hotel staff to foster a festive environment. Some of them wore convention shirts while others makeshift hats resembling elves or gnomes. The bartender's eeriness had been the most convincing. It didn't explain how he knew my name but that must have been it.

Strange as he may have been, the following morning I followed his advice.

The vendor room was like nothing I'd ever imagined. Stalls of hand-crafted clothing, weapon replicas, and artwork were tightly packed between book vendors and independent authors. I dove in, intent on buying shirts that didn't immediately mark me as a con virgin.

I began to understand the hierarchy of the congoers. There were con virgins, like me. We dressed in mundane, drab garb from the world beyond. A rookie mistake. Additionally, our con badge was unadorned aside from a single ribbon that we'd been given upon entry.

Next there were the experienced and casual attendees. They wore witty shirts that displayed their fandom, and their badge had a long beard of ribbons. Some were lengthy showing the breadth of their nerd scope. Others were focused, narrowing in on exclusive ribbons that set them apart from their peers.

Then, above them all, were con icons. These people wore fanciful garb and established aesthetics as identifiable to their persona as their name. Their badge either had a flowing tapestry of exclusive ribbons or no badge at all.

This must be the highest convention status, the level to which most aspire; to be known without a badge was to be royalty.

I envisioned what it would be like to be so well known. I imagined being that well known that when a con virgin asked, 'Who is that?' people answered. I dreamt of not even needing a badge. It was this level of convention status I knew I must achieve, no matter the cost.

Attending the panels would be my start.

I set forth, garbed in my witty fantasy shirt (a misquoting of characters in an obvious way that would invite conversation) and armed with a handmade notebook I'd purchased from a sweet older woman who told me she'd been coming to this convention since she was little. I was ready.

I was also lost.

My first hurdle was finding the panel room. I became grimly certain that hotels were designed by Greek Gods, and, at any moment, I'd stumble into a minotaur. Finally, I found the room after deciphering the small map on the physical pamphlet and comparing it to the updated room assignment from the phone application. I was certain this must have been how Turing felt upon breaking the Enigma machine.

I entered- late.

I stood in the back, not wanting to interrupt the panel. The conversation had already started, and I missed all the introductions but the last.

Corinne Vanderbrook was just as I'd imagined her. She wore a flowing knit shawl and sat straight-backed yet at ease at the far end of the table. She'd let her hair gray, and she looked even more established and confident for it. Thin-rimmed glasses sat towards the end of her nose, and she peered over the top at those who spoke with a thoughtful expression.

Yet, even more, there was about her a command of the room and the nuances of public speaking that marked her in a way that made her seem larger than life. Her responses to the moderators' questions were considered and she'd pause briefly, as if formulating her thoughts. Then, with an acuity that drew me in with each word, she'd approach every topic in a way that made complexity simple.

"The lightest darks are always darker than the darkest lights," Corinne said, speaking on how there were shades in shadows, degrees of dark. "It's the task of the artist to understand the depths of shadows, and to draw the eye where it needs to go. It's in the shadows that we're truly drawn. It's there that the world of imagination comes to life."

Then she seemed to stare at me. The room blurred into a haze, as if the walls spun like a top around me. The audience blurred, twisted until they were contorted in inhuman shapes. Their mouths sat agape in an endless, silent scream.

I flung myself back and stumbled against the wall.

The moment passed as quickly as it'd come, as if it'd never been. Corinne fixed her attention back to the moderator. Sweat beaded on my brow. I looked around, breathing heavily. Nothing was out of place, nor the audience bothered. The moderator opened the floor to questions. Hands raised.

I stood stone-still.

Had I not been so uneasy, the questions people asked would have either irritated or amused me. Over half were not really questions. Instead, people raised their hands as if they themselves were panelists and they'd address the room with a point to be made. Often, poorly.

But I was too troubled to pay close attention, nor in that moment care. The abnormal moment had left my mouth dry, my questions were stuck to my sandpaper tongue and locked in my sluggish mind.

A water dispenser sat on a table at the end of the room with dixie cups stacked neatly beside. I filled one and drank until the edges of the plastic paper were soggy and the shape of the rim had failed. The water gave me a reprieve but did little to calm my mind. I needed a drink.

A proper drink.

Not until later, after several panels passed, did I make my way to the bar. I sat at the far side of the room and avoided being in eyesight of the uncanny bartender (as best one can when a place is full, and options limited).

"Join me," a now-familiar voice said as soon as I sat down. I craned my neck. Corinne sat in a booth behind me. She crooked a finger and her voice carried over the hum of conversation. "No need to sit alone."

The urge to run tugged at me. But this was why I'd come in the first place. Networking. There was little point to being here, to taking the mockery of friends and family, if I didn't seize the opportunities presented.

I pressed down my worry, stood, and joined her. "I saw your panel today." It was perhaps the most simple and inane thing to say, but I didn't really know how else to greet her.

She smiled and dipped her head to the empty seat. "Yes, I noticed. You were at three more also but always in the back of the room."

"I'm new." I plucked at the graphic t-shirt. "Apparently this hides the fact."

She laughed. "Masterful disguise. Then again, most are in disguise here until...well that doesn't matter." Leaning back, she spread her hands. "Are you an artist?"

"Trying to be one."

"You either are or aren't."

"Well, I've not sold anything or been in a show or—"

"You're mistaking the act of creation with success. They're not the same. Terrible artists can be professionals and wonderful ones have never sold a thing. What kind of art do you do?"

"Book covers," I said in a lame voice. How many others have said that? A hundred here alone, I wagered.

"Good. Then that's what you shall be."

Slowly others came to join her table, and one by one she introduced me as a cover artist. No one questioned it, nor me. My nervousness must have been apparent to them. Who was this stranger who came from nowhere? But no one asked. Instead, they gave a polite nod of acceptance before engaging with Corinne or others. They were the ones that mattered— yet I was there, sitting among them.

A waitress delivered a glass of scotch to me. The amber was dark, almost black in the low light. I glanced to the bar. The bartender stood, watching. A thin smile curled his lips before he turned and was lost in the crowd.

"He's a master of dark waters," said a heavily bearded writer whose name, like the others, I'd only briefly heard and promptly forgotten in the chaos of introductions.

"Pardon?" I asked.

"The bartender. No one mixes drinks better."

The conversation died down. Everyone watched me. My mouth felt dry again, but my water glass was empty and the decanter in the middle of the table had long since been poured. I raised the glass to my lips and sipped.

They resumed their conversation, appeased.

On my third day, I resolved to avoid panels and the bar entirely. I lingered in the art gallery and watched the silent auction. I studied the way the artists spoke, the way they'd nod and go over each other's work, and the way they held themselves. It was a strange mix of confidence and anxiety, as if each was sure of their work while simultaneously feeling as they were there by mistake.

A petite, almost waifish woman my age spotted me and came over. Her hair was dark blue, almost violet, and the tattoos on her arm were symbols I couldn't place in a language I didn't recognize.

"Is this your favorite?" she gestured to the painting of octopus reaching out from waves I just happened to be standing beside.

"I don't have one" I said. "Honestly, I just was trying to stay out of the way."

She smiled and quirked a brow. "That's not the reason."

"I've heard that more than once here."

"Then it must be true."

I snorted. "Everyone seems to know my reasons better than I.. Is that part of conventions? Everyone's a mind reader."

She rose to her toes and leaned towards me. The scent of her perfume tugged at something deep in the recesses of my mind, wrapping its tendrils around something so primitive inside me that I dared not dwell upon it. Her voice was barely a whisper. "Yes."

My pulse quickened. "I..."

"No!" She laughed, rolling her eyes. "Of course not. As if anyone or anything could truly read minds."

"Oh, I knew that."

"Mmhmm." Her eyebrow quirked, matching the skepticism in her tone.

Very much wanting to change the subject and trying hard to keep the embarrassed blush from my cheeks, I said, "Then you tell me, what am I doing?"

"Besides creeping in the corner?"

"That's not particularly flattering."

She scrunched her nose at me. "True, though."

"I—"

"—need to relax?" she finished for me. She took a breath. "I'd guess that you were seeing how this is all done? You're an artist, and this is your first convention." She tilted her head and continued. "You're by yourself— that means your friends and family aren't part of...this."

"Decent guess," I said. "But maybe they're just at a panel or something?"

"Could be but it isn't. Your girlfriend certainly isn't."

I squinted. "No, she's not- but how did you know I have a girlfriend?"

"Because you were nervous when I leaned in." She smiled sweetly. "And you don't strike me as shy. You're taken but she's not here. This isn't her place."

"Not really, no."

"What does she do?"

"She's a senior account representative."

"What does that mean?"

"She um... handles accounts."

"For old people?"

I chuckled. "No, she's the most senior of her team."

"Let me guess. You sit at overpriced bars with these teams as they talk about what?"

"Accounts."

She clicked her tongue against her teeth. "Well, you're safe now."

"Safe?" I asked. I felt anything but safe. "I didn't know I was in danger."

"Of course you were. You were drowning."

"And now I'm not?"

"No," she winked. "Now, you've drowned. It's why you're here. They tolerate your fun, little hobby. Just don't bring that hobby up around the other senior account managers, right? That's how it is, isn't it?"

I wet my lips. "It's not quite like that."

"Liar."

"I think you've gotten the wrong impression about me," I said. She hadn't, not at all, nor of things outside of this place. I felt bare in a way that made my skin prickle.

"We know our own." She squinted. "I'll just wait for the next part."

I swallowed. "What next part?"

"When you know, find me. Thelxie is my name. The short version, anyways."

"An unusual name."

"An unusual place. It fits." She nodded back to the cashier table. "I'll talk to you later, Seth."

It was my turn to squint. "How did you know my name?"

"The bartender told me." She swirled on her heel and giving me a little wave. "Welcome home."

I watched her go, not trusting my voice, not knowing what else to say. Throughout the rest of the day, I tried to ignore the conversation. I had learned some of how things operated here, made a contact, and that was good enough for a first convention. Yet, I felt tethered here. Oddities clung to me. Questions seeped into my mind.

The real world felt distant, distorted as if I was looking up at the sky from the bottom of a pool. I tried to focus on the simple, boring details of my job but they felt somehow even more dry. The perfunctory words and corporate speak I'd so been accustomed didn't come. The more I struggled the dryer my mouth became.

That night passed restlessly in a half dream. I tried to force myself to sleep but only lay awake. The rain against the windowpanes, which normally lulled me into rest, brought no comfort.

Between the pattering rain and my own breathing, a voice sung. Whenever I strained to hear, it quieted. When I lay still, sleep almost finding me, it grew louder, waking me back into a restless wakefulness.

The song called to me.

She called to me.

I had to leave.

Finding no rest nor respite, the song lulled my mind but not yet my soul. I rose from bed and hurried into my normal clothes. I smoothed the sports jacket. I found my keys and my phone and watch. I left the rest, fleeing from the room.

The hallway felt empty and longer than I remembered. I hurried down the corridor as the song grew but when I looked back I saw no one there. The song seemed to come from everywhere and nowhere at once, as if I'd been dipped in the honeyed voice and left tethered here to be consumed.

At long last, I reached the windowed corridor that connected the wing of the hotel from the lobby. Rain cascaded down the windows. Dark clouds hung low, touching the tops of hotel buildings. The lamplights had gone out in the parking lot, and the cars were obscured in the black. The normal sounds of the hotel and its guests were gone. No echo sounded behind me nor whispered before. There was only silence.

I walked alone down the corridor. Then I ran. Pride didn't matter. I needed to get to my car. I needed to leave. The lobby had to have people in it, didn't it? They'd get my car from the valet at this time of night.

They must.

But the front desk stood empty. No one waited at the valet. The gift shop doors were open, the checkout unmanned. I called for someone, searched for anyone, and peered inside the employee's room. I even rang the little bell. Once. Twice.

Silence answered.

From the bar I heard the jingling of glasses. I crept towards the sound, my breath clenched in my chest. I feared what I'd find around the corner, but the silence was so unnerving that even the specter of the bartender felt like a reprieve.

His back was to me, and he stood in the halo of a yellow, overhead light. Yet his shadow cast impossibly against the wall beyond, a black shade dimmer still than the dark corner.

It wasn't his shadow— it couldn't be.

The shadow coalesced into inky tentacles, ethereal and sickly. They curled around the bottles of gin, caressed the vodka, lingered along the labels, until they stopped at the scotch. Then, all at once, they recoiled back into his form.

"Have you found it?" he asked without turning. He poured the glass of scotch and held it out with his left hand towards the seat I'd taken the first night. "Do you understand the truth of why you're here?"

My voice trembled. "This is a dream."

"A lucid dream is more than just a dream." He turned and bade me to sit. I complied without thinking, as if my legs were not my own, compelled by either his voice or my own curiosity. "The real world isn't real." The bartender then gestured to the convention with a slow wave of his hand. "It's this- in a way. Everything is an illusion of either our comforts or fears. One is no less real than the other. Drink?"

I shook my head. "I was just about to leave."

"Were you now?" his voice was amused.

"I was."

"And where were you going?"

I tried to wet my lips, but my mouth remained dry. "I was going home."

"You are already there. Didn't Thelxie say that?"

"This isn't home. I'm not—"

"An artist?" He finished for me. "Didn't you say that's

what you wanted to be? So Corinne made you one."

"I was wrong."

"Resistance is natural. People always fight against their nature, they're hesitant to be consumed." He pushed the glass towards me with two fingers. "Do you think by leaving you'll forget about this, all of this, once you get back to the normal world."

I nodded. "Yes." His smile was thin, eyes unblinking as always. My skin crawled yet I didn't run. I sat, realizing the lie of my answer without needing to be told. "I mean… maybe."

"Say why you come here."

"To be an artist."

"No." He leaned forward. The shadows crept from his back, trailing along the counter towards me. His voice was stern, reprimanding. "Say it."

I struggled to find the answer. My mind worked frantically. Inch by inch the tentacles reached for me until the shadows wrapped around my petrified arms, cold as death. I had come here to be an artist! I came here to be… I came here to be. What did I come here to be? Was it an artist? What did I come here to be? Not what I was outside. That wasn't it.

To be something, meant I wasn't anything already. I wasn't anyone. I was tolerated in parts, accepted in measures, moving from one faux acceptance to another. Doing what I should do for those I shouldn't care to impress. Yet, that was all I did. And in doing so I had become nothing— and nothing has no place.

My throat was dry, and my fingers pressed into the wood of the bar. "I came here to be…"

He slowly nodded.

"I came here to be…to be…to belong."

The shadowed coils of death, of misery, of something as base and primal as a wordless scream withdrew. The bartender set the glass before me. "Yes," he purred. "To belong."

My chest heaved with each breath. "Yes."

The smile was thin, and his voice dripped in a venom that I eagerly lapped. "Now you understand."

"What now?"

"Drink."

"I don't want to." It was my last resistance. A final retort as I splashed franticly against the tide of the conversation.

He reached into his pocket and withdrew a card. "Corinne's number. She has a job for you. One of many." He placed one corner of the card on the bar, rotating it slowly. "Thelxie's number."

The low song hummed in my ears as if saying her name summoned her.

"I need to..." I trailed off.

"To belong."

For a long moment I stared at the card that now rotated on its own before me in an impossibly empty hotel. The bartender loomed before me; every bottle consumed in its shadow. My mouth was so dry.

I summoned my will to stand but, as I met the creature's gaze, memories stirred. I remembered how my friends would laugh and how they would talk about the congoer and how they'd mock the illusionary world I now lived in. It was a world bereft of normalcy and made even more comforting by its absence.

I picked up the glass of scotch. What was one more drink to someone who'd already drowned? A blissful descent.

END

GIVE A DOG A BONE

OLIVIA BAXTER HUDSON

About the Author: OLIVIA BAXTER HUDSON lives with her totally radical family in the great PNW.

She has a long history of writing to amuse herself, but she is always fiendishly delighted when someone else is amused with her writing as well. Her other pastimes include muttering curses in the general vicinity of her sewing machine, brewing odd concoctions to pour into jars, communing with the random creatures that haunt her yard, and attempting to persuade her kids to listen along to her otherworldly music collection.

She also owns one suspiciously eldritch Jack Russell terrier. (Seriously folks, consider yourselves warned).

She would like to thank Greg, Tracey, and Greg's

trusty bike pannier for loaning her the gnarliest grimoire she's ever seen.

And she would like to give Trek a big hug and a squirrel. He knows why.

GIVE A DOG A BONE
OLIVIA BAXTER HUDSON

I've reached a point where I can tell that a convention is coming when I find my claws being trimmed.

Which is what is currently happening. And I am not amused, for it is breakfast time and by all due rights I should have a belly full of meat by now.

The man crouched before me refers to himself as "Dexter." At least, he insists on doing so when other humans are present. As far as I am concerned, he is both caretaker and Caretaker. Both of us have our roles. And that is all I need to understand. Names have come and gone. Or altered. Or buried by time.

I had an ancient name, once. This morning, I cannot recall it. But it will return. It always does. A bellyful of meat would surely summon it back home.

My stomach growls. I allow myself the satisfaction of pushing the growl through my throat and into my mouth, where it comes to perch on my tongue like a spiteful imp. It is time for this nail-trimming to end. And so, in turn, I growl at Dexter.

He is not moved. He does not outrank me, but neither is he subordinate. And he knows this well. He fixes his cold, gray eyes on mine, and silently extends his hand for the final forepaw. Which I give to him. It would be easier to carve a tombstone with my tongue than to argue.

"We've finally done it this time," he says to me. "This is the opportunity we've been waiting for. Everything must proceed as planned! Did you think that all of this preening was for the benefit of those mortal wretches? For all their earthly follies that we have tolerated? That was merely practice!"

I will not bother myself with a reply. Dexter loves nothing more than to listen to the sound of his own voice. Even now, he's regaling himself with another lecture about how hard it was to market our dwelling as an ideal convention site.

I feign interest for a few seconds. Then I imagine an itch and begin to gently scratch behind an ear with a hindleg. This always helps to muffle the sound of Dexter's voice. Small wisps of my coarse black fur begin to fall away from my head. Out of the corner of my eye, I watch them float downwards to land on the cold stone floor.

These flagstones are remnants of our original temple; deep underground, where none of our so-called guests have ever ventured.

To Dexter's credit, he has delivered on his promises, even decades after the last of our priests told us to seclude ourselves. The world wars did not go as planned for our kind. The powers that fed our cults were overthrown. There would be no more aid from our brethren in Europe.

I have forgotten some things, but this I remember as if it were yesterday.

In 1945, a final message came for us, penned tenuously by one of our sect. Dexter read it aloud to me. "Remain in New England," it said. "Hide. Obscure yourselves. Wait for an era of excess. Glamour and novelty will reign supreme. Men and women will sell their souls for material goods. Flatter their vanities. Bait them with their own desires."

While I chewed the bones of the tiny fiend that had delivered the letter, Dexter fumed and flipped through dusty grimoires, searching for solutions to our problems.

As the years passed, Dexter stripped our temple's shelves and walls of its artifacts and trophies and hid them away down underground. Then he began to make subtle alterations to the building itself; the most notable of which was adding some windows to usher in more daylight. These were festooned with thick curtains crafted from old ceremonial shrouds, but even these familiar objects could not fully obscure all the new sunbeams in my home. It was utterly ghastly, so I began spending my days in the basement.

But in the nighttime, I continued to hunt along the banks of the river that flowed around our property. The only trappings I cared for were bones.

Then one morning, Dexter told me to stay inside. Men were coming to repair the driveway between our home and the bridge over the river, and I must not stalk them. "A hotel," he explained, as we watched them work from a window. "This is what we've been reduced to."

Later, I was told to take a bath. Dexter had filled a tub with soapy water. I snarled and I howled. How dare he treat me like a common cur!

"But how dare you!" Dexter had retorted. We needed the money. And—if the soothsayer's words were to be heeded—practice at luring the unsuspecting. He pointed his finger at the river and told me it was either that or the tub. I took the river, just as I already had for countless years. After all, I am a water dog.

Then Dexter took his clippers and his brush to me and introduced me to the concept of "maintaining pretenses."

Brushing. Ugh. That's what Dexter was doing now. He must have finished the nail clipping while I was distracting myself.

That's enough of this, I think. Judging by the pile of fur at Dexter's feet, I must be adequately groomed by now. Before Dexter can give me his leave, I dart like a rogue phantom out of his reach and sprint along the cold flagstones and up our secret passage.

There are some bits of machinery and pipes at the end that must be skirted, but they serve a dual purpose by helping to conceal our hideaway. The door at the end has a long handle that I can grasp easily in my jaws. It opens into the hotel's kitchen. Dexter explained to me years ago that the words on the door read "Boiler Room Access" because most humans take no interest in the working bowels of a building. Therefore, they would not be inclined to linger too long looking for the hidden route to our private chambers.

And we have ways of circumnavigating problems with trespassers. There was once a traveling salesman who became rather too curious about   the inner workings of the hotel. Fortunately for Dexter, it is remarkably easy to hide a car when you've got a convenient river outside, already swollen with winter rains. And our Master always ensures that the river keeps our secrets.

Otherwise, I found it unfortunate that the salesman himself had carried a disappointing aftertaste of cheap cologne.

But here and now, in the kitchen, I can smell traces of blood. I nudge away the fake service door and begin sniffing out my breakfast. Our drudges have already materialized, and they are busy preparing the food that Dexter has ordered for the upcoming convention.

One of them is getting ready to place a rack of roasts in the oven. I growl thickly at it to get its attention. It turns its shadow-head towards me, nods, and slowly flings a chunk of meat off the tray.

The roast lands on the floor and slides with a red streak towards my feet. It is merely beef. How dull. However, I am ravished. I snap it up quickly and lick the trail of blood off the floor.

Then I pad my way past the drudges and out into the hallway that leads to the grand foyer. It is long and tall, with arched rafters, and beneath my feet are the dark wooden planks that were once the floor of our temple. The guests will frequently inquire about it. "Could it be mahogany?" they ask, as they admire the rusty-red tones in the wood. Dexter never directly conceals the truth. Instead, he flatters them like so: "You must have an eye for craftsmanship, sir! The boards under your feet originally came from an ancient place of worship in Europe—back from a time when architecture was an artform! Just look at the work that went into staining the wood! It has a rather bewitching beauty, don't you think?"

And, while Dexter talks, I lounge under the check-in counter, and I silently congratulate myself. Those stains were some of my finest handiworks.

At the present time, the foyer is vacuous and unoccupied. It reminds me of the beginning of our hotel days. At first, there were only sporadic visitors. Mostly hunters, and people interested in bird watching. A ragtag mushroom hunting society. Quiet people who didn't overstay their visit. Dexter politely took their money and surreptitiously reminded me not to stalk them.

But then, late one evening when he was tidying a room in the west wing, Dexter picked a magazine off the floor and let out a gasp. It was a sound I'd never heard him make before, and it alarmed me.

"This is what we've been waiting for!" Dexter hissed with excitement. My concerns quickly turned into eagerness as Dexter translated what he was reading. "Look, there's some professor of economics in here who's labeled the nineteen-eighties as the 'Era of Excess' because people are spending money on frivolities at a higher rate than ever. They want gadgets. They want parties. They want something called 'fast fashion'— whatever the hell that is."

And that was how, for the first time in decades, I was left alone one day while Dexter journeyed to the nearest town. He returned home with a box full of magazines and spent several days reading. He told me that he was doing research. That he'd been ignoring the nuances of human society for too long.

"Conventions," he told me one morning. "That's how we pull them in."

The first one was maddening. It was a large group of mostly children, walking around the foyer manipulating colorful cubes with moving sides that they would twist over and over again with little click-click noises. I couldn't tell if the objects were toys or religious talismans. Or possibly both? All I knew was that I hadn't seen such tender young things in such a long time. I spent most of that week hiding in the kitchen; mostly to evade Dexter, who reminded me in no uncertain terms that humans tend to throw loud fits when their offspring go missing. And if I was going to drool all over myself, I could do so in the kitchen where the drudges could clean up after me.

Then there was the convention where a large group of dashing young men congregated, sporting objects that looked like bricks of plastic and metal that had all been festooned together into one lump. "Mobile phones," they explained to Dexter. "Fashionable and functional!" They proceeded to run about looking for 'service,' which had me perplexed because they seemed to think they would find more of it outside the hotel rather than inside. Dexter pointed to our old barrow and recommended they "try the hilltop." This solution seemed to satisfy our guests, and they spent the good part of that weekend dragging various contraptions up to the top of the barrow.

And every evening after these guests had retired indoors, Dexter prevented a calamity by performing a few quiet rites at the base of the barrow. Too many tramping feet, too many beating hearts, too many electrical contraptions; and some of our dead might stir. I did recall that some of the foundation sacrifices had been particularly surly. And in the mornings that followed, Dexter muttered to himself in the mirror as he shaved: "Ridiculous way to communicate. Utterly ridiculous. Just draw a circle on the floor and light some candles." I grunted the merest of agreements as I lay on the floor with my legs in the air and uncomfortably digested the bats and rats that had come careening out of the barrow.

But the worst convention was the one with all the blaring music. Something about new waves. I was confused. Our hotel is nowhere near the ocean. Perhaps our river attracted them? Which made no sense to me because the river is so deep that it rarely ripples at all. Unless, of course, our Master wants it to. To this day, I don't so much remember the guests as much as I remember Dexter clutching at his ears, while wriggling tendrils of his dark aura threatened to burst through the cracks between his fingers . . .

But what's this? A dark spot crouching inside the shadows of a heavy curtain. I can see it out of the corner of my eye. One of the grotesques from the old temple must have broken out of Dexter's containment rooms in the basement. Excellent. I could use a hunt.

Slowly, I walk past the curtain, pretending not to notice anything amiss. Then I spin and lunge! There is a shrill squeak of alarm, and the grotesque is off and running. I chase it down the full length of the foyer. I snap at its heels—so close!

There is a small rectangular hole in the wall near the floor by the grand hearth. The grotesque darts inside before I can close my jaws around its stony little head. I cease my pursuit. My left hip is hurting, and I can't help but limp around as I sniff the air. There are damp underground vapors wafting up through the hole, filled with tantalizing smells from our old lives.

"Not getting any younger, are we?" Dexter asks me. He has followed me down the length of the foyer, rubbing his wrists as he approaches. Grooming me always stirs up his arthritis.

He crouches by the hole, examines it closely, and scowls. "This used to be where the blood sluice was positioned," he comments. "Right over the basin room in the basement. What clever little fiends we have. Clever, and restless. Remind me to let them out for a bit of exercise after this convention is over."

Dexter straightens, grabs a heavy armchair, and drags it over until it blocks the hole.

"Since you're up and about," he says to me, "go do some rounds through the building and make sure we don't have anything else lurking in the shadows that might disturb our guests."

I agree wholeheartedly. It's the closest thing I'll get to a hunt without going outside. And so, I begin to roam through the antechambers and hallways, sniffing everywhere for more grotesques. But I found none. Then I roam some more, this time sniffing for more mundane creatures such as rats and mice. But there are none of those either.

I return to the grand foyer, but I don't see Dexter. Eventually, I find him in the dining room, preoccupied with setting up the carts and warming trays for convention meals. I am bored, and my hip still aches. I make my way underneath the check-in counter and lay down on the fluffy dog cushion that Dexter purchased not so much for me but for his "pretenses."

I wake later to an odd sound. Something is making a noise akin to the squawks of a large bird, yet it is communicating with actual words. I raise my front end off the dog bed and peek upwards at Dexter.

Over the top of the counter, he is listening to what I presume is a human woman. She is dressed completely in black; from the large, gong-shaped hat above her head, to her shiny heeled shoes. Her clothing looks quite comparable to Dexter's suit, yet her shoulders appear ridiculously large and pointed, as if she were hiding a spade under the berm of each sleeve. There are strands of white in her hair, the same shade as the pearls around her neck. Otherwise, the only other colors I could spot on her were streaks of flame-red on her thin lips that matched the long nails on the ends of her fingers.

Overall, she put me in mind of the crows that circle the aftermath of my hunts.

"And my Lulu only eats white meat," she is saying to Dexter. "Anything too rich upsets her delicate tummy."

I look at Dexter, who is wearing his best placid expression. But there are tiny fumes of aura escaping from the back of his shirt collar, so I can surmise that this woman must have been irking him for a while before I woke.

"Madame," Dexter begins, "Our kitchen has always been well stocked with an astonishing variety of meats. And I can assure you that I would never offer your precious Lulu anything that I wouldn't be prepared to eat myself."

The Crow pauses for a moment, considers Dexter's words, and opens her mouth to reply. Then she spots me.

"Good heavens!" she shouts and clutches her collar. "That is the largest dog that I have ever seen!"

Dexter turns, and spots me for the first time. He shoots me a meaningful look. I know, I know. Pretenses.

Wearily, I rise to my feet, and rest my chin on the counter. I gaze up at the Crow with one ear tilted comically, just the way Dexter taught me. "Woof," I say in my mildest tones.

"That would be Fido," Dexter informs the Crow, his voice dripping with something approximating affection. "He's my oldest friend."

"Is he . . . some sort of Newfoundland mix?" she asks Dexter.

"Oh, if I recall correctly, his dam was one, yes. But

between you and me, I'm quite sure that his sire was a bit of a hellhound . . . if you get my meaning," Dexter replies, and he flashes the old bird a charming smile.

That smile. It's been ages since I've seen it. I remember the priestesses in the old temple would do anything Dexter asked when he used it on them.

I watch as a sickly shade of pink flushes across the Crow's cheeks. She's blushing! Well done, Dexter, I think with a silent snicker.

"Oh yes, I think I know what you mean," the Crow replies. She releases her grip on her collar and begins to toy with the string of pearls around her neck, her bright red fingernails clicking along each little sphere. "Animals will be animals, after all."

Dexter gives me a swift glance and reaches for the canister on the counter. Damn it! Not the bones! Curse you, Dexter!

"Here," Dexter says, and presents the canister to the Crow. "Would you like to give him a bone?"

"I'd be delighted," the Crow says, smiling back at Dexter. She reaches into the canister and pulls out a phallus-shaped atrocity.

Of course, I have no choice but to take it from her. I reach out and delicately bite the so-called treat out of her hand. It tastes like pig flavored tree bark. I wag my tail to show a cursory amount of thankfulness, then turn and walk down the hall and into the kitchen.

I spit the bone into the nearest garbage bin, and then I bully one of the drudges into giving me something better. When I'm sated, I make my way through the fake service door and down to my underground quarters. I've done enough play-acting for the day, and my real bed is calling to me.

I wake again at twilight. Dexter is nearby in the inglenook, cooking his dinner in a sturdy crucible. I rise from my bed of skins and amble towards him. He is muttering to himself about the Crow.

"Suits with padded shoulders! You call that stylish? Who do you think you're fooling; running around trying to look like a man?" Dexter gives the contents of the crucible an overly vigorous stirring. Some of the viscous liquid comes sloshing out and lands on the fire below. A couple of salamanders dart out from under the cinders and begin to lick the sizzling drippings. I drool with anticipation as I watch them.

"Bah!" Dexter continues. "Last generation, girls were burning their bras! Rejecting all that stuffy Puritan nonsense. The priestesses would have approved of that! Not that they ever bothered themselves with fashion. Or clothes, for that matter! Heh, heh, heh!"

Dexter has his odd little mannerisms. But he also has giblets.

Dexter sets a bowl of raw giblets on the floor for me, and proceeds to serve himself out of the pot.

"Don't stay out too late tonight," he says, "You've got a busy day tomorrow. Got some serious contenders to choose from. I should know, I checked them all in this afternoon."

Of course I know. This is the opportunity we've been waiting for all these years.

But that doesn't mean I'm going to forgo my nightly swim in the river.

"And mind you don't track any mud across the foyer when you come back," Dexter reminds me as I slink away.

The following morning comes too soon. I stayed out far too late last night, and my left hip is acting up again. But today is an important day, so I must rise.

Dexter is nowhere in sight, but that is understandable. He is the face of our façade and will undoubtedly be upstairs catering to the guests.

I shamble through the dark passage and into the kitchen, where I demand breakfast. Dexter has given the drudges the semblances of human faces and some drab uniforms. The spell is weak but should hold long enough for the duration of the convention. One of them is preparing to wheel a large cart out the kitchen door, so I follow closely behind.

The drudge parks the cart near a wall, and I crouch behind it for cover while I investigate the scene. Someone has hung a banner that reads: "Welcome Lady Dog Lovers Society" in large letters. And indeed, the dining room is packed full of both ladies as well as dogs.

They are every size, shape, and color; human and canine alike. Most of the women are dressed in a fashion similar to what I saw on the Crow yesterday, in sleek suit jackets with overly exaggerated shoulders. Some have taken pains to make themselves stand out. One woman with kinky bleached blonde hair has crimped the fur of her Afghan hound so that they match each other. They are sitting at a table with a woman who has completely covered herself in neon colors, and her Schnauzer is sporting a bulb-studded collar that flashes rainbow lights.

Brash. Self-absorbed. Gaudy beyond belief. Once again, the nineteen eighties had spewed forth its decadent bile all over the inner chambers of my domicile.

And yet, we had finally managed to bring in dogs.

I watched them all intently from my hiding place. There were tiny dogs, jittery Chihuahuas and yippy Pomeranians. I could have snapped them up in one bite if I'd so desired. There were medium sized dogs; retrievers and setters that appeared healthy and strapping but would never survive trying to outswim me in my river. No, it was the big dogs I wanted.

The first one I saw was an Irish Wolfhound. But too old. A bit wheezy in the chest, with a body that looked like it was being held together by sinew. Stringy. No good. There was a Bernese Mountain dog being hand-fed pills stuffed into cheese cubes by a fussy woman. Heavily medicated and possibly ill? Disqualified.

Finally, I spotted a large black poodle. She was sporting a snakeskin collar with the name "Chanel" spelled out in rhinestones. Her fur was glossy and well cut. Quite an ornate bitch.

Admittedly, she was slightly smaller than what I was hoping for, but she had an impressive chest. Well-muscled. Lots of meat on her bones. Absolutely delicious.

Chanel. She would be the one to watch, I decided, then I slunk my way out of the room.

On the second day of the convention, I made some important discoveries. The poodle belonged to the Crow. Also, the Crow introduced her dog to other humans as "Lucretia," though "Lulu" was her affectionate nickname. Perhaps the "Chanel" collar was some sort of mortal attempt at apotropaic magic? If so, it was a pathetic ward. It certainly didn't work on me.

Not that it was a relevant matter in the grander scheme of things to come. What was important was that I learned that Lulu craved beef. She sat by her mistress's side at the dining table while she was spoon fed pureed chicken. But it was the slices of roast on the Crow's plate that had her begging like a pretty little fool. To which the Crow indulgently responded: "Now darling, you know that meat is far too rich for you."

And so it was, that on the third and final day of the convention, I snuck inside the room where the Crow was giving a presentation titled "Assessing your canines dietary needs by examining their stools." The lights had been dimmed so that the audience could view a projector screen. Not a soul saw me creep through the shadows along the wall. Just moments before, I had procured a fresh t-bone steak from the kitchen drudges, and now I carried it in my mouth as bait.

Lulu had been tethered to a table leg off to the side of the room. The leash contained more frippery than metal, so it didn't require much work on my part to release her. One sniff of the meat in my maw was all it took to convince her to abscond with me.

Out of the room she follows me, down the hall, and through the foyer. We pass Dexter at the reception counter. He gives Lulu an appraising look and says, "Interesting choice. Well, have it your way then. There'll be hell to pay tomorrow."

I simply nod my head in agreement. My mouth is too full of beef to reply anyway. I continue into the kitchen and through the doorway to my underground lair, with Lulu trailing at my heels.

Dexter was not exaggerating at all when he said there'd be hell to pay on the morrow. He woke me early in the morning and instructed me to make my way to the foyer as soon as possible. He'd dragged my bed out from under the reception counter and placed it innocuously in front of the hearth. I was to play the part of "good old boy resting his bones in front of the fire," so that no one could accuse Lulu of running off with the caretaker's dog.

The foyer was soon filled with soppy women and their yapping beasts, all taking their turns at   consoling the Crow over her "poor lost Lulu." A policeman materialized around noon and lazily wrote down a description of the missing dog. Dexter reassured the policeman and the frantic women that he had searched the grounds thoroughly but was more than willing to take the Crow with him on his next perimeter sweep.

All the while, I lay upon my bed and tried my best to ignore the idiotic mongrels who occasionally wandered over to sniff at my hindquarters. At this point in the game, it would not do at all to lose my temper and chomp one of their little heads off.

After an arduous eternity, evening arrives. Dexter makes a big show of announcing that the Crow is welcome to stay, free of charge and as long as necessary, until her dog is found. And so, one by one, the women are reluctantly checking out of our hotel. When they are all gone, the Crow dabs grateful tears from her eyes and allows Dexter to escort her on a tour of the grounds.

The following morning, I rise to an overcast day. There is not a single sunbeam on the foyer floor. Just the way I like it.

I push open the door to the lawn and pad my way down to the riverbank, where I sit and bask in my own self-satisfaction.

After a while, Dexter appears, leading Lulu on a sturdy leash. He walks her towards the sheltered dog run he has built for her, and he leaves her inside to dine upon a bowl filled to the brim with prime cold cuts. All beef, of course.

Then he joins me at the riverbank, and together we gaze longingly at the meandering water for a while.

Dexter is the first to break the silence. "The spell worked perfectly this time. The trick is to find a master who adores their bitch as if she were their own child. Stronger bonds make for stronger magic."

I yawn with mild derision. Dexter is not telling me anything I don't already know.

"There should be several pups that take after you in this litter. You'll have your own little army again in no time," he informs me, a sly grin creasing his face. "Well done, old Shuck."

Shuck. Dexter only calls me that when he is truly pleased. It was a name that humans gave me, ages ago. As if naming a terror could lessen its grip!

Shuck.

But it was not, I think, my original name.

What was my name? I turn to Dexter and prepare to ask him if he remembers the answer to this question.

However, Dexter has begun to gag and cough, one hand pressed to his mouth. A tiny patch of crimson appears, and my hackles rise as I sniff the air for traces of blood. Instead, I find only the man-made stenches of plastic and lacquer.

Dexter lowers his hand. Cupped inside, there is a fingernail. It is long, and pointed, and flame red.

With a grunt of contempt, Dexter flicks the nail into the river. For a few moments, we watch in tandem as the bright object floats slowly downstream.

The tip of a large tentacle surfaces; dappled and hoary. It snatches the fingernail, then descends just as quickly as it appeared.

Our Master has always enjoyed our little mementos. END

Star Crossed

Rhiannon Louve

About the Author: Rhiannon Louve is a freelance writer. Professionally, she writes short stories, video game dialogue, table-top role-playing books, and privately commissioned fiction. She hopes to soon add novels to the list. With her MA in Applied Theology, Rhiannon has taught World Religions at the college level, and published Pagan thea/ology essays. Rhiannon's published short fiction is mostly steampunk so far, while her current video game gig is with State of Decay 2, about surviving post zombie apocalypse. Most of Rhiannon's table-top RPG work is in traditional fantasy, though not without horror and Lovecraftian elements, such as her contribution to the award-winning Elder Evils D&D 3.5 sourcebook. Rhiannon has a strong interest in Lovecraftian fiction, but comes at it from a weird fantasy or dark fantasy perspective, fascinated most by the mythos itself and the psychology of such a world. Outside work, Rhiannon mostly games (table top, analog), including a Bleach-inspired shinigami game, using her own homebrew version of Exalted. Her other hobbies include scholarly study of primate behavior (including humans), and learning languages (she speaks French, some Spanish, and minute amounts of Japanese and Irish). Rhiannon rarely watches television in English, and has written scholarly papers on manga and anime.

STAR CROSSED
RHIANNON LOUVE

Friday Morning BridgeCon Bulletin

Welcome to the first day of BridgeCon 47! If you're new to the hotel, be sure to get a map and visit the info desk early and often!

A list of cancellations and room changes follows.

Today's special shoutout goes to our volunteer team! They really went all out this year, and the hooded uniforms they've put together were all on their own, in celebration of this year's super fun End of the World theme!

In addition to this year's Last Dance in History and Apocalypse Masquerade, be sure to check out our special End of the World programming, like our Crisis Preparedness panels, our Heat Death of the Universe panel, and our Best Mid-Apocalypse Fiction panel!

We've added some brand new staff this year. Warm welcome to new members, especially our new hotel liaison who got us the best deal we've ever had on room rates! Big thanks to the "old guard" staff stepping down, for keeping the con alive all these years!

Have a Great Con everybody!! --Miriam Lyle, Chair, BridgeCon 47

***

Robin Daley looked up as Eowyn Smith passed the single-page bulletin with its subsequent list of corrections

231

and questionable humor to him.

"I can't believe they're still wasting paper on these things," she said. "For a con about fictional futures, it sure hasn't changed since I've been away."

Robin laughed. "The little crossword looks fun," he said, toying with his waxed mustache. His beard was finally growing in properly, and he was starting to feel quite vain about his neatly trimmed goatee and slim handlebar mustache. He hoped Eowyn found them sexy. As a short, tubby individual, he figured his facial hair was just about the most manly aspect of his entire appearance.

From what he could see of the other con-goers in the halls so far, he did feel like he might fit in pretty well here. He judged himself to be a bit less tubby than attendee-average, and quite appropriately dressed in jeans, a nerdy t-shirt, and a random sport coat. He hoped Eowyn was right that there would be more costumes in the evenings.

They reached the head of the line and stepped up to check into their rooms. When the clerk started the room-location process, Robin nudged Eowyn.

"Remember the weird wing," he whispered.

"Oh right!" Eowyn said. "Can we have one of the rooms from two-fifty-seven to two-seventy-seven?"

The hotel clerk frowned. "That wing hasn't been included in the BridgeCon package most years . . ." she began.

"Wow, you've been working here a while," Eowyn said. "Most hotel staff never know what deal the con has on the rooms."

The clerk laughed. "Yeah, I always enjoy working with this con," she said. "Bit of a geek myself. Oh! Look at that. It's included this year. Con room rate. There you go, room two-seventy-one. Let me get you your keys."

Later, on the way to the "weird wing", Robin felt the

need to speak up. "You're just messing with me, right?" he asked, as he and Eowyn pulled to a stop at a second bank of elevators. "I know you said this hotel is laid out weird, but this is not a rational route we're taking."

Eowyn laughed and showed Robin the map. "That's why the weird wing is the weird wing," she said. "It looks like you should be able to get to it by walking west from the front desk and then going upstairs anywhere after this point here." She poked the map for Robin's benefit. "But these elevators don't even go to that floor. We can go outside and around to here," she poked a spot on the far back end of the hotel, "and take the stairs up, or we can take this route I learned from the other con kids like ten years ago."

They'd gone *north* from the front desk instead of west, down a flight of stairs, east to an elevator, up three floors by pressing an unmarked elevator button, *then* west down a dim hallway with plainer carpeting that *really* didn't look like the public was supposed to be here, to their second set of elevators, at which point Eowyn had pressed the "down" arrow and Robin had suspected a practical joke.

"There's also the service stairs here," Eowyn pointed on the map after they'd stepped into the elevator and pushed the button for floor 2. "But they're usually locked."

"It's not possible that a real world hotel could be designed this badly," Robin protested.

"I heard it was a remodeling mishap, and it's just been too expensive to fix all these years," Eowyn said. "There's actually nothing on the floor below us in this wing. Like, nothing at all." This, too, she demonstrated on the map.

Robin could only shake his head and laugh. "Must be where they keep the dimensional anomaly that makes the weird wing so weird."

"Right?" Eowyn laughed. "I think . . ."

But then the elevator doors opened, and the two young con-goers were confronted by the wildest pair of eyebrows

Robin had ever seen.

"What are you kids doing here?!" growled the man behind the wickedly up-brushed eyebrows. They were grey, and matched a long, shaggy goatee and mustache beneath them, with a large pair of thick, aviator-framed glasses in between. The human wearing all this was of average build, in black jeans and a black t-shirt, scrawled with white-lettered jargon in (presumably) a nerdy joke too obscure for even other geeks to decipher. The personage looked to be in perhaps his fifties, with crazed eyes made huge by his coke-bottle glasses.

Robin stifled a squeak at the apparition's sheer intensity. He took an involuntary step back.

Eowyn held her ground. "It's good to see you too, Howie!" she cried, though Robin didn't think her tone indicated actual joy at the reunion. "We're just headed to our room."

Howie narrowed his eyes and did not give way. "Are you the Smiths' kid? You should know full well to avoid this wing at night," he said. "New liaison got *everything* wrong! You go tell the hotel to give you a different room!"

As Robin adjusted to the man's presence, he seemed to loom less large and look more just old and weird. Robin stepped up to Eowyn's defense, even though he was the shorter man by several inches. "Look," he said, emerging from the elevator even though that brought him within old Howie's somewhat booze-scented bubble. "We're not superstitious, and our room is none of your business. Have a good con, okay?"

Howie glared down at Robin, but he made no move as Eowyn slipped out of the elevator past him. Shaking his head, Howie and his eyebrows turned away, muttering. The words sounded to Robin like, "Come find me before it eats you," but he was sure he heard wrong. Howie stepped into the now-empty elevator and hit a button. The doors closed.

Robin and Eowyn exhaled in unison.

"What the hell?" Robin asked, allowing himself a little chuckle.

"I don't even." Eowyn shook her head. "That guy has always scared me a little. He's been with the con since the dawn of time, I guess. Used to always be hotel liaison. My dad said he was the most amazing source of weird trivia—seemed to really like him back in the day." She shrugged. "He's got this, like, natural villain-laugh, though. It's wild."

She started off down the hall, in the direction indicated by the wooden hotel sign. Robin was sure that sign couldn't possibly be pointing them in the right direction, according to his understanding of the map, but he figured all the up and down and back and forth had just left him disoriented.

"So this guy really believes the weird wing is dangerous?" Robin asked, scurrying to keep up with Eowyn's longer stride.

Eowyn shrugged. "He has a bizarre sense of humor, I remember," she said. "For all I know, he was trying to make sure we had more fun scaring each other tonight." She spotted their room number and stuck her key card into the slot. It didn't open, so she tried again. "I mean," she added, "why was he even here unless this is where *his* room is too, right?"

That did sort of make sense. Robin nodded warily, but something felt off. He didn't know this Howie guy, but the man had looked dead serious to Robin.

On the fifth try, the door unlocked for Eowyn. She stepped on into the room.

Robin followed her in and looked around.

It was eerie.

Don't let that guy get to you, Robin told himself. Sure, the room was dim and empty, but hotel rooms always were when you first walked in. And yeah, the lamp in the corner was flickering a bit, but this was undoubtedly an easily explained phenomenon. A short in its wiring perhaps, or an old fluorescent bulb.

The abstract wall art, in browns and golds, looked vaguely monstrous to Robin, but was that really unusual as hotel art went?

Beside him, Eowyn shivered melodramatically. "Wow, this place does feel kinda haunted," she said. "I can see how the stories got started."

"How would it be different from the other rooms, though?" Robin asked. He set down his bag and started poking around. An unusual light fixture in the bathroom ceiling threw weird prisms all over the walls and shower curtain. For a moment, it seemed like the curtain was moving, but when Robin looked directly at it he saw no indication it had been anything but an optical illusion.

"Good point," Eowyn said. "Old Howie must have rattled me back there. Do you want the window bed or the one by the bathroom?"

Robin kind of wanted, suddenly, to go back to the front desk and ask for a different room. But he'd been so excited to sleep in the "weird wing" of Eowyn's childhood con adventure stories, he felt pretty stupid backing out now.

"I'm easy," he said. "Let's get ready for that Last Dance in History."

The dance was basically a bust. The room stood almost empty. An old man in a unitard and multicolored feathers undulated alone on the dance floor, to an eerie remix of an 80s rock song. Robin found the performance hypnotic at first, and then surreal and frightening. The only other people in the room were the DJ—zoned deeply into his task and largely hidden behind his equipment— and three people at a table in dark hoods that obscured their features.

Robin glanced at Eowyn.

"Yeah, the dances used to be a bigger deal," she said. "Huh. Let's go check out a panel or something."

The late night panel on the Fictional History of Arcane Ritual, once they finally found the circuitous route to the hall in which it was located, had three panelists. Two of these had fascinating things to say about H. P. Lovecraft, Algernon Blackwood, and the general ethnocentric bigotry of early portrayals of Indigenous and Pagan practices. The third remained silent and stared at a wall. Occasionally, her lips moved.

Eowyn seemed to calm down while listening to the scholarly and real-world-grounded panel, in the brightly-lit, boring little meeting room, but Robin couldn't help staring at the third, silent panelist. She didn't have a nameplate, and they'd arrived too late to catch the panelist introductions. Something about the way everyone else ignored her made Robin wonder if she was even really there, or if he was just seeing things.

At the end of the panel, the two speaking panelists gave their final thoughts and then confirmed the third panelist's existence by turning to her and asking for her closing remarks.

"It's stirring in its slumber," she said. Her voice was soft and faraway, but the whole room hushed to hear her. "Something is wrong. The wrong robes will stand before the altar."

"Um, Annie?" asked one of the co-panelists.

The white-haired woman blinked and looked around at the room. "Um, yes," she said, sounding perfectly normal. "Ritual can have great power if you use it right. Have a good con everyone!" Then she stared directly at Robin.

Robin blinked and looked behind him, but there was

no one else she could be looking at. When he glanced back her direction, she'd stood up and now appeared to be engrossed in conversation with a man in a wheelchair. Robin looked to Eowyn.

Dressed for the dance in black lace and a cheap faux corset, Eowyn looked even more beautiful than usual. Robin really hoped she liked short guys. He adjusted the bowler he'd donned for the dance, and made sure his old-fashioned tie was tucked properly into his Edwardian vest. He knew he looked as dapper as his little, roundish form could look in this outfit. He hoped it mattered to her.

She flashed him a knee-melting smile. She was no great beauty by outside world standards—a bit gawky and plain, with not nearly enough curves to distribute her extra nerd pounds in a stylish manner—but Robin had loved her from the first day of their first term of physics at the local community college. She'd referenced Terry Pratchett in a discussion of quantum phenomena, and Robin had absolutely swooned.

To his tastes, at least, she was ethereally beautiful.

Robin shook off his lingering fears and sense of the surreal. At least he was here with Eowyn.

"That was an awesome panel," she said. "Gives me some great ideas as a gamemaster!"

She was wonderful.

@@@

The rest of the evening was nice enough. Eowyn introduced him to old friends they met in the halls, and they attended a lively panel on Sci Fi and Sex, and eventually made the long trek back to their room. This time Eowyn showed him the longer but more-direct outdoor route, and they took the stairs up to the weird wing.

The darkened nighttime parking lot was much less creepy than the convoluted indoor route—if a bit windy and cold—and Robin had almost forgotten his previous desire to switch rooms by the time they both tumbled into their beds, all tuckered out.

Much as Robin might have loved an invitation to share a single double mattress, he ultimately ended up on the window bed, and Eowyn did not.

At 3:47 in the morning, according to the blood red light of the hotel alarm clock, Robin awoke and needed to pee. Around him, in the dark, the room seemed entirely the wrong shape and size. Robin ignored this and concentrated on making his way to the bathroom without waking Eowyn.

Halfway around her bed, he looked over to her sleeping form. A host of thick shadows swirled around her, pawing at her. They had clawlike appendages and curling tails. Eowyn tossed in her sleep, but didn't wake. The shadows bent to kiss her nose and mouth, and Robin knew they would suck away her will.

He dove toward her bed to chase them off her, and . . .

Woke up.

His mouth was dry and tasted awful. He still needed to pee. He stood up and started to make his way around Eowyn's bed. The numbers on the hotel alarm clock looked to be running with blood. Trembling a little, Robin went back for his wire-framed glasses. The clock read 3:52. Robin couldn't explain why this terrified him so much, but he would have preferred a clearer discontinuity between his dream and reality.

He peed without incident, and Eowyn seemed to sleep peacefully throughout his awkward and fumbling bathroom trip, but as Robin climbed back into his bed it seemed as though the shadows beneath the furniture reached out to claw at his feet. He whipped his legs safely up onto the mattress and under the covers, feeling foolish and very young.

Around him, the darkened room really did look to be the wrong shape and size. Robin wished desperately to turn on the lights, sure it would dispel the illusion and return normal geometry to the world, but Eowyn was asleep. He didn't want to disturb her. He didn't want her to think he was a coward or a dork.

But the walls looked wrong. No matter how Robin stared at them, he couldn't shake the perception. Their angles made no sense. And the shadows in the corners were a great deal darker than they should be.

Shivering cold, Robin huddled under the covers and squeezed his eyes shut, hoping the weird shadows wouldn't touch him.

***

Saturday Morning BridgeCon Bulletin

I hope everyone had a great dance last night! As usual, there was a long line at the info desk, yesterday. We promise, the program maps really are accurate, even where they don't seem to make sense. Con veterans can also help you to navigate. We swear the rooms don't really move when you walk away from them.

A list of cancellations and room changes follows.

Today's special shoutout goes Boris and Kraken of the security team! They found and retrieved four lost children yesterday, and the grateful parents wanted to make sure we thanked them properly, so here's to their heroic rescue efforts!

The weather's taken a turn for the stormy, so stay safe inside today, and don't miss tonight's Apocalypse Masquerade!

Keep Enjoying the Con!! --Miriam Lyle, Chair, BridgeCon 47

***

Eowyn and Robin had a great morning together. They both put on their best hall costumes, and Eowyn thought Robin's "Steampunk Robin Hood" was just about the cutest thing she'd ever seen. She wondered where he'd found that forest green derby, and whether he'd had the rest of the outfit personally tailored. He was really such a cute little man. She had no idea how he afforded all his excellent nerd gear.

Eowyn normally avoided comparisons between herself and the namesake her nerdy parents had chosen for her, but since Robin was being Robin Hood today, she went ahead and wore her mom's old "warrior princess" armor with a few flourishes she hoped made the outfit more Tolkieny. Robin took pictures and told her she looked amazing, and for once Eowyn found herself not minding so much to be praised for something as shallow as her appearance. Robin just knew how to phrase it right, she supposed.

The hotel breakfast buffet was nice, and the dealer's hall was fun. Robin bought her a fancy new dice set, and she bought him a CD from her favorite filk musician, who manned his table personally and charmed Robin's socks off when they met.

It was a much better morning than last night had been. Oh, the con parts had been all right, other than the depressing dance, but that weird wing room . . .

Eowyn knew it was all in her head. The old stories, and Howie's practical joke (it had to have been a practical joke, right?) . . . it had just gotten to her. But those nightmares last night had been so realistic—Robin's eyes glowing yellow, and that shadowy, watery hole gaping open in the floor . . .

Eowyn shuddered. She didn't think she'd ask for the weird wing again. Next year they'd both be 21 and could have more fun staying up late in the party wing anyway.

They finished browsing the clothes, jewelry, games, and mostly-micro-press books of dealer's hall, and emerged into a different part of the main corridor than Eowyn expected. But the con hotel had always been like that. It was just that disorienting a layout.

"Where to next?" Robin asked.

"Definitely the art show," Eowyn decreed. "There's always some amazing local pieces." Luckily it was near the dealer's hall, and not too hard to find.

It was, indeed, a good art show this year. Eowyn was happy to see that Robin seemed completely engrossed in each artist's section of the labyrinthine rows of sci-fi and fantasy art on their tall, folding, pegboard display panels. There were dragons and spaceships, diaphanously-clad fairies, portraits of geeky movie and TV characters, weird space art, grotesque monsters, and impressive geeky handcrafts in every medium around the outer walls. As always, Eowyn wished she could afford to bid on every single silent auction entry.

She was happy that Robin wanted to take in the show a bit slower than she did, really savoring each display, but her mom's old faux-armored boots didn't quite fit her right, and it hurt to stand still for long. Eowyn left Robin behind to peruse the show at his own pace and decided she'd make two passes herself, to hopefully get the same amount of detail.

Besides, there was always a hushed, reverent sort of quality to the art show. It was almost meditative to experience it alone. Robin didn't even seem to notice when she wandered away.

The show seemed larger than usual this year, and Eowyn soon found herself disoriented, completely uncertain which direction she'd been walking, and whether or not she'd already seen the displays around her. She picked a random direction and ended up in a corner near the far back wall.

The hotel's ceiling light was dim and flickering in this corner, so it was several degrees darker than the rest of the art show, and inconsistently so. On tables along the wall stood the most amazing, weird, faery-inhabited trees—crafted from driftwood, shells, pretty stones, and leaves sculpted in green glass and wire. In the shifting light, the branches and little stone goblins seemed to move. Eowyn loved them.

Then she turned around to view the paintings on the nearby pegboard panel.

They were actual oil paintings, not even prints—all of dark, swirling waters, strange aquatic life, and . . . was that one abstract? Or some kind of underwater portal?

Eowyn looked closer. She felt drawn to the image and repelled at once. Its colors were ugly and muddy. It seemed amateurish. And yet . . . she found she couldn't quite look away. Its waters seemed to roar all around her. She felt she might be swept away in its deep, filthy current.

She gasped for air, and water seemed to fill her lungs instead.

Eowyn blinked and looked around her. She seemed to be down on the hotel's lower level, near where they always kept "Hospitality" (the free food room) cleverly hidden. How had she gotten here? Where was Robin?

Eowyn fumbled out her phone and checked for messages.

How the hell is it 10:30!?!

Her hand started to shake. There were no messages. Fingers trembling, she texted Robin, which wasn't easy. After she hit send, she saw she had no signal down here anyway. Her parents used to complain about that, she recalled, back in the day. Cell phones barely worked inside the hotel.

In a daze, and since she was already almost there (and starving), Eowyn wandered on into hospitality. Maybe someone there would know where to find Howie.

Wait, Howie? Why Howie? Eowyn did remember how much her parents had respected Howie Hoskins, but—

was Howie really the answer? Or should she just find Robin and get out of here? Her mind felt fogged. She couldn't think.

Hospitality was crowded with vampires and airship captains, bellydancers and anime heroes, as well as a lot of nerds in jeans and t-shirts. Their conversation seemed surreal and alien to Eowyn, which—as a geek born and bred—was the most upsetting part of all. Cons were Eowyn's childhood home!

I'm just worried about Robin, she thought.

She threw together a sandwich with random cheap ingredients from the Hospitality buffet tables and, while stuffing it into her face, went looking for a seat in the dining area.

Then she saw him. Off in a corner by himself, hair in his eyes and hat askew, was Robin.

***

"Are you okay?" Eowyn was asking him.

Robin rubbed his face to clear his head. He blinked at his friend. She had mustard on her nose. She'd never looked more beautiful "Yeah," he said. "My, um, brain's a bit tired. I've been gaming."

Did he really want her to think he'd spent this whole time gaming?

"I mean," he scrambled to add, "I looked for you first, all over the place. But then I found the game room."

In fact, after that one weird exhibit in the art show, Robin didn't remember a thing until finding himself alone in the board-gaming room, where random strangers had soon cajoled him into a game. He hoped Eowyn hadn't been worried about him all this time.

Everything felt so strange. Robin knew he was in a room called "hospitality", and that he'd been given food here, but he wasn't quite sure how he'd gotten here, or where his new gamer friends had gone.

"I'm so sorry!" Eowyn pulled him into a hug. "I don't

know what happened. We were at the art show, and then . . . I just lost you.”

Robin wanted to enjoy the feel of her hugging him, but his head felt full of sand, and his body felt strangely far away.

“Robin? Are you mad?” Eowyn was asking. “I understand if you are, but . . .”

“What? No!” Robin realized he'd been spacing off. She thought he was mad because he was acting weird. “No, I'm just glad we're together again. Should we go check out that Masquerade?”

“I . . . think we missed it. I'm sorry,” Eowyn said. “Robin . . . Something's wrong with the con this year. I . . . want to get out of here.”

Robin felt betrayed, and he couldn't explain why. “What are you talking about?” he asked. “There's so much more to do!”

“The dance was dead last night, and we've seen dealer's and the art show,” Eowyn argued. “We're too young for the party wing, so all that's left is panels and gaming, and you said you've been gaming all day!”

“There was still stuff I wanted to buy at the dealer's hall,” Robin heard himself mutter. He wasn't quite sure what he was upset about, or even what he wanted.

“We can come back in the morning,” Eowyn said. “I don't want to sleep in the weird wing again.” She stood and offered him a hand up. “We can already say we did it, so come stay at my place tonight?”

At Eowyn's place?

That . . . didn't sound so bad.

Robin took her hand and stood up. Her skin was warm. He wanted to keep touching her, but she slipped away quickly and out into the hall.

“Let's at least get our stuff from the room before we go,” Robin insisted. “I don't want to have to get it in the morning. Plus, I'll want clean socks tomorrow.”

Eowyn froze. She looked like she might be trembling, but she did nod her agreement. "Yeah, I should change out of these boots anyway," she said.

000

Eowyn flatly refused to take the convoluted indoor route to their room, and Robin wasn't certain why he wanted to see it again so badly anyway. He agreed to the outdoor route, which, from the lower floor where Hospitality lay, was already convoluted enough. East to take the stairs up, or was that west? Robin was all turned around. And then a long, curving hall, and then Eowyn announced *she* was lost and they had to backtrack until they found the dealer's hall again, and then they finally found the right hall and went down it for what felt like miles before reaching the outer door.

Outside, once the howling wind allowed them to open the door at all, the trees danced and creaked dangerously, and rain poured down so hard it felt more like standing in a waterfall.

Robin clutched his instantly-soggy hat onto his head and scurried after Eowyn. "Are you sure we need to go this way?!" he yelled over the storm.

"We're almost there!" was all she yelled back. They splashed through a puddle so wide and deep it probably qualified as a duckpond. Robin's beloved green steampunk boots were soaked through. He hoped the leather wouldn't be damaged.

They finally reached the desired entrance, but the doors were locked for nighttime, and the magnetic strip for their key cards refused to work six times for Eowyn.

"Key must be demagnetized!" she finally yelled. "Try yours!"

"We can go the other way!" Robin called back, still unsure why he wanted to.

"Try first!" Eowyn insisted, so he did.

It still took three tries, but then they were inside,

cold and dripping, and the doors re-locked behind them, shutting out the howling of the wind.

"Wild storm," Robin said, shaking off his hat.

Eowyn nodded, looking pale. "I'm freezing." She hurried on toward the stairwell. She looked soaked to the bone, her costume gone see-through in several places. None of it was horribly revealing or sexy, but Robin still found it cute. He wished he could help her dry off with a big, fluffy towel.

As they squelched up the stairs, though, Robin could see his companion going paler and paler with each step.

She was frightened. He felt bad for dragging her back here.

They reached the second floor and stepped into the hall. It was wrong. Robin wondered if someone had slipped something into his water. The walls and floor seemed to ripple and bend around him. The shadows all looked misshapen, and far too deep.

Their room door opened for Eowyn on the first try, which elicited a startled little cry that Robin barely heard. He did see that her hands shook as she pushed open their door.

Inside, the room seemed enticingly normal, but as the door ker-thunked shut behind them, fatigue engulfed Robin completely. He stumbled to his bed and fell over onto it, face-first.

"Yeah," Eowyn said. "Let's lie down . . . just a minute."

The next thing Eowyn heard was the chanting. Five or six voices in unison. She didn't understand the words, so it shocked her all the more to realize that she herself was chanting along with the others.

The words felt filthy in her mouth. She shut her mouth and tried to look around her.

The light was dim, but as the chant continued, the

altar in the center began to glow a sickly yellow. In that hideous light, Eowyn could see the other chanters, all in the hooded robes this year's volunteers had been wearing. She couldn't see their faces. When she looked down at herself, she saw she'd been given a hooded robe as well.

And she was chanting again, even though she'd decided to stop.

The altar in the center of the dim, echo-y space glowed a little brighter. Eowyn could see writing scrawled all over it now, in some hideous, unearthly alphabet that seemed to squirm and seethe at the edges of her vision. The sight made her sick to her stomach, and she clamped her jaw shut on the chant that kept boiling up out of her lungs.

She tried to step back, out of the circle, but her hands turned out to be tightly clasped in those of her neighbors. She couldn't break their grip.

Struggling to break free, her wild eyes fell on her neighbor to her left. She caught a glimpse of his face inside the deep hood. It was Robin. His eyes glowed the same ugly yellow as the altar. It was just like her nightmare.

The sight shocked her motionless.

The instant she stopped struggling she started chanting again, as if it came more naturally than breathing.

Robin chanted too, beside her, but a single, yellow-tainted tear rolled down his cheek.

Eowyn wanted to throw up, but she couldn't seem to stop chanting anymore, even by biting her tongue.

The altar before them glowed brighter and brighter. Above it, in mid air, a swirling darkness began to take shape. It looked like the painting in the art show. Like brown, filthy water—the swirling depths of the most corrupted eddy in a sick, polluted river.

It stank like rotten garbage.

Eowyn's stomach heaved, but all she vomited out were the hideous nonsense words of the chant, over and over.

She tried to move again, tried to shake free of whatever

evil magic held her here, but it was no use—like one of those half-lucid nightmares where you know it's a dream but you can't wake up.

Except that she was already awake. There was no escape.

The floor beneath her began to shake. The unseen walls and ceiling rumbled. Glowing yellow cracks appeared along the altar, and the swirling mass above it grew and grew, reaching filthy, wet tendrils out toward the chanters.

Far above Eowyn's head, as if miles away, there came a rhythmic thumping, like a sledgehammer on old wood.

Eowyn tried to look toward Robin again, but she couldn't seem to even turn her head anymore. She wrenched her eyes downward and caught a glimpse of one green-toed boot beneath Robin's robes.

The thumping overhead was soon drowned out by the roaring of filthy water, and the rumbling of the quaking floor.

Ice cold fluid seeped into Eowyn's ill-fitting shoes, sliming the space between her toes.

She tried to scream, but her chanting only grew louder. Everyone's did.

We're all screaming, Eowyn realized. *It's all we can do.*

With a thunderous crack, a hail of dust and ceiling fragments rained down on Eowyn's head. She and the other robed figures could do nothing but chant, more frantically than ever.

Light streamed in from above, bright and normal.

The swirling filth recoiled before it, but then surged back, lashing out toward its source. Within seconds, Eowyn saw a heavy emergency lantern drawn down into the mass and be swallowed whole.

Darkness returned, lit only by the sickly-glowing altar.

Something thumped to the ground behind Eowyn, but she couldn't turn around to see what.

Hot tears burned down her cheeks, but she could only keep chanting.

"I'm too late," a despairing voice said close behind her. "This is so much worse than I thought."

The speaker chuckled then—an old, familiar, mad villain chuckle. It was Howie.

Was he here to save them? Was there anything he could do?

At her feet, Eowyn felt the corrupted floodwater rising. Her mom's old boots were completely submerged. It felt so much worse than any real water. It seemed to seep into her bones, claiming her flesh for its own.

She wanted to die.

"Sorry kids," came Howie's voice behind her. "It's too late for you and me." He sounded sad, but determined. "I can still save the city though."

Somehow—over the groaning, rumbling roar all around them—Eowyn heard a lighter flick open right behind her. Blue light sparkled and fizzed. A ball of blueish white sailed over her head and hung in the air for a long moment.

At the sight of it, Eowyn's mind cleared. She didn't know how or why, but whatever was in that ball, it broke her spell. She stopped chanting. Much to her relief, she heard Robin do the same. The chanter to her right let go her hand and began to scream, but Robin held on tighter.

Eowyn tried to run, but something was wrong with her legs. They no longer felt like legs. She and Robin fell together into the disgusting water below them.

Howie was right. It was too late for her. For either of them.

But that blue ball of light overhead lit Robin's sweet face. His eyes no longer glowed, and his sad smile was full of love.

He was beautiful.

The moment passed. The ball of light continued its arc

toward the seething mass above the altar.

Eowyn smelled anise.

The world exploded.

***

Friday Morning BridgeCon Bulletin

Welcome to the first day of BridgeCon 48! We're at a new hotel this year, so please be patient with us as we learn the new layout.

A list of cancellations and room changes follows.

Lots of changes this year, and lots to mourn after the horrible events of last year, when the con hotel and surrounding properties crumbled suddenly into the river. All our gratitude to the heroic con and hotel staff who got so many of us to safety that night. A memorial for those lost will be held this Saturday evening in the main ball room.

It's hard to move on in the face of such a disaster, but we know in our hearts that the best way to honor the fallen is to keep the con spirit alive, so our theme this year is Rise From the Ashes! Be sure to check out our special programming on Disaster Recovery and Urban Futurism, and don't miss all the gorgeous phoenix-themed art in this year's art show!

Let's make this a BridgeCon our lost loved ones can be proud of.

Have a Great Con everybody!! --Miriam Lyle, Chair (yes, again), BridgeCon 48

END

Room Party Fit for an Elder God

Elizabeth Guizzetti

About the Author: Elizabeth Guizzetti is an author and illustrator best known for her demon-poodle based comic, *Out for Souls & Cookies* and the novels in the *Vampires of the Paper Flower Consortium* universe. She is also the creator of the comic books: *Lure and For Blood, Bones, & Biscuits: Legend of Walnut Razorfang*. She enjoys writing stories with a dash of ordinary reality mixed with horror. Guizzetti lives in Seattle with her husband and dog, Walnut. When not writing or illustrating, she loves hiking, reading, and birdwatching.

ROOM PARTY FIT FOR AN ELDER GOD
ELIZABETH GUIZZETTI

Sarah looked proudly at the ancient runes she'd drawn on large tarps affixed to the suite walls. "Do you think They will come?"

Josh did not answer her; he was busy counting bottles. They had a full bar, plus he had made three barrels of special glowing punch that was said to be a favorite drink of the Elder Gods. They also had ordered 200 fancy cupcakes in a variety of flavors, including Chocolate Sardine.

Elder Gods liked cupcakes, right? The text said ritual sweet bread.

Sarah had gotten most of her information from a compilation of newer and ancient texts which suggested Their likes and dislikes from previous room parties. Of course, the Gods did not care about humans as a species. We were nothing to the Gods. Yet, her research uncovered They did enjoy human rituals and ritual foods.

"Josh, do you think They will come?" Sarah asked again.

"You must have patience. Pray to Them if you are nervous!" Josh said.

At that moment, Sarah didn't have time to pray.

Underneath the strange hotel, the river flowed deeper than any human eyes could fathom. There was a crack which led to the Void. And Elder Gods enjoyed leaving the Void from time to time. Room parties were especially a pleasant diversion.

Her district cult was known for their room at Cthulhu FhCon, but their converted numbers were falling. A room party graced by the presence of an Elder God would bring those numbers right back up. However, if another room party from a different cult was graced by a God's presence, but the God or another did not grace Sarah's suite, she and Josh would be shamed before their cult. Worse, their cultists might leave and join a different cult with better room parties!

Of course, she did not know Who would answer. The fact there were many Gods was part of the challenge. What she did know was Gods enjoyed this suite; the high ceilings and symmetrical layout at the end of a long corridor almost gave it the feel of a temple. Moreover, the suite overlooked the ancient river which flowed underneath the hotel, so any visiting God didn't have to move through the hotel but could enter the party directly.

She opened the windows and the screen door.

"You're letting flies in," Josh said.

"Yes, but Gods shouldn't have to knock on the patio door," Sarah said.

"They will come or They won't. Either way, you created an amazing party," Josh said.

She knew he was trying to be encouraging, so she thanked him.

Sarah was pulled away from her worries when the two men who had volunteered to be bouncers arrived. They were non-believers who came to the convention for fun and volunteered for the badges. No matter.

Josh explained how ID checks and drink tickets worked. Red bracelets for under twenty-one, green bracelets for over. Josh explained they had several non-alcoholic options for the underage party goers and teetotalers alike. Whether or not an Elder God showed up, a room party always had to remain on the right side of the law to protect the convention.

Josh also explained they had ribbons for con attendees to remember what was unrememberable. Sarah was proud of this year's ribbon. It was not only the perfect purple to match the trim on her robe, but a willing cultist created the image of an ancient rune over rippling water. It was so well drawn that if one looked at it one way, the water appeared to move.

The sun sank into the west and the clouds created orange stripes over the river. Weather forecasters claimed these were caused by clouds blocking the trajectory of the sun's rays as the sun lowered in the sky, but Sarah knew it was a sign.

Not that it mattered, either way. Soon, the sky would be inky black.

Knowing she would need her strength and this bite of food might be her last, Sarah sank her teeth through fluffy white icing down into a chocolate truffle cupcake. Ravenous, she finished it in three bites. Wanting salt, she ate a handful of pretzels and chased that with a red cup full of water.

Then she used the toilet for what also might be the last time.

She placed her peerless white and purple robes over her shoulders. She placed her badge with the party ribbon around her neck. She checked her reflection in the mirror and smiled at herself. It was time.

As the sun sank below the river, Sarah sang an ancient melody. Her voice called over the raging river below. Every syllable, she uttered praise to the Old Ones.

The doors opened to no one in the hall, but she would sing alone.

At 8 PM, the first cultists arrived. Behind her, she could hear the bouncers make a suitable line in the hall to conform to fire-code.

Attendees pocketed their drink tickets or got a drink and came to the balcony. Their long white robes billowed from the night wind.

Behind Sarah, the cultists added their voices to her ancient song.

She did not turn when someone behind her screamed. The screaming became a fevered pitch. A young woman had jumped (or was tossed) into the river. Her hands reached upward. Her eyes and mouth opened wide as she hit the water, went under, and was carried away by the current.

Sarah undulated her hips and rose her arms, still singing. She had learned this ancient dance from her text. Hopefully, she could get the others to do it. If not, they too could be sacrificed to the Gods.

Behind her, as if the cult was under her spell, they did the same.

Her dancing grew faster.

Below, the water level was rising.

"A God approaches!"

The cultists cheered.

She threw up her arms in abandon as bodies crushed against hers, pressing her toward the handrail of the patio. Her muscles spasmed from exhaustion, but she could not stop dancing.

She saw the glimmer of primordial matter break the surface of the river.

Please come to our room party, she thought.

A tentacle sliced the air in front of the patio. It transfigured into something else as it slid back into the water.

A giant head crested the water below. They passed the patio where Sarah and her cultists sang to Them. Their giant eyes did not even turn towards them. She sensed the crowd behind her disapaite. They headed to the bar to turn in their drink tickets, but she knew they would head over to another district's party once loaded.

"Keep dancing," she shouted. "Sing louder!"

"If anyone isn't singing, throw them to the God!" Josh shouted.

The people who turned away, turned back, and began to sing loudly.

Another sacrifice was tossed to God, and a giant eye turned to the patio. A tentacle grabbed the human form in midair and covered it in some primordial ooze. The tentacle transformed into a weird humanoid shape covered in irregular writhing pustules. It reminded Sarah of dancing worms. Sarah changed her rhythm to match them.

"We have cupcakes!" she shouted though she didn't know why. "The fancy kind!"

They, now, had the God's attention.

A giant wave splashed over the patio as They approached. Many people stopped chanting and clung to each other.

Sunday cultists! What did they expect! Sarah thought.

But the God's tentacles swayed and writhed like boneless serpents matching the rhythm of the dance. Sarah's throat grew raw, and her muscles ached. She could not stop dancing now if she wanted. Her body was in time to the God's. She did not know if its music came from its heart or a nameless organ, but she felt it in her very soul.

Primordial unearthly oozed towards them and transfigured and reshaped as it entered the room. The weird pustules popped. Wriggling pieces of confetti landed on the crowd of people. The transfigured God's humanoid neck extended outward. On what might be called a head, sharp claws cut into the nearest humans and pressed them into a gaping terrible maw filled with mottled teeth which had petrified long ago into stone. Rancid breath filled the room.

Saliva dripped onto the floor between bites of cultists. Then the tentacle stopped at the cupcake table. A giant eye filled the patio window.

The tentacle grabbed a chocolate sardine cupcake and tossed it in Their mouth. They swallowed so fast, Sarah could not be sure if They even tasted it. Maybe it didn't matter.

On the next serpentine head, only a large eye peered at the bar. Josh handed the walking God a bowl of glowing punch and ducked away. This, too, went into the maw.

Sarah's dancing grew more erratic as the tentacles slithered around the room. She felt as if she were hallucinating, yet she danced as pustules broke open and followed the rhythm of the confetti worms. Her feet ached and her lanyard began to rub at her neck as it shifted with her dancing. She ignored it. She felt the heat from more human bodies as the room began to fill with non-believers and cultists from other districts.

Tentacles pressed against the cultists who were transformed by Their touch. They screamed both in terror and in devotion as they became part of the timeless God.

Yet Sarah as a priestess, it was her duty to convert, not transmute.

She sang until her voice failed her. She danced. Her feet and calves screaming in agony. Her hip muscles spasming. She danced when black spots covered her eyes. The constant pounding of the badge against her chest sliced open her robe and then the tender skin of her chest. The lanyard rubbing her neck broke open her skin. Yet, she danced until her head fell forward and she collapsed.

When Sarah awoke, the day's sky was covered with the gray clouds of morning.

All around her was wetness, broken bones, and torn flesh and hair lost in the struggle. The runes were gone from the wall. Only blocky text remained on the still-wet tarps. LOVED THE CUPCAKES! PUNCH NEEDS MORE KICK. GREAT ROOM PARTY!

Sarah heard a low moan. She rose to her aching feet and was met by the sour smell of urine. It grew worse as she peeked over the bar. Josh lay in the corner, his entire body shuddering and spasming. His shirt was soaked in sweat. His pants were wet. *Thank the Old Ones, I insisted on tarps behind the bar too.*

"The God liked your cupcakes," he said dumbly as he poured her a cup of water. "They ate all the chocolate sardine ones."

Leaning on the bar, she sucked down the liquid which burned as it plummeted down her throat.

She checked the bathroom. The door was locked. She knocked. "Hey, party's over."

Four men and a woman peeked out. They looked up at her in terrible fright and wonder. Their mouths made mumbling sounds until they found English.

"Priestess, we saw your God!"

Sarah had seen the wild look in their eyes before. They had come as unbelievers, but now were converted.

She answered them in a raspy voice: "They are your God too."

"They are?" one asked.

"Yes. Come with me and I shall teach you to teach others."

Their formerly-sane eyes gleamed with passionate wild purpose. They would bring others, convert them. But for now, she told them to scrub the bathroom and ensure the surfaces were not sticky.

Sarah heard a whimpering in the closet. She found three young women, their t-shirts covered in cupcake crumbs and stained with punch. They were also converted by the sight of a living God. The three helped with cleaning up by wiping down the tarps and folding them neatly as Sarah instructed.

Outside, the two bouncers were muttering nonsensical phrases and holding each other. They had seen echoes of the Void in the writhing tentacles. They had completely lost their intelligence. That happened sometimes. Such converts were next to useless with cleaning up after a party, but they were useful as they often would throw themselves to the God on command as others had done the night before.

Most of the drinks had been drunk, and all the cupcakes had been eaten. Several cultists were missing as they had been sacrificed or merged with their God. And former non-believers converted! Moreover, there was very little physical damage to the room or plastic-covered furniture. She was sure she would get their deposit back.

She smiled at her triumph. Her room party had been a great success.

END

Curious Volume of Forgotten Lore

Paul A. DeStefano

About the Author: Paul A. DeStefano lives on Long Island, NY, with a strange menagerie that includes a dog, a few cats, sugar gliders, lizards, and his family.

After graduating Hofstra University with a split degree of English and Acting, he worked in the boardgaming and roleplaying industry for decades, including officially licensed projects for Star Trek and Lord of the Rings. He did not win the Origins Award for Best Miniatures Rules in 2004 and has totally forgotten that bitter defeat.

Paul's work was narrated by James Cosmo (Lord Mormont from Game of Thrones) for the multimillion dollar fantasy game Oathsworn: Into The Deepwood, which is the highest rated game ever at Boardgamegeek. com. When not actually playing and working on games, he can be found touring internationally, giving lectures on worldbuilding and character design.

Being a professional full-time blacksmith for several years made him realize how much less painful it was to go back to writing. He's been lucky enough to hold the Top Humor Writer badge at Medium multiple times, and has several traditionally published paranormal novels for his Riftsiders series.

It is also worth noting that having never taken any lessons in bassoon, he still cannot play one.

Denny clutched the pale canvas package to his chest and kept his other hand on the handle of the luggage trolley, glancing and quickly counting the cases again.

"Sir."

The cases and packages hadn't moved. No one had touched them or come near him at all when he was in line in the lobby. He looked behind him to a man wearing sunglasses, even though it was raining outside. The man crossed his arms and licked his lips.

"Sir," the tired voice came again from the other side of the convention staff table positioned next to the check-in counter.

He wasn't sir and had never been called such. It took him a moment to realize that he actually was the one being addressed. Denny snapped his attention back.

"Sorry," Denny said, his word reverberating off the high ceiling. He then turned to the man with the crossed arms behind him and apologized to him as well.

"This is your dealer's badge," the con staffer said, sliding a plastic laminated card across the table. It was printed to look like curled and poorly kept parchment. Denny checked the spelling of his name, nodded, and tucked the card into his wallet. Briefly, he let go of the luggage trolley, but kept a careful eye on it.

Not loosening his grip on the canvas package, Denny wrestled to flip his wallet closed and stuff it back into the pocket of his khakis. The wallet splayed open, flapped like a rabid bat and slapped to the floor, sending a rainbow of credit cards and discount vouchers to game shops he would probably never visit again spewing across the floor.

"Sorry," he said, bending to retrieve the contents of his wallet from the marble floor. The smooth surface made it almost impossible to get a fingernail under his drivers' license. The license evaded his grasp and spun several feet, whirling like a puck on an air hockey table to land wedged under the combat-booted toe of the man with the sunglasses.

Denny wiped the hair from his face and scrambled to retrieve the license.

"Thanks," he said, glancing up at the man, using the combat boot as a wall to lift his license. "I mean, sorry."

Denny crawled like a monkey on three paws, still clutching his package to his chest and retrieving the other scattered cards. He examined his luggage and tugged the trolley with his cases over to the check-in counter next to the table with the convention banner on it.

The desk clerk sat on the brass stool behind the counter, a tight-lipped smile on her face, politely ignoring the chaos of Denny trying to force his restuffed wallet into his pocket.

"Sorry," Denny said, three of his fingers now trapped in his pocket, wedged uncomfortably between wallet and cloth. He looked to the luggage trolley, tried to pull his hand free and decided to just stand and await further instructions as his fingers were imprisoned half in his pants.

"Quite alright," the clerk said. "Will you need help with storing your packages?"

"Help?" Denny flinched. "What? Store? No. No one touches. No. Why do you think I would need help? No,

I'm fine. No. Thank you. Good to go. Why do you need to store my stuff? I'm fine."

The clerk raised her eyebrows, then nodded. "We had you at late check-in, which is not for another three hours. I'll give you a call when the room is ready. You're welcome to wait in the lounge until then. With your luggage."

Denny looked across the ornate lobby to the busy hotel bar where peals of laughter had been pouring from his whole time in the lobby.

"There?" Denny asked. "Yes. Yes. Sure. I'll wait. And you'll call. Yes."

One herculean tug freed his hand from his pocket, sending his knuckles rapping harshly to the granite edge of the check-in desk.

"Sorry," he whimpered, eyes watering and sucking in his bottom lip.

He gingerly wrapped his hand around the trolley handle and tugged it with one startlingly loud and squeaky wheel to the lounge.

Tiffany lights hung from the ceiling of the lounge, each displaying a different stained-glass flower. Every stool at the bar was taken. Denny tugged his luggage trolley to a booth next to the bar, the only empty table he spied. He slid his linen package into the bench, pushed it all the way to the wall, and sat next to it. He drummed his fingers on the wrapped surface for a moment, then tugged a menu from the holder at the wall and placed it carefully in front of him.

He started reading in the dim lighting but a wild-eyed girl suddenly slid into the bench on the opposite side of the table.

"The burgers suck," she said. "But the Cajun fries are pretty good."

Denny froze. He looked behind himself for a moment, sure she was speaking to someone other than him, but saw only the wall.

Her hair was a black pixie cut with blue metallic highlights that matched her glitter-touched nails. Dark eyeliner surrounded eyes made red with cosplay contacts. One shoulder was bare, torn fishnet hanging over the front of an elaborately-laced black leather corset. Her nails tapped the table. She turned her head slightly, looking at him, pursing her lips to the side. He knew she was expecting a reaction of some sort. Someone at another table laughed at a joke he didn't hear.

"Sorry?"

"You a dealer, Denny?" she asked, leaning back in her bench, popping a bubble gum bubble loudly.

"I'm sorry? What?" Denny's eyes darted around the room, looking for security. "Why the? How? How do you know my name? Who are you?"

"Relax," she said, sliding his dealer badge across the table. "You left this in the lobby on the floor after your wallet exploded. Has your name. Quite a show you put on out there."

"What?" he said, looking at the badge, which he vaguely recalled having seen when the con staff member handed it to him. "Wow. Sorry. Thanks. That's great. I'm usually not... these are so hard to get, you know. It would have been forever to replace. Rare. Very rare. You have to prove you're a dealer and tell them what you're selling and you have to pay for the table in the dealer room and all that and without the badge, I mean, wow, thanks. Sorry about that."

She scratched her lip with her thumb for a second and looked at him. In a fractioned moment, for the slightest flutter of a butterfly wing, her eye twitched, almost glancing down to Denny's side, but stopping. He put his hand to the package on the bench next to him.

"What do you sell, Denny?" she asked.

"Rarities," he said. "You know. The real hard-to-find stuff. Horror. Gaming."

"Stuff perfect for a horror convention," she said.

He nodded enthusiastically.

"Creepy hotel, right?" she said. "Easy to get lost. All out here in deep nowhere on the river. Did you see the river? Did you look into it?"

"I kind of just came straight in to the hotel with my stuff when I got here."

"Did you look into it?" she urged. "Did you look into the river?"

"I mean, I guess, maybe. Sorry. I don't think so. It was kind of gray and mucky out."

"So, you looked into the river?"

"I don't know." Denny shrugged. "Maybe. I guess so."

"Did it look back?"

Denny froze, his lips not moving. Not a quiver. No breath taken. He didn't blink and stared at her.

"I'm Lulu," she said, breaking the silence and reaching out a hand wrapped in torn fingerless black fishnet gloves.

"Denny," he said, slowly reaching to take her hand in his. "Sorry, you knew that. Never mind. I mean, I'm still Denny. But you knew. Thanks for the card back."

Another pop of bubble gum snapped through the room over the sounds of adjacent conversation. She turned to the bearded waiter that approached.

"Ready to order?" the waiter rumbled, unceremoniously dropping napkin wrapped silverware to the table.

Lulu tilted her head and looked to Denny. Denny broke away from her stare to look to the waiter, then back to Lulu. Then he looked to the menu. He picked up the dealer badge she returned to him and read his name on it. He looked into her red eyes and back to the waiter.

"Cajun fries," she said. "Fried calamari app. And two colas. Thanks."

"Very good," the waiter said. He nodded, turned on heel and left them.

"I'll take that as my reward for returning your badge,"

she said. A loud pop of bubble gum startled him. She grinned. "That okay? We sit here and you buy me some food?"

"Sure," he said. "I guess. Yes. Yes. That's okay. I can't go to my room. It's not ready. I have the dealer badge. But no room. I have to wait. They have to call me when my room is set. I mean ready. Ready. Set."

"Then we can wait together."

If she had asked to discuss the bell curve of success rolling two twenty-sided dice in an advantage roll, Denny could have spoken for an hour. He hadn't anticipated facing a cosplay goth girl alone in the hotel restaurant. He rubbed the linen of his package, trying to coax comfort from it like a purring kitten. He stopped moving his fingers over the surface when it was clear that her eyes twitched that time, looking to his hand over the table, peering. Prying. Leering. Scrying.

He sat back and pulled the package tight to his thigh. Sodas were placed between the silent couple. She picked hers up and stabbed a straw into it. Lifting the glass in a mimed toast, she sipped from the straw.

"Pretty valuable, huh?" she said, indicating the package with a nod.

"Pretty valuable," he said.

Her fingernails scratched the dark wooden tabletop. She inhaled deeply and looked to the bench next to him and then into his eyes.

"Show me," she said, accenting the end of her sentence with a snap of bubblegum.

"What? Here? No. No way. There are too many people. This is too valuable. This is for the dealer's hall, where there's like security guards and stuff and I can lock it in a display case. Not here. No."

Lulu nodded slowly. Again, they sat and looked at each other in silence, surrounded by other travelers, couples who knew how to engage in casual conversation and convention goers waiting for their rooms. Dice clattered pleasantly on one table, followed by a roar of dismay. A large clock behind the bar was ticking by seconds far slower than seconds could possibly take. The waiter came over and placed two plates between them.

"You like calamari, Denny?" Lulu said, pulling silverware from her napkin.

"What?" he said, looking to the plates. One, a steaming pile of heavily seasoned hand cut potato wedges, the other a pile of golden battered squid and tentacle segments. "Sure. Yes. Yes, I've had it. It's good."

She plucked a tiny squid, hung it for a moment from between her lips and took it into her mouth.

"How do you eat with gum in your mouth?" he asked.

She laughed. "By the Gods, he can actually engage in conversation. Look at that. I was beginning to lose hope of you being someone to hang with for the next few days here. Yeah. Special skill, right? Chew gum and eat at the same time. Let's just put it down of one of my very special and unique talents. What's in the package, Denny?"

He froze, a French fry in hand, half the way to his mouth. He turned and slowly looked to the carefully folded linen next to his side.

She looked to him and leaned forward. "It's a book, isn't it, Denny? It's shaped like a big book of some sort. What you got in the book, Denny?"

He shook his head. "Sorry."

She snatched another calamari piece and popped it into her mouth. "Not here, right?"

He chewed the fry and nodded.

"Too many people, right?" she added.

He sipped his cola and nodded.

"That all yours, Denny, all that luggage? Yeah? Horror convention is three days. That's a whole lot of socks for three days. Is that all your product? Anything cool in there? Anything else really valuable?"

"I have a lot to sell," he said. "Some is just, you know, stuff. I'm a dealer."

"Established, but thanks for the reminder. You think it's safe having all this stuff here in this bar? I mean, all these people. And, what, ninety percent of them must be here for the con, right? All looking for some cool deal, some souvenir. Is it safe?"

"What do you mean, safe?" He glanced around and saw the man in sunglasses was at the next table with two others.

"Well, you can't possibly keep an eye on it all, right?" She pointed to his luggage with a potato wedge. "What if you had to go to the bathroom? You're not tugging all that crap in there with you, am I right? The book, maybe. You could bring that book. You need someone to keep an eye on things. Otherwise, this truly is a whole lot of stuff to just have lying around here where someone could maybe grab one of those boxes."

"I'm pretty sure I won't lose my stuff."

"You mean like your dealer badge, Denny? You didn't even know it was gone."

Bubblegum snap.

"I'll keep my own eye on my own stuff, thanks, Lulu. My room will be ready in a few hours."

Bubblegum snap.

"You know, Denny," she sighed. "I have a room already. I got in yesterday. Wanted to have some time to explore the hotel and look into the river. Have you looked into the river?"

Denny shook his head and buried his attention in the Cajun fries. They were on the edge of being too salty, but some sort of sweetness and biting spice tempered the seasonings. He reached with his fork for a piece of the calamari, but found the plate was already cleared. A sip of soda later, he reached for another fry and found that they had finished those as well. He looked for the clock behind the bar. Somehow, they had been there for just under an hour. A bored busboy shuffled over and started clearing the table. Lulu looked to the busboy and smiled. The busboy smiled unevenly back and retreated with the plates.

Denny's phone rang. He struggled it from a pocket.

"It's the hotel," he said, showing Lulu the number on the screen. "I wonder if my room's ready."

"You're supposed to answer it," she said over the repeated ringtone.

"Right," he said, putting it to his ear. "Hello, this is Denny. Oh. That's OK. I'll wait. Thanks."

"Sir," the waiter approached, holding out the bill.

Denny nodded and squirmed in the seat to put his phone away and tug his wallet out. He opened it and rifled through the plastic cards there.

"Psst," Lulu said. He looked to her. She held his debit card between the fingertips of her first and second finger and offered it to him.

"How?" he said, more to himself than the curiously discomforting girl or the waiter, looking at the card for a moment and handing it over with the bill.

"Fell out when you put your dealer badge away," she said.

His brow scrunched, struggling to remember a moment when he put the badge away, watching the waiter run the card through a portable reader.

"Your card, sir," the waiter said, handing it back. He turned and bumped into Denny's trolley.

"Sorry," Denny said, sliding to stand and pulling his linen package with him. He tried to slip the debit card back into his wallet with his one free hand.

"Come on, let's get out of here," Lulu said, tugging his luggage cart.

"Hey," Denny said, standing and forcing his wallet back into his pocket. "Don't. It's okay, I got this."

"Like your debit card and your badge?" she said, pulling the cart behind her and leading him from the restaurant. "Relax. You bought snacks. Just helping a friend out."

"A friend?" he asked, trailing her into the lobby. She pulled his luggage in front of the elevator, next to the man wearing sunglasses.

"We can't go to my room," Denny said. "It's not ready yet. They said I have to wait a bit. They're busy and short staffed."

The door to the elevator slid open and two men stepped out, nearly bumping into Denny. He danced between them, watching Lulu pull his luggage in behind her.

"Not your room," she said. "We're going to mine."

Denny felt his body jump in shock. He turned to the man in sunglasses. The man gave a slow nod and thumbs up to Denny, stepping back to allow Denny into the elevator. Denny stepped in to grab the luggage cart back. He looked to the still nodding man as the doors started sliding shut between them.

"Wait," Denny said to the man. "You're not coming? Please?"

The doors hissed, gently thudded together and the elevator pulled them up.

"Do I make you nervous?" Lulu asked, looking around the luggage stacked between them. Strange gold lighting from the elevator ceiling made the blue highlights of her hair look more like hardened and cracked jade.

"Very," he said before he could think of not saying it. "I mean. Not more than usual. I'm always a bit. No. No, you don't. That's just me. You're cool."

"Thanks, Denny," she said, tugging his luggage into the hall after the doors reopened.

"You know, I'm good, this is good. We don't have to go to your room or anything."

He looked up and down the empty hall, holding his

package tightly to his chest and following her as she guided the trolley along.

"Where will you store all this stuff until your room is ready then?" she said, shouldering her door open and pushing in. He watched his luggage disappear into her room.

"How old are you?" he called in over the luggage. He watched the luggage turn a corner and stepped in. He had no idea they had such large suites at the hotel. He assumed his room would be too tight to even comfortably walk around the bed. Lulu's suite had a kitchen. The bedroom was off to the side, luxurious in dark blue and green tones highlighted by a copper headed bedframe under a painting of a whaling ship. She pushed the luggage cart against a wall of the central room.

She wiped her hands on black and ripped jeans, smiling up at him.

"I promise," she said, heading to the sink in the kitchen and filling a glass of water. "I'm older than you think. So much older than you think."

The click of the door to the hallway shutting echoed like a cell door from Alcatraz in Denny's ears.

"Water?" she asked, holding the glass to Denny.

He shook his head. She finished the contents and placed the glass in the sink.

"Now," she said, walking toward him. He stepped back. "Show me what you're selling."

"I can't," he said, tightening his hug on the canvas package. "We're alone."

She rolled her eyes. "You can't show me downstairs, it's too crowded. You can't show me upstairs, it's not crowded enough. Seriously, Denny. How do you expect to sell anything if no one ever gets to see it?"

"It's not that. It's more like—"

She held up her hand to cut him off. "I'll show you mine if you show me yours."

The words he thought he was saying was 'really, what, no'. The sound his mouth made was closer in his ears to 'R'lyeh wgah'nagl'.

She laughed, stepped forward, put her hand on top of his hands clasped tightly over the packaged book, and shoved.

Denny yelped at the surprising force she put against him. He stumbled back and fell to the bed. She stepped into the bedroom and flicked the switch on. An elaborate crystal chandelier sparked the room to life, casting fractured shadows to the dark curtains.

"Interesting choice of room, Denny," she said, her arms to either side of the doorframe, blocking his way.

"What? No. You pushed me."

"Show me what you have."

Denny's eyes widened and he struggled to a sitting position against the overly thick and soft blanket that threatened to engulf him. He was sure his room wouldn't have incredibly thick and soft blankets.

"The book, Denny," she said in an inky, slithering voice, taking a single step toward him." Show me the book."

"Why?"

She moved to the curtains, slid a slight opening between them and peered through, a gray outside light flooding her face. She looked down and then let the curtains fall closed.

"Have you looked into the river, Denny?" she asked, pulling on the curtains to straighten them. "You ask why. Why do I want to see your secret book? I'm a collector. A collector of rarities, Denny. Show me. Wow me."

"It's unfair," he said, squirming off the bed. "It's going to the dealer's hall. This is special and I need to make sure I get the best price I can. I can't let anyone see it before then. That would be unfair. This is special. I'm taking offers. In case another collector has another deal."

276

"What if I bought it from you right here?"

"No," he said, stepping away from her. "I might get a lot more on the floor."

"Or less," she said, deliberately walking toward him by the foot of the bed with measured footsteps. "I would make a very generous offer I promise. If what you have fits my collection, I have the power to offer you a great deal."

"You don't even know what I have in here."

"Because you won't show me," she said, pushing her bottom lip out.

He took another step back as she reached to put her hand on the carefully grasped package. He looked at her. The contact lenses were not the same. It wasn't just red irises now. At some point, she had switched to scleral lenses that covered even the whites of her eyes as large glistening red orbs.

"Show me," she said, her voice the rushing sound of foam on a darkened beach.

He slid back and his heel struck the wall. She reached out and put a hand over his, still grasping the package. She slid her hand slowly up the pale linen wrapping. He looked down to his treasure, her glistening fingernail poking over the top. The finger that followed, pressing down on the book, was dark, slick and oily. It vibrated and split. A tiny mouth opened on the gray fingertip. Her other fingers followed, squelching and sliding over the top of the book, small writhing eels, black and visionless eyes opening on the sides of each, pushing through the rubbery surface of her skin.

"Have you looked into the river?" she asked again, her head swaying unnaturally. She brought her face close to his over his book. Her nose had retracted, leaving a strange wet indentation pulsing in the middle of her face. He turned, repelled by the appearance and the sudden strong stench of rotting lobster on her breath. Her eel-like fingers crested over the top of the book, probing to the folded opening of the linen sack to pull it open and down, revealing the green leather top of the tome he had been hiding.

"What is it, Denny?" she said, the words sliding from between too many needle-like teeth. "What are you hiding from us?"

He tightened his grip and watched a long black whip of a tongue circle her lips.

"It's magic," he said. "Okay? It's magic."

She wrapped her eel fingers, sparkling and damp, tiny teeth nipping, around his wrist and pulled with a strength he had never felt before, leaving him cradling the half-unwrapped book in one arm.

"It's just magic," he said, shaking his head and pressing back into the wall behind him. "Rare magic. That's all it is."

She leaned to him, one putrid hand holding his wrist helpless and away. The long black tongue lashed out and licked his cheek. Her bulbous red eyes blinked vertically and she smiled. She released his wrist and the five black warted eels that were once her fingers latched into the flesh around his neck.

Pinning him to the wall with one hand, she pulled the book from his grip with the other. She shook the linen wrap free to the floor and lifted Denny against the wall, his feet dangling. Her red orbs looked to him and she grinned the smile of an angler fish. The eels opened their mouths and she released him. He crumpled to the floor, gagging, trying to catch a gulp of the rotten ocean scented air that filled the room like a choking miasma.

She moved sinuously and smoothly as oil on the surface of the ocean, to settle on the bed, his stolen treasure in her drenching hands. She flipped the cover slowly opened. She lay the book before her, mouth a wide surprised O, taking in wet and raspy breaths as she beheld the contents. Her eel fingers probed and danced over the plastic laminated pages, blind eyes seeking.

"Denny," she breathed, looking to where he struggled to his hands and knees in the corner of her bedroom. "Is this really an unplayed alpha edition black lotus? And the mox set? Oh, my God. The whole power nine?"

"I told you." He coughed, rubbing his neck and drying it. "It's just rare magic cards."

"Dude, I'll buy them all, book value plus twenty percent," she announced. Lulu bounced off the bed, glided to the doorway, turned and blinked red eyes at him. "I have my blue-black deck in the other room for the tournament, but I think it still needs tweaking. Get up. We gotta play."

END.

The Call of Hastur

A.R.R. Ash

About the Author: A.R.R. ASH is a lifelong fan of both science fiction and fantasy, though he typically focuses his talents on writing dark, epic fantasy (some would say grimdark). His first independently published novel, *The Moroi Hunters*, is available digitally and in print through www.LMPBooks.com. His story, "Chapter 16," appeared in the anthology *Socially Distant: The Quarantales*, also by Impulsive Walrus Books. He has received a Silver Honorable Mention and two Honorable Mentions from the L. Ron Hubbard's Writers of the Future Contest. Those stories are available to read at the above website. *Xy: Descent*, the first book of his *The First Godling* trilogy, is undergoing editing, and he continues to make progress on *The Tribe of Fangs*, a prequel novel to *The Moroi Hunters*.

In other trivia, his favorite dishes are burgers and sushi (but not together), his favorite series is *Dune*, though *The Expanse* by James S. A. Corey is making a run for the title, and his sense of humor is decidedly an acquired taste.

THE CALL OF HASTUR
A.R.R. ASH

I.

The moonlight glinted off the water, turning the ferry's wake into a glittering trail of liquid diamonds. Standing at the ferry's gunwale, Phelicity breathed in the night air and the spray from the Providence River. In the fog-shrouded distance, she could just descry the imposing black shape of Hastur Manor, revealing itself like one of the eternal creatures out of the mists of time from the cosmic horror stories that Asher liked. Phelicity couldn't believe that it had once been someone's home—the structure was enormous, easily large enough to double as a hotel.

Asher, Phelicity's boyfriend, settled beside her, resting his hands on the railing, his shoulder lightly brushing hers.

"There it is!"

Phelicity felt his excitement transferred through their light touch. "Mmhmm."

"I've wanted to visit for years. I know Cthulhu isn't your thing, but I'm really glad you came." Asher wrapped his arm around Phelicity's shoulders. The heat of that embrace not only comforted against the chill February night but spread a warmth beneath her chest as well.

Contrasted with Asher's black T-shirt depicting an, admittedly, creepy squid-like creature, Phelicity wore, beneath an unbuttoned, long-sleeved, flannel shirt, a light blue tee that reproduced the cover of Nirvana's album *Nevermind*.

Phelicity rested her head on his shoulder. "I've never been to anything like this, so…who knows? Maybe it'll be my thing."

The ferry docked along a quay extending from the island on which Hastur Manor was the only structure. The manor sat atop a low, stony hill not far from the rocky shore; the remainder of the island was covered in loose stone, grass, and sporadic trees.

Dressed in smart blue slacks and a clean, white, short-sleeved Polo, a crewmember on the ferry opened a gate set into the bulwark and lowered a short plank onto the concrete-piled quay. The passengers began to disembark.

Phelicity and Asher walked hand-in-hand, each pulling a single, wheeled suitcase along the short pier. From the dock, a simple, paved path led up the stony slope and to the manor.

Phelicity shivered. "Did it seem to just get much colder?"

Asher shrugged. "Must have been the wind."

The throng of excited con-goers crowded around them and, eager to enter the manor, passed them. Asher squeezed Phelicity's hand, looking at her and smiling his goofy, enthusiastic smile. Just off the path before reaching the front doors of the manor was a rectangular plaque, set at a vertical slant atop a squat pedestal. Phelicity paused to read the plaque in the glow of the single light ensconced above the door:

Hastur Manor was home to Randolph Carter (born 1874), founder of the Lovecraftian Association. Upon Carter's death in 1980, in accordance with his will, the annual conventions of the association, previously closed to all but inducted members, were opened to the public, and

Hastur Manor was converted into a hotel to accommodate the increased guests.

"Huh," Phelicity said, her lips parted slightly in mild surprise.

"What?" Asher prompted.

"This place has a long history is all. I didn't expect that."

"See?" Asher flashed a wide smile. "I knew you'd start to like it."

Phelicity chuckled. "Let's not get ahead of ourselves."

The two large black doors of the hotel were embossed with a black sigil in the shape of three angular tentacles extending from a central oval. With the hotel's black stone construction, crossing the threshold gave Phelicity the impression of entering the maw of some awesome, stony beast.

"The Sign of Koth," Asher said, nodding his chin toward the sigil.

"Huh?"

"It's used to seal doors against unwanted entry," he explained as if it were the most normal thing in the world.

Phelicity didn't know how to reply to that, so she allowed the silence to stretch until offering a response would have been more awkward than not.

As they walked the hall, Phelicity became distracted by the architecture and décor within the hotel. The flooring shone from the highly polished, plain, dark wood, and matching wainscotting covered the walls. Light shone from black-iron wall sconces and chandeliers in the form of nightmarish interpretations of real-world animals—bulls, monkeys and gorillas, vultures, hyenas. Black-iron balustrades, wrought in intricate designs like those of the sconces, lined the curving, wooden staircases. The ground floor was open and spacious, though higher stories had narrower hallways and lower ceilings.

After checking in at the front desk, Phelicity and Asher took the stairs to the third floor—the manor-turned-hotel had no elevator—and settled in to their quaintly appointed room of old-style carpeting and simple furniture for a short nap.

@@@

II.

The scheduled events of Cthulhu FhCon were held during the night, leaving the day for sleep and recuperation. Phelicity and Asher left their room just after 7:30 PM and headed to the banquet hall that served as the opening session for the con.

Some two hundred attendees squeezed into the hall. Phelicity looked with wide eyes at the assortment of polypous, tentacled cosplay. She even saw at least one Conan among the crowd. Asher wore his grin like a costume and pointed out the creatures he recognized: "That's a Xiurhn. There's a Brown Jenkin. And, oh, she's Pherol the Black!"

Phelicity didn't know what any of those words meant, but she smiled and nodded as if it all fascinated her.

They found two seats together near the center middle of the room and delicately made their way past the snaking, protruding appendages of the seated con-goers.

"Oh, excuse me," Phelicity said with an embarrassed smile upon stepping on an oversized, clawed foot with an eye atop.

Once seated, they didn't have long to wait before three bizarre forms took the stage at the head of the hall. The audience greeted their appearance with a buzz of enthusiastic conversation.

A shiver of disconcertment traversed Phelicity's spine. The three on stage were quite tall, standing well over seven feet, and had trilateral symmetry, with three long legs, three arms, and three eyes. Their skin was squamous, like that that of a fish, and showed many different colors that blended into one another.

"Wow!" she said breathlessly. "Those are incredible costumes."

"I know, right?" Asher agreed. "They're amazing! They're supposed to be Antareans, an advanced race of spacefarers"—his voice assumed an air of authority—"but I think their crests are a little off."

Once the excited drone of speech calmed, the middle form on stage spoke, its voice watery and tinny, as if passed through a synthesizer, "We welcome you all to this, the fifty-fifth annual Cthulhu FhCon."

A round of cheers went up from the crowd.

"Some of you are new faces, some we recognize from years past. You are all welcome to this celebration of a mind who grasped cosmic secrets most couldn't begin to imagine.

"Please, enjoy the panels and gaming rooms. On Monday, the fifty-fifth day of the year, we invite everyone to attend the closing ceremony. We promise an unveiling you'll not forget."

Phelicity could feel the building kinetic energy of the crowd, a frenetic excitement that the enclosed space of the hall could barely contain. Despite her own ignorance of all things Cthulhu, Phelicity felt a rush at the shared experience and could feel herself being swept away by the impassioned wave of emotion.

"Before we release you," the strangely modulated voice continued, "join us in The Call: *Ph'nglui mglw'nafh Hastur Aldebaran wgah'nagl fhtagn.*"

Phelicity had no inkling what the gibbering, jarring sounds meant, yet she found herself repeating them along with everyone else in the hall. The inhuman-sounding voices of the hosts droned in perfect time, the sound of their voices almost naturally complementing the bizarre utterances.

Upon completion of the recitation, Phelicity shook her head and blinked a couple times, as if starting into consciousness after nodding off. Glancing at Asher, she saw recognition rekindle in his glazed eyes as well. Indeed, the whole crowd appeared to be awakening from a trance.

Nevertheless, the sensation lasted but a moment, and, soon, the buzz of conversation and the sounds of sliding chairs, lifted bags, and moving bodies again filled the hall.

Asher took Phelicity's hand, squeezed, and, walking slowly among the press of bodies, led her from the room. Once outside the hall, the crowd began to disperse as everyone headed to their chosen events. Moving off to the side, Asher pulled a folded schedule from a pocket and perused the events.

"Hmm. They have a panel on recurring themes in Lovecraft's writings," Asher read. "One on Lovecraft's influence on the genre of cosmic horror. The gaming room is open. Ooh, tomorrow is the costume competition. We have to go to that!"

Phelicity smiled politely, not experiencing the same giddiness as her boyfriend. *His* excitement was palpable, though, and she felt vicarious enjoyment through him.

They spent the next couple hours listening to panelists present serious, scholarly, well-thought-out commentary on the metaphysical meaning and social effect of Lovecraft's corpus. Phelicity was surprised to find that the same parts of her that loved grunge music were fascinated by the motifs of angst, alienation, and isolation in his works—albeit focused on the more universal sense of humanity rather than on a personal level as in grunge.

The last forum they attended that night was a speculative fan panel about the possibility of a Hollywood movie based on "The Call of Cthulhu." Though morning was yet an hour off, Phelicity and Asher started losing their battle against sleep and decided to turn in for the day.

However, despite her exhaustion, she slept fitfully, with dreams troubled by visions of strange tripodal creatures and awesome, tentacled, world-devouring beasts.

III.

Phelicity and Asher awoke, yawning, in the late afternoon. Showering and eating quickly, they made for the banquet hall where the costume contest would be held. For hours, they sat in rapt attention as contestants displayed one impressive costume after another: An antehuman—a species of tall, lanky, super-intelligent humans who predated Homo sapiens—followed an Antarean—which was a shabby reproduction beside the costumes of the three hosts—leading into an alien-insect hybrid creature. The hosts, serving as judges, voted a fleshy batrachian as the winner.

Following the contest and a hastily consumed snack, Asher was intent on visiting the gaming room.

"Okay, I'll meet you there. I just want to go get some water from the vending machine," Phelicity said in response to Asher's statement of his intention.

"Bring me one too, please."

"Will do."

They leaned in and gave one another a peck on the lips. As they parted, Phelicity's head swam in a sudden, inexplicable premonition. It wasn't a specific prescience, just an acute sense of wrongness. However, it was gone as quickly as it came, and Phelicity shook her head as if that could clear it of the memory.

Phelicity ascended to the second-floor landing, where a vending machine—seeming so incongruous beside the gloomy, bleak interior design—nestled in the corner. She pulled fifty cents from her blue jean pocket, the coins clinking as they descended the chute, then pressed D21.

"Ugh!" D21 wasn't even available; she'd meant to press D12. She must have been distracted by the lingering disconcertment from the earlier sense of foreboding. However, when Phelicity pressed the coin return button, she found herself jumping backward in alarm when the vending machine swung outward revealing a low opening in the wall.

"Huh? What?" Phelicity tentatively peeked around the corner to look into the dark passage beyond. In the light from the landing, she could see that stairs descended from the opening.

Above the portal someone had inscribed a bizarre symbol, similar but different from the sigil on the front doors of the hotel. It was yellow, outlined in black, and just its appearance caused Phelicity to shiver and brought to mind ancient profanities best left undisturbed.

Phelicity chuckled at her own inarticulate, irrational fear. She was at a con filled with obsessive fans of a long-dead author of strange horror. Of course the people running the convention set up some game like this for the attendees. Indeed, the threefold design of the yellow sign reminded Phelicity of the—what did Asher call them?— Anteans.

Phelicity shrugged, took a deep breath, and stepped through the portal, ducking her head beneath the lintel. As soon as she passed the threshold, the vending machine swung back into place, blocking the light from the landing. Phelicity's heart skipped in momentary panic before strips of lighting along either side of the stairs flared into a yellow glow.

Phelicity slowly descended the wooden stairs, keeping one hand pressed against the wood paneling to her right. Her breathing echoed, the lone sound in the stairwell; her heartbeat quickened in a mix of excitement and fear, like when riding a roller coaster. The air smelled of dust and old wood.

After Phelicity descended to at least the level of the ground floor, the wooden stairs ended, and stone steps, seemingly carved out of the ground itself, began. The wood-paneled walls transitioned into gray rough-hewn rock, and the odor of rock dust replaced the woody smell. The illumination strips continued with only a small break at the transition.

"This...isn't creepy at all," Phelicity said aloud in an overt attempt to calm her growing sense of unease. "How deep can these stairs go?"

Just before she decided to turn back, Phelicity heard voices ahead. She couldn't make out the words, but they resembled the underwater-synthesizer sound of the Antean-costumed hosts. Despite the lesson from every horror movie she'd ever seen, Phelicity found herself continuing, reaching the bottom of the stairs.

A corridor led from the right. She stopped and peeked around the corner. No one—though she could still hear the voices reverberating down the tunnel bored through solid stone. Her Doc Martens crunched on the ground of the tunnel floor as she crept down the passage.

Several other passages branched off, but the voices led her unerringly on. Finally, she came to an opening to a path descending around the perimeter of an open, circular chamber.

The smooth, gray walls of the chamber reflected the glow of the lights embedded along their circumference. Phelicity ran her hand along the interior wall—cold metal.

On the metallic floor of the chamber, the three still-costumed hosts stood around a circular column, about human height. Three vertical control panels of a technology Phelicity didn't recognize were mounted around it. Otherwise, the chamber was empty.

Phelicity ducked back into the corridor, though she inched her head around the corner to observe the trio in secret.

"The time is upon us. Just one day more." The watery, electronic voice reverberated around the chamber, and Phelicity felt the sound in her bones.

"Will they be enough?" a second asked.

"My calculations are flawless," the first replied.

"Then, soon, The Unspeakable One will have Its deserved victory over the Dread Lurker."

Phelicity didn't know what to make of any of this. Was it some sort of LARPing?

One of the hosts tilted its head upward, and Phelicity jerked her head back into the corridor. In that instant, she saw real malevolence in its prismatic eyes. She gasped and put a hand to her mouth. Whatever this meeting was, Phelicity was sure of one thing: She hadn't been meant to see it.

A burst of frenzied, computerized speech came from below, and Phelicity, with no thought to subtly or stealth, ran back the way she came. Despite the seeming awkwardness of their costumes, Phelicity heard the inhuman voices behind her getting louder as the distance closed. Phelicity pushed herself, breath coming in heavy gasps and calves burning as she took the stairs two or three at a time. She didn't dare look back for fear of tripping or slowing. The stone steps became wooden, and still she didn't allow herself to pause.

The voices grew louder and more urgent. Phelicity reached the top and pushed against the back of the vending machine.

It didn't move.

Frantically, chest heaving, she ran her hands over the surface and looked for a release. She felt a small handle, and moved it upward, then heard a faint click. Phelicity put her shoulder against the vending machine, pushed, and squeezed through the opening. Sliding closed the machine, she ran downstairs in search of Asher.

As she searched the gaming room, all she could do

was hope that the three hadn't seen her clearly. She found Asher sitting at a long table with a small group of players and rolling a pair of polyhedron dice over a game board in the design of a cavernous dungeon.

When he saw her, Asher's wide smile was spontaneous, though his features quickly fell in concern. "I was worried. You were gone so long."

Phelicity looked around the room as if expecting to see her pursuers at any moment. "I'm okay. I just need to talk to you about something."

"Now?" His voice raised and cracked, like a child who thought he was about to be punished or was being told that he had to stop playing and clean his room.

She nodded. "Yeah."

"Bu—okay." He set down the dice and, looking at the other three players, shrugged. "Sorry, gotta go."

They nodded or mumbled farewells, but they didn't interrupt their game.

Phelicity took Asher by the hand and led him from the room.

"Whoa, your hand is really sweaty, Phelicity. You sure you're okay?"

"Mmhmm."

"Where are we going?" Asher asked, confusion and worry in his voice.

"Our room." Phelicity was brusque in her response.

"Ohhh." Asher gave a goofy smile, his amorous thoughts plain on his face.

"Ugh, not now. I have to tell you something."

Asher's entire body seemed to deflate. "Okay."

Back in their room, door bolted, Phelicity allowed herself a moment's respite and calm. She sat on the bed, and Asher settled beside her.

"What's wrong?" he asked, taking her hand and looking into her eyes.

"I saw—I heard something. I didn't mean to." Phelicity

stumbled over her own words as she tried to organize her thoughts.

"Oh?" he prompted.

"Something strange."

Asher gave an amused scoff. "This is a Cthulhu con. Strange is the norm."

"No! No." Phelicity bunched the comforter in her fists in frustration. She took a deep breath, then began again. "I found a passage behind a vending machine—"

"Huh, where?"

Phelicity didn't pause in her account. "I went to explore and heard voices. I saw the three hosts, and they sounded like they had something strange planned. Something... bad."

Asher's face scrunched in confusion. "Bad? What did they say?"

Phelicity sighed, shook her head. "I don't remember... exactly. Something about calculations and an unspeaking person."

Asher chortled. "Calculations—now, that does sound scary." Phelicity narrowed her eyes at him, and he hurried on, "Hmm. Unspeaking person? Unspeaking...do you mean *unspeakable*?"

"Yes!" Phelicity's whole body lifted off the bed momentarily in the forcefulness of her exclamation. "That was it."

"I mean, there is an Unspeakable One—Hastur—in the Cthulhu mythos, but I'm not sure what they'd be referring to."

"I'll show you the passage," Phelicity said, face lighting in vindication.

Asher patted the air. "Tomorrow. I'm sooo tired."

Phelicity, briefly, pouted her bottom lip, ready to argue. However, in the quiet shelter of their room, the earlier fear seemed far away, and she couldn't deny the weight of her own exhaustion. "Okay. Tomorrow."

IV.

Phelicity awoke surprised at the soundness of her sleep, but, then, fear was an exhausting emotion. Asher was still asleep, and she shook him awake. "Get up. Let's get going."

"Wh-what? Already?" His words slurred as if inebriated. When Phelicity opened the old yellow curtain, he put an arm over his eyes to block the incoming light.

"Come on," she insisted.

"Okay, okay, but I need something to eat first." He yawned and rubbed his eyes.

After their morning ablutions, Asher took a light breakfast of fruit, bagels, and lox, then Phelicity led him to the vending machine on the second-floor landing and repeated the procedure that had opened the way to the passage.

When the machine again swung outward, Phelicity sighed, having hoped, in the lucid light of day, that she had imagined the whole episode. The open corridor before her meant it all hadn't been a dream—she wasn't sure if that made her feel any better.

"Whoa, cool!" Asher grinned, and his eyes opened wide.

Phelicity frowned. Asher might think it was all fun and games, but she thought more was going on. "Come on."

Hand in hand, they entered the passage, and, like the previous night, the lights came alive and the machine swung closed behind them.

"Awesome!"

Phelicity squeezed Asher's hand as if to reassure herself of his presence and reality. They descended the wooden stairs, though, where Phelicity expected them to transition to stone, the passage turned and leveled off.

"Huh? That's not right." Phelicity stopped and looked around in confusion.

"What?" Asher looked around as well, though he couldn't know what it was she looked for.

"The passage didn't turn like this. It kept going down," Phelicity said as if accusing the passage of participating in a conspiracy against her.

"Hmm. Are you sure?" Asher's tone was dubious.

Phelicity released Asher's hand. "Of course."

"Umm, well..." Asher shrugged and raised his hands questioningly.

Phelicity huffed and continued down the passage; Asher followed. The passage continued in a straightaway for some time, then up, down, up, down, left, right, seemingly without end.

Asher stopped. "Okay, this is weird." His voice held a tremulous quality. "No way all of this could be inside the hotel. Let's turn back."

Phelicity nodded, silently thankful that he had been the one to suggest it, so that she wouldn't seem like the fearful one. However, the return didn't follow the reverse of their entrance, rather leading them down, left, up, right, left, straight, and, ultimately, to a dead end overlooking the hall where the closing ceremony was taking place.

Both looked through the grating to the assembled con-goers below and the two—only two?—Anterean hosts on stage.

"Huh? How long were we wandering around?" Asher asked out loud, though appearing not to expect an answer.

One of the tripod-like creatures was speaking, "We want to thank everyone for making this such a successful convention."

The crowd cheered.

The aqueous-electronic voice continued, "Now, if you'll join us in another Call to mark the end of the festivities." It spoke the words in the jarring, inhuman tongue: "*Y'ai 'ng'ngah, Hastur h'ee – l'geb f'ai throdog uaaah.*"

In a loud, reverberating chorus, the crowd recited the

words. As the recitation ended, the collective voices of the crowd rose in a new sound—anguish. Even as Phelicity and Asher watched, the bodies of everyone assembled began to shrivel, to desiccate, and the room filled with rising, misty, undulating forms.

The second host on the stage made a sound like someone cackling into a submerged microphone. "We thank you for your sacrifice. With your life energy, we can power this vessel to Aldebaran and lead He Who Is Not to Be Named here, that It might destroy Its half-brother, Cthulhu, while the Sleeper of R'lyeh slumbers."

The individual vaporous forms moved in unison, like an eldritch cloud, toward the grating where Phelicity and Asher hid. Both yelped as the mist passed over them, though they felt nothing more than a shiver as from a blast of cold air from a vent. Soon, the cloud had disappeared down the passage.

"Let's get out of here!" Asher grabbed Phelicity's hand, and he nearly dragged her back the way they'd come.

Again, the corridors had changed, though, this time, after descending a wooden staircase, they found a door. At a turn of the knob, the door opened without resistance. Exiting, the two found themselves in the lobby of the hotel.

Phelicity was sure a door hadn't been there before, but she didn't waste time considering the anomaly. They ran out the front doors of the hotel and down the path toward the quay.

The entire island shook, knocking Phelicity and Asher to their hands and knees; the loose rocks bit into their palms. Behind them, the hotel collapsed. From the rubble rose a sleek, metallic ship, shaped like an elongated bullet with four long fins running its length and placed equidistant around its cylindrical fuselage.

As Phelicity and Asher watched, the vessel hovered horizontally above the island, then shot off into the night sky.

...And now for something completely different...

SHAOLIN TENTACLES

PETER J. WACKS

About the Author: PETER J. WACKS was born Jebediah Jason Zarathustra Janney Shults, then was quickly reminted the next day to a saner name on his second birth certificate. After that intro, he never really established normalcy in his life. Peter (or Zarth, whatever, it's cool) has traveled to thirty-seven countries, hitchhiked across the United States (very funny, no, he didn't hitchhike to Hawaii), and backpacked across Europe. He loves fast cars, running 5Ks, space travel, and armchair physics. In the past, Peter has been an actor and game designer, but he loves writing most and has done a ton of it, which can be found by looking him up online (even if it seems a little cyber-stalkery, don't worry, go for it!) Since he doesn't think anyone reads these things anyway, he will mention strawberry daiquiris, Laphroaig, great IPAs, and really clever puns are the best way to start conversations with him. Are you still there? The bio is over. Go read.

SHAOLIN TENTACLES
PETER J. WACKS

Madness takes a toll, but no greater than that of sanity. John Doe slung the convention badge lanyard around his neck and headed out of the hotel to the riverfront. There was barely 100 feet between the rear doors and the water, an embankment covered by lush grass and foliage. On the towpath he knelt, placing a hand in the river, feeling the cool waters wash over his fingers. It was electrified by the power of the rune the river happened to mimic the shape of; something a mortal would never sense, and the reason he had to be *sure* there was no other presence here. Closing his eyes, he whispered, "⟨runes⟩." Water swirled, glimmering droplets climbing, merging, morphing through shapes as glowing beads revealed a hooded figure. "⟨runes⟩!" he shouted, slapping a hand through the visage and dispersing it with a splash.

Somewhere in this hotel, obviously built by cultists, was the Servant God. The only being in the universe both awake and with the means to awaken all of the Great Old Ones. Every cult that comes close to success, he's always behind them... and his presence would mean a horde of cultists here.

John thought back to Berlin, and the seven dead actors there. He'd had to collect from their corpses, and his preference was a live specimen. That had been just cultists, without a being like the

Servant even there. Precision was his modus operandi. But cultists... they were the wrong type of fanatical. It always went poorly when they popped up.

The collection could not be endangered, and John could think of no bigger threat than who the waters had just shown him.

He headed back to the hotel, pulling out his phone. His call went straight to voicemail and he grunted in frustration. "Dammit Fuu. Where are you?"

Unnoticed behind John, the same figure the watery spell had shown melted out of the background. In the flesh, he had skin darker than midnight and wore a deep green cloak and long twin daggers slung from his back. He stared at the water, then back toward the Red Lye Inn. A slow smile spread across his features in stark contrast to the madness and malice glowing in his eyes.

Fuu cursed the traffic. It was rather ineffectual, as she had no power to enact a curse, and even if she had such power, it would only have served to further slow her. But... it did make her feel a modicum better. Bumper to bumper cars stretched endlessly, a Machiavellian obstacle course of modern civic engineering. It reminded her of the M25, surrounding London... down to the same feel of hopelessness and despair grinding out evil...

Realization slapped her across the face.

That was *exactly* what it felt like! She hit her flashers and hopped out of her crème white 1963 Volkswagen Beetle—named Heart of Gold. Heatwaves rising from the asphalt distorted her view, and she could even smell the rot of low-grade annoyance wafting from the blistering motorway. The gray Oldsmobile behind her honked and she paused, throwing her hands wide. "What? It's not like we're going anywhere!"

The driver of the other car, a David Duchovny clone with extra 5 o'clock shadow, rolled down his window, "Fine. But if traffic starts up again, I'm not letting off the horn till you move!"

"That's fair, thanks!" Fuu gave her best smile, flashing a sideways peace sign. She kicked back a heel, then made a beeline for the front of her car to open the hood, which was, in this type of car, the trunk. Her luggage, containing a mix of clothes for the convention and supernatural detection devices, filled the space.

She rummaged about till she found the psychometer. The device was a long, thin, metal casing made of something she'd never been able to pinpoint, with dull light bars surrounded by rune etchings along it. The runes were, "⌇⊨⊰'⊱ ⫟⊬⊰⬦⤬" and she had no idea what they read, just what they meant overall—bad news. All five bars were glowing red.

"A-Ha!" It confirmed her suspicions. This *was* a massive psychic event generating pure evil. She'd always known traffic jams were bad, but this one wasn't just low grade normal; it was truly evil. And if it was tuned to her, then...

The Oldsmobile driver laid into his horn. Sure enough, as soon as she'd pegged the freeway for what it was, the damn thing was trying to move her. She grunted in exasperation and jammed everything back into the boot of her beetle.

True to his promise, the other driver didn't let off his horn till she was back behind the wheel with her butt planted squarely in the seat. Rather than flip him the bird—thus contributing to the mounting psychic bomb—she gave him a polite 'thank you / I'm sorry' wave. They inched forward about thirty feet, just long enough to distract her from what she had been doing.

With an overly dramatic sigh, she pulled out her phone. Of course. No bars. What the hell was John walking into? She shot off a quick text, relying on the cell towers to push it through once she was expelled from this hellish loop of misery.

Growing up as the daughter of two physicians, Fuu's environment had been all about academic pressure. As a little girl she'd pushed against her parents, taking up martial arts—and throughout her life physical discipline had served her well to relieve mental pressures. Fuu settled in, focusing on her breathing and practicing what Tai Chi forms she could in the small driver's seat of her beetle, knowing that she wouldn't be able to do anything to reverse the diabolical ritual slowing her down.

Frakking traffic jams.

꓅ꓹꓮ ꓦꓰꓨ ꓅ꓹꓩꓮ �

John stared innocently at the Red Lye Inn—instead of the man he'd been tracking for the last ten minutes—the hairs on his arms standing on end. The man bumped him as he passed, heading to the parking lot, and all of John's senses were on red alert. What he had just touched was the filth of the other. That sealed the deal.

"Sorry," The stranger seemed distracted, glancing around nervously, with eyes both darting about and unfocused simultaneously.

"It's fine," John replied.

The man hurried on.

John paused a beat, then followed. The building was built onto the bank of the river—the same one he had just moments before cast the reflection spell on the banks of—right along a bend that shaped the whole into the ancient rune ra'kham. Moving along the line of cars in the lot, they grew inexorably closer to the edge of the building, and the river.

Of frakking course... John thought. *He's a cultist.*

Sure enough, once they rounded the building, the man began tracing out a rune with what looked to be a vial of blood and chanting, *"Am-il-lak... Am-il-lak..."*

John walked up from behind and clasped a hand on either of the cultist's temples. "See your own mind," John hissed into his ear "and the scorpions that fill it." The man screamed and crumpled to the ground, shivering and drooling.

While the cultist contorted on the ground, John scuffed out the rune with the sole of his shoe. Job done, he walked back to the parking lot, into the bright afternoon sun. Where there was one, there were bound to be a horde of them.

He sighed and, with a quick flick of his wrist, flipped open the arms of a pair Blinde "Elipse" 136003s. He slid them over a carefully groomed face till they rested in place above his perfect 5 o'clock shadow and chiseled jaw line. Over toned arms and abs of steel, he wore a tight black t-shirt—with a simple red Cylon eye in the center— complementing matching red skinny jeans which showed off legs that went all the way to the ground. Though well-muscled, he was still lean, a little too thin and bony.

He walked over to his '67 Impala. Magically, in a packed parking lot, the spaces to either side were empty. No one ever parked near him. Popping the trunk of the car revealed a stash of weapons and occult raffia. He dug about till he found a particular amulet, then pocketed it.

On the way back in, he walked past Black Widow and Kakashi Hatake sharing a smoke to the side of the entry, under a cheaply printed banner that read *"Welcome 29th Annual Con-vacation Fandom!"* The hum of power, a vibration only he could feel, grew stronger.

The man in the green cloak strode into the dealer hall, beelining to the 501st recruitment booth. All fire and madness, his gaze pierced their white helmets and locked directly with their souls.

"Yes, sir!" Both snapped to attention.

"There is another here. An ancient enemy. We must ensure preparations are completed immediately."

One of the troopers reeled back in surprise. "Eff me gently with a chainsaw... how are we supposed to—"

"No excuses!" The man barked. "Delay is failure. That little bit of your hindbrain that says it can't be so...make it so. Or I unmake you."

The troopers trembled. "We will spread the word. When tonight?"

"Midnight, the dreaming hour. The death of a day, and the birth of a new holds power. He will be distracted but I will draw his focus." He paused, fidgeting with his cloak, "We are dastardly. We are evil. Tonight, we embody that. Let's be bad guys, villains, harbingers of darkness, and open the gates before our opponent is ready for us."

"Yessir!" they chorused in unison, with a malevolent flare in their auras visible only to the man in green. He was satisfied.

〜⚡✕⟠⚡🜚〜

Fuu exited the freeway, finally free of the grind. Honking—and a palpable air of frustration thicker than peanut butter—receded as she coasted down the off ramp.

"Right," she said to no one in particular. "Time to figure out what the hell is going on."

With a quick left she pulled below the overpass, parking on the shoulder. Shadows beyond those usually formed. The late-afternoon angle of the sun filled the available space with gloom, a psychic layer of sticky, venal vichyssoise, virulent vices made tangible.

Fuu shuddered, "Gross."

Instead of the human smells she would have expected, there was instead an overpowering olfactory oppressiveness, decay and hopelessness made pungently physical.

She pulled out the psychometer, walking back forth below the freeway. Sure enough, it went off the charts while directly below the frustrated motorists and dropped to normal background levels of evil as she emerged from the oppressive gloom. Well, only one way to sort out what the hell was going on.

Digging around the car's boot, she found her runestones. She began a slow set of movements, imagining a ball between her hands, with the stones in the center. Green tracers of light strung between the small rocks as she moved, and they floated in place, the center of the invisible ball she manipulated. Her movements sped up and the energy brightened, arcing from her hands to the underpass wall, where the mystic ritual took hold, and the electrical discharge burned a message into the wall.

She pulled out her pocket notebook, flipping to the alphabet John had scribbled, and looked up each of the runes. "Yuggoth." She knew that word. Someone was channeling energy from the steppingstones of the elder gods to this solar system. For what purpose, she had no clue, but John would know.

Of that, she was sure.

Narrowing her eyes, she thought for a moment. One of the things that made Fuu so unique was that she frequently resisted the impulse to do something, choosing instead to stop and think. It may not sound like much, but if you, well, stop and think about it, resisting the impulse to react favoring instead pausing and figuring out *what* to do is a rarity. As Fuu thought, musings morphed into ideas.

Energy was energy, and just like a human body converted chemical energy to mechanical energy when ATP is hydrolysed during cross-bridge cycling for muscle contraction, this energy was contracting a massive, metaphysical muscle, drawing something or things from Yuggoth. It followed, then, that the trick would be to drain off some of that lifting power and try to make sure there wasn't enough left to finish the job.

Fuu had learned a thing or two about cultist rituals over the years of travelling with John. To channel something this huge, someone used blood. A lot of it. So, she was going to need enough blood to paint runes large enough to fully cross the ceiling of the four-lane overpass.

...And a way to spray it.

Even were she willing, she didn't have enough blood to power that. Instead, she was gonna have to hack the ritual... She studied Heart of Gold, thinking, muttering to herself. "Blood... What is blood? Glucose, hormones, proteins, mineral salts, fat, vitamins... You can do this, Fuu."

Positioning the Heart so its butt was pointed at the overpass, she got to work. When you drove a '63 beetle, you to tended to carry a *lot* of backup bits and parts.

From under the overpass, she knocked over a 55-gallon drum, dumping its contents and rolling it out to the beetle. She righted it, then poured in all her backup radiator water, only a couple gallons. It took a bit of effort, but Fuu bent scraps scavenged from the random detritus in the dark corridor into a sluice, positioning it to feed into the barrel.

She then pulled out leftovers from various stops on the road trip and laid them along the sluice —half a steak, a chicken sandwich; adding a few high protein energy bars selected based on the minerals and vitamins they contained. Finally, she wrestled the spare battery to the sluice's top.

Stabbing the battery with a screwdriver, she ran behind the beetle for cover. Having never tried it before, she'd rather be safe than sorry. In theory, battery acid would pour down the sluice, liquifying the meats and energy bars, then pouring into the water. That part would produce a *lot* of heat, but it only took a mix of about 2 to 1 to make battery acid inert, and this was like 30 to 1. At the end of this, she should have a few gallons of stew made up of glucose, hormones, proteins, mineral salts, fat, and vitamins. Not in a cellular structure but, maybe with a catalyst...

Once the hissing and sputtering stopped, she grabbed her med-kit to add said catalyst—some of her own blood. She stirred the solution, then took a second to carefully apply a Hello Kitty band-aid to the incision on her forearm.

Popping off the radiator hose, she drained it into the empty water bucket and refilled it with the synthetic blood—which had come out more brown than red, but she had confidence it would work. Twisting the key in the ignition, Heart of Gold rumbled to life and Fuu pointed the hose at the ceiling above, using it as a high-pressure sprayer. It took a couple tries and used up all the faux blood—with most ending up on the road—but she managed to roughly paint 3 runes across the bottom of the motorway, stretched from edge to edge.

The three letters phonetically spelled out her name. She had to tear down the rig quickly—Heart of Gold was already choking and overheating, making pre-emptive death-rattles.

Gathering her supplies, she tossed them onto the passenger seat and jammed the car into first gear, sputtering out from the ritual-oppressed area toward the convention hotel. She just had to hope her little beetle would make it before the slop-tainted fluids circulating through the coolant system overpowered it.

"Two thousand, nine hundred, seven. Two thousand, nine hundred, eight." John counted paces, matching them against his Fitbit step count, measuring the distance of the hotel. The rune stretched a mile, end to end, and the exact center seemed to be the check-in desk, but that was an artefact, a trick of the building's design to fool the senses. Another little way to drive mortals mad, without ever noticing something awry. In truth, the center lay in the bar—just off the grand ballroom, where the parties and cosplay contests would be held. He grunted. This would interfere and the final piece of the collection was arriving tomorrow... this had to be dealt with.

He needed to think.

He headed to the hotel lounge, taking a seat at the bar.

"What'll ya have?" The bartender came over, wearing a white button-down shirt, untucked, with an ID badge that identified him as part of the Nerd Herd.

John grunted. That collection of mortals was already complete. "Burger. As close to a Big Mac as you can make it. And a Coke."

The man nodded and headed to the POS.

As John sipped his Coke, he contemplated, albeit briefly, before being interrupted.

A man clad in a dark green cloak settled on the neighboring stool. "Hi, John."

"Hello, Nyarlathotep." John responded. "What name are you going by these days?"

"Same as always, I've no need to hide behind aliases. I'd heard rumor you were awakened. How are you enjoying being in the world?"

John took another sip of his Coke, then spoke, "Well enough."

"I hear you switched sides."

"Sides? I've never played for anyone but myself." The bartender wandered back by, checking on them as John continued, "You know—"

"I'll try a Gargle Blaster off the convention menu." Nyarlathotep leaned forward and clean interrupted John.

John's knuckles went white around the Coke, but his composure held. Were one an elder god, creature from beyond, or other extra-dimensional being the casual conversation would have looked more like this:

The astral plane was filled with gossamer ghosts of desires, dreams, and imaginations tangling and tangoing, so many blind dancers colliding. Some tethered to people, some to locations… other, stranger, ones to deeper realms only glimpsed via fractured madness behind the looking glass.

Central to the landscape were two figures, the focus

of all the chaotic activity. One was humanoid, at least in overall shape, its skin the black of space only found beyond the expansion of the universe, the place light cannot yet reach. A swirling cloak surrounded him, made of jet-black fabric—boring compared to his skin tone. He held a staff, from the end of which hung 6 star-metal forged rings.

Opposite stood a monstrous anthropomorphic octopus with bat wings and tentacles for lips. Each of the tentacles, and indeed both scaly green wrists, were bound in shackles of a different darkness. The fetters reeked of decay, death, a rotted fetid imprisonment in the chains of mortality. The beast roared.

Back out, for a nonce, to the reality most perceive. Comparison reveals each traded word at the bar as a blow sent along the highly turbulent psychic plane.

Back to it then, on the astral plane. The monstrosity lurched forward, tentacles hungrily grabbing.

"I'll try a Gargle Blaster off the convention menu." Nyarlathotep leaned forward and clean interrupted John.

The humanoid of void-stained darkness swung the staff in a low arc, then, thrusting the weapon upward. As the rings made contact, sweeping aside the tentacles, a shockwave hammered the realm.

The beast flipped backward, absorbing the impact, and landed with one hand and one knee on the ground. It reared its head back, maw open wide, but uttered only silence.

Realizing quickly that it was quieted, the octo-anthro-monstrosity focused on the physical attack, sliding its foot along the ground in a wide, sweeping arc that connected with the staff as it landed. The weapon spun sideways, twisting itself out of the Nyarlathotep's grip.

"Regardless, you are here. I have no intention of letting you interfere. This is an undertaking of decades. This is not your place, not your domain."

As the beast swung about, the midnight man used the distraction of the weapon to launch a series of strikes, left right left, repeated in sequence, against the torso of the beast. Shivering, the monstrosity cowered as the blows rained down.

"I name thee intruder, you have no dominion here."

The beast collapsed, defeated, unable to stop the assault.

Returning to the hotel, to the twisty reality that so many reject in favor of what they can see with their own eyes—and nothing more—it was a different scene.

The bartender dropped off John's burger and fries. John slumped forward, ignoring Nyarlathotep, and tore into the burger. He barely alternated, or chewed, as he jammed burnt cow and ketchup-soaked fries into his mouth.

"Pitiful. You couldn't even summon your voice and fight back. To think I was worried." Nyarlathotep slammed his drink. "You don't have the energy to stop me. I don't know what's shackled you, but you've grown weak, my dulcet little monstrosity."

John shot baleful side-eye at him but kept the calories coming in.

"Tonight at midnight. Come for us. We will be waiting. Your pride assures you will, and yet, your blood will, in the end, strengthen my ritual." He traced a finger along John's masticating jaw—which was ignored.

John finally finished, then turned to his enemy.

Nyarlathotep eagerly awaited the ancient Dreamer's response.

John wiped his mouth with a napkin. "Whatever, dude." He tossed a hundred on the counter and walked away.

Ryan laughed, from the bottom of his belly. "Delightful!"

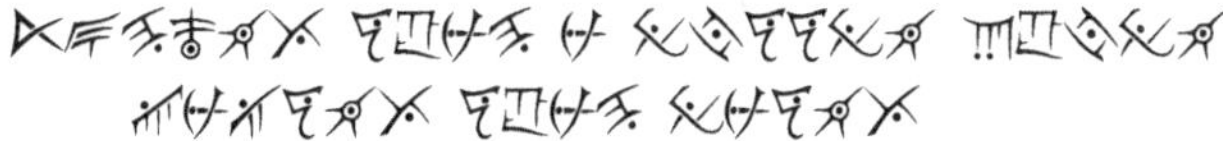

Fuu pulled up to the convention, under the cover of post 10 PM night, drifting on inertia alone. Heart of Gold had rattled her last rattle about half a block back. Somehow, she managed to roll into a conveniently open parking space next to John's Impala. Mostly. With a little bit of elbow grease and grunting, she got Heart parked fully.

Her best friend had been waiting, and lord only knew what trouble he had gotten up to—especially with the insanity happening on her way here. John was fanatical about adding to his collection, and tomorrow... tomorrow was really important. The First would join the collection. Also, he was complete rubbish at dealing with humans without her.

That he was alone wasn't by itself a problem. More worrisome; he hadn't replied to any of her texts since two that afternoon. Normally, John was punctual and polite. A truly great friend. She strode with purpose behind her gait, but still tried to remember to be a normal convention goer and avoid attention. Ever since messing with the ritual, her head had been a little whooshy, and she was feeling off.

A cosplayer zipped by her.

"Nice costume dude! I love the way you have the cloud on a hoverboard to make it look like you're floating!" She squealed.

He spun around, detouring to zip back her way. "Thanks!"

She paused as a couple storm troopers passed, then headed to the convention check-in.

A fan sat at the table, helping late-comers retrieve badges. "Hi there! Did you preregister?"

"Sure did!" Fuu nodded.

"Great," the volunteer slid over to a long box filled with alphabetized badges. "Can I get your last name?"

"Kasami, K-A-S-A-M-I," she spelled it out for him. As he rifled through the badges, she made small talk. "This is awesome. It seems like everyone is in cosplay!"

"Yeah, there's some really great costumes. It isn't quite this much most of the time, but the costume parade is starting in the main hall. A-ha!" He yanked a badge out, grabbed a program book, and handed it all to her. "Here you go, have fun!"

"Thanks again!" The halls were a flurry of activity, people jostling by each other nonstop. Fuu breathed it in while she headed towards the bar—always the first place to check for John. It was so exciting, every one of these conventions. Even though they were literally at a different one every weekend... it never got old for her.

She got to the bar, and it was awash with voices and laughter, people having a good time. Off to the side, a large group was clustered around someone she couldn't see—apparently the life of the party. She watched a bottle of McCallan 25 get pulled from the top shelf and delivered to the cluster of people.

Definitely not John.

But a quick sensory scan left her with the impression that he'd been here, and recently. *Hmmm.... Where to go?* She strode out, back into the packed hall. People were bumper to bumper. Between the bar and the hall, people were packed so tightly the temperature was at least 10 degrees higher. Normally, she would have been super into it, but her concerns about John overrode the normal frenetic fervor of fanatical excitement that fermented in her soul.

Instead, she followed the feelings she had, tracking John. Ahead, past the swelling cosplay masses of convivial convention goers... he was *there*.

"'Scuse me! Pardon me," she pushed through the folks filling the hall. "Behind you!" Urgency beset her, a hound howling at the moon, primal and feral. Something was wrong. John was hurt, she could feel it in her jellies.

Something called, dragging her attention toward the back. The rear lawn had far fewer people on it, though there were still enough that the low hum of conversations filled the night air. Down closer to the river, she spotted a lone figure sitting, staring at the night sky.

John.

She hurried over and sat next to him, the damp grass immediately soaking through her pants and getting her butt wet. "John. Are you okay?"

"I'm hurt," he replied without looking. "One of the Great Ones is here. The Servant God, son of the ender of all things. He's been slowly draining me all day." He held up a hand and Fuu noticed a black ethereal shackle was shimmering in and out of existence. "He'll try to finish me at midnight."

"Oh hell. Not good. It must be connected to the ritual." She glanced at her watch; midnight was fast approaching.

"Ritual? How do you know about that?"

She explained the insanity on the way here, and what she had discovered under the freeway.

"You are sure it said Yuggoth?"

She pulled out her phone and showed him a picture.

"Interesting. Nyarlathotep is the child of a being trapped beyond the gates. Were he bringing that here, it would not be via Yuggoth. It could be Rhan-Tegoth, Tsathoggua, Ghizghuth, Zstylzhemgni, Hziulquoigmnzhah, possibly even Gla'aki. Or he is doing something else completely with the energy."

"Uh. 'Kay. How is that connected to this hotel?"

"The hotel is a rune, shaped from a language more primal than even Ancient. From your description, I suspect he's using the same trick he used in London during World War II—ritualizing roadways to create the shapes of runes he needs—with this building at the center. Germans were flying overhead and bombing the city, providing the blood he needed."

"So. Overwhelmingly strong bad guy, minutes left on the clock, and no real resources to call on… how do we beat him? You're about to collect the First, we can't let him stop that."

John's jaw clenched. "My collection must…" he shook his head. "I don't know how to beat him, Fuu."

"Do we run?"

"We can't." John grimaced, rubbing at his ribs as he shifted. "Nyarlathotep is a creature of evil. Markedly different from most. He relishes in madness and pain on the human level. Whatever he is doing will have dire consequences for the world." He pulled the amulet out of his pocket. "Are you ready for this?"

"Yup. You think I'll need it tonight. Okay, I'm game."

"Indeed. I wouldn't risk it if you weren't ready." He struggled to his feet with Fuu's help. As he grabbed her hand, a strange look—somewhere between curious and shocked—crossed his face. "Are you feeling okay?"

Fuu cocked an eyebrow at him. "Yeah, fine. Why?"

"No reason," the tiniest hint of a smile flitted across his lips. "I know what we need to do now. Help me get to the bar."

Fuu pulled his arm over her shoulders and helped steady him while they walked.

The bar had quieted down substantially, most folks having taken their drinks to the dance party following the costume contest. Seconds ticked by, slicing the remaining well of John's life-force in sharp and precise increments of inevitability.

John sipped a Coke, waiting by the bar.

Fuu stood a couple feet away, watching the entry. Even in here, the loud music from the grand ballroom vibrated the air. There was nothing they could do about the few other people here. In less than ten minutes, the clock would slice that last second away, and on that stroke, as midnight rose for one day to die while another was born, the ritual would complete.

If this had been an Old West saloon, rickety batwing doors would have swung to either side as the theme to *Rawhide* played from some mysteriously unseen source. But this wasn't. Instead, Nyarlathotep strolled in through the wide-open entry in a moment of complete silence. He paused and locked gazes with her. The next song at the party started thrumming, and Nyarlathotep casually sauntered across the space toward Fuu and John to a muted *Na-na-na-na, na-na, na...*

Pink's *So What* kicked into full gear as Nyarlathotep stepped up to Fuu.

"What are you, little mortal?"

"Me? I'm just a girl."

"No ordinary girl could be a companion to *him*," he juked his chin at John, "without going mad."

"He," Fuu mimicked his motion but kept her eyes glued to the man before her, "is John. He's my friend. And I won't let you touch him, you deep-space-other-dimensional or whatever the hell you are S.O.B."

Taunted, Nyarlathotop sprung forward, sliding one of his blades out. The long dagger was a cruelly hooked thing, shimmering with an unearthly sheen to the metal and glowing sigils etched along the blade.

Instinct took over for Fuu. As he lunged, she slid a foot to the side, centering her balance, and her hands shifted to a defensive pose, one palm up with a raised arm, the other down, low. As the blade raced in, she struck with her lower hand smoothly jabbing upwards with a bent wrist. It connected with his forearm and the blade shifted its course, missing her by inches. She danced to the side, throwing three quick blows into his wrist, elbow, and shoulder.

The blade fell to the floor. Nyarlathotep was no amateur though, with eons of bloodlust having shaped him. He dropped into a roll, springing up and pivoting, throwing himself at her.

She dodged to the side again but still took a blow to the ribcage. Though it knocked the wind out of her, she recovered with a wide circular motion, sweeping his arm aside to throw a rapid series of strikes at his face.

Right as she connected with his nose, his foot lashed out, catching the side of her knee.

As black blood dripped from his nose, Nyarlathotep let out a bestial roar, unlike anything a human throat could produce, and swung a mighty backhand.

Fuu crossed her arms in a block, but the strike was fueled by a strength from beyond and she went flying, smashing into a table that collapsed under her. A couple of other patrons in the bar moved to help, but the palpable malevolence of Nyarlathotep's will locked them into place.

While she was down, Nyarlathotep grabbed the second blade and darted forward, stabbing John, then jumped back, turning to face Fuu again.

John held the blade's handle, staring in shock at the knife plunged into his belly. Fuu scrambled up and threw herself between John and Nyarlathotep. She wiped the blood from her lip with the back of her sleeve and stared down the elder god. Behind her, John slid off the barstool and slumped against the low wall below the counter. "The amulet, Fuu..." he spoke weakly.

Fuu yanked her necklace off and snapped the medallion in half, tossing the pieces to either side. Dead black shackles of Aether coalesced from the firmament of realms beyond, manacling her wrists. Calm descended, stilling the cacophony of raging thought swirling in her mind. She smiled, popping her neck by rolling her head to the side. Centering her weight, she slid one foot back, then slowly spread her hands wide, beckoning.

Nyarlathotep's eyes narrowed as he studied her. His senses screamed that he could snuff her life force like the bug she was, calling forth shadows and creatures or purest hunger to consume her... and yet. At the same time, she held no fear. Nothing to latch onto. She was balanced, light and dark, madness and sanity, and the ancient being felt something he'd never felt before.

Fear.

He backed up, sending out a call on the psychic plane. It was time. The ritual was seconds from complete and now he could achieve his aims, so long as he could avoid this woman.

Cultists across the hotel answered his call.

Fuu launched herself forward, flipping sideways as her foot lashed out and caught the surprised Nyarlathotep across the jaw. He stumbled backward.

Behind her, John smiled, struggling up to one knee. "Thank you." On the stroke of midnight, he collapsed forward, plunging the blade the rest of the way into his abdomen. The chains that bound the god of death shimmered around the ethereal form superimposed over his body. His corpse, already dead, could not be dead again. Instead, John was released—temporarily—to use the full extent of his power.

And use it he did.

Cthulhu stretched its mighty wings, sharing its dream of madness across the hotel, infecting everyone that was not a cultist for

Nyarlathotep with the madness of how he had come to be what he was. He slid into the sleep of the half dead, and everyone else awoke as they shared the dream...

"Am-il-lak... Am-il-lak... Am-il-lak..." the robed figures chanted. Echoes of the droning intonations dopplered off distant walls in the dim subterranean chamber. Tiers of stone platforms circled the space, moving slowly as ancient machinery spun them along their orbit, each carrying a chanting cultist. Far out, past the stone monoliths, blackness swirled. Filled with shapeless congeries of protoplasmic bubbles, faintly self-luminous, and with myriads of temporary eyes forming and un-forming with pustules of greenish light all over; slithering across the glistening walls and floor that it and its kind had swept so evilly free of all litter.

Bones and all.

If 'ere there was a creature that lived up to cleaning their plates after a meal, it was the Shoggoth—and though cultist and monstrosity alike served the same masters, the robed fanatics were just that. A meal.

Shadowy tentacles snaked into the inner area, wrapping around passing zealots, crushing them as they chanted with their brethren. The blood of cultists pooled in silver urns locked below the moving stone tablets as their remains were dragged into the shadows.

On a slab at the center stood a single figure, arms raised. She wore a black velvet robe, as opposed to the brown of the surrounding acolytes, with red silk edgings along the soft fabric. She alone spoke different words, "BYAGOONA, master of the dead, arise! *Klatoo Veratta!* Come to us, faceless one! We call to you with our blood, our life force, ARISE!"

"Am-il-lak... Am-il-lak... Am-il-lak..." the chant continued over her ritual.

Below the grinding gears, the shadows boiled. Something else, not of this world, rested in a slumber deeper than death. But now it stirred. Screams could be heard below as it fought through its torporic fugue, passing into a dream state as it moved from death to life. But dreams… were the domain of another. A stronger, older one…

The Dreamer consumed, on reflex, the entity that dared pass through, and Byagoona, faceless one, god of death, became a meal. It may be an old saying, and it may be trite, but you are what you eat.

Cthulhu found itself being ripped from the dream as Byagoona's essence filled it, and the Dreamer awoke. With that infusion, Cthulhu found itself bound to the rules governing the summons. It felt itself being ripped through planes of reality, dragged toward a gate… it fought to recapture the dream, but the infinite worlds of imagination rejected it.

Far above, in the frigid basement of the medical school building of Miskatonic University, located in the sleepy town of Arkham, Massachusetts, was a set of tiles organized into the floor in the shape of the rune of ra'kham. The rune erupted in light, and the energy of Cthulhu, unleashing a draconic roar of frustration, was dragged into the closet vessel. In this case, it happened to be a corpse laying covered on a steel gurney in the morgue. Cthulhu filled the vessel, reanimating dead limbs, its essence being tied to that of the former cold meat. Neurons fired. The heart once again beat. Blood rushed through the veins.

It sat up, the cloth slipping away.

Across the morgue lounged a medical examiner, watching a small TV on her lunch break. A ham sandwich dropped from her fingers to the floor, splatting as it hit the frigid tilework. Her jaw hung open and her eyes were wide.

The corpse turned and looked at her.

"Hi?" She squeaked and blinked, wondering if it wanted to eat her brains, perhaps to learn about the world through absorbing her memories…

It blinked back, trying to figure out if she was a follower, or if perhaps it should just eat her essence and drive her to madness—

though that decision hadn't gone particularly well a few moments ago.

"Um. I'm Fuu. Fuu Kasami. Do you want to watch Battlestar Galactica with me?" She pointed at the TV with a shaking hand.

It ambled off the gurney and looked at the box she had indicated. On the small screen a jumpsuit-clad man spoke "... you know, we need to figure out which side we're on."

Another man replied, "Which side are we on? We're on the side of the demons, Chief. We're evil men in the gardens of paradise, sent by the forces of death to spread devastation and destruction wherever we go."

The being—trapped in the body it was—didn't understand enough to know who or what these characters were. What it did understand was that in this little box were eternal dreams, a kind of madness all its own. And in the words laid such delicious intent.

"Yes," it figured out how to work the vocal cords. "I do want to watch Battlestar Galactica with you."

"Swell!" Fuu gave a mental sigh of relief. The zombie wasn't going to eat her brains. "Say, who are you?"

With names come power; they can define and make a thing greater or knock down and make a thing less. In this moment, still bound to the rules of the death god, Cthulhu chose a name. A human name. And thus was defined.

It, now he, looked at himself. His eye alit on a tag hanging from his toe, and he yanked it off, reading it. "I am John Doe."

In the bar, John rose, strength flowing into him through icy veins of madness. The dream shared had awoken him. He was not Cthulhu, not Byagoona, but John. John Doe—a being which was both of those things, but human too. Something more.

So much more.

Lightning cascaded outside the hotel, jumping from the roadways and shattered the sky like a giant inky black chrysalis. What emerged was not a being, but a pillar of fire and purple lightning that slammed into the hotel.

In the bar, the pillar of raw energy ripped through the ceiling and slammed into the floor. Nyarlathotep threw back his head and laughed. "I don't know how you escaped death, John, but it's all over now!"

"Seriously, dude. Did you not watch enough movies in the nineties or what? You need better banter." Fuu retorted. "How about this; never go in against an ancient one when *death* is on the line!"

"Insolence!" Nyarlathotep roared. Lightning danced and jumped along the rune shaped Red Lye Inn, micro portals to Yuggoth opening in penumbral shadow. Swirling bubbling beasts, amorphous monstrosities—all tentacles and frenetic darting eyes—left viscous trails as they emerged. To these beasts Earth was, in essence, a cosmic drive-through—with humanity the main item on the value menu. The viscid congeries of insanity were ready for a meal, but Cthulhu's dream, and this was of utmost import, had been shared.

And after sleep comes...

Convention goers across the hotel woke into the deepest slumber, the power of names, the power of insanity, freeing them. The madness of deepest truth roamed wild and rose, as cosplayers became that which they had named themselves. Passion rose to meet despair, and its light pierced the darkness.

In the hallways, Darth Maul grinned evilly, flanked by storm troopers. His double-bladed lightsaber slid into being with a distinctive hum. Gloom bubbled behind the cultists, now clearly visible by the dark auras the force revealed... and in the murky corners, eyes and tentacles swirled as Shoggoth coalesced into being, feeding off the ritual set into motion by Cthulhu's blood.

Behind him, Goku rose into the air, a golden glow surrounding him...

Klingons took attack positions, bat'leths at the ready...

Neo and Trinity struck kung fu poses, ready to deal with agents... an army arose, ready to battle with cultists and beasts from beyond.

Just outside the bar, a cultist—about to come to Nyarlathotep's aid—screamed as they were swallowed whole by the Shoggoth.

Fuu and John stood opposite the laughing god.

...and then the last thing any of them expected happened. A leonine roar was followed by a bellowed "FOR KAHLESSSSSSS!" and those present heard something never heard before.

A Shoggoth yowled in pain.

The pillar of energy began to hum, not just the vibration of power, it yearned to speak a word...

Miles away, three hastily etched runes on the bottom of an overpass glowed in all the tones of the psychic spectrum... coruscating in a frenzied dance of purple, blues, reds, and blacks emitting a dark light of their own.

The vibration of the energy pulse finally snapped into clarity, the word it hummed becoming crystal clear. "*Fuuuuuuuuuuuu...*" It leapt across the room and slammed into her midsection. The shockwave blew John and Nyarlathotep back. Fuu threw her arms wide, rising in the air while lightning and fire merged into her.

Nyarlathotep howled in rage. "What the hell have you done?!"

John regained his feet. "I've driven them mad, of course. But madness mixed with passion is so much more than simple madness. I've freed them. And she... well... spoilers."

John sprinted forward. Unlike Fuu, he was untrained, thoroughly unused to this form. But what he lacked in discipline, he compensated for with fervor. He jumped, launching a good ten feet through the air before landing on the other god with a downward haymaker. The blow caught his target across the jaw as bone crunched under John's fist.

Unfazed, Nyarlathotep bear-hugged John, slamming him to the ground, and the two grappled.

In the maelstrom's eye, Fuu's consciousness spread across the town, clawing for comprehension. Throughout the hotel, the tide of the swarming Shoggoth found... resistance. She could hear the battle cries of the mad set free.

...“Super-sayan!”

...“Chidori!”

...“by Grabthar's hammer!”

Hundreds of people came for battle, set free by Cthulhu to become the heroes and villains they cosplayed, and fought back the wave of Shoggoth slithering into this realm.

Finally, Fuu understood. She stepped into the psychic realm, a being of light amongst the shades, to stand next to the bat-winged monstrosity that was Cthulhu against the being of night. The combat began.

The three other patrons in the bar, suddenly released from Nyarlathotep's psychic death-grip, lunged forward. The one in the center, a sharp looking man of about 50—wearing a Caprica Special Blend tee while holding a glass of the McCallan 25 that had been brought out earlier, led the charge, a hockey stick materializing in his free hand. The other two, a younger couple, wore matching red shirts that had the letters Fe arranged in a circle on them.

Cultists swarmed, dodging blaster bolts, only to be intercepted by the group of three protecting Fuu and Cthulhu's backs.

Nyarlathotep warily watched his twin opponents. This was not how any ritual had ever gone before. Ever. This was... *madness.*

Fuu landed, feet spread wide and one hand on the ground to stabilize her. The raw force still cascaded over her body, singeing the tiles of the floor, but the tether was gone. She stood slowly, her glowing eyes staring down the thing across from her, and stretched her hand out, palm up. She curled her fingers in a come-hither challenge.

John stood and dusted off his shoulders. Stepping to the side he forced Nyarlathotep to track separate targets.

The ancient walker, son of Azathoth—destroyer of all things—threw his arms wide. His skin bubbled, wickedly hooked tentacles trying to burst forth from extra-planar subdermal pouches as he revealed his true form. But it didn't work. He stood there, arms wide, then finally blinked in confusion. "What the hell?"

John smiled. "Newp. No cheating. You're in my dream now." He snapped his fingers, and the music, which had ground to a halt with the earlier shockwave, picked back up. This time it was the opening bars to AC/DC's *Back in Black*.

Fuu launched forward with a lightning-fast low sweep. Nyarlathotep lifted a foot to dodge, and she sprang up into a spinning backfist.

He brought a forearm up to block. With each strike and block, black, purple, and red sparks leapt, showering the area around them.

John didn't miss a beat, darting in from the side, feinting with a left haymaker, then hammering Nyarlathotep with an uppercut when he blocked wide.

Nyarlathotep crashed through the outer wall of the building. It wasn't enough to slow him down. Faster than any mortal could have, he sprang back through the detritus and lashed out with strikes of his own.

Brian Johnson belted out, "because I'm baaa-aa-aack..." as the three traded blows in a dance macabre.

Along the psychic plane, Fuu spun and leapt the hypnotic dance of her Tai Chi forms. Inky pockets of blackness, each connecting to a micro portal, were swept up by her energy, fusing until only gossamer strands created a web with her at the center.

Nyarlathotep launched forward, blows raining down so fast that Cthulhu and Fuu could do nothing but defend. Fuu flipped out of the way of a low sweep and Nyarlathotep rotated up into a two-hand dragon strike, catching Cthulhu squarely in the gut and chest. John went flying across the room, sliding to a stop at the very spot Fuu had earlier broken his amulet in half.

Fuu's dance ended, and she moved in place, working a ball of pure blackness between her hands—a compactified soccer-ball sized nuclear core of pure evil.

"Now!" Fuu yelled.

John grabbed the rent amulet, sprinting toward Nyarlathotep.

Fuu flung her hands wide. The energy infusing her arced to Nyarlathotep, bridging the distance between them with a brilliant display of lethal power. John slammed the fetish's halves back together, capturing the arc discharge.

A sonic boom blew out pieces of walls and windows throughout the hotel, and as it hit each shadowy corner the portals to Yuggoth cracked and deliquesce, then evaporate... Cosmic gateways across the hotel winked out of existence, sucking confused Shoggoth—the few that still survived—back to Yuggoth.

Injured and bloody cosplayers across the destroyed hotel cheered in jubilant victory.

In the bar, Nyarlathotep collapsed. All the cosmic energy, the weight of evil, the ritual energy, was gone. He was, barring the eons of malevolent wandering across the universe, now just a human. "What have you done?"

John looked around before responding. The hotel was a wreck. Walls were collapsed, dust and soot everywhere, windows shattered... there was more debris than structure. It was a marvel the building was still standing. "You gave us a hell of a lot of energy, so we used it. Welcome to mortality, friend; we drained your essence."

"Oh, and one last thing... run." He threw the medallion in the air, and a shimmering portal appeared. A giant squidlike tentacle lashed out of it, filling the room with scent of rotted deep ocean, wrapping around Nyarlathotep and pulling him through the portal. "Failure," a deep voice boomed, shaking the still standing bits of wall.

"Father! Noooooooooo," screamed Nyarlathotep as he was dragged away. The portal vanished, and the amulet clattered to the floor, lifeless, devoid of energy.

Everyone in the room, excepting John, sat, exhausted, wiping sediment and blood away. Fuu met his eye, smiling, and in a subtle motion jerked a thumb toward the man with the hockey stick and glass of scotch.

John keyed on him and he walked over to the weary battler. "You."

The man looked up, meeting his eye, "Yeah?"

"You are the First. I am here to collect you."

He cocked his head to the side. The knuckles of hand holding the hockey stick went white as his grip tightened. "Collect me?"

"Yes." John reached through the Aether, pulling the compendium of his collection to him. A black leather folio appeared in his hand, which he proceeded to flip open. "You are the first I saw as I entered this life. Chief Tyrol, on Battlestar Galactica," he flipped open the folio and presented the man with a headshot and pen. "Can I have your autograph, Mr. Douglas?"

Aaron smiled and took a sip of his scotch. "Sure thing, buddy."

End.

9 781952 971075